EXECUTION EVE:
—And Other Contemporary Ballads

BY THE SAME AUTHOR

God and Man at Yale
McCarthy and His Enemies (with L. Brent Bozell)
Up from Liberalism
Rumbles Left and Right
The Unmaking of a Mayor
The Jeweler's Eye
The Governor Listeth
Cruising Speed
Inveighing We Will Go
Four Reforms
United Nations Journal: A DELEGATE'S ODYSSEY

EDITOR

The Committee and Its Critics
Odyssey of a Friend: WHITTAKER CHAMBERS' LETTERS TO
WILLIAM F. BUCKLEY, JR.
Did You Ever See a Dream Walking?:
AMERICAN CONSERVATIVE THOUGHT IN THE
TWENTIETH CENTURY

CONTRIBUTOR

The Intellectual
Ocean Racing
What Is Conservatism?
Spectrum of Catholic Attitudes

William F. Buckley, Jr.

EXECUTION EVE:

—And Other Contemporary Ballads

G. P. PUTNAM'S SONS
NEW YORK

SBN: 399-11531-5
Library of Congress Catalog
Card Number: 75-17593

"On the Wind's Way" and
"Memoirs" © 1973/1975
by The New York Times Company.
Reprinted by permission.
"Reflections on the Phenomenon" first appeared in
Esquire magazine in October 1974.

PRINTED IN THE UNITED STATES OF AMERICA

For Sophie Wilkins

Acknowledgments

My THANKS to the proprietor of: *Esquire, Harper's, National Review, New York,* the New York *Times, Playboy, Redbook, Sports Illustrated, Travel & Leisure,* Washington *Star* Syndicate, *Yachting,* for whom I originally wrote the material in this book.

Contents

Introduction   13

I. Détente

To China with Nixon: Is There a Road Back?   21
Vive la Différence   42
Solzhenitsyn at Bay   44
The Victimization of Owen Lattimore   47
Soviet Justice, Soviet Law, Soviet Gas   49
The Impact of the Soviet Jew   51
The Chinese Exhibitionists   53
The Coils of Détente   56

II. The Campaign of '72

Humphrey vs. McGovern   61
He Lost It in California?   63
McGovern and the National Mood   65
Altered Prospects for George Wallace?   67
Convention Preview   69
The New Religion.   71
Hate the Rich   73
After the Ball   76
The Eagleton Impasse   78
The Limits of Decency   80

8

The Republicans' Achilles' Heel   82
McGovern's War on Wealth   84
McGovern on Crime   86
Remarks by WFB at a Debate with John Kenneth
    Galbraith   88
De Profundis   94
Advice for McGovern: A Return to Innocence   96
The Morning After   98
The Schlesinger-Galbraith Entrail-Reading Service   100

III. *Watergate*

Watergate Developments   105
Watergate Perspective   107
Is Nixon a Fool?   109
Reflections on Nixon and Impeachment After
    Listening to the Speech   112
One Down for Senator Buckley   122
As It Might Have Gone   124
Democratic Strategy   126
Watergate Professionalism   128
The Dean Memorandum   130
The Presidential Tapes   133
The Awe-full Senator Weicker   135
Are You Sorry You Voted for Nixon?   137
A Tendency to Distort   139
Nixon and Resignation   141
Senator Buckley's Proposal   143
The Paralysis of Mr. Nixon   146
Destroy the Tapes   148
The Jesuitical Benediction: Too Much   151
Meanwhile, Questioning Gerald Ford   153
The Senators Prepare for a Trial   155
Going Down   157
Let Him Go   158
Julie at Bat   160
Nixon in Perspective   163

IV. *Travels . . . Complaints, Impressions*

Fiddlestix	171
French Summer	173
An American Exhibit in Russia	175
Midsummer Mexican Notes	179
There'll Always Be an England	181
Getting About in Italy	184
Overweight?	186
Post Office Collapse	188
So Much for 1974	190
Travel Notes at Christmas	192

V. *The Mideast*

Israel and American Policy	197
The Uses of Blackmail	201
Talking Back to the Oil Monopolists	203

VI. *African Sojourn*

Johannesburg	207
Salisbury	209
Nairobi	211

VII. *Sports*

Reflections on the Phenomenon (An Introductory Essay to *Esquire*'s "Super Sports Issue")	217
On Being Rescued by the Coast Guard	227
Strange Bedfellows	237

10

Reflections on Skiing   244
The Ocean Race of William Snaith   248

VIII. *Freedom—Backing Away*

AFTRA Backs Down   255
CBS on the Line   257
A Post-Watergate President   259
The Consequences of Disestablishment   261
Are You Against the Handicapped?   264
The End of the GOP?   266
Ford and the Impossible   268
The Decline of Patriotism   270
To America with Love   272

IX. *The War on Business and Property*

Down the Businessman   277
Professor Galbraith's *China Passage*   279
Economic Damnation   282
The Economics of a New York Assemblyman   284
Galbraith and Inflation   286
Economics via TV   289
A Congressman Objects   291
Oil and the Demagogues   293
Middle-Class Poverty   295
Palm Coast and the Knee Jerks   297

X. *Notes and Asides*

XI. *Taming the Kids*

Generals and Kids at Yale   375
Secretary Fonda   377

11

The Students: What Is Their Problem?   379
Crisis in Princeton   381
Sex and Ideology at Princeton   384

XII. *Morals, Manners, Mannerists*

Vietnam Blindness: What Is Morality?   389
Reexamining the Pot Sanctions   391
The Perils of Thinking Out Loud About Pot   393
Capital Punishment   401
Lenny   403
The Ennobling Dirty Movie   405
On the Use of "Dirty" Words   407
The Disintegration of the *Playboy* Philosophy   409
The Shocking Report of J. Edgar Hoover   411
The Problem of Unbought Tributes   413
Truth in Packaging   415
Death to Textbook Sexism   418
Bad Manners in China   420
The Poop-Scoop War   422

XIII. *The Press: Mostly Personal*

The Theory of Jack Anderson   427
The Proposed Shield Laws   429
What Are the Russians Up To, and How Can
   We Tell?   431
The Ethics of Junketing   434
On Leveling with the Reader   436
Columnists Are People   438

XIV. *Religion*

1. Chuck Colson and Christianity   443

2. Abortion
   New Thoughts on Abortion 445
   The Court on Abortion 447
   How to Argue About Abortion 449
3. The Court
   Impasse on the Schools 451
   Dead End with the Court 453
   The Need for a Constitutional Amendment 455
4. Anglican Agony 457
5. A Personal Statement 460

XV. *Personal*

Lillian Elmlark, RIP (A Eulogy) 465
Dennis Smith the Fire Fighter 467
Shockley and Shockleyism 471
Harry Truman, RIP 473
Lyndon Johnson, RIP 475
H. L. Hunt, RIP 478
Frank Shakespeare, a Testimonial 480
Sir Arnold Lunn, RIP 482
Henry Regnery, a Testimonial 489
Jozsef Cardinal Mindszenty 493
Death of a Christian 497

Index 501

Introduction

I AM A YEAR LATE in producing this book, but my publisher accommodated me inasmuch as, in the interval since my last collection (*Inveighing We Will Go*), I gave him, and he published, two books. In any event, I have had three years' material, unpublished in book form, from which to select what went into this volume, and those years, to say the least, have been active. The danger, in republishing material written on the spot, is that it should appear frenetic in that aggravating sense that it puts off a reader who, the season having changed, has recaptured historical perspective. I leave it to others to pass judgment on whether that problem is here coped with, while urging those who nowadays wonder that anybody, in 1972, should have been so excited by the prospect of a victory by George McGovern to remember that his nomination *was* an exciting act, anticipated by—no one.

A few concrete matters.

In the summer of 1972, I wrote for *Playboy* magazine a piece on Mr. Nixon's trip to China, on which I accompanied him as a member of the press contingent. In writing it, I used a great deal of the illustrative material I had sent out from China to my newspaper syndicate. Much of this was republished in my previous collection. Although the *Playboy* essay, with which I launch this book, was conceived and executed whole, I beg the indulgence of the reader who finds in it allusions he might already have become familiar with.

Tucked into this book, in a short essay I think I shan't, with your permission, identify, are four paragraphs lifted from my book *Four Reforms*. I found myself, accosting a particular theme one morning, going to extravagant lengths to avoid

13

plagiarizing—myself. Enough of that, I thought: so these paragraphs are reproduced here even though they have previously appeared between hard covers. They occupy less than one page of this book.

Concerning Watergate, I reproduce essays giving (as I do in every case) the date on which I wrote them. The reader will discern an odyssey of sorts. I think I am correct in saying that I was the first journalist to mention the possibility of impeachment over Watergate. Even so, I was stoutly maintaining as late as May of 1973 that our experience with the Constitution of the United States and the institution of impeachment suggested the unwisdom of impeaching Richard Nixon. You do not, I contend, impeach an American President merely to *punish* him. You impeach him in order to *get rid* of him. A year later, I had come to the conclusion that we needed to replace Mr. Nixon, but I thought it better that he should resign than be impeached; and in due course he deprived us of the alternative.

Reading over the Watergate copy turned out to be quite the opposite of what I expected. It did *not* bore or distract me, nor do I find (surprise!) that my reflexes were creaky. Perhaps it is true of most of us that we tend to suspect the man who arrives more quickly than we do at any conclusive position respecting someone's guilt. No doubt there are, among us, men and women greatly gifted with powers of intuition—such that, on looking into the face of Richard Nixon a single time, know with the force of certitude: *That man is guilty.* I admire the faculty, but if I disposed of it, I do not think I would ventilate my intuitions publicly. A journalist or commentator is always at least one part juror, and must reserve judgment. However, his attachment to due process becomes a partisan device when he refuses to conclude that which abundant testimony requires the open-minded juror to conclude; or when he fails to extend the same procedural courtesies impartially.

In this connection I should note something I have not written before. It is that in December 1972 I received a telephone call from E. Howard Hunt, ten days after his wife was killed in an airplane accident. It transpired that she had named me the alternate executor of her estate, a precaution against the incapacitation of her husband should he be found guilty (which one month later he was) of conspiring to burglarize Democratic headquarters at Watergate. As it happens, although I am the godfather of the Hunts' three older children, I had not seen Howard or his wife for several years.

Hunt arrived at my apartment in New York, and in two hours told me the story of Watergate—as far as he knew it. He had no knowledge of any complicity by the President. Now this was *before* Hunt delivered the famous communication about which in due course everyone would spend months arguing whether it was "blackmail," and whether Nixon had succumbed to blackmail. In any event, I was for several months privy to details about Watergate and its auspices which were not publicly known until, little by little during the following spring and summer, they were teased out of reluctant witnesses, or proffered anxiously to the Justice Department by co-conspirators seeking either to avoid prosecution or to mitigate their crimes. During that interval I was, in respect of certain matters, greatly encumbered, having received confidential information on which, however, I could not act, or affect any knowledge of in my writings. The problem was to avoid disingenuousness. That became less and less difficult as, little by little, what Howard Hunt confided to me in December became public knowledge. I cite the incident for those who may wonder at certain blurs in what I wrote in the spring of 1973, or who may wonder why certain allegations were not more directly accosted.

There is, in this volume, one feature brand-new to my books. For the first time, I reproduce items that first appeared in the "Notes and Asides" column in *National Review.*

That is, in effect, the editor's column, but it is rather unusual. It consists, primarily, of letters written to me in my capacity as editor of *National Review,* or as a columnist or author or television host, about—anything at all. To these letters I sometimes reply in print. The "Notes and Asides" section is also used to transact business among the editors which is of general interest to the reader. It is used, too, as a bulletin board for arcana of general or particular interest. I occasionally publish short speeches there, scholarly differences of opinion about the meaning of a phrase: that sort of thing. Whereas the section, as it appears in *National Review,* consists mostly of material written by others, in the form of letters to me, those excerpts I have gathered together here are necessarily mostly written by me, this book being, after all, my responsibility. But I do make exceptions, and, for instance, republish a rather long but superb put-down (of me) by a Princeton classical scholar, which conveys nicely the flavor of the section. Some items are rather prickly. For instance, there is one heap-acrimonious exchange with Arthur Schlesinger, Jr. In arranging it, I found that the 52 items could be classified loosely under the headings: NR Staff, Kookdom, Pedagogy, Up Yours, Setting the Record Straight, Very Personal Observations, and Sui Generis. But on reflection, I did not group them rigidly. Instead, I cut a bolt of cloth from one section, go on to another, and another, and then return to the first—all this for the sake of variety, and pungency. On the whole I find it successful, and hope you will too, and that you will see in it something of the animating spirit—the crotchets, the ideals, the superstitions, the tenderness, and the toughness—of a journal I dearly love.

*   *   *

I am grateful to Frances Bronson, Agatha Dowd, Robin Wu, and Joseph Isola for their editorial help. To Walter Minton of Putnam's for flogging this collection out of me. And to those of you who, by your hospitality to my other collections, impregnated this one.

W. F. B.

Stamford, Connecticut
April 1975

Execution Eve:
—And Other Contemporary Ballads

I.

Détente

To China with Nixon:
Is There a Road Back?

January 1973

WHEN RICHARD NIXON suddenly grabbed the television mike to announce not only that we were ending our ostracism of Red China but that he would himself visit China sometime before the following spring, the shock waves were every- where palpable; but Mr. Nixon knew enough about his con- stituencies, voluntary and co-opted, to know that he might safely proceed from the television studio to a fancy restau- rant in Los Angeles, there to celebrate his diplomatic tri- umph in a highly publicized private dinner at which the champagne corks popped in complacent harmony with the impending public elation. A few precautions were taken, as if by a master electrician running his eyes over the fuses. I sat viewing Mr. Nixon's television performance in the relaxedly hushed living room of Governor Ronald Reagan in Sac- ramento, with my brother Jim. We were together not only because of ideological consanguinity, or because we are friends, or because we thought foresightedly to man the same fortress at a moment when President Nixon would say something we were alerted to believe would be more than his routine denunciation of wage-and-price controls. But the coincidence was happy—we could reflect now together on the meaning of Mr. Nixon's *démarche,* without pressure.

The governor turned off the television after the network commentators began transcribing the delighted stupefaction of the international diplomatic community. There had been no comment in the room, save one or two of those wolfish whistles one hears when someone on one's side in politics says something daringly risqué; kinky, even, gauged by the standards of Nixon-straight. The television off, there was si- lence in the room for a second, not more—the telephone's ring reached us. The butler appeared. "Dr. Kissinger," he said to the governor, who got up from the floor and went to the sequestered alcove where the telephone lay. He wasn't gone for very long, but even by the time he returned, somehow we knew that the question *Did Richard Nixon say something he shouldn't have said? Did he undertake a course of action he should not have undertaken?* was somehow not up for generic review. Nixon had pierced the veil, and the defloration was final. Henry Kissinger had, within five minutes of the public announcement, reached and reassured the most conspicuously conservative governor in the Union that the strategic intentions of the President were in total harmony with the concerns of the conservative community. We sensed, all of us, the albescent tribute to Mr. Nixon's solid good sense.

The balance of the evening was given over only glancingly to the great catharsis, which not many months later, by compound interest, would emerge as a Long March jointly undertaken by the United States of America and the People's Republic of China. The dissenters were much more than helpless; they were paralyzed. In a matter of hours the political emotions of the country were permanently rearranged. Nixon had done it. Surely Nixon is *our* bargaining agent, the old anti-Communist community reasoned. I thought of the mine workers, who on one occasion were surprised when John L. Lewis announced the agreement he had reached with the operators. The terms appeared dismaying. But it is easier on such occasions to reason a priori, from faith in the leader. *John L. Lewis will not make settlements strategically disadvantageous to his constituency.* No more Richard Nixon to his. To be sure, we lisped out our reservations. Senator Buckley issued his cautionary notes. I broke wind with heavy philosophical reservations. A fortnight later a few of us met in Manhattan and decided, as a matter of historical punctilio, to suspend our formal support for President Richard Nixon. The press, though visibly amused—as if Grandfather Bonaparte had come in from the village to disown the young emperor—gave the story attention, faithful to the spastic journalistic imperative that anything that might conceivably embarrass Richard Nixon is newsworthy. But that was about it. There was the formal gesture by Congressman John Ashbrook, who ran primary campaigns against the President in

New Hampshire, Florida and California. But it was much too late. The *Zeitgeist* was so far ahead of us it had time to stop and laugh as we puffed our way pot-valiantly up the steepening mountain. And soon the great day came when, glass raised high in Peking, the President of the United States toasted the Chairman of the People's Republic of China; after which we disappeared from sight.

PRINCETON, NEW JERSEY, March 10, 1972. One important effect of President Nixon's trip to China [the Gallup Poll reported today]—and the period leading up to this historic event is the far more favorable image the U.S. public has of the Communist Chinese today than they did in the mid-Sixties. Respondents [to the poll] were asked to select from a list of 23 favorable and unfavorable adjectives those which they feel best describe the Communist Chinese. The terms "ignorant," "warlike," "sly" and "treacherous" were named most often in 1966, the last time the measurement was taken. Today, however, "hard-working," "intelligent," "artistic," "progressive" and "practical" outweigh any negative term used to describe the Chinese.

It was mid-January in New York and I was lunching with friends, among them Theodore White, already embarked on his industrious monitorship of a Presidential year. Someone asked White whether he would succeed in getting a ticket on the coveted flight to Peking accompanying Nixon. You might as well have asked the queen whether she would get a ticket to the coronation. "If I don't get one," he said excitedly, "I might as well give up writing my book! How can one write a history of the making of the American President in 1972 and not travel to Peking with Nixon?" He elaborated, most discreetly, on the measures he had taken—the strings he had pulled, the people he was prepared to exalt, or to strangle, according as they proved helpful, or obstructive—in transacting his application. His eyes lit on me suddenly, and the pointed mirth that makes him such good company fastened on the subtle reticulations of my own position. You son of a bitch, he said, if *you're* on that plane and *I'm* not, I'll never speak to you again! That afternoon I wrote and applied perfunctorily for a seat. Five weeks later, White and I were facing each other across the aisle of the Pan American press jet, en route to Hawaii, the first leg on what we were repeatedly reminded was a historical voyage, a presumption none of us doubted. I had had a call, in Switzerland, from the White House—did I *really* want to go? . . . Yes, I said, over the transatlantic phone, I was most anxious to go. Forty-eight hours later Ron Ziegler reached me to say that I was among the chosen. Forty-eight hours and twenty minutes later, Herbert Klein called me to say the same thing.

The mood aboard the press plane was mostly muted, inquisitive in an unobtrusive way; languid like the professional athlete on the eve of protracted exertion. The buildup was subtle, but palpable. Mr. Nixon paces himself carefully, with an eye on the relevant coordinates: his health, and television prime time. He does not believe in arriving anywhere unrested, uncomposed, or unobserved. Though he is capable of staying awake all night, he does not chart his trips so as to make this likely. It was only on the fifth night that, experiencing impasse with Chou En-lai, he stayed up until dawn, pressing his position—presumably on how to phrase the vexed question of Taiwan (he might as well have stayed in bed). Accordingly, we spent a day and a half in Hawaii, which we left at dawn, destination Peking. The President left with us, but to go only as far as Guam, there to "overnight," as they put it.

Safely on board, Teddy White was Buddha-happy, sitting with a pile of news clips on his tray whence from time to time he would pluck out an anti-Red Chinese tidbit and offer it to me playfully in return for anything favorable to the Red Chinese I might supply him from my own pile, gentleman's agreement. Now he beamed. "I have a clip here that says the Red Chinese have killed thirty-four million people since they took over China. What will you offer me for that?" I foraged among my material and triumphantly came up with a clip that said the Red Chinese have reduced illiteracy from 80 percent to 20 percent, but White scoffed me down, like a professional pawnshop broker. "Hell," he said, "I have that one already. *Everybody* has that one." I scrounge about for more pro-Chinese Communist data, and finally tell him, disconsolate, that I can't find one more item to barter for his plum; he smiles contentedly at his tactical victory, and I wonder if he hasn't, however, lost the war.

We merely refueled at Guam and went on ploddingly to Shanghai. Guam–Shanghai is only four hours, Guam–Peking six. But all along we had been directed to stop over there, before flying into Peking, giving eighty-five out of eighty-five reporters the opportunity to wire back the knowing historical observation that the purpose of the stopover was indisputably to wrest from us a jet-age facsimile of the traditional obeisance of the visiting dignitary who, on his way to an audience with the emperor in the Middle Kingdom, was made to pause at the hem of the imperial gardens to beg leave to proceed. But it is also a Chinese tradition that official guests are not made to stop merely in order to water their horses. So therefore there was a grandish meal at the airport, prefiguring the routine that lay before us—one official Chinese seated next to every American around the round tables; like the other Chinese we would meet, functional in English, but not very much more than that. White, who had left Harvard three years earlier to devote himself to Sinology, could not suppress his curiosity about the great city of Shanghai, which he had not seen since before "Liberation" (October 10, 1949), and went on with his questions. "What has become of the old racetrack?" he asked. "It—is—a—people's—park," said his host measuredly. "A people's *horses'* park?" another reporter asked solemnly, confident that the satirical turn the questioning had taken would go unnoticed (it did). "No," said our host, not quite getting it, but sensing the danger, "a people's park." Walter Cronkite turned to White and explained matter-of-factly: "They race people there." That too passed without difficulty. But White was not to be deterred. He gave up finally only when on asking "What will we see in Shanghai?" he got back the answer, "A city of ten million people." Cronkite, responding to the many toasts that had been offered to us at four- or five-minute intervals during the long lunch, rose gravely, glass in hand, to toast a "most auspicious beginning."

Back on the plane, the final leg of the trip, to Peking. We are boarded onto buses, making our very long way to the Nationalities Hotel, beyond the Great Square of the People.

There is no other traffic, only bicycles, and the drivers use their horns as routinely as safari drivers plying their mosquito swatters, to keep the road clear of the blue-suited bicyclists, half of them wearing white gauze masks over their mouths, a native precaution against the spreading of germs. Why doesn't the cold kill the germs? I wondered. Or why don't the germs kill the cold. . . . I was slipping into fantasy, under the torture of fatigue after seventeen hours' journey. In the hotel lobby full of bags and people and confusion we found we were expected to eat yet again. I went to the dining room with Bob Considine, who asked, in the best manner of W. C. Fields, "Do you have a bar?" The comrade in charge of the dining room answered, "Yes. You want olange juice?" "No," said Considine; "whiskey . . . wheeskee . . . glub glub glub," he motioned with his hand on an imaginary highball glass. "Ah," the functionary smiled, "beeh?" "Take me," Considine turned austerely toward me, "to the nearest war lord." We stumbled off to our rooms. Large, utilitarian, mid-Victorian, comfortable, dimly lit, plenty of hot water, chocolates and hard candy and fruit on the table, instant service at the press of a button. I do not know whether Considine rang for a war lord. I was within seconds sound asleep, snug in bed in the capital of Red China. When you are very tired, and your bed is warm and your room is silent, nothing else matters. Nixon had a point, though, staying over in Guam. Nixon always has a point.

They ask you, What did you find in China that surprised you? Or—more often—What did you find in China that surprised you most? But one is better off asking such a question of someone who has just returned from terra altogether incognita; from those parts of the Upper Amazon (I take it there are still some) about which we have all learned from *National Geographic* that no human being from the civilized world has ever traveled there (interesting question: What is the "civilized" world? What does the word nowadays mean?). Mysterious China, during the period since Liberation, has not been mysterious in the *National Geographic* sense. There have been travelers to China all along, even during the convulsions. Much was seen in China even during the Cultural Revolution, that was not laid on for foreign visitors to see.

The control of visitors' movements, during the Cultural Revolution, was less thorough by far than the control after the
Cultural Revolution; than the control today, when by contrast with pre-Ping-Pong China, it is considered a country
relatively open to discreet inspection by foreign journalists.
But even during the twenty years largely closed to Americans, there were others who went there, others who reported
on China in our own language, among them some who measured China by Western values. Clement Attlee led a delegation of Englishmen there eighteen years ago, one of whom
wrote a mordant little book called *No Flies in China,* urbanely
mocking the only absolutely verifiable revolutionary achievement in the city of Shanghai—in fact, the reporter hadn't
seen a single fly. But then possibly he wouldn't have noticed
the absence of flies if their absence hadn't been remarked to
him, and if he hadn't read somewhere that Shanghai used to
be full of flies.

What *would* have surprised us?—traveling to China a few
months after Ross Terrill of Harvard did, and James Reston
of the New York *Times,* and William Attwood of *Newsday,*
and dozens of Canadians and Australians and, for that matter, French and West Germans, whose reports we had read.
"Have you noticed about the dogs?" one journalist asked me,
four days into the trip. No, I said, scratching my head. Were
the dogs class-consciousless, I wondered? What had I
missed? . . . "There *are* no dogs," he said. I hadn't noticed,
but it was true. True, more exactly, that we hadn't *seen* any
dogs. Not true, necessarily, that there *weren't* any, someplace—it would not have done for President Nixon to have
presented the Peking zoo with two dogs. Another journalist,
after three days in Peking: "Have you noticed about the
grass?" Same thing. There was no grass. I mean, *there was no
grass.* The explanation may be simple. Maybe grass is extremely hard to grow in the climate around Peking. On the
other hand, grass grows all right in Maine and in the Lauren-
tians, where it is also very cold. No doubt there is another explanation, on the order of having to use all the available
earth for food, or perhaps there is a positive cultural antipa-
thy toward grass as conspicuous horticultural consumption.
But I hadn't in fact noticed it.

What the questioner is really asking, after a trip of this nature, is: "What surprised *you* that didn't surprise the newsmen who have previously reported on their travels throughout China?" But even that question generates an answer only on the assumption of the incompetence or venality of your predecessors. This cannot safely be assumed, mostly because in conspicuous cases the people who had been to China were neither incompetent nor, all of them, beholden to the Communist myth. Of the ideological sycophants there were of course a number, but their writings, though distracting, are disregarded by the practiced reader as automatically as the lesser stars by the navigator. One does not examine the reports on China of a Felix Greene, except as one is interested in ideological pathology. It was a problem for years where Russia was concerned, and although it's true that there are people around who are willing to say gaspingly about China the same kind of thing the boys used to say about Stalin's Russia, in China, on the whole, observers have been at once more cynical and more wise. The more cynical—the Wilfred Burchetts, the Felix Greenes—presumably know what they are doing but are willing to do it anyway. Joseph Stalin had his apologists even after the Moscow Trials were exposed. The typical journalist visiting China is as I say at once wiser and more jaded, so that on the one hand he does not automatically accept on their terms the representations of his hosts, but on the other hand is world-weary about applying only standards of conduct that would have satisfied Woodrow Wilson, or the Committee for Cultural Freedom.

What *would* have surprised us? Well, we'd have been surprised if, say, a political prisoner had been tied to a stake outside our hotel and shot for breakfast. We'd have written home about that. We'd have been surprised if, turning a corner during an unaccompanied walk through the streets of Shanghai, we had bumped into a corpse in the middle of the street, dead of undernourishment, or boredom. We'd have been surprised if the secret police (they call them the Social Affairs Department—the Maoists are really *wonderful* on terminology, though after a certain amount it cloys, like Franglais) had come in one night to the hotel and dragged Barbara Walters off in handcuffs—you could have counted on us to cause a hell of a good row.

But that kind of thing didn't happen. So what was it that did surprise us?

Leaving out the nonexistence of dogs and grass, and the trivial anomalies that strike each observer differently—what was it that surprised all, or nearly all of us?

If you winnowed down the list ruthlessly, I think you would have something very nearly like general agreement on the following.

It surprised us that the airport greeting given to President Nixon was so scandalously spare. There were present at the airport (1) an honor guard of a couple of hundred soldiers; (2) a diplomatic retinue of several dozen Chinese, led by Chou En-lai; and (3) us. One journalist, struggling to assimilate the implications of it, ventured the ingenious explanation that perhaps the Cultural Revolution had been so successful, this was in fact all the Chinese that were left. Americans are good at absorbing social shock. Richard Nixon proved superb at it.

Ten hours after he landed he went to the microphone to return the toast of Chou En-lai, and oh, what a crafty toast it had been. It drew its strength from the implicit friendship between the American and the Chinese people. Alas, *"Owing to reasons known to all, contacts between the two peoples were suspended for over twenty years."* Chou En-lai went on to say, in the principal banquet hall of a capital city in which the Chinese people did not at that moment know even that the President of the United States was physically present in their city (they would learn it the next morning, when Nixon's picture appeared in the papers, visiting with Mao Tse-tung), in a country in which the people haven't the liberty: to choose what they want to read, or to write what they want to write, or to express themselves in behalf of the kind of society they want to live in, or to take the job they want or leave a job they don't want, or to practice the religion they want to practice, or to leave the city for the country or the country for the city, or to travel to another part of China, or out of China . . . said Chou in his toast, "The people, and the people alone, are the motive force in the making of world history." And he toasted the health of the President.

The surprise came when Richard Nixon did what he did. He could have got up, a genial, wizened smile on his face, to thank Chou for whatever efforts he was prepared to make to further the people's interests, the world over; to encourage him to join the United States in a joint search for peace; to toast the health of all leaders of the People's Republic of China, and of the people of the People's Republic of China . . . and have sat down, smiling. Perfectly proper. Impeccable.

We could not believe it, what he did. I mean, there was no one there who was unsurprised—except, maybe, those who had projected rigorously how Richard Nixon characteristically does things: the imperative fusion of Quaker rectitude, and political exigency. . . . He began, under the shadow of that reception at the airport, by thanking Chou for his "incomparable hospitality." Then Mr. Nixon talked about bridging the differences between the two countries. Then, in a breathtaking gesture of historical ecumenism, Mr. Nixon talked about undertaking a "long march together." The Long March being Red China's Bastille, Winter Palace, and Reichstag fire, the invocation of it by Richard Nixon as historically inspiring could have been matched only by Mao Tse-tung's bursting into the hall and saying that he wanted to be there passing the ammunition to Richard Nixon the next time America faced the rockets' red glare. Then Nixon quoted Mao himself, in tones appropriate to Scripture. Then he toasted not the *health* of Mao and Chou but, directly, Mao and Chou.

Nor was that by any means all. President Nixon did not return to his table to sit down. He returned only to pick up his small glass of liqueur, armed with which he strode to the adjoining table, crowded with Chinese officials, and paused, effulgently, to toast each one of them individually, his cheeks flushed (with grand purpose—Nixon is to all intents and purposes a teetotaler), and on to yet another table of Chinese dignitaries, to do the same. I commented in a dispatch cabled that evening that I would not have been surprised if Mr. Nixon had lurched into a toast to Alger Hiss. My comment was taken amiss here and there. When I wrote it, I had no reason to know that the next morning UPI would report that the widow Snow had just released the text of a letter received from Richard Nixon during Edgar's last hours on earth, expressing hope for his recovery and saying, "It will strengthen you to know that your distinguished career is so widely respected and appreciated." Edgar Snow had been a full-scale Communist apologist, writing from China, during the forties and fifties, as only a Communist sympathizer could. But there could not have been any observer of that extraordinary scene in the Great Hall of the People who understood the raised Presidential glass as motivated other than by a pure transideological desire to touch the soul of Chinese Maoists, in a way poor Nixon has never succeeded in touching American Democrats. It was an astounding gesture, freighted with innocence. But he would have had a hell of a time explaining it to the Committee on Un-American Activities.

Anyway, *that* surprised us.

We were surprised the next day when they took us off to see the ballet, the *Red Detachment of Women*. It was a small hall, and we had our only glimpse of Chiang Ching, Madame Mao Tse-tung, whose displeasure over a ballet in 1965 that showed insufficient servility to the thought of Mao Tse-tung had triggered the Cultural Revolution. There was *no* chance that the *Red Detachment of Women* would trigger anything among American viewers surrounding the President of the United States other than contempt, tempered by pity. It was as if the President had called together the chiefs of the black republics of Africa to a ballet in the White House on the theme of Little Black Sambo. What surprised us was not so much the hard-drug ideology—we are a country that absorbs Jane Fonda—as the curious social effrontery. The Chinese had nothing at all to gain, but unmistakably something to lose, from a concentrated display of agitprop as art to a conscripted audience of Americans who sensed the restraints imposed upon the President by the diplomatic situation; and worried both that he might visibly fret under the strain; and that he wouldn't. (Oh, how much R. N. might have accomplished, the following night, in his next public toast, by an urbane reference to the *Red Detachment of Women*. How easy, how effective, how inspiriting, how just!) There could not have been anyone in the audience who didn't think: Orwell. Rose Macaulay, on reading *1984*, commented late in her life that she really didn't understand how George could have written such a book, because such a society as he described was simply unthinkable. I thought of Rose Macaulay. There was no *need* for our hosts to make us think of Rose Macaulay. After all, they had taken the trouble not to shoot dissidents outside our hotel room. Why should they do it to art, a few feet away from us?

And—remember, the list is as compressed as I can make it—there was surprise over the affair at Peking University. Every morning we had a choice of five or six tours to take— typically, a visit to an army unit, or a cooperative, or a hospital, or a museum, that kind of thing. It happened that on this morning, the day after the ballet, the majority of us signed up for a tour of Peking University, the center of learning in pre-Liberated China, where at about the time of the Versailles Conference a young assistant librarian, Mao Tse-tung, is said to have steeped himself in learning, the better to compose his visions of a New China.

So there we were, thirty or forty of us, on that hallowed ground, in the cold, cold rector's office, wearing our overcoats, and seated in a great semicircle. A translator was giving us in English the rector's dreary account of the noble aims of Peking University under the patronage of Chairman Mao. The whole mechanical business was exasperatingly slow, in sodden harmony with the text, which was boiler plate Mao, as revised by the Cultural Revolution. The reporter next to me leaned over and whispered, "That guy"—pointing to the rector—"speaks *perfect* English. He sat next to me at the banquet last night. Hell, he got his PhD at the University of Chicago in the twenties." It was so, and in quick order all of us knew it, and it became evident that he was not speaking in English only because of the Red Guards, who, it transpired, were still in control of the university, and who didn't understand English. Two of them, chunky, unsmiling twenty-year-olds, flanked their seventy-six-year-old rector, ears cocked for ideological error. He committed none.

Does anybody get dismissed from PKU? was one question.

No, nobody gets dismissed.

Do you ever decide that a student should return to farm, or work?

We have no such cases.
Do students pick their own specialties?
Their choices are combined with the needs of the state.
What was it that was wrong with PKU before the Cultural Revolution?
We were imitating the elitist practices of Russia.
What did you do to remedy that situation?
A Mao Thought Propaganda Team came in the fall of 1968, stayed a full year, and then left a revolutionary council to run PKU.
What is it that PKU now has that it didn't have before?
Sufficient class-consciousness, and a proletarian spirit.

The rector, tall, thin, gray, wore his authority as naturally as Robert Hutchins, spoke a little anxiously, and after a while, sensing that we all knew that he knew English, began discreetly helping his translator. Hearing him, a doctor of science from Chicago, say what he said, was a deeply saddening experience. It would have helped if he looked like Carmine De Sapio, but he looked like H. B. Warner. A little like Pasternak, who died more or less trying. The rector at PKU chooses to live and to hang on to power, and has to pretend he can't speak English, and presides over a university gutted of spirit and intellect which, Sinologist White concluded, after surveying the curriculum, offers fewer courses in Chinese history than any important university in the United States. We were surprised. Not so much that PKU is as it is but, once again, that we should have been allowed to see it under the circumstances. We were surprised, but I began to get the idea; and the idea is deadly.

The long march for America has been away from Wilsonianism in foreign policy, but we have not meditated what else it is that we are losing along the way. We did not make the world safe for democracy—Wilson's stated objective—by our venture into the First or the Second World War. In fact, a very good case can be made for the idea that the more strenuously we sought to export our democracy, the less democracy flourished, and perhaps it wasn't coincidence. It was well before Nixon's China trip that we gave up on that illusion, reducing our general position by one gigantic step. Now we committed ourselves to making the world safe for those countries that wished to resist subjugation by a major Communist power. Call it, if you will, the Fulbright Reservation. It was neatly stated by him a few years ago: "Insofar as a nation is content to practice its doctrines within its own frontiers, that nation, however repugnant its ideology, is one with which we have no proper quarrel." The corollary of the Fulbright Reservation was that we *did* have a proper quarrel with any nation that was *not* content to practice its doctrines within its own frontiers, though I think the Senator would have wanted to refine that just a little, to read: subject to United States resources, and to our evaluation of the strategic implications of a defeat of the country resisting the exportation of a foreign ideology. It was, of course, the application of the Fulbright Reservation that brought us to war in Korea and Indochina, and to the brink of war in Quemoy, Berlin, Lebanon and Cuba.

The China trip did much to dislodge the Fulbright Reservation, though Fulbright himself, and many others, had meanwhile done a great deal to put pressure on the dam Mr. Nixon yanked open. They did this by seeking to explain, or, if you prefer, to explain away; by managing to understand, and then to tolerate, that which was formerly thought of as quite simply repugnant. And, at the other end, by seeking to disparage, and otherwise abuse, that which was formerly accepted, if not as ideal, quite clearly as nonrepugnant. In this endeavor much of vocal American society has engaged over recent years. Martin Luther King said about America that it was "the greatest purveyor of violence" since Hitler, even as some historians were discovering that the Cold War could not truly be said to have been primarily the fault of the Soviet Union. At the barricades in American academies, students and professors were denouncing this country as militarist and materialist and racist, while we began indulgently to understand certain historical necessities, certain quite understandable practices, under the circumstances, in Russia and China. The young American president of the National Students Association went to North Vietnam to broadcast to the South Vietnamese the news that theirs was the worst military despotism in *history*. Professor Noam Chomsky and likeminded folk were saying you could not believe a word uttered by the government of the United States, while urging us to accept the word of the government of the Soviet Union on everything from statistics on genocide to the control of atomic testing and production. A perfect equilibrium was finally reached, in the egalitarianization of Them and Us, in a speech given in the spring of 1971—by Senator Fulbright. General de Gaulle prefigured it all when he used to refer to "the two hegemonies," but most people put that down as sour grapes from the junior varsity. Fulbright now was talking about our unnecessary fear of the growth of Soviet naval power in the Mediterranean. "This is not to suggest that the Russians are lacking in ambitions in the Middle East," he said. "There is no doubt that they desire to maximize their 'influence' in the Arab world and that they derive gratification from sailing their warships around the Mediterranean. This, however, is normal behavior for a great power: it is quite similar to our own. We too keep a fleet in the Mediterranean, which is a good deal farther from our shores than it is from the Soviet Union; and our main objection to Soviet 'influence' in the Arab countries is that it detracts from our own. Were it not for the fact that they are Communists—and therefore 'bad' people—while we are Americans—and therefore 'good' people—our policies would be nearly indistinguishable."

There, now.

Professor Ross Terrill, an Australian teaching now at Harvard, moved rather more philosophically into the question in two brilliant articles published in the *Atlantic* immediately before President Nixon's trip. They were, reportedly, closely examined by all of us, and although Terrill's personal biases were instantly apparent and sometimes even schoolboyish (it was "Mr. Chou," but just plain "Rogers"), he did not attempt to disguise, in the manner of the Stalin apologists, the lack of freedom in China, as conventionally understood: with emphasis on the qualifier. "Turning back toward the hotel, I pass a Protestant church—its closed gates bearing the banner 'Carry through the Cultural Revolution to the end.'" Sometimes he tried to explain a particular deprivation. "Wherever I walk, there is a People's Liberation Army man with boyish grin and fixed bayonet. 'Back the other way.' Well, it is a sensitive area. . . . There was an openness and a practical root to nearly all the restraints that met me in China." But the effort is halfhearted—there wasn't, after all, any readily understandable explanation of the practical root for the refusal of any news vendor to sell him the morning papers. Nor does Terrill tell us that the straitened freedom is otherwise compensated for, say by meritocratic integrity. "Another PLA [People's Liberation Army] officer, a tough, cheery man who confessed his total ignorance of medicine, was head of a Peking hospital." He does not even begin to suggest that there is cultural freedom in China. "I found cultural life far more politicized. . . . Public libraries, and museums too, are closed. Churches are boarded up, empty, and checkered with political slogans. . . . In 1971 you simply do not find, as you could in 1964, segments of social and intellectual life around which the tentacles of politics have not curled." The propaganda, in the style of the *Red Detachment of Women,* is altogether relentless. Terrill confirms that in Shensi, with a population of 25,000,000 people, 100,000,000 Mao works were published during the Cultural Revolution. A little liberty, perhaps, for the people liberated on Liberation Day by the People's Liberation Army of the People's Republic of China? "I inquired of the spokesman of the factory Revolutionary Committee, 'Can a worker transfer work by his own individual decision?' I might as well have asked if the leopard can change his spots." Terrill, too, knew about the plight of higher education. "At PKU I saw the English class, which was reading, and discussing, Aesop's fables. . . . They received me with clapping—though few, I found, knew what or where Australia is."

But after all that, the breath-catching evasion. The cement poured on the floor Senator Fulbright seeks to stand on. "People ask, 'Is China free?'—but there is no objective measure of the freedom of a whole society." He explains that there are differences in ours and the Chinese historical experience that account for many differences in attitude. But he agrees that yes, "at one point we and China face the same value judgment. Which gets priority: the individual's free-

dom or the relationships of the whole society? Which *unit* is
to be taken . . . the nation, trade union, our class, my cro-
nies, me? This is the hinge on which the whole issue turns."
(Those who hear a familiar ring are right—the implied doctrine is undiluted fascism.) Terrill gives examples. He has
told us already about Professor P'u Chih-lung, a scientist inclined to the study of pure science, who however was recently
instructed by the state to devote himself entirely to pest control. "Professor P'u Chih-lung . . . did not make his own
decision to take up the problem of insect pests—it was handed him. Is that wrong?" He recalls the writer Kuo Mo-jo, who
used to satisfy himself, before Liberation, writing books suited to his own taste, for small audiences. The government
decided he should appeal to wider audiences. "The
writer . . . cannot now do books for 3000 or at most 8000
readers, as Kuo used to in Shanghai in the 1930's, but must
write for the mass millions—and he's judged by whether he
can do that well or not. Is that wrong?"

Is that wrong?
Wrong! What *is* wrong?
What's *right* is things like Eliminating Graft. (Why, then,
oppose Mussolini?) "The elimination of these conditions in
China," writes historian Barbara Tuchman, exultantly, "is so
striking that negative aspects of the new rule fade in relative
importance." The loss of every known freedom is defined,
now, as a Negative Aspect.

We have been fifty years discovering the limits of Wilsonian politics, our experience as an imperial power having
taught us, fitfully, that the Wilsonian idea simply didn't
work. But we never tried to do without it altogether. The
Wilsonian idea, during its brief golden age, was not only a
mandate for concerted action by the good states against the
bad states, which mandate foundered in its first major test
against Mussolini's Italy for invading Ethiopia. The Wilsonian idea, for all that it was impractical, like the United Nations
Conventions on Human Rights, at least preserved a loose set
of criteria concerning the human condition that are epis-
temologically optimistic. Wilsonianism believed there were

ways societies should behave toward their citizens and shouldn't behave. Very well. If we cannot march in to save the Tibetans from being overrun by the Chinese, who proceed genocidally to extinguish a religious creed, we *can* express ourselves on the heinousness of the act with philosophical and moral security. We will try hard not to be censorious, let alone priggish, in making judgments, and we will be scrupulous as to the form in which they are pronounced. We will be worldly enough, for instance, to recognize the probability that Ghana will move quickly from emancipation as a colony of England to self-rule as a one-party state. But never so worldly as to dismiss the subsequent torture and murder routinely practiced under Nkrumah as merely a Negative Aspect—who knows, perhaps even . . . appropriate?

The retreat from Wilsonianism toward ideological egalitarianism is quite general, though there are interesting exceptions, mostly arising from polemical opportunism. George McGovern has railed against the Greek colonels and against President Thieu with a fervor he never summoned against, say, Tito, or Ho Chi Minh or, for that matter, in recent years, against the devil. He minded it greatly when Agnew went to Greece and to Spain, not at all when Nixon went to Romania or to Yugoslavia. There is something there that seems to say: it is the higher duty to suspend criticism of any power that is strong enough to initiate a world war. You see, it is still fashionable to inveigh against undemocratic societies but only provided that they are (a) weak and (b) allied, in some general way, with the West. The further they recede from the family's orbit, the less we criticize them. This is so for reasons that are psychologically understandable. You castigate Cousin Joe when he starts hitting the bottle, but the alcoholic at the other end of town is a statistic. And then—no question about it—there is the racial point. Arthur Schlesinger remarked somewhere that he finds it disquieting that his fellow intellectuals seem to be saying that Communism, which would never be tolerated here (read: among civilized white Americans), is somehow OK over there (read: among uncivilized yellow people).

But now, with the Fulbright-Terrill-Nixon offensive, even those words of Mr. Schlesinger, uttered only a few years ago,

seem strangely reactionary. They rely, after all, on acquiescence in the proposition that—
But *is* Communism wrong?

We were in Hangchow, and of course there was a banquet. We were restless. Tired and a little bored: demoralized and a little ashamed. There were so many vanities to be indulged. Chinese vanity had us flying in from Peking in *two* shifts because they wouldn't let us use our own big Boeing jet, insisting that we use their little jet, which was Russian at that. Our deadlines for filing copy meant that the first shift couldn't leave before 1 A.M., the second therefore not until 4 A.M. The hotel in Hangchow, hailed as a tourist center ever since Marco Polo, proved to be too small to give us each the indispensable solace of a single room. The day was gray and cold. There had been no hard news. The night before, Nixon and Chou En-lai had been up until dawn, chewing the impasse. We did not know what was the nature of it and were tired of sending speculation back home. Then—sensing something amiss—the President invited us all to his villa at 4 P.M. We got there, wandered about a bit in the ornate gardens and quarters, and found finally the outdoor patio where we were expected. It had been rigged for one of those group pictures, planks on light scaffolding, with a cavity in the center, which meant he would be posing with us. We lined up, already shivering from cold. Mr. Nixon entered, beaming, and we all posed. Then he turned around to face us, spoke genially and said: I'm sorry I can't give out the details of what we're working on, but you must understand that in order to help you do *your* duty of reporting the news well, I cannot risk doing *my* duty, which is diplomatic, badly.

So help me that was *all* he said, but it took him twenty minutes, during which the wind and the cold went to work lasciviously on our bones and our spirits, as we stood silently there on the scaffolding, eighty titans of the American media, chin just above the head of the man in front, four tiers of us, like cadets having one last docile session with the drillmaster, before graduation. Then, the briefing at an end, Nixon said, sort of teasingly, that if any of us wanted to present our spouses with proof that we had indeed been in China with the President, not, er, elsewhere doing something else, he would be glad to have his picture taken with each of us individually. End Sulk. Eighty-odd grand masters lining up to have their picture taken with the President of the United States, making self-conscious conversation as the line moved forward slowly.

The indignity, all the more biting for its having been self-inflicted, hung heavy in the stomach two hours later in the banquet hall, where we reported as told to do promptly at 7:45. There we stood, waiting. Nixon and Chou arrived *forty minutes* later. The predinner booze was the same Chinese syrup, with zero anesthetizing power. For the first time I was asked a provocative question, by the Chinese official standing next to me, waiting, as we all were, for the principals, and for the first (and only) time, I answered a Chinese shortly. He had heard, he said, that I was "a conservative." What was an American conservative? I answered crisply: Someone who believes in individual freedom and in—I reached for the most incendiary word—capitalism. Did I *really* believe in "capitalism"? he asked mockingly. Yes, I said, "and for all anyone is permitted to know, you do too." He feigned ignorance of the allusion to his intellectual paralysis, and smiled as sickly sweet as the Chinese wine he brought to his lips to toast me with. Joe Kraft said he was going next door to the bedroom to fetch something (the banquet hall abutted the hotel). He came back two hours later (he missed a splendid meal) and in plenty of time for the toasts, which were just beginning. "Where on earth have you been?" I whispered. "Sleeping," he winked. *Très* cool. We were listening to the usual business from the Chinese toastmasters. We were relieved to learn from Chou's toast that the Chinese people still feel friendship for the American people, and that nothing had happened to change that since last night's toast. Then came Nixon, and by God, he was likening the revolution led by George Washington to the revolution led by Mao Tse-tung. But after all, why not? As Terrill would say, is that wrong? Both were revolutions, weren't they?

Albert Jay Nock wrote a line that never leaves the memory. I paraphrase him: "I have often thought that it would be interesting to write an essay on the question: How do you go about discovering that you are slipping into a dark age?" In any such essay I think you would have to reflect on the special problems a democracy has in mobilizing public attitudes in such a way as to inform foreign policy in directions that are essentially moral. The great totalitarian systems do not have this difficulty. It sufficed that China should publicize a picture of Mao Tse-tung fraternizing with President Richard Nixon to satisfy the people that a friendly relationship with the United States was the right thing to do. Only two years ago, Chairman Mao pronounced that "U.S. imperialism is slaughtering the white and black people in its own country. Nixon's fascist atrocities have kindled the raging flames of the revolutionary mass movement in the United States. The Chinese people firmly support the revolutionary struggle of the American people." The speech in which that passage presumed was still being passed around (in several languages) while we were there. I got my copy in the hotel lobby. As easily as Mao now redirected the public on the proper attitude toward America, he could redirect it back to where it had been, as Hitler and Stalin twice changed attitudes toward each other, on either end of the Ribbentrop-Molotov Pact.

A free society cannot do this kind of thing. And America— young, inexperienced and moralistic—can do it least. When we fought hand in hand with Stalin, Churchill had said he would make a pact with the devil himself to defeat Hitler. In America, our leaders, far from thinking of Stalin as a devil, began to find great qualities in him, who before long became "Uncle Joe." Thus have the Chinese Communists been transformed, under diplomatic exigency; so that now the polls tell us that the American people, assimilating the Nixon trip, have discovered that the Chinese enterprise is "intelligent," "progressive" and "practical." To be sure, the Chinese don't do things the way we do, but their distinctive ideas on how to do things are understandable—and anyway, who are we to criticize? Who ever said we were so great?

And then too, a free society makes decisions concerning its own defenses with some reference to what it is that it seeks to defend itself against. Our own defense budget is a great extravagance—unless it is defending something that is indeed worth $80 billion a year defending, and at the risk of a nuclear war: That is the logic implicit in owning and manning 1,000 multiple-targeted nuclear Minutemen. As the differences between what we are and what we might become in the absence of an irresistible defense system diminish in our mind, so does the resolution diminish to make the sacrifices necessary to remain free—the tacit national commitment that the risk of death is better than the certain loss of liberty.

Nineteen sixty: "Do you believe that the United States should defend itself even at the risk of nuclear war?" Yes, 70 percent—of the student body of Yale University, in answer to that question.

Nineteen seventy: same college, same question—"Do you believe that the United States should defend itself even at the risk of nuclear war?" Yes, 40 percent.

Is that wrong?

Well, of course, it depends. Presumably if the people in the Dark Ages had known it was dark and why it was dark, they'd have done something about it—let in the light. As a matter of fact, eventually they did. "If the whole world is covered with asphalt," Ilya Ehrenburg wrote, "one day a crack will appear in the asphalt: and in that crack grass will grow." How will we know then that it is grass?

I have not worked that out.

Vive la Différence

March 13, 1972

IN THE aftermath of the Peking Summit the distinction-crushers are hard at work insisting that, after all, what is the difference between having affable social relations with the governors of China, and having affable social relations with the governors of Taiwan, Spain, and Greece? One has the feeling that some of the people who make the comparisons really do not know the difference, unlike those others who are merely polemical opportunists. A gentleman who broadcasts from Long Island, to give an example, amused himself at the surprise expressed by some of us over the enthusiasm with which Mr. Nixon threw himself into the business of toasting the person of Mao Tse-tung. Here is how he put it. Why be "appalled at the sight of the President drinking toasts and exchanging civilities with the despotic rulers of Red China"? Because of the "embarrassment [caused to] our friendly client despots on Taiwan? As if Mao and Chou weren't the moral equals of Franco, Papadopoulos, and other dictators toasted and praised on their own home grounds last October by Vice President Agnew."

And of course for years now it has been chic to refer to the "so-called free world," the idea being that much of the world on this side of the Iron Curtain is no more free than the world at the other side of the Iron Curtain. The gentlemen who slur the distinction spend, on the whole, not enough time . . . thinking.

In Taiwan, in Greece, and in Spain, a human being can: (1) practice his religion, (2) quit his job, (3) join a labor union, (4) leave the country, (5) travel within the country where he wants to, (6) enter into contracts, whether to buy or sell a loaf of bread, exchange a piece of land, or provide a personal service. In those countries, (7) what he owns is his. (8) He is free to buy all but a very few books, and in fact he can get these by the mildest exertions. (9) He may say anything he wants to say: except that he cannot attempt to bring down the government—he has no political freedom.

In China, you may not practice a religion, you may not change your job without permission of the state, there are no labor unions to join, you cannot leave the country, or travel within your country except by special permission. You may not engage in contracts except by leave of the state, which owns all your services. You may not own property, outside the toothbrush category. You will find to read only accepted works of Communist theology. You may not criticize the state nor, obviously, attempt to bring down the government.

At a positive level, you are required to submit to hours of instruction every week in the state religion, to fawn on its leaders, dogmas, rituals, and hope (but not pray) that you will find yourself aligned with the winning faction during civil uprisings.

There should be differences enough there to be visible to most people. To be sure, Mr. Nixon has not greatly helped. His perfunctory references to our "different systems" make him sound as though Americans like calico, while the Chinese Communists like gingham. Still, people who influence opinion ought always to distinguish between the despot and the totalitarian. Papadopoulos is a despot. Mao is a totalitarian, which is a stage advanced from the tyranny about which political philosophers have written from the beginning of time.

Papadopoulos did not take power in order to tyrannize. He took it, as Franco did, in an intractable social and parliamentary situation. That they haven't yielded more of their power is either a discredit to their integrity, or a tribute to their perspicacity (closer to the former, I judge, than to the latter). J. S. Mill taught that under certain "conditions of society . . . a vigorous despotism is in itself the best mode of government for training the people in what is specifically wanting to render them capable of a higher civilization." But only "provided the end be their improvement," which is to say their introduction to liberty. Such liberty as is despised by name by the Communists, who seek explicitly to crush it wherever it raises its head, as for instance in Czechoslovakia. That is the difference.

Solzhenitsyn at Bay

January 12, 1974

THE NEW VOLUME of Aleksandr Solzhenitsyn raises policy questions for the West which, if we answer them wrongly, will bring down upon us that curse of history reserved for those despicable men who, though knowing everything they needed to know, declined to act, thus contributing to a crucifixion. Solzhenitsyn is only an individual, but there was never in human history a clearer identification of an individual and a class. Martin Luther King as representative of the American Negro recedes alongside the authority of Aleksandr Solzhenitsyn as representative of the 200,000,000 people of Russia who have suffered, and continue to suffer, at the hands of the creed-ridden tormentors of that wretched country. The Soviet government does not disguise its feelings about Solzhenitsyn, any more than the establishmentarians disguised theirs toward Jesus. Now, on the publication of *The Gulag Archipelago,* they have begun their offensive. It is clearly launched with a certain tentativeness—else they'd have simply yanked him from the streets and shipped him off directly to Siberia, or to a convenient warren in the cellar of the Lubyanka, there to receive a little lead in his stupefying, awe-inspiring mind. Though Solzhenitsyn is only one man, his elimination would amount to an act of genocide. It is now as if, thirty-five years ago, Adolf Hitler had released, for the convenience of the next few editions of the *World Almanac,* the projections of the diminishing percentage of Jews alive and well in Germany. Would the West, in such circumstances, do anything about it? Or would that be to interrupt the rhythm of détente?

Permit a drastic truncation—in just a few sentences—of the experience of just one Soviet victim—this one an American citizen who, incredibly, has been living in Maryland since 1971. It required that we should learn of his existence from Aleksandr Solzhenitsyn. His name is Alexander Dolgun. He was a clerk with the American Embassy. In 1948 he was seized on the streets of Moscow and would spend eight years in Soviet camps, and another fifteen years in civilian detention. A cheerful representative of the Workers' Paradise, second in charge of Soviet security, called Ryumin, called in young Dolgun, who had declined to confess to crimes he had not committed.

"'And so,' said Ryumin politely, stroking his rubber truncheon which was an inch and a half thick, 'you have survived trial by sleeplessness with honor. So now we will try the club. Prisoners don't last more than two or three sessions of this. Let down your trousers and lie on the runner.'

"The colonel sat down on the prisoner's back. Dolgun had intended to count the blows. He didn't know yet what a blow with a rubber truncheon is on the sciatic nerve. The effect is not in the place where the blow is delivered—it blows up inside the head. After the first blow the victim was insane with pain and broke his nails on the carpet. Ryumin beat away. After the beating the prisoner could not walk and, of course, he was not carried. They just dragged him along the floor. The remnants of his buttocks soon swelled up to the point that he could not button his breeches, and yet there were practically no scars. He was hit by a violent case of diarrhea, and, sitting there on the latrine barrel in solitary, Dolgun laughed. He went through a second and third session, and his skin burst, and Ryumin went wild, and started to beat him in the stomach and broke through the intestinal wall, in the form of an enormous hernia where his intestines protruded. And the prisoner was taken off to the Butyrka hospital with a case of peritonitis, and for the time being the attempts to compel him to commit a foul deed were broken off."

The reason Brezhnev et al. are so much afraid of Solzhenitsyn is that his indictment isn't of the man Stalin, or even the man Lenin, whose atrocities figure greatly in this book. His indictment is a universal: an indictment of totalitarian society. Brezhnev can no more convincingly denounce Stalin than he can denounce his own aorta. The governors of the Soviet Union cannot break with their own past without walking, unmanacled, to Red Square, to set a torch upon themselves.

This is the moment not for bureaucratic response, but for gallant response, and those of us who know Henry Kissinger pray that he will take the initiative—no one could do it better.

If a hair of the head of Solzhenitsyn is harmed:

One. The United States of America will suspend all cultural exchange with the Soviet Union beginning immediately.

Two. An absolute embargo, for a mourning period of one

year, will be imposed on commerce of any kind with the Soviet Union, and against any purchase of goods of any kind from the Soviet Union.

Perhaps Solzhenitsyn requires martyrdom, fully to anneal his work to the service of humanity. Perhaps, even, he desires it. But we cannot willingly play the role of Pontius Pilate.

The Victimization of Owen Lattimore

February 19, 1974

THE PEOPLE'S REPUBLIC of China has done something that gravely imperils the cause of détente. It has uncovered Professor Owen Lattimore. It has been said of him that he is a "reactionary historian" and—"an international spy."

Many years ago Senator Joseph R. McCarthy—it was his most famous charge—said that Lattimore was a Communist spy. There was a lot of investigation, and as the power of McCarthyism waned, the reputation of Lattimore rose. So that one never runs into his name nowadays without some reference to his having been "vindicated."

That would hardly appear to be the word for it. Apparently, all this time, while more or less pretending to be pro-Communist, he was really an anti-Communist. More, an international spy!

Owen Lattimore wrote a book shortly after the war called *Solution in Asia.* The jacket of that book described the contents neatly. "He [Lattimore] shows that all the Asiatic people are more interested in actual democratic practices such as the ones they can see in action across the Russian border, than they are in the fine theories of Anglo-Saxon democracies which come coupled with ruthless imperialism. . . . He inclines to support American newspapermen who report that the only real democracy in China is found in Communist areas."

That was pretty rank stuff, and no doubt, in saying it, Lattimore convinced the Communists that he was really on their side. Indeed, only two years ago Chou En-lai gave a big party in honor of Lattimore in Peking, so convincingly had Lattimore presented himself as sympathetic to Mao during this last generation.

However, since it is the practice of the CIA never to disclose the identity of its agents, one fears that Lattimore will not be betrayed as an American superspy. Accordingly, he will have to fight to establish his innocence of Peking's charges. What can he do? Everyone knows that there is no freedom in China, none to speak, to organize, to emigrate, to practice religion, to seek out a job of one's choice, to study what you want where you want. These deprivations haven't bothered the legion of admirers who in recent years have swarmed over China: Barbara Tuchman, for instance, or John Kenneth Galbraith, or Harrison Salisbury, or Seymour Topping, or James Reston. The Cultural Revolution in which a million or so were killed, following on the heels of the purges of the preceding decades, didn't in the least undermine the enthusiasm for Mao. But now, what if Owen Lattimore accuses the Chinese Communists of—McCarthyism!

What would Barbara Tuchman say? Or John Fairbank? Or Arthur Schlesinger? I mean, we all want peace in this world, sure. And we can afford to be understanding if the Chinese revolution requires an average of 1,500,000 victims per year, and an absolutely totalitarianized society admitting of no human freedom—that's okay. But McCarthyism we cannot accept. If Owen Lattimore persuades the Eastern Seaboard Establishment that Peking is McCarthyite, they'll impeach Nixon not for Watergate, but for having gone and made friends with Chou En-lai.

This poses very grave questions of public policy. While I am ordinarily sympathetic with the iron code of the CIA that its agents are never uncovered, I for one think that in the case of Owen Lattimore an exception should be made. After all, we live in dangerous times. A nuclear war could dash the hopes of mankind. East and West *must* meet. And anyway, why should the CIA suffer from the exposure of just this one operation? After all, they had McCarthy fooled into believing Lattimore was a Communist, and that was twenty-four years ago. You can't expect to fool all the people all the time, and Peking's discovery reminds us we've got to stay on our toes. Let's swallow our pride like a man, decorate Owen Lattimore for his services as an international spy, and pull together for détente, by making it clear that the Chinese Communists may do a lot of things we don't agree with, but it is wrong, and unfair, to accuse them of McCarthyism.

Soviet Justice, Soviet Law, Soviet Gas

February 22, 1974

ON OCTOBER 16, 1973, the Union of Soviet Socialist Republics deposited with the Secretary-General of the United Nations its instrument of ratification of the International Covenant on Economic, Social and Cultural Rights, and the International Covenant on Civil and Political Rights, which covenants are the legal embodiment of the Universal Declaration of Human Rights.

As regards Aleksandr Solzhenitsyn, ejected yesterday from his homeland and dumped in Switzerland, here is the relevant language of the Declaration:

"Art. 2. Everyone is entitled to all the rights and freedoms set forth in this Declaration without distinction of any kind such as . . . political or other opinions.

"Art. 5. No one shall be subjected to torture or to cruel, inhuman, or degrading treatment or punishment.

"Art. 9. No one shall be subjected to arbitrary arrest, detention, or exile.

"Art. 10. Everyone is entitled in full equality to a fair and public hearing by an independent and impartial tribunal, in the determination of his rights and obligations and of any criminal charge against him.

"Art. 11. Everyone charged with a penal offense has the right to be presumed innocent until proved guilty according to law in a public trial at which he has had all the guarantees necessary for his defense.

"Art. 12. No one shall be subjected to arbitrary interference with his privacy, family, home, or correspondence, nor to attacks upon his honor and reputation. Everyone has the right to the protection of the law against such interference or attacks.

"Art. 13. (1) Everyone has the right to freedom of movement and residence within the borders of each state. (2) Everyone has the right to leave any country including his own, and to return to his country.

"Art. 15. (2) No one shall be arbitrarily deprived of his nationality nor denied the right to change his nationality.

"Art. 18. Everyone has the right to freedom of thought . . . this right includes freedom to change his . . . belief . . . either alone or in community with others and in public or private to manifest his . . . belief in teaching, practice, worship, and observance.

"Art. 19. Everyone has the right to freedom of opinion and expression; this right includes freedom to hold opinions without interference and to seek, receive, and impart information and ideas through any media and regardless of frontiers.

"Art. 30. Nothing in this Declaration may be interpreted as implying for any state, group or person any right to engage in any activity or to perform any act aimed at the destruction of any of the rights and freedoms set forth herein."

Mr. Andrei Gromyko, Minister of Foreign Affairs, addressing the UN General Assembly on September 25, 1973:

"The [Soviet Union] actively contributes to putting into practice everything of value that can be produced by the collective wisdom and experience of [the United Nations]. Indeed, just a few days ago, the Presidium of the U.S.S.R. Supreme Soviet ratified two important documents of international law pertaining to respect for fundamental human rights and freedoms, protection of human dignity and the interests of society as a whole. These . . . covenants not merely express wishes and recommendations of a declaratory nature but provide for quite specific obligations of the participating states. We are calling on countries which have not yet signed or ratified the said covenants to follow suit and take steps for these covenants to enter into force as soon as possible."

The Impact of the Soviet Jew

September 29, 1973

WHAT I'D LIKE to know is, What do we do after the Soviet Union runs out of Jews?

An appropriate thought, set down during this Jewish holiday period—when one considers that the toughening of our cultural, and perhaps now economic, positions on the Soviet Union is exclusively to the credit of the Jewish community. It is they who have demanded, by means mostly fair, though by some (the Jewish Defense League) foul, that the United States do something, short of war, to alleviate the plight of Jewish citizens in Russia who seek to emigrate.

The Senate sponsors of the Jackson Resolution have magnanimously required, in the draft of their resolution, that the Soviet Union also permit other Russian minorities the right to emigrate, but everybody knows that that insistence will die of neglect after the last Russian Jew who wants to leave the Soviet Union has done so.

How I wish there were some Jews in China who wished to emigrate. I have yet to hear one Congressman call for the application of any sanctions at all against China, where at least it can be said that the government of Mao Tse-tung applies its repressions on strict nondiscriminatory grounds. I.e., everyone is discriminated against. No one can leave the city to go to the country without special permission, or vice versa; let alone leave the People's Republic to go to a country where human beings are permitted to breathe.

When the subject comes up of trade and credits for China, I shall raise with Senator Jackson the question of applying his reservation to China in behalf of China's Christians, but I know that the good Senator, for all that I love and admire him, will not return that telephone call.

Christians are born to be martyrs, and mostly martyrs of the silent kind. Jews have had quite enough of martyrdom in this century and are resolved to fight back, and today, writing on the feast of Rosh Hashanah, I pay them tribute with all sincerity, and go so far as to say that if the Christian community today, let alone a generation ago, had displayed one one-hundredth of their tenacity and courage, the persecution of the Christians in East Europe, in Russia, and in China would have been inconceivable.

Professor Kissinger has an entirely plausible point when he says that he is embarrassed by pressures from "my co-religionists" which impose upon his schematic foreign policy national encumbrances. Indeed he reminded the Senate Foreign Relations Committee that up until a few years ago the academic community considered it axiomatic that a normalization of relations between the United States and Soviet Russia would itself constitute the principal pressure on the Soviet Union to relax its controls over its serfs.

Mr. Kissinger is correct that that was the current assumption. But the thaw with the Soviet Union began not with the Nixon Administration but with the Eisenhower Administration, in 1957 with the summit conference, and then with all the cultural accords. In 1957 the Soviet Union left off jamming our broadcasts, permitted the publication of Solzhenitsyn's *A Day in the Life of Ivan Denisovich,* and seemed to be headed toward liberalization.

Successive crises, internal and external, changed all this. But there is no more reason to suppose that the crises were responsible for the hardening of the Soviet spirit than there is to conclude that the progressive totalitarianization of Hitler's Germany grew out of our full contacts, economic, political, and cultural, with it.

Most important of all are the arguments of Solzhenitsyn and Sakharov, that economic and diplomatic success by the Soviet Union at this juncture and on their terms can only fortify the regime in its determination to crush all dissent, like butterflies on the wheels of American technology. It is a pity that Senator Fulbright did not think to ask Mr. Kissinger to explain his reason for supposing that he is better informed than Sakharov on this matter of Soviet behavior.

Meanwhile the pressure on the cultural-political front intensifies. Professor Hans Morgenthau has discovered that Soviet leaders probably believe their own propaganda. Anthony Lewis, having absolutely established that the Soviet Union is miles removed from Indochina, has come out for a hard line. I pray that every Jew in Russia will be permitted to emigrate. But I pray also that one (1) Jew will elect to remain, while pretending he wants to get out. Otherwise there will be a collapse of our foreign policy, of Congressional sanctions, and of our Army, Navy, Air Force, and probably our national anthem.

The Chinese Exhibitionists

December 11, 1974

FOR MANY DAYS it was a well-kept secret. But as the moment came for the preview, a decision had to be made. The National Gallery of Art was faced with two alternatives. The first was to examine the credentials of every newspaperman or critic who came to the door. If it proved that he was a Taiwanese, a South Korean, an Israeli, or a South Vietnamese, he was to be denied entrance. The second alternative was to cancel the preview altogether.

Needless to say, even our State Department, which had been in hectic consultation with the gallery officials, advised for cancellation. It was too late to advise all the newspapermen and critics who had been invited. They came to the door of the gallery and were told, simply, that the preview had been called off.

That night there was the banquet. Mrs. Gerald Ford was present, most conspicuously. But a few others declined to attend, in protest against the exclusionary principle that the officials of the People's Republic of China, as that playground of a handful of Chinese ideologues is so playfully called, had laid down. Among those sensitive enough to stay away were Mrs. Graham, the publisher of the Washington *Post,* and Mr. James Reston and Mr. Clifton Daniel of the New York *Times.*

Now we probably view the episode as a victory of sorts for our side. After all, we declined to meet *their* terms, they declined to meet *our* terms: so the preview was canceled. But it was no more a victory for us than it was a victory for the Chinese. Because they themselves said that unless their terms were met, there would be no preview. So that canceling the preview was as much the Chinese solution as it was the American solution. Call it, if you will, the Chinese-American solution.

Later that day, at the banquet, Mrs. Ford made a little speech and raised her glass to toast the exhibition as "an important symbol of the growing ties of friendship between our two peoples." That is cant to begin with, there being no visible signs of an increasing friendship between the Chinese and the American people for the perfectly straightforward reason that no American can visit China without getting a special visa. And these are vouchsafed sparingly and, in most cases, with much attention given to the political background of the applicant. But Mrs. Ford's toast under the special circumstances of the canceled preview was a little worse than routine cant. It brushed up against perversity. Don't blame her: she just reads the stuff the State Department gives her to read.

The entire political ballet reminds one of the despondent fact that there is no such thing as a cultural exhibition where the Communists are concerned. There is only psywar. It surpasses the understanding why we put up with it.

In Peking, in 1972, the President and his press party were made to endure the world's worst ballet, the *Red Detachment of Women,* on the theme of the triumph of Mao's Army of Liberation against the capitalist-imperialist forces of the bourgeois world. I walked out after the first act. Poor President Nixon stayed and then talked about how he had seen ballets all over the world, but had never seen a better one than this one. It was good training for his future statements on Watergate.

The question before the house is, really, What is the reason for letting them get away with it? If the President of the United States is forced to see a ballet on the theme of the decadence, materialism, and sadism of the non-Communist world, why can't he say: "I thought the thing was lousy—agitprop posing as art."

If the Chinese bring an exhibit of art treasures the current government had nothing at all to do in creating (the exhibit reaches millennia back into Chinese history), why do we permit the Chinese to use it as an occasion for humiliating the Jews and those Orientals with whom we have fought side by side during the past generation?

Why didn't the State Department close down the exhibit, cancel the dinner, and tell the Chinese to ship their treasures back home, and bring them back another day when they had grown up sufficiently to contain their horny appetite to make vulgar political points. I ask this with all seriousness: *Why don't we do that?*

The answer is that we don't do it for exactly the same reason that we are, really, losing all over the world. Because our spirit is enfeebled. We still have a lot of hardware, but the national pride is oozing away, and our tanks and missiles are derelicts.

The Coils of Détente

January 25, 1975

SENATOR JACKSON is in disrepute because of the refusal of the Soviet Union to accept American economic credits. Indeed, Senator Jackson and his colleagues were publicly scolded by President Ford when he delivered the State of the Union address a few days after the Kremlin huffily announced that it could not be expected to be forced into the indignity of observing human rights for mere money. No, it would take a great deal more than that to force a proud leadership to renounce its principled opposition to human freedom.

Mr. Kissinger of course joined President Ford in lamenting the turn of events, and one can, in a purely technical sense, understand, and even sympathize with, a Secretary of State who is trying to negotiate with a foreign power and finds himself saddled with extrinsic considerations by Congress. Because they are, of course, extrinsic: that is to say, a Soviet respect for human rights is not an aspect of détente in any formal philosophical sense. Winston Churchill said he would make a pact with the devil to accomplish his objective (the defeat of Hitler) and proceeded to do so. Willy Brandt said that human rights in the Soviet Union had nothing whatever to do with his policy of *Ostpolitik.*

What Mr. Kissinger has not commented on is the *failure* of détente—in Indochina, for instance. What is happening in Indochina is that the Soviet Union and the People's Republic of China have been hypo-ing an already ravenous North Vietnamese Communist appetite for taking over South Vietnam with military hardware on a huge scale. Peace in Vietnam was held up as the first fruit of détente. And, for a flickering moment, Peace in Vietnam was understood as meaning peace in Vietnam. Presently, the Orwellian meaning of the phrase became clear. It meant: American military withdrawal from Vietnam, and quite literally nothing else. If I were one of those people who are always looking for excuses to label Westerners as "racists," I would use the Nobel Committee as a prime exhibit. The Nobel people awarded a Peace Prize to Mr. Kissinger and Le Duc Tho for stanching the flow of WASP blood in South Vietnam. Gooks don't count. They continue to be slaughtered at the conventional rate. And Mr. Kissinger's diplomacy proves helpless in stopping the flow of arms that makes this possible.

So Congress stepped between Mr. Kissinger and the Russians and insisted that economic concessions to the Soviet Union could not be made unless the Soviet Union permitted free emigration. But the integrity of this humanitarian impulse on the part of Congress is suddenly clouded as Congress sits by, refusing to appropriate the dollars necessary to help the South Vietnamese resist the advancing Communists. Moreover, unlike the Russian situation, it was established American policy to help South Vietnam defend itself against the Communists.

Congress cut in half the pledged military appropriations to the South Vietnamese, and in doing so accomplished more than the depletion of the South's military reserves. It has gone a long way to accomplish the demoralization of the South Vietnamese, who find that they were leaning on so slender a reed as the word of the United States.

Meanwhile, no doubt, Israeli strategists observe Congress insouciantly prepared to deliver South Vietnam to the North Vietnamese. That is the same Congress that voted to insist on the rights of Jewish emigration from the Soviet Union. The hypocrisy is transparent, and no doubt the Israelis are saying to themselves: There, but for Israeli intransigence, would go Israel. If the United States will not spend a pledged extra $300,000,000 to defend an ally with which it fought arm in arm in a great war, what will it do to help us, when the going gets tough, and the concrete of isolationism in the American spirit hardens?

I, for one, yearn for the days of the Cold War. Because international tension is fun? No, because international tension is there in any case, and it is healthy to recognize it as such, in the sense that realism is healthy. Détente is impacted diplomatic hypocrisy. We're not spending any less on defense on account of détente, and in fact we should be spending more. We have not achieved freedom for Eastern Europe. We have not brought peace with honor to South Vietnam. What has détente done for us except provide a backdrop for the exchange of toasts between American Presidents and Communist tyrants? Neville Chamberlain and Adolf Hitler were able to contrive a situation that permitted the use of champagne. We should keep ours in the cellar until there is something to celebrate.

II.

The Campaign of '72

Humphrey vs. McGovern

June 1, 1972

THE SECOND debate between Senator McGovern and Senator Humphrey, it seems to me, confirms this: that George McGovern is going to get the Democratic nomination. I cannot imagine that Mr. Humphrey knows less well than other political analysts what the fates have decided. That no doubt is why, on television, George McGovern looked so cool and confident, while Hubert Humphrey sounded so raspy and edgy. And no doubt Mr. Humphrey's desperation was in part responsible for his disastrous performance. This isn't to say that McGovern came out of it with all the marbles, but for all his vagueness, his non sequiturs, his banalities, there was an air of assurance which is the smell of the victor.

Mr. Humphrey began with an apology. In his prime, he'd have known that it would probably emerge in the headlines. The apology was utterly unnecessary. And it sounded unnecessary even as Mr. Humphrey spoke it. Political exchanges are not lapidary models of the syllogistic art. Granted, in the classroom it goes this way: (1) People who believe in confiscatory taxation are fools. (2) George McGovern believes in confiscatory taxation. Therefore, (3) George McGovern is a fool.

It was rather painful hearing Mr. Humphrey explain that "if" people took what he said about George McGovern as being "personal," then he wanted to "apologize" to Senator McGovern, who is a "fine" man. Rigorous thought would have required him, instead, to say that *if* people believed that Hubert Humphrey *was* being personal about George McGovern, the people were wrong. Or, he might have said, the people were foolish. But then at the third debate I suppose he'd have had to apologize to the people for calling them foolish. After all, the people are fine. Hubert Hum-

61

phrey has known people all his life, and he's here to tell us they are fine, the finest people he ever knew.

Then the Senators began exchanging statistics, dealing in the billions of dollars, and the craft began to show. Hubert Humphrey was out to suggest that the calculations of George McGovern were irresponsible, and of course they are irresponsible, but it doesn't sound very convincing when Hubert Humphrey suddenly puts on the toga of guardian of the exchequer since for years Hubert Humphrey, like Eleanor Roosevelt (in the fleeted phrase of James Burnham), has tended to treat the whole world as his own personal slum project.

He did score off McGovern's infatuation with the military-industrial complex in California. George McGovern being brave in California reminds me of Bobby Kennedy's being brave in New York, when, running for Senator, he dropped the scheduled passage on closing down the Brooklyn Navy Yard when he got a sniff of the crowd—at Brooklyn.

Humphrey skewered another of McGovern's tergiversations very neatly when he asked how come McGovern was against subsidies for Lockheed, when he was in favor of subsidies for American Motors. Well, ah, uh, said George McGovern, America believes in competition. Well, said Humphrey, shouldn't there be competition among the airplane producers also? Here McGovern showed a superior skill, because although Humphrey made the point, McGovern slid off it in the direction of some social vapidity or other and Humphrey let him get away with it.

McGovern's most adroit maneuver was to rush in to identify himself exactly with Humphrey's views on busing. Humphrey's views on busing being absolutely unintelligible, that is where George McGovern is most comfortable. To say that busing is "only one of many tools to effect integration" is to say something as arresting as: paper is only one of the constituents of pornography. It is to say nothing at all, which both candidates are most in favor of saying about busing.

But not about Vietnam. Humphrey, who a while ago was telling the South Vietnamese face to face that we would never let them down, is now in favor of cutting them off "flat." It is "my judgment," he said, that "they are capable of their own defense." In that event, of course, his judgment is very bad, because the South Vietnamese are not capable of their own defense, any more than the North Vietnamese are capable of their own offense. But the climactic worst came, appropriately, at the end of the debate, when Senator Humphrey announced his brave solution for the war: turn the problem over to the United Nations. "I've lived too long," Senator Humphrey said a couple of times, leaning on his favorite opener, "to be taken in by"—this, that or the other. By the end of the evening, the audience was agreeing with the opener, and yawning at the rest.

He Lost It in California?

June 7, 1972

HARVARD YARD. A great big Greyhound bus, surrounded by disconsolate young passengers with their bags. They thought all the expenses had been provided but now, all set to go, the company agent is requiring $2,000 in insurance—a very reasonable premium, one would think, in case this busload of Radcliffe girls and Harvard boys dehydrated in Death Valley, or fell into the Grand Canyon, or whatever: picture the lawsuits! And of course the parents wouldn't be suing George McGovern, in whose behalf the children were bent, to canvass for him in California, but the poor old bus company. Anyway, the agent was absolutely firm: that bus would rot in Harvard Yard and not move an inch, unless the McGovern Kids came up with $2,000, cash.

At this point an economics professor strolls by and catches the signs of distress. He quickly collars every member of the faculty he can put his hands on, and gets $300. That isn't enough. But he happens to have in his pocket a check for a lecture fee, appropriately enough for a lecture delivered the week before in California, so he resignedly signs it over to the bus company. Within seconds, the motor roars, and the bus moves on. And the professor muses that in a lifetime of contributing money to political causes he has never yet experienced so direct a sensation of causality. Like putting a nickel in a turnstile and instantly unfreezing it. Nice sensation. Nice story.

And part of a growing legend which was strangely arrested in California. They were talking, quite seriously, about a two to one vote, McGovern vs. Humphrey. It was very very far from being anything of the sort. At this writing the lead is not 25 points, but 5 points. And this notwithstanding the biggest political romance in modern times. The manager of the McGovern campaign, Mr. Pierre Salinger, said that he doubted there had been as many volunteer workers, as much enthusiasm spent, in any primary in the history of the United States. The McGovern organization, a humming coordinated miracle, with as many moving parts as a Saturn rocket, seemed to sweep the state. McGovern, the poor man's candidate, spent money like Nelson Rockefeller. McGovern, the pollsters' waif only two months ago, showed a solid 20 percent lead in the guessing polls, right up to Primary Day.

Hubert Humphrey, by sharp contrast, was apparently lost in confusion. An account of his experience in Santa Barbara, from a correspondent not unfriendly to him, is suggestive. "Incident here, blacked out of all media except local paper: HHH was to address the Channel City Club, which in Santa Barbara's terms is *the* prestige audience. Its founder twenty-five years ago, and president ever since, a banker, found out he and HHH had just two days before shared a birthday. So he boxed a slice of birthday cake for presentation to the ex-Veep. Ex-Veep's schedule characteristically snarled from talking too much somewhere else. Channel City Club stall, chat, finally eat their lunch, finally get up and leave.

"At 1:25 HHH arrives at the door in a scream of tires. Hand outstretched, he starts to alight. Why is everyone leaving? 'We adjourn at 1:30.' At that moment Mr. Channel City Club steps up with his box of birthday cake, starts to present it. HHH bangs the car door in his face and the auto leaps off to the next stop, leaving behind a humiliation for Mr. Channel City Club and perhaps 300–400 people who are unlikely to think of voting for Humphrey. One puts it down to campaign nerves. G McG is making serious inroads on the Humphrey cool."

It could very easily, we now see, have been the truly major upset of the season. If anything had been subtracted from McGovern, he'd apparently have lost. If there had been less than the organization he took a year to build. If the polls had less assertively discouraged the Humphrey people by giving McGovern such a way-out lead. If the children had been required to wait until they were as old as Abraham Lincoln was before *he* was permitted to vote. . . .

Nevertheless, McGovern won, by what may turn out to be about as narrow a victory as Goldwater's over Rockefeller in the critical election of 1964. Still, even as Goldwater won, McGovern won. For Goldwater, it proved to be his last major victory, the significant difference between Goldwater and McGovern being that Goldwater's cause was my cause, wherefore, just, noble, and eternally inspiring.

McGovern and the National Mood

May 24, 1972

THEY ARE saying (Scotty Reston is saying: ergo They are saying) that George McGovern might actually become the President of the United States. The reasoning is simple-complex. To begin with, nothing is happening the way it ought to have happened. Three months ago it was not thought by any professional that Ed Muskie could be stopped. Ed Muskie! As well nominate Harold Stassen, at this point. And what did he do to earn such sudden, permanent oblivion? Nothing at all, just act normal. Moral of the season: Act abnormal.

That is what George McGovern has for the most part been doing. Going left left left, ostentatiously alienating the middle people, who are supposed to be indispensable to a true victory. Upsetting the labor union leaders, defying the bosses, ignoring the great social issue of busing, saying things like: "I still think Henry Wallace was right," a statement of such breathtaking perversity as to render George Romney's famous self-disqualifier about having been brainwashed positively unnoticeable by contrast. But it doesn't stop McGovern. Nothing stops McGovern. I doubt if McGovern would lose a primary if he said that on second thought he wishes the Arabs would take over Israel. Or has he said it already, and nobody noticed?

So . . .—they are saying—who knows? Are the American people just being perverse, backing a nice man to whom it would be thought risky to entrust a college seminar? What then if you add the balls Richard Nixon is juggling, one of which he might drop? Suppose that in October the North Vietnamese topple the Thieu government, by military or political pressure? Or that unemployment and inflation begin to gnaw deeply? Or that the dollar is sold down humiliatingly? There are other possibilities, of the sort that would undo Mr. Nixon, and crystallize the national mood which seems to be saying: Better not to bear the ills we have, than to shrink from others we know not of.

I do not doubt that Vietnam is hugely responsible for the general frustration. Subtract from consideration of it, for the moment, the cost in human life: the human agony. Think of it only, if you can, as a national enterprise. It is as if we had launched an Apollo missile to the moon every month for the last seven years, and every one of them had failed, though they cost $1 billion each and the scientists kept telling us that the next one would surely work, and the President proclaimed that confidence in American technology absolutely required that we proceed.

The reversal of our SST program is not unrelated to the national mood—that lack of self-confidence which is the principal psychological hangover from the Vietnam War, and I for one wish that we had never entered Indochina, rather than conduct ourselves as we have conducted ourselves there. There are those who believe that disillusion with the Cold War was inevitable, that it would have come to us via some other instruction, some other defeat. Perhaps. Meanwhile, it has become thinkable that someone will be elected President who quite clearly desires second-class international status for the United States. There is no reason growing purely out of pride why we could not be happy as a second-class nation. The pride of a Swiss is at least the equal of the pride of an American. But to be an American and a second-class power means that the world will belong to the Soviet Union, and in our day, a world that is dominated by the Soviet Union would be a world intolerably bitter to first-class spirits. First-class spirits are those that America has uniquely nurtured, with our concern for freedom, for the individual, for the underdog, for national sovereignty. There are those ready to give all of that up provided the government will send them a check every week and pay the medical bills and take away H. L. Hunt's money.

Indeed anything can happen, and a lot of it certainly will if the McGovern phenomenon goes on. And though by orthodox analysis the Republicans are entitled to cheer every McGovern primary victory as edging the incumbent further and further along the road to a landslide victory, they'd better watch it. The Gadarene swine, as Mr. Muggeridge observes, are frisky.

Altered Prospects for George Wallace?

May 22, 1972

THE HEADLINE reads: "Again a Gun Alters the Politics of the Republic," but in fact I do not see that this is the case. The alternatives for Governor Wallace have always appeared to be few. Mostly he is doomed to ineffectuality, like the assassin manqué, who has given us a human tragedy, but has not in fact altered the politics of the Republic.

What now can he do? Well, assuming that Governor Wallace were whole, what could he do? Let us postulate that the one inconceivable development is his nomination by the Democratic convention. That was never possible. It would not have been possible if he had won every primary. George Wallace is a protest candidate, of overwhelmingly regional cast, distrusted by truly conservative Americans, and for good reason. George Wallace is a man who did touch pitch, and is forever defiled. The genealogy of his stand on busing and states' rights is suspect because of its segregationist animus.

John C. Calhoun could speak about the concurrent majority or about the doctrine of nullification out of a sense of respect for constitutional principle. George Wallace came around to his positions because he wanted a fancy argument for Jim Crow. It is true that he has changed his rhetoric, that the racialist lint is now almost all gone. But only one person can serve as President of the United States, and the country would simply not turn to a man with a past such as George Wallace's; nor are his qualifications otherwise remarkable. He is a great stump orator, period. He was never moving seriously into Presidential contention.

Nor is it safe to assume that George Wallace could deliver his following. Everyone knows that personal political allegiances tend to be nontransferable. FDR discovered that, as did General Eisenhower. If George Wallace were to request his followers to work for the election of, say, George McGovern, it is by no means obvious that they would do as ordered to do. For one thing, Wallace would lose credibility. Notwithstanding the strange identity in the appeal of the two men to what one would suppose to have been irreconcilably disparate voters, George McGovern emerges as something on the order of the socialist candidate, and George Wallace's supporters are not, for the most part, socialist.

Wallace's popularity is related to his candor, to his refusal to accommodate. To suggest at this point to his followers that they vote now for the one man in Washington among Presidential contenders most closely identified with the ideology of busing and the growth of the central omnipotent government is asking too much. Martin Luther King could not have got his followers to vote for Wallace, and Wallace can't get his to vote for George McGovern.

Or Hubert Humphrey, though the problem would be a lesser problem. No, either George Wallace will run on his own, as he did in 1968, or he will help Nixon. If he runs, it is not obvious whom he will hurt. A recent New York *Times* survey insists he would hurt Nixon most. The general assumption is that he would hurt the Democrat most, depriving him of critical support in some of the big cities, among blue-collar workers in particular. The question is unresolved, and the fact that it is unresolved greatly diminishes Wallace's strength. If it were obvious that he could cost one or the other candidate the election, his strength would be greatly enhanced.

What Wallace probably could do is: guarantee the reelection of Richard Nixon. In order to make his backing even of Nixon credible, he would need to get from Nixon one or two headline-making promises. In the field of busing; something about taxation; and maybe something on law and order. Not too difficult, in fact, since there are many points of contact here that Mr. Nixon without ideological embarrassment could trot out and back with total sincerity. What he would be left with is the stigma of Mr. Wallace's support. There is a little of that still left around, enough as I say forever to disqualify Wallace for the Presidency, but not to disqualify someone backed by Wallace for the Presidency. This the assassin did substantially accomplish. It is in this sense only that he might prove in some way to have altered the politics of the Republic.

Convention Preview

June 12, 1972

THEY TALK about stopping George McGovern, and who knows, they may succeed in getting William Scranton to present himself at Miami to spearhead the effort. But let's face it, it isn't going to work. But between you and me, I hope that the effort itself to stop McGovern fails, and here are my labyrinthine reasons why.

Well over one-half of the people going down to Miami are quite conventional Democrats, decent, law-abiding, paunchy, New Dealers. But about one-third of them are political Hell's Angels bound and determined to rip off tradition, the Constitution, the whole thing. These are young people who have burned with enthusiasm for George McGovern for months, some of them for over a year. They have undergone the most extraordinary privations in order to bring out the vote for McGovern. Some of them have even forgone fornicating in public places, such being the fever of their dedication, making their predecessors who resolved merely to be Clean for Gene summer pilgrims by comparison.

Now this army of zealots doesn't want to arrive in Miami and find nothing to do, no walls to push against, nothing to sate their ideological passions. They need a good fight, a good victory. They need to crush, let us say, a last-minute attempt by Hubert Humphrey to take the nomination away from George McGovern. Or they may need a dark horse to vanquish: a desperate move, say, to give the nomination to an establishmentarian dreamboat: an Earl Warren, Jr., type.

Failing that, what will they do in Miami?

What they will do is fight the old order via the credentials committee, of course. But primarily they will fight over the platform.

And that is what we Republicans want to see. Hour after hour of it on national TV.

How about a raging floor fight on the question of permissive abortion vs. compulsory abortion? I suppose I'd want, under the circumstances, permissive abortion to win out, but I'd want the victory to be narrow. A real squeaker.

Or how about a demand by the leader of the Massachusetts delegation, who for all we know is only a year or two older than Shirley Temple when she discovered the Good Ship Lollipop, delivering a rousing call for Free Marijuana? Why should marijuana go only to the privileged few? Those who make use of tax loopholes? Those landowners who have the wherewithal to grow grass? Those supereducated who alone can afford to buy catalogues telling them how to grow it? Who says marijuana should be smoked only by people who can read instructions?

As regards foreign policy, why not get somebody to stand up and say that the time has really come to close down on tax loopholes? I can hear it now: Stop the tax exemption for the United Jewish Appeal!

Secretary Laird has testified that to adopt the defense budget proposed by George McGovern would be quite mad. Instead of spending the proposed $50 billion per year on defense, said Mr. Laird, we might just as well spend $1 billion to buy white flags which we could hoist all over the world. Surely, in endorsing this proposal, a McGovern delegate could insist that $1 billion for white flags is a typical military-industrial extravagance? White flags shouldn't cost that much money. Are the Republicans suggesting that they all be loomed on Senator Eastland's plantation?

That, as I say, is the likely scenario if the delegates don't find themselves caught up in mundane movements involving the naming of a candidate. That is why, if I were George McGovern, I'd be spending my time urging Hubert Humphrey to stay in the race and to try to make a tough fight out of it. Already we have seen that Humphrey's resolution has gone to the point of publicly considering the possibility of George Wallace as a running mate. A complementary gesture, by George McGovern, would be the public consideration of Shirley Chisholm. His failure to do so suggests to me that at this moment what he desires least is to overwhelm Hubert Humphrey, and now we all know the reasons why.

The New Religion

July 11, 1972

MIAMI BEACH. There are those who say that the politics of George McGovern is a new politics based on great shifts in ideological sentiment. Professor Galbraith, using to be sure a kind of shorthand, says that the new issues are (1) global Communism, (2) the redistribution of wealth, and (3) economic growth. Concerning which the Democratic avant-garde believes (1) that we have done quite enough of containment, (2) that we should have more of it, and (3) that it isn't a cure to all human problems.

But there is something else in the McGovern Spirit, and it is quite palpable here in Miami. It is the sense of absolute, total self-righteousness. It is manifestly intolerant of different opinions, and disposed, toward those who hold them, to dismiss them as cretins. It was worth noting, for instance, the attitude of typical young McGovernites toward Hubert Humphrey. They hate him.

It seems an odd word to use but it is something like the appropriate word. They feel an utter contempt for him. I attempted to probe this attitude, in talking with a young delegate who is highly placed in the youth-McGovern hierarchy, and I said to him: Why are you so very much opposed to Humphrey? After all, his ideological rating, as handed down by the Americans for Democratic Action on the basis of his lifelong record, is 97, which is higher even than McGovern's 93. Ahh—said the young man quick-wittedly—but the record in question was earned during the period that Senator Humphrey was a Senator, mostly before he took the Vice Presidency in 1964. We hate him for the positions he took while he was Vice President.

This of course has to mean the position that Humphrey took on the Vietnam War, since on all domestic matters, Lyndon Johnson was an exemplary liberal. So I said, but isn't it to be expected that a Vice President will take the same position as the President? That has been the case since the great disengagement of Vice President Calhoun from President Jackson. Well, said the youth, but the fact of it is that Humphrey took Johnson's positions enthusiastically. Well, I said, Humphrey takes every position enthusiastically—it is his mode. One could hardly stand up before a crowd as Vice President to President Johnson and speak listlessly one's praise of President Johnson's policies.

No, the thing of it is that Hubert Humphrey opposes George McGovern, and in the New Politics that isn't as simple as that Humphrey's emphases are different from McGovern's. What it is—is sacrilege. McGovernism is something of a religion, and the test in the days ahead will be whether the McGovern shock troops can move with sufficient tact.

It will have to be a cultivated tact. It will not, that is to say, come naturally. Because they do not feel it naturally. The young man in question told me that he would desert the Democratic Party rather than back Humphrey, in the event the convention chose him. Note the interesting failure to mediate the symmetry. The distance between McGovern and Humphrey is no greater than the distance between Humphrey and McGovern. Yet although they expect that Humphrey people will work for McGovern they would not make a commitment the other way around. The reason is quite simple: they are right, the others are wrong. It is to be expected that the heathens will work for the saints if the saints are anointed. It is not in prospect, failing that, that the saints would turn to the cause of the heathens.

Now George McGovern, notwithstanding a great seismic fault in his temperament, knows how to be conciliatory. And he is going to have to do a lot of that kind of thing in order to conceal from the mass of Democratic voters the priggishness, the ethical chauvinism, of his followers. It is off-putting to be asked to vote for McGovern as a religious exercise. It is one thing to seduce the Humphrey Democrat by appealing to his party loyalty or to his disapproval of Richard Nixon. It is something else to try to co-opt him into a new religious order.

Hate the Rich

July 12, 1972

MIAMI BEACH. Scene: BBC studios, at Convention Hall. The British anchorman, Robin Day, is tapping his fingers on the desk. The time is 2:58, and opposite him is an empty chair. At exactly 3 P.M. the satellite lodged high in the heavens by the military-industrial complex is scheduled to vouchsafe one of its beams for the purpose of transmitting the thoughts of Professor John Kenneth Galbraith from Convention Hall to the British people. And when a satellite bestows its favors on you, you need to put plenty of nickels into the slot.

Three P.M., no Galbraith. Three fifteen, no Galbraith. Finally he comes in, at 3:22. His trouble was that the security guards wouldn't let him into the Booth Section of the hall, because he didn't have the proper pass. That was a little bit like denying Peter the Great access to St. Petersburg. There are few precedents for that kind of thing, though in future years John Kenneth Galbraith, in a sense the father of the McGovern Convention, might wish to have been spared it, even as M. Guillotine must have wished to have been spared access to his invention.

Galbraith, as I say, is probably the principal intellectual patron of the McGovern Convention. He has given his enormous prestige to popularizing the kind of populism that George McGovern has ridden in on. Where else, except in Galbraith, can you find someone who is at once president of the American Economics Association, past president of the Americans for Democratic Action, author of the best-known economic treatises since John Maynard Keynes', and principal dispenser of the kind of snake oil they have been drinking here in Miami Beach?

The principal domestic enthusiasm here is Redistribution. And Professor Galbraith touches on the subject in an article in the current *Saturday Review* called "The Case for George McGovern." Mr. Galbraith takes great pains to dissipate the miasma that hovers droopily over all McGovern campfire meetings. It is the slogan: "McGovern is the Democratic Goldwater." Galbraith spots that as very dangerous to Democratic morale, so he proceeds to explain the principal differences between McGovern and Goldwater. "Goldwater was urging change in favor of the few and the rich. It was Barry Goldwater's romantic thought that the poor wanted more done for the rich, less for themselves. He wanted more freedom, which, generally speaking, meant freedom for the privileged to expand their preferred form of plunder. He is a nice man who brought a marked passion to his program for enriching the rich."

Now never mind that that account of Goldwater's candidacy is preposterous, however amusing. It is even internally contradictory, since if enhancing the rich was the principal meaning of the campaign, it is hard to understand how come Goldwater got 27,000,000 people to vote for him, unless there are a lot more rich people in America than is generally supposed. More likely, they understood themselves to be voting for a principled man who believes the government ought to get to work and do what it's supposed to do better than it's been doing (curbing crime, providing for the national defense), and get its cotton-picking hands off what is no business of government (telling your children where to go to school and why, subsidizing everything from illegitimacy to ballet). But the myths are comfortable, unlike the demagogues and the college professors, and here is how they sound when they are written into campaign platforms. . . .

"Deconcentrate"—says the Democratic draft platform— "shared monopolies such as auto, steel and tire industries which administer prices, create unemployment through restricted output and stifle technological innovation." That passage precedes the usual stuff about the rich, and it is breathtaking in its effrontery, describing as it does the immunized practices of the large labor unions, protected in their monopolies by sweetheart laws not one of which has caught the critical eye of George McGovern—or his mentor, John Kenneth Galbraith. It is so much easier to sit back and talk about taking it from the rich who, by the way, are defined by the working of McGovern economics as anybody who earns $12,000 per year.

It is strange that, in Miami Beach, they talk about "new" and "progressive" policies. Professor Galbraith's discovering of redistribution as a campaign issue comes some time after the discovery of it in Athens by the hoi polloi, and the rediscovery of it at quite inexhaustible length by Beatrice and Sidney Webb. It is very very old hat, and one regrets the reactionary influence from Professor Galbraith on the McGovern Convention.

After the Ball

July 18, 1972

COMING HOME, pursuant to Senator McGovern's instructions. It is a very good feeling, coming home. The mood in Miami, at the McGovern Convention, was elated. These are the happy people, and it is obvious why. Jimmy the Greek, who is the actuarial Delphos in America, was brought down and interviewed on network TV, and he said that he had put the odds against McGovern's nomination, as recently as last December, at 50 to 1.

Now McGovern is nominated, and Jimmy the Greek shifts gears and puts the odds against McGovern's election at 4 to 1. Jimmy has traveled a long distance, and the McGovernites at Miami, a harmonic arrangement of kids, intellectuals and ethnics, are as confident as the early Christians. Chiliasm is in the air, and He is George McGovern, whose incarnation will be effected by the voters in November. Then, to quote from the peroration in McGovern's acceptance speech, America will have "come home."

I do not know whether George McGovern will be elected President. I do know that the McGovern Convention was an ideological joyride. And—no matter what happens in November—the moment of rapture will not turn to bitterness. George McGovern, in an incautious public flirtation with megalomania, spoke of his nomination as a "sweet harvest." Thus it will remain in the memory, win or lose.

However, the legions intend to win. They hope to reify George McGovern's dream. They are the political alchemists, who will transform hatred into love, poverty into plenty, the Soviet Union into Switzerland. One finds oneself hoping, less that Nixon will win because it is important for the safety of the Republic that he should do so, than that he should win in order to spare the young McGovernites a direct experience with power.

When John Lindsay made his victory speech, back in 1965, he told his followers that he would transform New York into the empire city, and he might as well have shot them all with a double jolt of morphine, so transported were they by the vision of it all. Yesterday, seven years later, the cameras did not trouble to focus on John Lindsay, sitting there unnoticed in the shadows that closed down on that rag-tag end of his boulevard of broken dreams. Eugene McCarthy, the bard of spiritual restoration only four years ago, came into Miami unnoticed except by those whose practice it is to notice the unnoticed. So it will be, not necessarily for McGovern himself: but for McGovern's dreams, surely; ineluctably. It is necessarily so for anyone who seeks to do what only God can do.

Speaking of which, the rhetoric of the last hours of the convention was exalted beyond even conventional idealism. Senator Kennedy said he had been "humbled" by the invitation to run for Vice President. If that is true, surely it will prove to be the most significant achievement of the McGovern Convention. Later, Senator Kennedy addressed the convention and said that it had returned to the ideal of "John Kennedy, who said ask not what the country can do for you, but what you can do for your country." A breathtaking announcement, uttered before a convention that sometimes seemed to be saying that the most you can do for your country is evade the draft, smoke pot, abort babies, have a homosexual affair, and receive, in return for nothing at all, $1,000 a year from your fellow citizens.

Senator Eagleton emerged as testimony to Senator McGovern's genius for discovering what nobody else had discovered, and he quickly, and amusingly, recounted the single trauma of his adult life, namely that, having mislaid his credentials upon presenting himself to the Senate after resigning his state job, he found himself, for a period of sixteen minutes during his adult life—off the public payroll.

If McGovernism triumphs, nobody will ever be off the public payroll, not even for a dreadful, reactionary sixteen minutes. Not unless the people's tribunal should happen to toll the dread words: "The great state of Idaho, home of the greatest potatoes in the peaceloving world, casts its twenty-two votes for taking John Doe off the public payroll." Cheers? When it happens, it will be John Doe vs. the McGovern Convention.

The Eagleton Impasse

August 1, 1972

I WRITE before the final solution to the Eagleton problem has been reached, in which connection a few observations:

(1) It is never more painfully clear than at moments like this that politics is a very rough game indeed. Probably it should be, when you are dealing with a set of people who aspire to fly about the world in their own Boeing jets, issuing orders to their subjects on everything from whom to make war with, to how much duty they should pay on imported soybeans.

It is something in the nature of an institutionalized hazing, preparatory to the long years when one's knees are supposed to tremble at the mere mention of the majestic office they occupy. "You want us to call you 'Mr. Vice President,' and maybe even 'Mr. President' if the old lightning strikes. Well, OK, meanwhile we will make savage jokes about you, even the good-natured among us."

"I don't see why Senator Eagleton shouldn't be Vice President," a prominent comedian meditated over the weekend. "After all, he's been playing Napoleon for years." The crowd roared, even those who are, in context of the joke, "pro-Eagleton." "I'm Just Nuts About Eagleton" became, just forty-eight hours after the news broke, about as dated as Lucky Strike Green Has Gone to War.

On and on they came, flushing out the American mood, which is suspicious, belatedly, about the kind of power we have conferred on the Executive. Irreverent jokes about the Queen of England are less savage because she has no power. Because she has no power, the public rises more quickly to her defense, as the whole world apparently did ten years ago when Malcolm Muggeridge pronounced his judgment on his monarch as being "frowzy, simple, and banal." If he had been writing a century and a half earlier about Prince William, who did have power, he'd have got away with it more readily. There has got to be a correlation between the intensity of the feeling, humorously turned on this occasion against Senator Eagleton, and the dreadful potency of the office he aspires to occupy.

(2) His apparent failure to have disclosed his medical background is at least surprising, at most dishonorable. In defense of the former interpretation, it should be said that he unquestionably considers himself to be totally cured, and that therefore even to acknowledge as relevant the medical treatments during the sixties, he disdained as paying obeisance to superstition—the superstition that once you have had a nervous breakdown, you are ever after unreliable.

On the other hand, I cannot share the general indignation against Senator McGovern for not having discovered Senator Eagleton's medical record. It is a sign of the highly nervous times that no one is supposed to accept anyone else on presumptive good faith. In America, the offices of the Good Samaritan would not nowadays be accepted without first testing the thesis that he might be engaged in entrapment. A functioning Senator from a large state who has run for public office for the past sixteen years, and concerning whom there is no derogatory information outside the compost heap of Jack Anderson, is not somebody whom one thinks to ask: "By the way, Tom, are you by any chance crazy?"

Senator McGovern may be faulted for a very full indulgence of the practices of politicians who say one thing and mean the opposite, but he should not be faulted for excusable negligence. It is already clear that what Senator McGovern meant by the word "irreversible," as in the sentence, "It is my irreversible decision to keep Senator Eagleton on," was "reversible." As in, "I promise to end the Vietnam War immediately," which means, "I promise to end the Vietnam War eventually."

(3) Senator Eagleton had a wonderful chance to test the organizational consequences of saying: "I won't withdraw, period." What would the Democrats have done about it? What is the legal situation? Even if you reconvene a convention, does that convention have the authority to withdraw a nomination once conferred? Granted, you are otherwise left with an incoherent political situation, one in which conceivably the Presidential candidate and the Vice Presidential candidate

are not on talking terms. Still, the impasse is conceptually fascinating. But, of course, the transcendent question is: If Senator McGovern is elected, who, four years later, will not have visited Mayo's?

The Limits of Decency

August 12, 1972

IT HAS been frequently quoted about George McGovern that he is "the only decent man in the Senate." Now that quote is the late Robert Kennedy's, and it does, surely, an injustice to the Senate. I am sure that there are other decent men there, not even counting the sainted junior Senator from New York, successor to Robert Kennedy in the affections of New York's constituents. And it is not the purpose of this essay to suggest that Senator McGovern is other than a decent man. It is rather the purpose to suggest that that which is decent about him is expressed other than in his political rhetoric.

But I fear that he has another image of himself than that which collectors of his remarks come up with, and before the campaign heats up, he should be reminded of it. Particularly before he sets his course to the deploring of the rhetorical excesses of Spiro Agnew.

Here is Nick Kotz of the Washington *Post* (May 17, 1972), commenting on Senator McGovern whom he had just interviewed. "As he talked in his office, McGovern returned repeatedly to the theme that he had tried to calm rather than incite the public to anger. 'I have sought not to whip up emotions, but to appeal to humanity and reason,' he said. 'There's plenty of anger and tension without our leaders adding to it. I think a conciliatory approach is needed. . . .'"

A conciliatory approach is not going to be tempered on McGovern rhetoric, and the gentleman's habits of harsh and uncharitable overstatement are not purely the accretions of a Presidential campaign. Back in 1964 (September 8, *Congres-*

sional Record, p. 21690) he was saying about another decent man in the Senate of the United States: "I regard Mr. Goldwater as the most unstable, radical and extremist man ever to run for the Presidency in either political party."

And about yet another decent colleague—from the same state—Karl Mundt of South Dakota: "I don't know how he [Mundt] felt about me . . . but I know I hated his guts. . . . I hated him so much I lost my sense of balance" (Robert Sam Anson, *McGovern: A Biography,* p. 93).

And one more time on a colleague: "But [Senator Henry] Jackson 'destroyed whatever chance he had of becoming the Democratic nominee by embracing racism,' in the anti-busing campaign, Senator McGovern said" (Chris Lydon, New York *Times,* March 19, 1972).

And after J. Edgar Hoover died, McGovern gave an interview (*Life* magazine, July 7, 1972). "Hoover had lived beyond the normal years, so I couldn't feel the pathos I would for a young man. I could feel nothing but relief that he was no longer a public servant."

On the Indochinese war, it is hard to think of Senator McGovern as stable. "I think the reelection of Richard Nixon in 1972 would be an open hunting right for this man to give in to all his impulses for a major war against the people of Indochina" (speech, Catholic University, April 20, 1972). And, "I've said many times that the Nixon bombing policy in Indochina is the most barbaric action that any country has committed since Hitler's effort to exterminate Jews in Germany in the 1930's" (interview with Gregg Herrington, AP, June 29, 1972). To liken Richard Nixon (and Lyndon Johnson) not only to Hitler but to the worst that Hitler ever did is, well among other things, perverse.

But that is characteristic when touching on the subject of Vietnam. President Nixon "has descended to a new level of barbarism and foolhardiness for no other reason than to save his own face and to prop up the corrupt regime of Thieu" (AP, April 16, 1972). And speaking of Thieu, he is a "corrupt dictator who jails opponents, a despicable creature who doesn't merit the life of a single American soldier or for that matter a single Vietnamese" (UPI, April 7, 1972). And "I want to be blunt about it," says Senator McGovern.

"[Nixon's] playing politics with the lives of American soldiers and with American prisoners rotting in their cells in Hanoi. He's putting his own political selfish interests ahead of the welfare of these young Americans and ahead of the taxpayers of this country who are bearing the burden."

To be blunt about it, Senator McGovern's animadversions on his fellow human beings are indecent.

The Republicans' Achilles' Heel

August 23, 1972

MIAMI BEACH. The jubilation of the Republicans has been very widely noticed, and the pollsters reveal that if the election were held tomorrow Richard Nixon would win very heavily. The complacency has generated the sense of caution to which President Nixon has alluded as at all costs to be avoided.

In Miami it was pretty much a carnival, and of course Democratic critics leaped to make a comparison between the Nixon Convention and the McGovern Convention. They did not reach back for further precedents because, indeed, the Nixon Convention resembles most closely the Roosevelt Conventions of yesteryear, when Roosevelt ruled supreme, though to be sure he took the precaution of checking things with Sidney. But as the Republicans survey the scene, they feel they cannot easily account for their blessings. For the Democrats to nominate McGovern, *and* for Wallace to withdraw from the race at one and the same time is simply—too much. So much too much as to cause them to lose their judgment? . . .

I have come across an omen of what I consider to be hard evidence that there is a little cool intelligence still at work within the Republican Party notwithstanding the euphoria. The circumstances are these. At the big gala on Sunday evening, the party charged $500 per person, for the worst dinner ever served since the discovery of fire, capped by a red wine perfectly suited to the meal. Well, we thought, the GOP needs the money; and then there was an evening's entertainment nicely emceed by Art Linkletter, who introduced John Wayne as a hero who had won all the wars he had ever fought in. Mrs. Nixon came in, escorted by Senator Dominick, under a floodlight, and on the way to her table was greeted so amorously by one male guest whose features we could not distinguish that the question arose: Who could he be? I volunteered the suggestion that the only proper speculation was: Nixon. But I was proved wrong—it was an old family friend. Mrs. Nixon then sat down comfortably at the table with Governor and Mrs. Rockefeller, but after all she has had very good training, having only a few months ago sat between Chou En-lai and Madame Mao Tse-tung.

I was about to tell you of the residual Cool Intelligence. Well, the next morning I came across a distinguished and very affluent Republican who was morosely strolling the hotel corridor shaking his head ever so slightly, ever so sadly. What was wrong? He told me that he had composed a special song, together with lyrics, for the Presidential campaign. The gentleman is very well connected and had no trouble at all in securing an audition at which, he told me, it was instantly agreed to inaugurate "The President's Song," as he straightforwardly called it, at the gala banquet the night before.

What happened?

Well, he said, unaccountably the master of ceremonies simply *forgot* to bring on the singer who was supposed to premiere the great political campaign song. At this point he reached from a mimeographed pile he was carrying and delivered it to me. I must share it with you.

"Good evening Mr. President I want to shake your hand/You fought a left-wing Congress four long years to stop our land/From going socialistic in the phony welfare way/Designed and planned by JFK and then by LBJ./You got us back upon the track but still there's much to do/So we're giving you a landslide vote November '72."

Before I had an opportunity to express my dismay at Mr. Linkletter's failure to launch "The President's Song," I was shown a second song. This one, my friend said, would make it unnecessary for Spiro Agnew to deliver an acceptance speech. He would need only to sing "The Vice President's Song":

"Good evening Spiro Agnew we are proud to have you here/You talk the sort of language real Americans want to hear/Straight from the shoulder no holds-barred, you don't beguile our youth/With sugar-coated fairy tales, you tell the honest truth./We want no handouts for sitting on our tails/This breeds a nation soft as dough instead of tough as nails/It's time our country's voters of all ages got the word/That welfare's no proud eagle but a soft permissive bird."

As I say, somebody up there still loves the Republican Party. At this point the only weapon the Democrats have that could conceivably give them a victory in November is "The President's Song" and "The Vice President's Song." Call it *their* Watergate Caper.

McGovern's War on Wealth

September 12, 1972

SENATOR MCGOVERN, who is the candidate of many of the intellectuals, continues to mystify by the arguments on which he lays so very much stress. Recently he was in Texas, and there he lashed out bitterly at John Connally, who has organized "Democrats for Nixon." Senator McGovern said that he did not care for the support of "Connally and his billionaire friends."

Now the point bears analysis. John Connally was several times elected governor of the state of Texas not by the state's billionaires. They number, I should guess, three. Or, if you wish to allow for hyberbole and assume that when Senator McGovern said "billionaires," he really meant "millionaires"—even as when he said he would support Senator Eagleton 1,000 percent he really meant he would support Senator Eagleton 100 percent—let us assume there are a few hundred, or a few thousand of them in Texas. John Connally got a clear majority of the voters of the state of Texas. Connally fancies himself a New Deal Democrat. He backed John Kennedy and Hubert Humphrey most vigorously, but drew the line at George McGovern, as one-third of the nation's Democrats propose to do. Why does that suggest to McGovern that Connally is motivated only by a concern for his "billionaire friends"?

But McGovern, who himself earned over $100,000 in 1971, is obsessed with the subject of wealth. He thinks of it the way the ladies who formed the Anti-Saloon League thought of booze: as inherently wicked, and the more of it you have, the more wicked you are. It is a point of view that is interesting pathologically, but hardly one that should commend itself to intellectuals who think of their academic training as having emancipated them from primitive fetishism.

Consider McGovern's ad hominem blast, on the same occasion in Texas, against one or two people whose salaries were enormously high last year, one of them the president of Dow Chemical, the other the president of the Ford Motor Company. George McGovern told lasciviously the story of the head of Ford, Mr. Iacocca, getting $400,000 last year. No wonder—McGovern drew out his tale—that the head of Ford should not have to worry about the rising price of hamburger, and so on and so on. A few minutes of that and you find yourself not only resenting the head of Ford but convinced that the system that permits him to get $400,000 is somehow evil.

I want to know why.

Let's say that Ford sells 2,500,000 vehicles in a typical year. Then $400,000 in salary paid to its president comes to 16 cents per automobile. Now $400,000 is a great deal of money, but what business is it of George McGovern if the directors of Ford feel that they would rather have Iacocca as head of Ford, even at the cost of 16 cents per vehicle sold, than someone else, at a lesser figure? Who is affected by that decision? The stockholders. But they can vote in new management if they want to. What business is it of the government to set a ceiling on salaries, or to confiscate salaries past a certain point?

Notice that Senator McGovern always offers up as an illustration of inordinate salary the high-priced business executive. The reason for that is obvious. People don't in general know just what it is that the presidents of Ford, or of GM, or of DuPont, or of Standard Oil actually do: and therefore high figures of compensation strike them as extortionary.

Last summer I endeavored to buy for my son six tickets to a Rolling Stones concert. The Stones were giving four successive concerts at Madison Square Garden, capacity 20,000 people. This was toward the end of a thirty-concert tour. I couldn't get them at the posted price of $6 per ticket. They had sold out on the spot. So, on a single afternoon, the Stones took in $120,000.

Should we resent this? The children and the shopkeepers and the fans who paid $6 if they were lucky, and bid up to $30 per ticket, didn't resent it in the least—they cheered the Stones as lustily as George McGovern was ever cheered.

When George McGovern goes lecturing, to eke out his living, he accepts a fee as large as the sponsoring committee offers. I have never heard him say that his fee is too large. It reflects, in a sense, his market value.

Mr. McGovern's aim is to stimulate envy and ignorance and greed, and to generate class envy. I invite him, next time he gives an illustration of unjustified reward, to use not the names of the presidents of corporations, but the names of the Rolling Stones, or The Grateful Dead, or Elvis Presley, or Elizabeth Taylor. That would introduce the subject in a soberer way. But that would not appeal to Bob & Carol & Ted & Alice, and they, plus Ken, are about all McGovern has left.

McGovern on Crime

October 22, 1972

SENATOR GEORGE MCGOVERN has discovered crime. To the considerable relief of his staff, his conclusions about crime in America are that there is too much of it, not too little of it, and to the relief of the rest of us, he has not yet blamed crime in America on the Vietnam War. What he does want to do, one gathers from his rather vague references to the subject, is to have Washington instruct the cop on the beat how to stop crime. As he put it, to "strengthen the capability of the police."

Actually, the police are pretty capable as they are. Sure, we need more capable police even as we need more capable Presidential candidates. But the problem isn't so much the police. Commissioner Patrick Murphy of New York City gave a resonant speech on the subject last winter. He was addressing the Bar Association of the City of New York and he used very direct language. He said: "This court system is in bankruptcy. It simply doesn't work. You all know this. I am not telling you anything new." The courts, he continued, must bear "the giant share of the blame for the increase in crime."

Commissioner Murphy ran his fingers over the ugly profile. . . . "In 1960 the New York City Police Department made 35,629 felony arrests. Last year we made 94,042 felony arrests. Exactly 552 of them went to trial, 552 out of 94,000." What happened to all the others? "The rest of them were, quotes, disposed of. Disposed of means dismissed outright, reduced to misdemeanors via plea bargaining, reduced to lesser felonies via plea bargaining." And so on.

Now why has the court system broken down? In part, to be sure, because in our licentious age there are more lawbreakers than ever. But there is also less punishment than ever, and the reason for this is that the Supreme Court under Earl Warren, by the narrowest margin, bequeathed us with interpretations of the Fourth, Fifth and Fourteenth Amendments which positively leer at law enforcement. Even so friendly an observer of the Supreme Court as the New York *Times'* Fred Graham acknowledges the correlation between the critical Warren Court decisions, and skyrocketing crime.

Recently in California the police homed in on a suspected dope peddler, and kept his house under surveillance. In due course the woman of the house threw out her trash, which was picked up by a truck. The police stopped the truck, inspected the trash, and found there narcotics debris—half-smoked marijuana cigarettes, etc. They arrested the guy, he moved to suppress the evidence and, you guessed it, following one of the Warren decisions (*Mapp* v. *Ohio*), the California courts ordered the case dismissed. Because searching the discarded trash without a warrant was a violation of the dope peddler's Fifth Amendment rights.

Now that case is being appealed by the State of California to the Supreme Court, which has granted certiorari (*Calif.* v. *Krivda*). I'd like to know: How does Candidate McGovern stand on the issues? Richard Nixon has certainly not stopped crime in America, but he has sent to the Supreme Court two realists who will almost certainly vote in a direction other than *Mapp*, or *Miranda:* in the direction of return to effective justice. In the direction, if you prefer, of Justice Cardozo, who on one famous occasion reminded us that the purpose of a trial is to determine whether or not the accused is guilty, rather than whether the constable has blundered.

Would the nominees of President McGovern to the Supreme Court treat the narrow and disabling decisions of Messrs. Warren, Douglas and Clark as aberrations, as grains of sand to be removed from the judicial gears? Or would they leave them there, and throw in a little more for good measure?

Bluntly said: Would he appoint men like Rehnquist to the Supreme Court or men like Ramsey Clark? My guess is that the next time the lady throws out the trash at the Krivda house it will include narcotics debris and McGovern stickers.

Remarks by WFB in a Debate with John Kenneth Galbraith

October 24, 1972

LADIES AND GENTLEMEN,
Friends and patrons of the New York Public Library,
Mr. Elliott, Mr. Buchwald, Mr. Galbraith:

It was way back last February that Mr. Elliott invited me by cablegram to defend, on this occasion, the Republican incumbent against Mr. Galbraith's advocacy of the Democratic challenger, whoever he might be. It happened that Mr. Galbraith reposed at that moment a local telephone call away, in Gstaad, where during the winter he pursues his study of skiing and economics. His skiing instructors are occasionally cheered by the news that Mr. Galbraith also has difficulties in mastering his other line of activity. I started to say his sedentary activity, but I am not sure that that would successfully distinguish it from his activity as a skier.

Anyway, Mr. Galbraith told me that he too had received the cable and had agreed to contribute his services on this occasion; at which point over the telephone there was a . . . pause. I thought, for the fun of it, to come flat-out at the most promiscuous end of what was then a technical possibility. "What will you do," I asked, "if it turns out that you will have committed yourself to appear before so distinguished an audience of New York liberals charged with the responsibility of advocating Senator Henry Jackson for President?" He replied with characteristic confidence that he could serenely predict that he would not be subjected to any such embarrassment; and of course he was right. The embarrassment to which he is subjected is of quite another nature.

There is no constitutional reason why Professor Galbraith cannot correctly predict what will happen in the short term, the long term having been dismissed by Lord Keynes as the point at which Professor Galbraith answers to the angels and the saints. In the spring of 1968 Mr. Galbraith predicted after the Tet Offensive that the government of President Thieu would be overthrown by the Vietnamese in six weeks. (The government of President Thieu was overthrown by Americans, not Vietnamese, and it took not 6 weeks, but 236 weeks.) Mr. Galbraith then divulged to me that he has a personal rule as regards Democratic contenders. The rule is that he will back the "leftwardmost"—I use his word—of the "viable"—again I use his word—candidates. What isn't clear, not even from the closest reading of his work, is whether by the qualifier "viable," he means the leftwardmost candidate who has a fighting chance to win the nomination and election; or whether he means "viable" in the sense of personally "tolerable" to Professor Galbraith. The latter, to be sure, springs to the mind of those who have studied Mr. Galbraith's propensities. On the other hand, if it had been Leon Trotsky who defeated Hubert Humphrey in the California primary, pleading perhaps superior experience on how to deal with the Kremlin, one is entitled to wonder whether the Galbraith formula would have locked him in, here tonight, to draw on his deep reserves of eloquence and ingenuity and cunning to sell us on the virtues of voting for Trotsky, as the—using his words—leftwardmost of the viable candidates? If you are out for ideological highs, you may as well use the purest stuff. Why not Trotsky?

The New York Public Library is manned by a worldly force, rather like the confessors at St. Peter's. But their cosmopolitanism sometimes runs ahead of their professionalism. Mr. Nabokov told me that a few years ago he came here after receiving a letter from one of those zoowatchers of the book stacks of years gone by, advising him that for all of Nabokov's vaunted originality, in fact a novel had been published in the 1880's entitled *Lolita*. He came here and found that the title did indeed exist—right here in the card file. So he scratched the index number down and presented it to the clerk. He looked at it, then over at Nabokov. He leaned over to him and said in an avuncular whisper: "That's not the *Lolita* you're looking for, Buster."

I submit to Mr. Galbraith that, really, George McGovern isn't the George McGovern he is looking for. George McGovern would not be a viable candidate even if he adopted the formal theoretical positions of Leon Trotsky. For the most part, to be sure, the backers of George McGovern back him as a pragmatist, whose utterances are nicely tuned to left-utopianism and left-hobgoblinization: who—to be sure—has suffered from the ignominy of the rites of passage of any American Democratic candidate, which stipulate that he visit, e.g., the LBJ ranch worshipfully, there to proclaim that that visit is "the most thrilling experience I have had"; and then to the city of Chicago, to visit there and to praise that extra-New York phenomenon, a functioning mayor; one who, a few years ago, recommended to the police that they simply shoot all looters, which advice said police for a while were accused of applying to Democratic delegates and their supporters who traveled to Chicago to support the candidacies of Eugene McCarthy and George McGovern. How could Mayor Daley know that the looters were simply anticipating the Democratic national platform of 1972?

Well, Mr. Galbraith, on the eve of the Miami convention, wrote an exuberant essay predicting that George McGovern would win the national election triumphantly. Mr. Galbraith's reasoning, way back during the elation of last July, was that the American people had a very simple choice before them—language that Leon Trotsky would have approved of, as fulfilling the formal dialectical requirements of class hostility—to vote for the candidate of the Rich People, or for the candidate of the Poor People. But three months later, the polls perplexingly suggest that, at this moment, approximately twice as many Americans would vote for the candidate of the Rich People. Does that mean, accepting Mr. Galbraith's rigorous formula, that there are twice as many rich people as poor people in America? Well, in a way that would make internal sense, in the Galbraith world, wouldn't it be so—if we believe that voters vote their self-interest, which is the spinal column of Mr. Galbraith's analysis of the Goldwater vote.

But it is unkind to press such particulars on him. True, he wrote in *The Affluent Society* that by the end of the decade we would have primarily the problem of what to do with our affluence. Now he tends to write mostly about things like endemic poverty, and unemployment, and inflation, the elimination of which is supposed to be the object of the science to which he devotes himself—with what effect, the poor people are entitled to wonder. But the polls then go on to tell us very strange things. They tell us that rich people will vote against McGovern, on the whole—though not by any means all of them: Mr. Galbraith is, certainly by Mr. McGovern's standards, rich, and he is going to vote for McGovern: unless he takes this auspicious opportunity to repent. But also the polls tell us that middle-income people intend, on the whole, to vote against McGovern. But then—get this!—the polls also tell us that the working class, on the whole, intend to vote against McGovern. And then—this is really getting to be too much—the polls tell us that half the faculty in the American academy intend to vote against McGovern. And, finally, that half the young people, even, intend to vote against McGovern.

What on earth is going on, you want to know: and so do I, and we can only hope that that which this evening will help to guarantee is that in the months ahead we will be able to come to the New York Public Library and find here, in its generous and nondiscriminatory archives, the resources wherein to find out: Why? Why did it happen this way, that the candidate of the majority party, running against a President with the smallest personal constituency since James Buchanan's, is going down to such an inglorious defeat? Will it prove to have been primarily a human problem? Or the pestiferous cultural lag that separates Mr. Galbraith from the People he labors so elegantly to serve! Will the facts, finally collated, say that it was the personal failure of the candidate that made the difference? Will the sympathetic clerk, sensing the anxiety of the young researcher, lean over and reassure him: "This isn't the McGovern you are looking for. . . ."?

Is this a way to approach the question, before such a gathering, in the twelve minutes we have been allotted? It is, I think, the preferable way. It would be somehow callous, and certainly tedious, to reiterate the progressive modifications of George McGovern on his domestic score, whose complexity has reached a point now that not even Leonard Bernstein could orchestrate it. Or to chronicle his adventitious discoveries: of Jerusalem, for instance. Imagine discovering Jerusalem only under the triangulating guidance of the three kings, Gallup, Harris, and Yankelovich. No doubt if the campaign lasted another month Mr. McGovern would move from recommending that our embassy in Tel Aviv should be moved to Jerusalem, to recommending that Moshe Dayan be named commander of an expanded Sixth Fleet (which by the way is not a bad idea). There is a very sad witlessness in the tergiversations of George McGovern, whether on income redistribution, or on bases in Thailand, or on Thomas Eagleton, or on defense policies, or on Mayor Daley, or on the

Mideast. Ronald Reagan, for instance, said it so much better two years ago when he recommended that we send to Israel at the end of every week exactly as many Phantom jets as the Egyptians claimed to have shot down during that week.

We are reduced, in defense of Mr. McGovern, to the most spectacular sophisms in modern journalistic history, the editorials of the New York *Times,* which proclaim clangorously the necessity of voting for George McGovern in protest—I ask you to believe me that I am quoting from last Sunday's editorial page—in protest against, for instance, the "budget deficits that have soared out of control" under Mr. Nixon. Therefore, vote for the man whose projected budget would increase that deficit by—to use the most generous estimate—$65 billion.

Or yesterday's effort by the *Times* to reveal that George McGovern, who twenty-five years ago deplored the Truman Doctrine and today deplores NATO, is the *true* internationalist. I have described New York *Times* editorials as Cotton Mather rewriting Eleanor Roosevelt, but I have to confess I do not know what I would do without them—they are as perversely cheering as the misanthropy of Scrooge, who, let's face it, ceased to be very interesting when he became wise and humane, like me, and Mr. Nixon. Besides, if you are looking for rainbows, you need only draw a line from the antecedent New York *Times* editorial on over to the historical development. I like the editorial during the last general election, the one that said about the beleaguered incumbent that his was "the voice of a public official determined to keep freedom from being assassinated by the ruthless night riders of the political right." Well, the night riders had their way and elected to office—the saintly junior Senator from New York. If that sweet disposition is the stuff of which the New York *Times'* nightmares are regularly made, we can all take heart.

Indeed in the worst of circumstances, one must take heart. And these are not the worst of circumstances, I should like to reassure you all, as witness the failure of the political crusade of George McGovern.

And let those of you who reason that four more years of Nixon is an insufferable prospect remind yourselves that, without Nixon, you would not get four more years of Buchwald on Nixon. That's what *I* would call intolerable.

De Profundis

October 24, 1972

I CAN SEE it now. They are preparing to take it out on the United States. I mean, the forthcoming victory of Richard Nixon. They will say that it shows that the country is irredeemable, that it proves that we are in a squalid state, incapable even of a lapse into decency. How they love it so. If truth be known, they really want Nixon to win because they find it easier to criticize America that way. If McGovern won, they would go into a sulk, because they wouldn't have America to kick around anymore. At least not for a little while. But of course they'd come back to it.

The current favorite in the anti-American festival is Kurt Vonnegut, Jr., the novelist who wrote *Slaughterhouse Five* and other wry books. He writes in a sort of idiomatic blank verse, and his message is really very simple. It is that war is evil, and people are inhuman, especially in America. His devices are rather orthodox: he juxtaposes the comfort of the wealthy and the powerful up against the tortures of the maimed and the neglected. Then he does things like dividing the world into "Winners" and "Losers," and saying things like "the fix is on" and—for this he is most famous—"so it goes."

He is a man of great wit and absolutely no humor. And in the current issue of *Harper's* magazine, reviewing the Republican convention in Miami, he strikes the tuning fork for the ululators, coast to coast. He mocks the alleged piety of Nixon and his supporters and in particular of one Quaker theologian. He dwells lovingly on gallows humor. He is skilled in draining the humor out of a story by telling it deadpan, the way some people can tell you a Polish joke and make it sound merely crude, instead of crude plus something else. Consider: "[Art Buchwald] told our table about a column he had just written. The comical premise was that the Republican Party had attracted so many campaign contributions that it found itself with two billion dollars it couldn't spend. It decided to buy something nice for the American people. Here was the gift: a free week's bombing of Vietnam." It is a technique anyone can master. Well, not quite anyone, but most people. The only inflexible requirement is that you postulate your own sensitivity and compassion, by contrast with the moral sloth of others.

That is what this gang is very good at doing. Norman Mailer, deploying those numinous phrases for which he is justly loved, talked in his piece on Miami about walking through the Democratic convention and suddenly realizing why it was an exhilarating experience: because he sensed only love among the delegates.

On reading that passage I thought of a young delegate (as it happened, an altogether amiable young man) who gave out the news to a reporter shortly before the convention that McGovern was going to win and that the reason why McGovern was going to win was that immediately after his nomination there would appear on the scene 5,000,000 young volunteers for McGovern armed with "hate." The hatred of Richard Nixon.

In fact the delegates to the Democratic convention were human beings with the strengths and weaknesses of other human beings, except that they were, as a lot, a good deal more arrogant than the Republicans. They had fire in their bellies, that hot ideological fire that says: We're going to change America and you, boy, are going to ride in the tumbrel to Execution Square, and we're going to enjoy your suffering. There was a good deal of that in the McGovern Convention, not much in the Republican convention, which was mostly dull, accepting the course of events, which was clearly: four more years of Nixon, the good that that means, and the bad that that means.

But the Vonneguts have had it with America. One wonders, Was it Vietnam that did it to them? But in fact Kurt Vonnegut's big book is about the firebombing of Dresden, not Hanoi: and that was an operation undertaken by people like Winston Churchill and Franklin Delano Roosevelt and Charles de Gaulle, whole encyclopedias before Vietnam which, a little carelessly, Vonnegut and the others now use as the principal crutch for their anti-Americanism. Nixon, of course, is the perfect complementary figure. Nixon/Vietnam goes down better than Churchill/Dresden. But it doesn't matter really. They will find reasons to say that America is intolerable, and they will say it quite deafeningly in the weeks to come.

Advice for McGovern: A Return to Innocence

October 29, 1972

IF I WERE at the side of George McGovern I would give him this advice. Try to recapture your innocence.

Or—if you are an anti-McGovernite who refuses to concede that there is an innocence there to be recaptured—I'd put it this way: Try, in the home stretch, to stop the rancor.

As it is now, George McGovern gets terribly in his own way.

Consider a few observations from his most recent broadcast.

He made a very great deal out of the effort by the Republican Party to collect a lot of money before the April 7 deadline.

Now consider this carefully. For years and years and years, contributors to electoral campaigns could disguise their identity and the extent of their contribution by a number of legal devices. So Congress meets and decides, finally, to close the loopholes. A law is passed that says that after April 7, donors must in every case reveal themselves and the exact amount of their contribution.

Now what would you do if you were the finance chairman of a political party? Exactly. And if you didn't do that you would be: not quite pure, but quite stupid.

What the Republicans did was send out an appeal to all known patrons of Republicanism which said: If you do not desire that your name be known, give NOW, before April 7, because after that the law requires that your name be published. This is in no sense different from the automobile dealer saying: Buy now, before the first of January, because after the first of January, the new retail tax goes into effect. It is not a circumvention of the law to buy now in order to save dollars. And it was not a circumvention of the law to give money before April 7 in order to guard one's privacy. But, at the hands of George McGovern, you would think that the Republicans had engineered the biggest swindle since the Donation of Constantine.

The Democrats did not do the same thing on a national scale for the very simple reason that there was no national Democratic candidate behind whom the entire Democratic organization could gather.

But—get this—the entire matter is put into personal perspective by George McGovern's own record on the matter of political contributions. He last ran for public office in 1970. During his campaign he reported zero political contributions.

Does that mean he did not spend any money? Of course not. It meant that he availed himself of a loophole that stale fish would find smelly. The law specifies that a candidate shall report contributions of which he is aware. George McGovern simply advised his campaign people not to advise him who had contributed what: that way, he didn't have to put down anybody's name. For someone who has inhabited a house as glassy as that to throw stones at Republican pre-April 7 practices is—worse than hypocritical. It is simply unconvincing.

Then he says that, under Richard Nixon, tax relief has been only for the rich. How heavily he depends on ignorance.

The 1969 law reduced the tax for those in the $3,000 or less bracket by 82 percent; for those in the $3,000 to $5,000 bracket by 43 percent; for those in the $5,000 to $7,000 bracket by 27 percent; for those in the $50,000 to $100,000 bracket by 1.7 percent. And—for those in the over $100,000 bracket, the tax was actually raised by 7 percent. Now: even so, this was not Richard Nixon's law. It was a law of the Congress of the United States. Congress is organized by the Democratic Party. And there is one man, head of the Ways and Means Committee, who is primarily responsible for the tax program. He is Wilbur Mills. Wilbur Mills is not only a Democrat, he is the man George McGovern has said he would appoint as his Secretary of the Treasury in the event he were elected.

What comes out of that distillery is 100-proof guile.

What, at this rate, will George McGovern have to look back upon? Barry Goldwater was tough without being hysterical or hypocritical or mean. Is it too late for McGovern to try? My answer is only partly political: It is never too late.

The Morning After

November 9, 1972

PROFESSOR JOHN KENNETH GALBRAITH remarked the day after the election that Richard Nixon's victory was actually hollow—because, he said, four years from now the Republican Party will probably be taking positions not very different from George McGovern's, so what does it matter, really, that the vision of George McGovern should be another four years or so in the realization?

Mr. Galbraith has a point, of course. There is social movement in America which is centripetal in character. More and more we ask the government to look after us. The great McGovern Interruption of 1972 may indeed be thought of in due course as nothing more than chronological presumption, rather like Norman Thomas coming out for Social Security ten years before Franklin Delano Roosevelt introduced it.

Galbraith and the brain trusters can see it now. It is the Democratic convention of 1992. A distinguished old man is introduced and the crowd goes wild. It's George McGovern. The man who ran in 1972 and was so greatly humiliated. But oh how his doctrines have triumphed! How they laughed at him then! How they honor him now!

That is what the boys—call them the Massachusetts boys,

in homage to Massachusetts' touching identification with George McGovern—are consoling themselves with. Incidentally, they may be right about 1992. It is of course quite another matter whether, in 1992, the land will still be bright.

What are the Nixon people telling themselves? For one thing that they are plenty smart political hombres. That would appear to be true, though it is easy to exaggerate it. No doubt future textbooks on how to score landslide victories will begin with the injunction: Get George McGovern nominated by the opposite party.

Nobody knows how it would have gone otherwise. If the Democrats had named Muskie, say. Or if the neurotic busboy from Wisconsin had decided to make love, rather than assassination. Richard Nixon, his skills aside, was very lucky.

What will he be thinking now?

We have to go someplace from here, and it is not all that obvious just where. Congress, really, is in shambles. There is confusion there, and bitterness. Some of the landscape is suddenly gone. After six years of frenzied talk about women's liberation, the only woman in the Senate is defeated. The rising administrative star of the Republican movement, Gordon Allott of Colorado, is beaten. Why?

In the case of Mrs. Smith, they say she was getting a little weather-beaten, and the voters were fractious. In the case of Allott, they are saying that pigheadedness in the White House was responsible: Nixon didn't bother to stop by and say hello, and a hello was all that Allott needed. Caleb Boggs of Delaware is down, and Jack Miller of Iowa.

The House of Representatives shows a little Republican gain, not much. A handful of liberal Republicans were reelected, and a handful of antiliberal Republicans. Here and there the voters seemed to be saying that they were voting for Nixon because there was no other way of expressing their distrust of George McGovern, but they were voting for Democrats other than McGovern to express their general resentment of the hole they had been put into.

How will such voters act in the future? And how will the Congress act toward a President who is disliked for ideological and personal reasons by many Democrats and mistrusted by many Republicans—who believe he turned the election into a prolonged and expensive venture in narcissism, without regard to the political party on whose cooperation he now depends?

There isn't, really, a feeling of satisfaction in the air. Mr. Nixon will fill the void quickly—or he will suffer the fate of Harold Macmillan, who in 1959 won the most triumphant reelection in modern English political history, and eighteen months later everything lay in ruins about him, a great story which SuperMac, as he was briefly called, is now engaged in recounting, in six volumes.

The Schlesinger-Galbraith Entrail-Reading Service

November 13, 1972

VINDICTIVENESS IS a bore, and I dwell here on some of the preelection vaticinations of Professors Schlesinger and Galbraith not so much because I desire to tease them, though I take the normal man's pleasure in doing that, as because I think there is something to be learned about punditry from meditating on them.

Mr. Schlesinger wrote an article for the New York *Times Magazine* (July 30, 1972), right after the nomination of George McGovern, called "How McGovern Will Win." Now nobody pays any attention to the man who rises on the convention floor to say: "I nominate the next President of the United States . . ."—after which sentence you can give out the name of Richard Nixon or of Lar Daley. The hyperbole is an accepted part of a ritual act, and is therefore altogether meaningless.

But Arthur Schlesinger is a professor of history. He was presumably writing altogether seriously for a major American magazine, using all his skills as a historian, in order to communicate what he sincerely believed. The man who so often explains America to us said: "To suggest this July that

George McGovern will be elected President next November is, of course, preposterous—as preposterous as to have suggested last November that he would win the Democratic nomination this July." In other words, not preposterous at all, as it proved not to have been preposterous to predict McGovern's nomination.

And he even went on to give technical details on how the victory would be constructed. "As Republicans reflect on the fact that Nixon won last time by only 600,000 votes against a bitterly divided Democratic Party, as they note McGovern's inroads into traditionally Republican areas, they must begin to wonder where the President is going to find support in 1972 that he did not have in 1968. He needs six or seven million new votes if he is to offset not just McGovern gains in formerly Republican areas but, above all, the Democratic potentiality among first voters. The Republican plurality of 600,000 four years ago could sink without a trace in this flood of new votes." In other words, McGovern wasn't merely going to win—that much historian Schlesinger knew even as he has known Certitude throughout his life. What he was telling us was that McGovern might very easily win by a *landslide.* John Kenneth Galbraith, who once said that he makes his reputation by thinking faster than the average person, and therefore penetrating reality before others do, was an entire month ahead of his old colleague Arthur Schlesinger. Professor Galbraith wrote "The Case for George McGovern" for *The Saturday Review* issue of July 1, 1972. Once again, Mr. Galbraith was not writing in the capacity of cheerleader. He went at the problem as scientifically as if he had been retained to predict the next turn in the business cycle. "If McGovern doesn't now adopt the Establishment view, it is asserted, he will do more this autumn to make Richard Milhous Nixon a statesman than Barry Goldwater did to make LBJ a pacifist. The comparison with Goldwater is a brilliant piece of political polemics. It certainly has taken hold. It is also nonsense."

Goldwater got 38 percent of the vote, LBJ 61 percent. McGovern got 37 percent of the vote, Nixon 60 percent. So that that which Galbraith pronounced in July as "nonsense" became history with near-flirtatious exactitude. But Mr. Galbraith had it all figured out. "[McGovern] will appeal to the unrich, unpowerful, and unprivileged majority, and, therefore, he will be elected." "The fact that McGovern has made it again and again and again in South Dakota—once the most Republican state in the Union—shows that he is highly electable." And just to make absolutely certain that the gravity of his prediction would not be misread, Mr. Galbraith put his reputation on the line. "For once, my credentials as a prophet are impeccable."

For once, we see how utterly incompetent is the judgment of many of our senior commentators. This does not mean, of course, that Arthur Schlesinger cannot go back a hundred years and wrest some truths out of the Age of Jackson, or that Professor Galbraith is any less interesting as a social moralist. It means, simply, that their political advice is not only shaky, it is, really, quite ludicrous. Professor Schlesinger ended his article in the New York *Times* by saying, "On the whole, pundits know very little about politics." The funny thing about it is he was talking about other people.

III.

Watergate

Watergate Developments

October 19, 1972

CONCERNING THE Watergate caper, a few observations:

(1) There is increasing indignation at the use of the word "caper" to describe Watergate. The indignation is one part genuine, one part opportunistic. It is true that as more is discovered about the circumstances surrounding the Watergate affair, the uglier the thing looks. It is one thing to break into an office of a nonsubversive American enterprise for the purpose of listening in on conversations and telephone calls (bad enough). Something else to hire a professional disrupter, as now it is alleged was done, and charge him to forge letters over the signature of Democratic candidates and to pose as the candidate's agent for the purpose of calling off meetings, and mixing up schedules. That kind of thing is totalitarian in tendency.

(2) Advocates of George McGovern are doing their very best to proceed on the assumption that the whole of the White House is guilty. They have nicely suspended, during the crucial interval between now and the election, the presumptions they guard so zealously in other situations. We are constrained to speak about the "alleged skyjacker" even after the jet has gone zooming off to Algeria, a man with a pistol in his hand held to the pilot's head. That man gets to be "alleged," whereas nowadays you will find McGovernites talking quite openly about "Nixon's" Watergate operation, and "Nixon's" political sabotage agents. One White House staff member is alleged to have told a former colleague on the Washington *Post* that he himself wrote the letter allegedly written by Senator Muskie that brought on the lachrymose encounter outside the offices of the Manchester, New Hampshire, newspaper. Read that sentence over again and leave out the allegeds, and you have put on your special McGovern lenses.

(3) The same gentlemen who are accepting the most venal versions of what happened are prepared to hold Richard Nixon directly responsible for them. Professor Kenneth Galbraith, who has been neglecting his economics—an infrequent act of philanthropy—in order to campaign for George McGovern, says it flatly: either Nixon was personally responsible for giving the orders to burglarize Watergate, in which case Nixon should be defeated for moral venality; or if Nixon didn't know about it, he should be defeated for incompetence.

As regards the first part of the proposed dichotomy: it is at least absurd to suppose that Richard Nixon knew that that kind of thing was going on. The expression "more royalist than the king" defined a relationship that survives in republican societies. Henry II said in a fit of exasperation, "Who will rid me of this accursed priest?"—and Henry's Dwight Chapin instantly attended to the assassination of Thomas à Becket.

If it happened that Richard Nixon was overheard to say in a fit of exasperation over, let us say, the burglarized minutes of his Cabinet meetings on the subject of Bangladesh: "I wish to hell I knew who the s.o.b. is who is getting our information over to Jack Anderson,"—one can imagine a young staff member deciding to take it upon himself to bug the Democratic headquarters thinking perhaps to identify the guilty party. But the situation would require that he not, repeat not, advise the king what it was that he intended to do. To say that nobody should be President who permits himself to have on his staff someone who is so resourcefully loyal is to say that Bertie Wooster should not be permitted to hire Jeeves.

(4) There is no question that justice should be done. Laws against illegal entry and eavesdropping were not written to be ignored. And a realistic view of the situation is that the Watergate set are in for a very tough time. They are no Ellsbergs, for whom half the legal profession in America volunteer their services. These are men whose blood the Democrats want, and whom the Republicans will most anxiously neglect. Compassion is not a political specialty.

But to suggest, (5), that it is appropriate to the crime to defeat Richard Nixon is the most audacious act of proposed highwaymanry of the century. The people of the United States aren't guilty of Watergate. Why should we be punished for Watergate? The American people seem to have made up their minds that a McGovern administration would be a national affliction. The American people will not turn to masochism in order to avenge the privacy of Larry O'Brien.

Watergate Perspective

December 12, 1972

WATERGATE IS coming up right soon now. As a judicial matter, before the relevant court, and as an extra-judicial matter, before Congressional committees that are raring to go, their thirst for justice no doubt stimulated by the happy coincidence that the Congressional committees are run by Democrats, and the victims are, at least putatively, Republican.

The entire episode requires, of course, a little perspective. It was hard to get that perspective during the campaign, in part because the McGovern people were elevating Watergate into a moral watershed. You were either dismayed by it, and therefore prepared to vote for McGovern. Or you were insensible to creeping totalitarianism under the Republican Party.

The challenge was hurled at me, in a public meeting, by the editor of the New York *Times Book Review* section, a most engaging and talented young man of old-fogeyish ideological inclinations, who, like the liberals with whom he increasingly identifies himself, disdains particular inquiry, and has not replied to two invitations to explicate his position, which was also George McGovern's: to wit, if you were opposed to the bugging of the Democratic offices at Watergate, therefore you should have voted against Richard Nixon. My point always was: perhaps they can dredge up a case for impeaching Richard Nixon. But even if that case were made, it does not add up to a case for voting for George McGovern.

Inasmuch as we all assume that the intention of the Watergaters was not larcenous in the strict sense of the term, one reaches for the context of the episode. Understand, I favor the application of the relevant penalties. But even as one believes in enforcing the law, say when it prescribes six months or a year for pot smoking, the context of the crime necessarily affects the judgment of the sentencing magistrate, and should. It is in this connection that one notices, with more than mere amusement, a feature story in the *Village Voice*, concerning one Dick Tuck.

"Tuck and his antics were shelved after Watergate," is one of the headline-insets in the article describing the "supreme humorist of American politics." It appears that Mr. Tuck has made a profession of interfering in Republican politics for very nearly twenty years, but when George McGovern decided to make a big issue over Watergate, it was thought wise discreetly to bench Tuck, and accordingly he was whisked away, to Spain, or somewhere.

You see, Dick Tuck has been an employee of Democrats for many years, and his running assignment is to embarrass Republicans by any means. He specializes in glorious improvisations, which are no doubt more damaging to Republicans than any conversation the Watergaters might have tapped over the telephone of Lawrence O'Brien could have been damaging to Democrats. At Miami Beach in 1968, for instance, Mr. Tuck arranged for a long line of banner-carrying demonstrators to move enthusiastically around the hotel in which Mr. Nixon was quartered, bearing the sign, simply, "Nixon's the One." So far so good?

So far so good.

But everyone carrying such a sign was a Negro female in advanced pregnancy. Tuck was delighted. So, one assumes, were his Democratic employers. So are we all, let's face it.

Four years earlier, Tuck penetrated Goldwater's campaign train, and foisted a young lady, who posed as a free-lance magazine writer, into the proceedings, which young lady proceeded to do everything possible to disconcert the Goldwater operation, including the sudden departure of the train seconds after Goldwater had begun to address an audience. The engineer had taken the signal of an impostor conductor who looked exactly like—Dick Tuck. And so forth.

If I were a member of a jury, I don't know what I would do to Dick Tuck, if ever the Democrats permit him to sneak back to the United States. For a brief interlude, after sabotaging Nixon's campaign against Pat Brown in 1962, he was temporarily hired by Governor Brown, and found himself aboard a nonpressurized DC-3 with the governor at an unhealthy 12,000 feet, avoiding frisky weather. Governor Brown was green at the gills, whereupon the irrepressible Tuck put on a parachute, opened the cabin exit, waved at the governor, who was at this point stark white, and said affably, "Don't worry, Governor, I'm just going out for help." Upon recovering his aplomb, Governor Brown fired Tuck, it is said with some relish. Tuck and his exploits, which included direct obstruction of Republican rallies and direct eavesdropping on Republican councils, were the joke of many who now put on their hanging robes and dropsied countenance, as they force the word "Watergate" through their chaste lips. Please write to Senator Kennedy, who is supposed to lead the investigation into Watergate, and ask him to subpoena good old Dick Tuck. If he can find him.

Is Nixon a Fool?

April 28, 1973

AT PRINCETON UNIVERSITY last week Professor Arthur Schlesinger, Jr., pronounced on Nixon and Watergate before a large audience. It is this simple, he said. If Mr. Nixon knew ahead of time about Watergate, he is a rogue and (such was the lapidary insinuation) should be impeached. If he didn't know about Watergate he proves by his mismanagement of the White Household that he is a fool and (such, again, was the insinuation) he should be—got rid of.

The formula reduces the complex situation to a dichotomy which one might expect to hear from a Rotarian fundamentalist, but which sounds strange coming from that breed of exquisite men who have spent their lives and developed their minds in Cambridge, Massachusetts, the better to penetrate the higher distinctions.

On the assumption that we are driven to the second of Mr. Schlesinger's alternatives by the simple act of rejecting the first, then Mr. Nixon is a fool. But what does that make Mr. Schlesinger? Richard Nixon outwitted the Democratic Party first in 1968 and then in 1972, defeating the candidate of the Democratic Party whom Arthur Schlesinger went out of his way to anoint. In midsummer of 1972 Mr. Schlesinger was predicting that George McGovern would win the election by a landslide. How would it have sounded, to a college audience, if one had said about Arthur Schlesinger that inasmuch as he is a trained historian and political observer, he was either a rogue (for flacking for McGovern even though he knew McGovern was trailing and would be defeated); or a fool, for so misreading the evidence. Surely charity would require that one meditate on alternatives, the most obvious of these being that Arthur Schlesinger was misled by his enthusiasm and loyalty for McGovern and McGovernism, even as one supposes that Nixon was misled by his enthusiasm and loyalty for Nixonites and Nixonism.

It is strange how commonly it is assumed that the man at the top is familiar with the least particular of the operation he heads. As a lowly publisher, I receive mail accusing me of invidious delinquency because someone receives his copy of *National Review* one week late. To be sure, Watergate was never a matter quite so detached from the proper concerns of the President, inasmuch as from the beginning one thing about Watergate was clear, namely that the operation was intended to benefit the reelection efforts of Richard Nixon.

As such it caught the attention of Mr. Nixon who proceeded (a) to order an investigation and (b) to brush aside with entire confidence suggestions that his own aides and confidants were involved in any way—an altogether routine profession of faith in the men he had chosen to surround himself with.

It is extraordinary that—thus far—Mr. Nixon should be thought to have behaved all that unusually. President Harry

Truman was forever professing his confidence in the probity of some of the scoundrels who surrounded him. It never occurred to President Eisenhower to doubt Sherman Adams, or to Lyndon Johnson to suspect Walter Jenkins. King Lear was the last to discover the treachery of his own daughters, and Nicholas II the last man in Russia to discover that he had become unloved by his subjects.

No, it should be phrased otherwise. Loyalty and fidelity can lead to *foolish acts.* But loyalty and fidelity are not the mark of the fool. Still, a President ought to be qualifiedly loyal. Nixon's loyalty to John Mitchell was always, and should always have been, contingent upon a level of performance. Mitchell, after all, worked not only for Nixon but for the American people. Nixon works for the American people.

The best way to view it, pending clarifications for better or for worse, is that Nixon was lax in taking the proper initiatives. The proper initiative, in the Watergate case, would have been the appointment of an outside investigator. It was on March 20 that James McCord wrote the epochal letter to Judge Sirica advising him that there had been pressure on the Watergate defendants to keep quiet. It would have been reassuring for those who believe Mr. Nixon's moral reflexes have become flabby if he had moved the very next day to question the whitewash we are told was given to him by John Dean, his own investigator, the previous summer.

That, at the present, is the case against Nixon. The case makes him neither a rogue nor a fool, however foolish his reliance on individual aides turned out to be.

Poor Mr. Nixon suffers not only from the excessive desire of his friends to please, but from the ravenous appetite of his enemies to harm. This appetite Mr. Nixon has over the years fueled by that curdling sanctimony that is his trademark; and by that articulate impatience with the imperfect performance of others on which he built his early career. But both sides should recognize that the stakes have become altogether too high, and they should retreat, pari passu: the Nixon loyalists by admitting that he has been very foolish, the Nixon critics by admitting that—he has been very foolish.

Reflections on Nixon and Impeachment After Listening to the Speech

May 10, 1973

I LISTENED to the President's speech at the faculty club of Stanford University. At the dinner were a dozen professors and a dozen students, and we sat at our places in the private dining hall and trained our eyes on the portable TV. There is no television regularly available at the faculty club of Stanford University, but when it was suggested that one be brought in, that was done and the dinner postponed without demurral. Nelson Algren once said that he was so removed from matters of the day that he would not step onto his own stoop even to witness the wedding of the man in the gray flannel suit to Marjorie Morningstar. My guess is that Algren was standing by at 9 P.M., EDT on April 30 watching the President with the same rapt attention as the professors and students at Stanford, who knew that the speech would be a historical occasion, if not in exactly the same sense that Richard Nixon is given to suggesting that history follows him about with a Polaroid camera, lest history miss something.

I don't know quite why we all assumed the speech would last only a few minutes, but we did. Restiveness set in when Mr. Nixon was done with Watergate, whereafter he enjoined us to meditate on other matters than Watergate; to remind ourselves that the Chancellor of the Republic of West Germany would be visiting with the President the very next day, in the very room from which he was addressing us, in order to discuss matters of great international concern. Going into emotional overdrive, the President divulged the inscription he had written in his inaugural memento to the members of his staff. Here his psychological sense of his audience proved astonishingly malfunctional. He had written on January 20 to his subordinates, he said, that there were 1,461 days left in his administration. Today, he said, looking directly at us, an audience skeptical of his representation and surfeited by his techniques, there were only 1,361 days left in his administration. It was as if the coach, seeking to encourage his long-distance runners after they had started on a twenty-mile marathon, had bellowed out, *"Come on, team! Only nineteen miles left!"* Then there were the distracting verbal slips, as when he announced with great dignity that he would give all his "intention" to the problems at hand, suddenly sounding less like a self-assured President who 174 days ago was elected by the biggest landslide of the century than like the befuddled CBS executive conscripted to microphone duty during the recent strike, sweating out the weather forecast and announcing that tomorrow there would be "mosterly easterly winds." When looking again into the camera, the President said "Two wrongs do not make . . .," a muted but fatalistic plea escaped me, as if to the headsman whose stroke is already committed, *"No! Don't!"* But it was ineluctable, and we were informed that two wrongs do not make a right; and then finally the President asked the blessing of God on each and every one of us, and it crossed my mind that on this occasion, we had truly earned it.

I was accordingly astonished and confused by the judgment of almost all those present, who pronounced it, in varying degrees, an effective speech. Oh, of course they didn't mean that *they* thought it was effective, but that the people *out there* would think it was wonderful—the heroic denials, the piety, the patriotism, the statesmanship. The theme was set by older members of the faculty, graduates of the Checkers speech, which they had thought quite awful, only to wake up the next morning to discover that it had moved the entire nation. I myself thought the Checkers speech extremely good and had not been surprised in the least that it had the intended effect. But I thought this one quite unmitigatedly awful; and probably ineffective. There was no immediate way of discovering which assessment was correct, and Mr. Nixon did not, this time, help us out. It would have been inappropriate, under the circumstances, for Mr. Nixon to suggest that telegrams be sent direct to the White House by those who supported him; and humiliating to suggest that they be sent to the White House in care of Price Waterhouse, to verify the count.

The rhetoric apart, I thought the speech mortally flawed by low analytical cunning. Mr. Nixon sought to construct an august scaffolding for himself, whence to preside over the restoration of the public rectitude. He produced a spindle, on which he impaled himself. The structure of the speech compresses into a single sentence: *"Although it is clearly unreasonable that I as President—laboring full-time to bring peace to our generation and to combat inflation and to make it safe to walk the streets at night—should be held responsible for the excesses and minor illegalities of the entire executive and political staffs, nevertheless, because I am that kind of man, I do accept responsibility, and I commence my discharge of it here tonight by firing two innocent men."*

Three days later, the President calmly informed the executive that conversations with him could not be divulged to anyone or anybody, and that no conversations with third persons about conversations with him could be divulged to anyone or anybody. The President's new counsel subsequently made an effort to fix the exact meaning of executive privilege, but, as of this writing, has failed to clarify the question of just how the privilege will be used. It is accordingly not clear what was the meaning of Mr. Nixon's assumption of responsibility for Watergate, the more so since he neglected to describe what penalties or humiliations he had exposed himself to by the act of assuming responsibility. The President did not say that if the Senate committee, having looked into Watergate, concluded that he had knowledge of the affair before he communicated that knowledge to the public, or to the Justice Department, he would resign. Or that, relinquishing executive privilege, he would now undertake to convince the Senate of his innocence; or even that he would accept, contritely, if the evidence militated against him, a motion of censure. He said, in effect: "I am, for the purposes of exorbitant propriety, accepting academic responsibility for Watergate, but I shall proceed so to shelter myself as to make it all but impossible to prove that I am in fact responsible."

Arguing passionately against those who opposed the projected Constitution of the United States—publicists who had been busily stoking the suspicions of wary republicans who had so recently fought their way free of the fetters of King George—Alexander Hamilton wrote (*Federalist,* 67) that the detractors of the proposed Presidency, "calculating upon the aversion of the people to monarchy . . . have endeavored to enlist all their jealousies and apprehensions in opposition to the intended President of the United States; not merely as the embryo, but as the full-grown progeny of that detested parent." He polemicized against the caricature his opponents had drawn. The President, he wrote, "has been shown to us with the diadem sparkling on his brow and the imperial purple flowing in his train. He has been seated on a throne surrounded with minions and mistresses, giving audience to the envoys of foreign potentates, in all the supercilious pomp of majesty."

Don't you understand, said Hamilton, pleadingly—striving to train the public's attention on the differences between an American President and an English King—"the President of the United States would be an officer elected by the people for *four* years; the King of Great Britain is a perpetual and *hereditary* prince. The one would be amenable to personal punishment and disgrace; the person of the other is sacred and inviolable."

It has not worked out that way. The President of the United States is much, much less than "amenable" to constitutional punishment. John Stuart Mill warned against American provisions for the selection of the chief executive. Not only would a President popularly elected prove less "eminent" than the parliamentary leader of a party, he said, he would be less easily disciplined. Early in the American experience, this proved so, though exactly why, the fiercely republican founders were unwilling to acknowledge, sensitive as they were to the notion that the President had ex officio acquired some of the spangles of the sovereign. Before very long it had become plain that the American arrangement, having taken hold, had, however tacitly, made appropriate institutional assertions.

So that while in Europe and Latin America under constitutional monarchs and parliamentary republics governments came and went, the American President proved miraculously stable. In England not long ago, the government survived by the slimmest margin under the stress of a single prevarication by the gentleman-pimp Profumo. In American history, there was meanwhile the single impeachment proceeding against Andrew Johnson, initiated in post-Civil War circumstances by the same ugly energies that beheaded Charles I, and it failed in the Senate, thanks to the grandeur of a single member. In due course it was quietly acknowledged that, having wedded the office of chief of state and chief of government, America was restrained from punctiliously meting out Punishment and Disgrace on its Presidents; restrained by the awful fear of the unknown, unspecifiable consequences of regicide. It is one thing to replace the government of Anthony Eden with the government of Harold Macmillan, or the government of Harold Macmillan with that of Alec Douglas-Home—the kind of thing the English can do without the piano player's missing a note. Another, to elevate the Vice President by removing the President. The Vice Presidential successor is confidently anointed in America only by popular election or by the assassin's removal of the legitimate President. After Andrew Johnson, resistance to impeachment as an available remedy grew as the office of the Presidency grew, in due course investing in the incumbent something of the inviolability Hamilton overconfidently assured the rustic republican community it would never acquire. The paraphernalia of the modern executive—the Transylvanian epaulets, the buglers' "Hail to the Chief," the Presidential seal extending, yea, even unto Lyndon Johnson's Levi's, the Oval Room's solemnity that eschews only incense—all this gives sensory confirmation to the reality, which is that the American Presidency is a republican production of the sovereign. Those who believe that Richard Nixon has introduced a unique isolation to the Presidency have not read the sad and bracing book of George Reedy deploring the isolation of Lyndon Johnson, whom he served, and of Presidents in general. The evolution of the Presidency slowly, but not less certainly, transformed the office and presented the Republic with an unwritten qualification. It is this: you must not impeach and remove a President *merely for the purpose of punishing him.* The Constitution, to be sure, speaks of the impeachment procedure as available against a President found guilty of "high crimes and misdemeanors," but the phrase in question was probably accepted at Philadelphia either because it was legal boiler plate (a misdemeanor, after all, is defined by the law as including a trivial misuse of the mailing frank, let alone the misuse of Air Force One for political purposes—it is inconceivable that a President goes a week without committing a legal misdemeanor), or as a sop to those whom, fearing the inchoate despot, Alexander Hamilton sought to reassure. It is not seriously suggested, this side of Ralph Nader—who has taken to rejecting Presidents as matter-of-factly as the ignition system of a Ford car—that a President should be impeached for a misdemeanor. "Nothing but [such crimes as] are dangerous to the safety of the state, and which palpably disqualify and make unfit an incumbent to remain in the office of President, can justify the application of this clause," Senator Garret Davis said in the Senate during the debate over Andrew Johnson.

What it is that constitutes a high crime, of an impeachable character, varies significantly according to the motive of the wrongdoer. When Judge Sirica imposed the breathcatchingly severe sentences on the Watergate conspirators, he was generally understood to be engaged in putting pressure on the defendants to talk. One of them did, and since then there have been developments in the Watergate case every day.

But one wonders what Judge Sirica would have done on the day he set aside, seven days after the original sentencing, to review those sentences, if the defendants had clung to the story that they alone were involved in initiating and executing the Watergate affair. Would he have confirmed his sentence of thirty-five years in jail against, say, Howard Hunt?

Judges generally weigh two factors in arriving at an appropriate sentence. They inquire into the motive of the wrongdoer, and into his record.

It is generally the case that the motive of a wrongdoer is personal gain, the gratification of greed, jealousy or lust. Howard Hunt cannot be reasonably suspected of desiring for his own purposes a record of the conversations of Mr. Lawrence O'Brien or (though the break-in was unknown to Judge Sirica when he handed down his sentence) the psychiatric record of Daniel Ellsberg. Hunt was never (nor were his confederates) a burglar-for-hire, available in the Yellow Pages of the underground. For one thing, at $106 per day, which is the consultant's fee he was paid when he became involved with the White House, the pay is simply insufficient for someone of his background doing work that risky. No self-respecting burglar with any experience at all comes that low, especially when the work is irregular. Hunt, like the others, knew he was engaged in an illegal enterprise—obviously—but in an enterprise he just as obviously must have believed was justified by higher purposes. Having spent more than twenty years with the CIA, he knew that the techniques of espionage are routinely employed for political purposes adjudged by the sponsoring governments to be justified. He understood, moreover, that the profession of the espionage agent is, however soft-spokenly, acknowledged as a part of the necessary enterprise of national sovereignty, particularly in an age of great-power tension.

As for a conventional criminal record, he simply had none. It is not established that he ever double-parked his car. The men he recruited as mechanics were deeply committed to the anti-Castro movement, had no criminal records and would not—so far as one is able to judge—have been in the least bit attracted to conventional criminal careers.

One must assume that Hunt was enlisted by the use of arguments that had a plausible ring for an inflamed patriot, and a compelling ring, perhaps, to an inflamed patriot who was merely being asked to employ techniques of a profession he had practiced for two decades.

What kind of arguments might his recruiter have used? Let us attempt to imagine them as they might have been laid on by an advocate both convinced and convincing. Probably such a man stressed, to begin with, a *particular* need, the need to discover who in the White House—who *wherever*—was feeding intimate details of secret policy meetings to the press, most specifically to Jack Anderson, whose transcriptions of the minutes of the National Security Council that met to consider America's role during the India-Pakistan war not only were sensational in that they brought headlines in papers all over the world, but affected the policy decisions of the warring states and, indirectly, the policies of the standby major powers. The chill that continues between India and the United States grew less out of any objective act of the United States during the war than out of the damage to the Indian national pride caused by the revelations of Jack Anderson. At all costs, the man must be found, our recruiter can almost be heard to say.

"However"—he might have gone on—"you cannot expect much help from the Establishment, because Jack Anderson is the kind of person who is not nowadays being reproached for doing that kind of thing. Far from it: he got the Pulitzer Prize for doing it. Don't you see, Howard, that is the attitude today of people who should know better but don't? Their hostility to this country and to its institutions is their first attachment. Did you see how they flocked to Dan Ellsberg when he admitted stealing our documents and giving them to the *Post* and the *Times*? They made a hero out of that bastard overnight, Howard. He's on trial now, and he has a pinko lawyer aching all over Hollywood for him, and he's going to get him off, and other little Ellsbergs will spring up all over the place, because they'll be saying there's no such thing as a national secret. The People—get that, The People, Howard, the kind of talk they use at Berkeley to justify burning down the joint—have a right to know. Wish to God they'd agree that the people have the right to a functioning government. They won't have a functioning government for very long if that madman George McGovern gets elected, that's for sure. Now let's discuss a practical problem. . . ."

I, for one, would have no difficulty whatever in imagining such an amplification coming from the lips of someone who happened to be in the Oval Office at the moment when, say, Anderson's column on Bangladesh was published, or when Jack Anderson was given the Pulitzer Prize. Perhaps it is easy for me to understand its happening because if someone had on the same occasions bothered to record my own mutterings, they would not have been significantly different, except that my commentary goes out quite safely in newspaper columns and on television, and is prettily laced with brooding historical references to a lowering American antinomianism. Is it so reckless to say that a lawless counterculture is likely to beget a lawless counter counterculture—to say this at the level of prediction, rather than of judgment?

Of course Hunt shouldn't have done it, and of course he should be punished. But the national attention is fixed now on whether the man who in the chain of command gave rise to such thoughts, volatilized by his subordinates into such galvanizing language as caused the Barkers to believe that by breaking into Watergate they were in their own small way pressing the war against Fidel Castro, did, by attempting to provide executive cover for his servants' servants, commit an impeachable crime.

Most of the critics who parlay Watergate into impeachment belong in the pulpit or in the academy, not in Congress. Congress, which has always been potentially supreme—it can deny jurisdiction to the Supreme Court, funds to the executive, and impeach the lot of them—is ultimately responsible for the stability of the nation. Under certain circumstances, the stability of the nation could require the removal of the President. But there is the lapidary distinction: the purpose cannot be to punish the President, only to effect his removal. This is the distinction that threatens to be drowned out in the fury of the current debate. They are still saying—even so august a conservative as Senator Barry Goldwater—that if Richard Nixon is "proven" to be guilty of having foreknowledge of Watergate, or guilty (which is worse) of attempting to obstruct justice, then he must be removed in deference to the office of the Presidency. In deference to the office of the Presidency, he must not be removed. Censured, yes; humiliated, yes. But to remove a President is to remove the sovereign. To remove him is to punish the citizenry who benefit from the national stability. The general point is underscored by the concrete point—the public is greatly divided on the fitness of Spiro Agnew to serve. That there are many Americans who would prefer Agnew to Nixon is not in point. There are many Americans who would not, and the narrow question must be framed around the primary question of whether the ascendancy of Agnew, the indispensable corollary to the deposition of Nixon, is justified. That is the way to put the argument a posteriori, for those who shrink from the abstract approach.

The moral question is whether the democratist idea of the same punishment for the same crime, no matter the station of the transgressor, is historically secure. Plainly it is not, and a meticulous constitutionalist could run his finger over American Presidential history and come up with cogent arguments for impeaching Presidents long since honorably buried whose crimes against the spirit of the Constitution were far removed from the chicken-thieving of Watergate; and yet they were left alone. Jefferson to suspend the Constitution in order to purchase Louisiana, Lincoln to override the Bill of Rights in order to wage war, Roosevelt to do his best to vitiate the judiciary by packing the Supreme Court.

Impeachment is a technical resource available against the President who becomes, or threatens to become, Caligula. Useful and usable against the despot, or the madman. Richard Nixon is neither. Assuming that every insinuation against him and his staff were proved to be true, it does not add up to Nixon as despot, or even to Nixon as madman, or even to Nixon as a plausible national threat to individual freedom by virtue of his exercises in managerial tyranny.

But there is a delicate corollary to the presumptive nonimpeachability of the President. The collision of two standards, not easily reconcilable, made for the bafflement, and the pathos, of the Richard Nixon of the April 30 speech. We hear much of the American tradition that a man is innocent until proved guilty. The distinction is correct in law, but has always been abstractionist as regards what it actually expects of a community toward an unconvicted defendant whom it believes to be guilty in plain fact.

We have now the extraordinary finding of the Gallup poll—that even before Nixon delivered his address on April 30, 40 percent of the American people thought him to have had foreknowledge of Watergate. The Stanford intellectuals' knowledge of the mind and heart of the booboisie notwithstanding, the television address had the astonishing effect of increasing, rather than diminishing, the number of Americans who believed that Nixon was not telling the truth.

The ethos, in America, demands almost fetishistically ("And ye shall know the truth, and the truth shall make you free") the whole truth. So here was the President, asking the people to accept as truth that which half of them did not believe. And here was the President trickily declining to furnish the data on the basis of which they might accept the President's accounting. It is better not to provoke the Puritan conscience of America at all than, having done so, to frustrate the mechanism by which it could arrive at a solemn judgment on the matter. This was Richard Nixon's great error of April 30. He asserted his innocence, then quickly maneuvered to inhibit the executive from cooperating fully with investigating bodies that sought to document that innocence. Thus he activated the Puritan conscience, which, after so much foreplay, is not easily denied.

Far better the blur, the vagueness, a formalistic contrition, the subliminal appeal to a postulated incorruptibility of the institution of the Presidency. Granted such a speech would have confirmed many in their suspicion of Nixon's personal guilt, even as the evasiveness of Senator Edward Kennedy after Chappaquiddick confirmed the belief of many in his guilt. But that way, the skeptical minority—or majority— could, with Nixon as with Kennedy, proceed to other business, acknowledging that Nixon is flawed after all and must be watched but that, after all, life has to go on; and, after all, Nixon has his strengths, even as Kennedy does, and the personal humiliation of their ordeals is probably enough punishment to shrive them—in this world, at least; which is the only world we govern. For which, among so many other things, we truly have God to thank.

One Down for Senator Buckley

May 10, 1973

THE NEW YORK *Times* has published on its Op-Ed page a statement about Mr. Nixon and Watergate by the sainted junior Senator from New York, James L. Buckley, which would better not have seen the light of day, however noble the impulses of the author. Its analytical thread is that the kind of thing being said about Richard Nixon transforms "the traditional, healthy skepticism of the American electorate" into a "morbid cynicism."

Really, I think it hard to justify that allegation. It is perfectly true that there are a few Americans—one thinks of the sick set in New York City, the same set that applauded a play in 1967 whose thesis was that Lyndon Johnson had murdered John F. Kennedy—who would gladly believe that Richard Nixon was the man who set fire to San Francisco and loosed the dikes at Johnstown. But it isn't they these days who are raising questions about the character of Mr. Nixon's involvement in Watergate and attendant skulduggery. How is it "morbidly cynical" to ask what are the practical consequences of Mr. Nixon's own declaration that he will assume responsibility for what happened?

Mr. C. Dickerman Williams, the eminent lawyer and scholar, published fifteen years ago a monograph on the Fifth Amendment in which he devastatingly rebutted the then fashionable notion that no invidious references of any sort were to be drawn from the pleading of the Fifth Amendment. Those were the days when Congressional committees were routinely asking people whether they had been members of the Communist Party, and when people routinely declined to answer, sheltering themselves behind the Fifth Amendment. It was Mr. Williams' point that it is one thing to permit someone to take the Fifth Amendment, another to ask that the community interpret a defendant's silence under such circumstances as meaningless.

The fact of the matter is that President Nixon has, in effect, taken the Fifth Amendment. He has not volunteered to answer questions put to him by, say, Senator Ervin. He has gone further and put fetters on members of his staff who are scheduled to appear before Senator Ervin and are even now appearing before grand juries, by advising them they are not to report on any conversations with the President, or on any conversations with anyone else concerning conversations with the President.

I have said it until I am blue in the face that in my opinion Mr. Nixon ought not to be impeached even if he is established to have had knowledge of Watergate before March, but it does not follow from that judgment, based on the superordination of the health of the state over the demands of individual justice, that Mr. Nixon's behavior is anything less than contumacious.

And it is preposterous to assume that a public 50 percent of which (according to Gallup) believes that Nixon is hiding things should be accused of a morbid cynicism.

For Senator Buckley to go on and on about Richard Nixon's accomplishments is a bad case of *ignoratio elenchi,* and did one not know the purity of the junior Senator's heart, one might suspect that it was morbidly cynical digression. The men who sat in judgment on Oscar Wilde did not deny his extraordinary literary achievements. But their assignment, at a given moment in history, was to judge him innocent or guilty of a particular breach of the law. If it had been established that in March 1865, Abraham Lincoln sold oil and gas rights in Alaska to his brother-in-law, it would not have undone the magnificence of the Gettysburg Address or lessened the quality of his compassion for the defeated South. Enough of that.

Senator Buckley urges "all Americans to give the President the support he needs and deserves in this troubled time." A proper modification of that sentiment is that all Americans should give the country the support it needs and deserves in this troubled time, and that support in my judgment requires us to reject impeachment as a convulsive expedient. But it is unnatural to suppose that curiosity concerning the factual story, a curiosity stimulated by President Nixon's tack in his April 30 address, is morbid. It is absolutely natural. And—up to a point we have not yet reached—wholesome.

As It Might Have Gone

May 15, 1973

I wonder how it would have gone over? . . .

Ladies and gentlemen: The events surrounding the so-called Watergate case bring me once again to report to you directly.

Last August I told you that an investigation had revealed that no one working on the White House staff was involved in any way in the Watergate case. At that time other rumors were floating about suggesting that the White House was also involved in discreditable tactics involving the Democratic primaries. On the basis of the disclaimers I made about Watergate you were entitled to assume that I was also denying any White House participation in, or knowledge of, these other tactics.

Later in the fall, in the height of the campaign, my press secretary Mr. Ziegler angrily denounced the Washington *Post* for suggesting that there was in fact a tie-in between Watergate and senior members of my staff.

Shortly after my second inauguration, a Senate committee began to look into Watergate, and later in March a grand jury turned again to the subject after receiving testimony from one of the convicted burglars. During that period my staff had been instructed not to give testimony, on the grounds that principles were at stake involving the separation of powers.

I am reporting to you tonight to tell you that I have been consistently mistaken in my attitude toward this case.

The Executive Department is, numerically, the major department of government. There are over 2,000,000 people on the payroll. In the White House there are 2,000 people. The Reelection Committee had thousands of employees.

But the fact of the matter is that I accepted the office of President because I was willing to take the responsibility of being the top man in this massive organization. Now as President, I depend on aides who in turn depend on aides. The line of responsibility extends from me to the civil servant hired yesterday to sweep the floors, and to the least volunteer in my political activities.

John Ehrlichman and Robert Haldeman have let me down. I say this with an overwhelming sense of sorrow, even as fathers are sometimes forced to say that their own sons have let them down. This is not the time or the place to tell you about their strengths and their virtues. It is an ugly but perhaps necessary part of the human story that at any given moment society concentrates exclusively on a man's transgressions. Under the circumstances I have no alternative than sadly to dismiss Mr. Ehrlichman and Mr. Haldeman. But theirs alone is not the blame. I am not your President because I am naïve. I should have suspected far sooner than I did a complicity between White House staff members and the initiators of the Watergate conspiracy and other practices. My own enthusiasm for my own reelection, my own contempt so frequently expressed in public and in private for the lawlessness of some of those who opposed administration policy, both during my administration and the previous administration, unquestionably transformed zeal into lawlessness.

There were signs all about me that I should not have mistaken. Examining my conscience, I can see that I should have acted earlier, that I should have interpreted things I heard differently, that I was deeply wrong to attempt to discourage the elicitation of the truth.

I have however been elected President very recently and by a huge majority of the American people, and I will not trivialize that election, or disrupt the stability of the Constitution, or convulse this administration by any heroic gesture of resignation.

But I have earned humiliation. If after the Senate committee is done investigating this sad, sordid affair, the majority of the members of the Senate vote to censure me for my role in it, I shall accept that censure with a heavy heart, but with full respect for the integrity of my judges. Thank you, and good night.

Democratic Strategy

May 19, 1973

IT IS TOO early to predict the strategy of the Democratic majority, but it is clear that the Ervin Committee seeks right away to erase any convenient blurs within which Richard Nixon and his diminishing company of servants and admirers can hide. If the public is persuaded that the Committee for the Reelection of the President was in fact an adjunct of the White House, then any crime or abomination committed by the Reelection Committee contributes to the obloquy in which, it is modestly clear, the investigating staff desires to suspend the Nixon administration. No doubt the staff believes that that is where the Nixon administration belongs. No doubt there is a special pleasure that attaches to the prosecution of the overbearingly righteous. I imagine that even among the ranks of retiring monks of great spiritual resolution, volunteers could have been got to touch the light on the pyre that consumed the saintly Savonarola.

Senator Weicker, in calling for the whole truth and nothing but the truth, was not doing more, really, than Mr. Nixon himself did in his television speech. That was probably the last chance the President had to steer the country in the direction of what one might call a Chappaquiddick solution. He thus stoked not only the healthy curiosity of his friends, but also the prurient curiosity of his enemies. The former, invited by the President to trust in the outcome of any investigation, could not easily suggest that an overweening curiosity about the significance of everything that passed from the White House to members of the staff of CREEP—every memorandum, every conversation, every innuendo—was unwarranted.

Meanwhile Mr. Nixon's critics, always willing to believe the worst about him, took the curdling sanctimony of his speech as a personal challenge to uproot any scintilla of evidence linking the President to Watergate, or to the subsequent effort to isolate the case. The Chappaquiddick solution of Senator Kennedy, with of course the appropriate modifications, would have disarmed Mr. Nixon's critics, and made the investigation a much more listless affair. Senator Kennedy, far from encouraging a meticulous public investigation of the Chappaquiddick affair, took refuge in a grand jury proceeding which in those days was reliably confidential and suffered a grave diminution of his reputation, but by no means a mortal one. The obmutescence of the President in the past fortnight suggests that he knows now the grave mistake he made on the evening of April 30.

There is something in Mr. Nixon that is at war with his generally sound political judgment. It is the compulsion to self-justification. He gave one other very bad speech during his Presidency. It was when he decided to send American troops into Cambodia. He begged, and even demanded, that the whole of the American public should endorse his decision, indeed that the American public should understand it as an act of great military and above all extra-military statesmanship.

Asked so to declare themselves, Mr. Nixon's critics, who ordinarily would have said simply, "Count me out," were driven instead to express their demurral by violently denouncing Mr. Nixon and his works. Today, Mr. Nixon's critics are showing a clenched-fist determination to dangle before the television cameras every conceivable datum that might substantiate a presumed knowledge by the President of Watergate and its squalid aftermath.

The senior Democratic leadership in Congress is remarkably restrained on the subject precisely because these are gentlemen who know that the success of the prosecutorial staff of the Senate committee may be in inverse ratio to the best interests of the Republic. What if, after a half dozen weeks of hearings, the only truly plausible conclusion is that Mr. Nixon was "guilty"? What then?

Isn't even a censure against an unwilling President something of a paralyzing awkwardness? Henry II presented himself before the altar to be flogged to atone for the murder of Thomas à Becket, and returned plausibly to his throne. This he could not have done if he had been dragged to the flogging post by force. And this is why in responsible circles there is little joy in the prospect of a protracted embarrassment of Nixon, and great concern about how, exactly, to chart the road back.

Watergate Professionalism

June 25, 1972

THE EARLY testimony of John Dean throws light on the risky uses of the term "professional." There was, for instance, the so-called Liddy Plan. This plan was unveiled by Gordon Liddy before John Mitchell and Jeb Magruder and John Dean in the early months of 1972. It called for doing a real job during the political conventions. In Miami, prostitutes would be loosed throughout the Democratic convention, to tease secrets from the politicians and delegates. In San Diego (where the Republicans were at that time scheduled to meet), the anticipated anti-Nixon demonstrators would be—presumably Liddy was talking about the ringleaders, though who knows, who knows—mugged, and others of them kidnapped south of the border to Mexico, where they would lose their appetite for anti-Nixon activity.

The enterprise, Liddy said, would cost $1,000,000. But—only professionals would be used. The very best girls. Presumably, also, the very best muggers, and the very best kidnappers. No amateur kidnappers.

And then Dean said that on one "social" occasion he had been told by one of the security people gathered around the White House about tapping the telephone of a "newsman." That was really something, the bugger had said to Dean. He remembered having simultaneously to hold the ladder for the technician who was installing the bug at the other end, while at the same time having to look to the right and to the left in case anyone showed up in the back alley in which they were doing their business. One could only think of Abbott and Costello installing a wiretap.

John Mitchell's reaction, said Dean, was to wink surreptitiously at Dean and Magruder while Liddy was solemnly going on about the kidnappers and muggers and prostitutes. Then—and here I think is a clue to the surpassing mysteries of Watergate—John Mitchell did what, Dean said, he characteristically did in any situation. He puffed on his pipe, and then said the most banal things he could think of, more or less to decompress the human tension. Bismarck, and one supposes J. Edgar Hoover, would have puffed on a pipe and then ordered the men in the white suits to come and take him away. John Mitchell just said that $1,000,000 was too much. It is only surprising that Liddy, who prided himself on thinking of every detail, didn't say that they could get the million back in ransom money for the kidnapped demonstrators.

So it went during that strange season. Somebody said that Senator Kennedy should be followed day and night. Somebody else said look, that's going to be rough, because it just isn't likely that you can follow a guy like Kennedy day and night without somebody noticing. In fact, the somebody who notices could very well be a security man assigned to protect Senator Kennedy and he might suspect that the people following Kennedy day and night are trying to kill him. So they report to the FBI. And the FBI comes and arrests the people following Kennedy—only to find that they are working for the White House. One gathers that the plan was most reluctantly dropped.

Professionalism! The entire lot of them, said Dean, didn't find out, as far as he knew, the name or the names of anybody who was leaking the security information to the press. It is as if one were to drop a hydrogen bomb on a small city with the intent of doing away with a statue, which was then spotted by aerial photography as the only artifact left standing. I remember the passage published a dozen years ago in a journal of opinion: "The attempted assassination of Sukarno last week had all the earmarks of a CIA operation. Everybody in the room was killed except Sukarno."

How does one cultivate professional skills in such activities as the Committee to Reelect the President, and the White House security people, were asking for? One hopes, and then sometimes wonders, whether other matters are being professionally attended to. For instance, the economy, which sometimes looks as if it were one of Gordon Liddy's lesser projects.

The Dean Memorandum

July 6, 1973

THERE IS a case to be made for Mr. Nixon's declining to enter into a dialogue with the Senate investigating committee, though I find it formalistic. There is no case at all, that I can see, to delay Presidential comment on the exchange of memorandums between Charles Colson and John Dean; and in particular, the memorandum from John Dean to John Ehrlichman, which will go down in the history of syntax, if not in the history of politics, as the memorandum on Maximizing the Incumbency.

Thus it began, with that perfect fidelity to bureaucratic pomp so appropriate to the bloated ego and the diminished mind. "This memorandum addresses the matter of how we can maximize the fact of our incumbency in dealing with persons known to be active in their opposition to our Administration." Get that "our Administration." And he was addressing, in this memorandum, the two top officials on the Nixon staff: Robert Haldeman, the chief of staff, and John Ehrlichman, the chief adviser on domestic political affairs. This wasn't the cleaning woman then, addressing the night watchman at the Metropolitan Opera, referring to "our production of Aïda." The memorandum went on: "Stated a bit more bluntly—how we can use the available Federal machinery to screw our political enemies."

Mr. Dean suggested a modus operandi. "Key members of the staff [he named top Presidential assistants] could be requested to inform us as to who they feel we should be giving a hard time. The project coordinator should then determine what sort of dealings these individuals have with the Federal Government and how we can best screw them (e.g., grant availability, Federal contracts, litigation, prosecution, etc.)."

In other words, a citizen who is listed as in "active opposition" to "our Administration" would pop up in the "project coordinator's" radar screen whenever he came into contact with a government agency. He might be a businessman seeking to deal with the SEC, or the FCC, or the FTC, or the CAB, or the OEO, or the DOD, to limit to a half dozen the hundreds of executive agencies with which a businessman might need to deal. Or he may be a journalist, filing his tax returns with the IRS, or seeking the aid of an embassy abroad while on assignment.

And finally Dean acknowledged the need to proceed with his plan to persecute people who are hostile to Our Administration with some care. "I feel it is important that we keep our targets limited . . . low visibility of the project is imperative . . . we can learn more about how to operate such an activity if we start small and build." Build means, presumably, to expand the list of people to be "screwed" by the Nixon administration for insufficient servility to it.

I have lodged a lawsuit against people who use the term imprecisely, a fact I mention only for the purpose of drawing attention to the holy precision with which I think the term needs to be used: *Dean's memorandum was an act of proto-fascism*. It is altogether ruthless in its dismissal of human rights. It is fascist in its reliance on the state as the instrument of harassment. It is fascist in its automatic assumption that the state in all matters comes before the individual. And it is fascist in tone: the stealth, the brutality, the self-righteousness. It is far and away the most hideous document to have come out of the Watergate investigation.

And the most serious, surely. Here, one repeats, is a document circulating around the offices immediately contiguous to the Oval Office of the President. There is no record, so far, that Mr. Haldeman or Mr. Ehrlichman took offense at Dean's memorandum, or that Mr. Colson did, who takes offense at the drop of a hat. No record of a repudiation of it from any of the dozens of White House staffers among whom it circulated.

Never mind that for a minute. Of course, we must assume that Mr. Nixon had not seen it. But we must assume that he has seen it now—a document written by his official counsel, addressed to his principal assistants. Why does he not denounce that document and the thought it embodies?

There isn't anything in the doctrine of the separation of powers that makes it inappropriate for the President to comment on a document issued from the bosom of his household, simply because that document was unearthed by another department of government. There is no reason for Mr. Nixon to delay in denouncing—except one, which I decline to consider.

The Presidential Tapes

July 21, 1973

CONCERNING THE Presidential tapes, a few observations:

(1) Should President Nixon have taped his conversations in the Oval Office? Some will say that is a point of purely academic interest at this juncture in the investigation of Watergate. Others will say it is more than that, that Nixon's having taped these conversations is one more ray of light into the dark neurons of the Presidential mind, increasing the public understanding of the dragon who sits in the White House.

It being so much the habit of his detractors to assume that modern sin is Nixon's invention, it became of course interesting to inquire whether other Presidents had taped some of their conversations, and the word came in at disconcerting speed from several quarters that the answer is yes, other Presidents have taped their conversations. FDR, for instance, LBJ as one would expect, and—JFK.

(2) Now this does not of course mean that Presidents should tape conversations secretly. It says merely that non-Nixons have done it.

The pressing point, pending a consolidation of the ethical position on Presidential taping, is whether Nixon should release the tapes to the Senate committee or, if not to the committee, to a panel of distinguished citizens who would report to the committee on whether these tapes corroborated John Dean's story of the implications of Nixon in the cover-up, or whether they corroborated Mr. Nixon's insistence on his innocence.

On the argument of executive privilege: It should be understood that a privilege can be improperly asserted. It always most greatly strained relations between other Christian faiths and the Catholic Church that the doctrine of papal infallibility was, in the judgment of the critics of Pius IX, based on circular argument. The Pope, they said, cannot be infallible because the Pope says he is infallible. The Pope's insistence on infallibility was in effect a deduction. Well, so is Mr. Nixon's insistence that the tapes are privileged a deduction. But whereas the Pope during the nineteenth century had absolute authority over the Church and could therefore ratify his own assertions, the President does not have absolute authority over the question of the division of powers, nor over the question of what the privilege is. And, of course, he mounts a confrontation under the worst conceivable circumstances, because it is everywhere assumed that he does so for self-serving reasons rather than for reasons that touch only on his concern for the integrity of his office.

A better argument, though not a sufficient one, is that private conversations simply ought not to be transcribed. For one thing they reveal mannerisms that are altogether inappropriate for the public print. Everyone knew, for instance, that President Eisenhower swore "like a trooper," as they so primly put it in the biographies, and this was thought to be a rather endearing detail. But nobody who was at the receiving end of one of Eisenhower's tirades thought it in the least endearing, and to read a transcript of such a tirade would be to reveal that which in the nature of things a man should be permitted to keep private. One needs to add to such obvious categories as spicy speech those colloquial characterizations of people which are death transcribed. I do not know just how, in the privacy of his chambers, Mr. Nixon refers to, say, George Meany; but if he knew Meany was going to be reading a transcript of his conversations Mr. Nixon would undoubtedly find himself saying to his aides, "Then there is the question of the silver-haired elder statesman of American labor, Mr. Meany."

Still, these difficulties could be coped with by the simple expedient of turning over the tapes to two or three men, perhaps retired judges, asking that they focus on the single question of whether Dean's conversations revealed Mr. Nixon's complicity in the cover-up. Said judges should then be asked to do nothing more than to check one of the following:

(1) The tapes substantially corroborate the President's involvement in the cover-up.

(2) The tapes substantially corroborate the President's noninvolvement in the cover-up.

(3) The tapes are ambiguous on the point.

Look, now, at the alternative. The argument of executive privilege is too abstract, and too implausible to capture the popular imagination. If Americans were unwilling to die for Danzig, they are at least as unlikely to want to die for executive privilege. Under the circumstances, they will take the President's refusal as grounds for properly drawing adverse inferences. It may be that the President's advisers console him with the bitter datum that the American people (71 percent) don't believe him anyway, so how can he be worse off as far as they are concerned? Here is how: There are only 18 percent who want the President removed. The figure can climb, and then the President might suffer from what one might call the Eagleton Effect: every day, a fresh voice calling for—the removal of the President.

The Awe-full Senator Weicker

August 16, 1973

How SHOULD one say it about Senator Lowell Weicker (R., Conn.)? He is my very own Senator, from my very own state, and I wish him all the best, but I do wish that before the Watergate hearings resume, he would go somewhere to dry out his lachrymal glands. If he weeps once more about the human condition on television, composing his features like a puppydog's, I would not be surprised to see a John Dean for President movement. Really, it is a wonder that Lowell Weicker can cross the street without stopping to bemoan the manners of motorists. If he had been the presiding judge at the trial of Willie Sutton, Willie would have died on the witness stand from old age. "Do you mean to sit there, Mr. Sutton, as an American, considering everything your country has done for you, back even before the Revolutionary War, and then the Civil War, and with all the traditions of honor, and justice, and respect for one's fellow man—Mr. Sutton, did you stop to consider all of that when you robbed the bank?" How one yearns, after a colloquy between Senator Weicker and a Watergate witness, for something of the flavor of the Sutton trial, of which a specimen exchange between prosecutor and witness was: "Why do you rob banks, Mr. Sutton?" "That's where the money is."

Consider Weicker interrogating John Mitchell who admitted that Gordon Liddy had come to his office with a set of bizarre counterintelligence proposals. Now everybody in the whole world, down to and including John-John taking his summer vacation in the Aegean, knows that John Mitchell was (a) head of the Reelect Committee and (b) formerly Attorney General. Here is what one has to go through on that point from LW:

"All right. Let's start at the beginning here, if we can, in going over the testimony that has been presented by you, and do some probing. I must confess, Mr. Mitchell, that as I have sat here and listened to your testimony the only difficulty I find with it is that it sometimes is difficult to realize that we have sitting before the committee not some administrative assistant to some deputy campaign director but we have the campaign director sitting before this committee, and indeed we don't have some deputy assistant Attorney General sitting before the committee, we have the Attorney General of the United States sitting before the committee. . . ." Can you, I mean, can you stand it?

Anyway, Mitchell listened to Liddy's plan, dismissed him, and proceeded to other pursuits. Senator Weicker seems to think it would have been more appropriate for Attorney Mitchell to push a button and call in an execution squad. He couched his indignation in Fanny Farmer nougat: "You mean after listening to what we would both agree are outlandish plans, that you were neither moved to great anger in your capacity as Attorney General of the United States, which certainly everything that he proposed runs contrary to what you were supposed to stand for at that moment? . . . I find it inconceivable, unless there seems to be at least some willingness to share a portion of the mentality, that you didn't go ahead and have the fellow arrested for even suggesting this to the Attorney General of the United States."

John Mitchell said, "Senator, I doubt if you can get people arrested for suggesting such things."

Senator Weicker would come back again and again. "Is there anything in this country, aside from the President of the United States, that puts you in awe, Mr. Mitchell?"

Mitchell. "To put me where?"

Weicker. "That puts you in awe?"

A. "There are very, very many things."

Q. "Do the courts put you in awe?"

A. "Very much so."

Q. "Does your oath as attorney, does that put you in awe?"

A. "Very much so."

It is only surprising that Senator Weicker didn't ask John Mitchell whether the Grand Canyon put him in awe. One wishes Senator Weicker were in awe of the aesthetic sensibilities of grown-up people.

Are You Sorry You Voted for Nixon?

September 6, 1973

ACADEMIC PEOPLE are for the most part disastrously easy to ambush, provided the wavelength is right, which is to say left. The New York *Times* has sprawled a great big survey across its pages. It is directed at scholars who permitted their names to be used in two full-page advertisements in the *Times* announcing themselves in the fall of 1972 as in favor of the election of Nixon over McGovern. With very few exceptions, the professors contacted by the *Times* fell like ninepins under the force of the inquisitorial grilling. Only one professor—Ithiel De Sola Pool of MIT—handled the reporter properly. "My mood is not a news item," he said.

There were, of course, a few professors who were forthrightly defiant. Professor Milton Friedman told the reporter, "I do not condone the Watergate business . . . but Watergate does not alter what a disastrous choice McGovern would have been." Professor Raymond Saulnier said much the same thing. And Professor George Stigler, the economic historian, spliced in a little of the irony for which he is famous by saying, "I signed for personal reasons, and I don't think I'd ever do it again. I think it's a minor fraud for a professor of economics, for example, to comment on all of a President's policies."

But most acted as though they were on the dock at a Moscow show trial. Professor Robert Nisbet, the world's kindest and brightest sociologist, said: "Would I have supported Richard Nixon if I had known the full extent of Watergate? No, a firm, frank no." And Dr. Thomas Szasz, the brilliant and provocative psychiatrist, said over the phone: "I'm so sorry. I wish you hadn't remembered me. I would not have signed it if I had known then what I know now. One looks very foolish in having supported what one thought was the better person."

Frankly, I think Dr. Szasz looks more foolish now than before. In the first place the contest was not between Nixon and McGovern in the sense that one might have a contest between John and James to determine which is the saintlier man. The contest was between a program of domestic and international convulsion versus a program, however wanting, loosely committed to Dr. Szasz's libertarian ideals.

And then, really, what is the New York *Times* up to? It— the world's major newspaper—didn't know about the Ellsberg burglary or about Dean's perjury or about Magruder's machinations last November. Why should American scholars have known about them? And because Watergate went on to explode, how does that embarrass people whose political judgments were made without any reference whatever to Watergate?

John F. Kennedy delivered an inaugural address more celebrated among the intellectuals than any since Lincoln's second. He intoned, "Let every nation know whether it wishes us well or ill that we shall pay any price, bear any burden, meet any hardship, support any friend, oppose any foe, in order to assure the survival and the success of liberty." That turned out to be the charter for the Vietnam War. Has the New York *Times* started telephoning Professors for Kennedy in 1960 to ask whether under the circumstances they have thought better of their endorsement?

As a matter of fact, it would save the *Times* a lot of phone bills if they would just pick up the intercom and telephone their own editorial writers and ask them how come they were against Otto Otepka leaking secrets to Congress, how come they were against Stewart Alsop publishing secret memoranda, how come they were in favor of resisting Hanoi . . . and have they repented? They could run a feature every day for months recording the misjudgments of their own editorial writers. Meanwhile, one wishes our brothers in the academy were a little less easily intimidated.

A Tendency to Distort

November 15, 1973

I DO NOT think the press is "distorted" or "vicious" in any categorical sense, but I do think there is a tendency in the press to magnify and thus distort: and unquestionably Mr. Nixon is frequently the victim of that kind of thing. Permit me to recount a personal experience.

Ten days ago I spoke at Kansas State University. In response to the question, What did I think the future held out for Mr. Nixon? I replied that the odds had now in my opinion changed, favoring the possibility of his resignation.

The next day I met happily with Senator Goldwater at the

annual meeting of a foundation of which he and I and a few other tigers (including Senators Tower, Thurmond, and Lausche) are trustees. After the meeting was over, Senator Goldwater and I drove to the airport together and, awaiting our flights, chatted together at the coffee shop.

A moment or two later a gentleman materialized who identified himself as being from the local CBS. He desired us to perform before his camera crew respecting Mr. Nixon and Watergate. We declined—ever so politely, and ever so firmly. Presently we got up, passed by the camera crew and the indomitable reporter to the boarding area saying, amiably, not a word.

The following morning, front page, New York *Times.* "Newsmen in Wichita, Kansas, reported seeing Senator Barry Goldwater of Arizona and William F. Buckley Jr., the conservative columnist, in 'deep discussion' at the airport there today. Mr. Buckley spoke last night at Kansas State University where he said that he believed Mr. Nixon would resign because of the Watergate scandal at the urging of Mr. Goldwater and other friends. Mr. Buckley and Mr. Goldwater were quoted by The Associated Press as saying they expected a startling development in the Watergate affair in the next few days."

In due course I received a telephone call from the New York *Times,* wanting to know more about the sensational development I had predicted. I replied that I knew of no sensational development, had predicted no such thing, nor had Senator Goldwater in my presence. On the matter of resignation, I explained that to say the odds favor resignation is different from predicting resignation. To say the odds favor rain tomorrow is not to predict rain tomorrow.

These nice distinctions were not reported back to the readers of the New York *Times.* Perhaps the distinctions are too nice. Professor Hugh Kenner has recorded that a newspaper is a "low definitional medium," and that it is unsafe to attempt in it a thought the accuracy of which depends on the correct placement of a comma.

Now, a week having gone by, I am receiving mail from all over the world, asking when would the news come out of the "startling development" that brought Senator Goldwater and me to make a "secret rendezvous in Wichita, Kansas," for the purpose of discussing the "mechanics of President Nixon's resignation."

In the first place, insofar as it concerns me, it is mysteriously flattering. I have no delusions about my own power to bring Mr. Nixon down. Who do they think I am? John Dean III?

In the second place, though at this point several newspapers have received from my own mouth the news that I made no prediction about any Watergate development, I have yet to see a single reference to said correction. This is the kind of thing Mr. Nixon is complaining about, if you see what I mean.

Nixon and Resignation

January 14, 1974

I PROPOSE, on completion of these words, to march them over to a printer, shrink them to penny-postcard size, and, wordlessly, to hand them out to elevator men, Hollywood stars, and corporation presidents who ask me, as everyone is asked these days, the one question: "Mr. Buckley, do you think Nixon will resign?"

If there were time, I would answer roughly as follows. . . .

There are several Nixons.

The first is the one that comes most readily to mind. About him the cliché is: he will never quit. It is uncharacteristic of him. He is a determined, stubborn man who fought most of his adult life to be President of the United States. He likes being President. He likes the power of the Presidency, the usufructs of the Presidency, and the romance of the Presidency.

You won't drive that man out of the White House until the limousine pulls up to the door on Inauguration Day, 1977.

That is Nixon One. Nixon Two is the political realist. He is the man who can coolly survey the political situation and draw the necessary conclusions, when there are necessary conclusions. It was that Nixon who, having expended himself at the Governors' Conference in Cleveland in 1964 trying to organize a Stop Goldwater movement, recognized it wouldn't work. Then, unlike the hapless William Scranton who went on to try to stop Goldwater and ended by looking like Harold Stassen, Nixon Two drew back, recognized Goldwater wasn't going to make it, and—supported Goldwater lustily. That single decision brought him the Republican nomination in 1968. Otherwise it would have gone to—Reagan; yes, Reagan. And Nixon knew that. This Nixon, the political realist, is capable of judging whether there is going to be impeachment plus conviction, and of either (a) acting to try to abort the case against him by hard political maneuvering; or (b) accepting the inevitable and resigning. He has not at this moment concluded that the political reality is that he will be deposed.

There is Nixon Three. Nixon Three is a withdrawn, moody, introspective man who revels in a pain that is often self-inflicted. It is the Nixon who works even harder than necessary to get the good grade, or to qualify for the football team, or to memorize the name of the ward leader. It is the Nixon who will make himself stay up all night before deciding on a Vice Presidential running mate, not so much because he is thereby better equipped to pick the right man, but because he likes to be able to say, "I stayed up all night worrying about this one." It is the Nixon who blurts out in the prepared speech that he will continue to work "sixteen to twenty hours a day, seven days a week," for his country. The Nixon who feels that all the proper people in the East resent him because he did not go to an Ivy League college and that therefore he will hew to the Rotarian company with which he feels comfortable. This Nixon feels that he is fated to suffer, must suffer; that suffering is good and that strength comes through adversity. This is the Nixon whose mind begins now to turn to the ultimate suffering: resignation. If, for the man on the make, power is an aphrodisiac, for the man facing the end, martyrdom is orgasmic. There is no other explanation for the smile on the face of St. Sebastian as the archers bent their bows.

And then, if you can stand it, there is Nixon Four. This is Nixon the human being. A recent New York *Times Magazine* has a million-page rehearsal of the entire Watergate business. One's eyes fasten on a single sentence. "He [Nixon] even deducted $1.24 in finance charges from Garfinckel's Department Store." Nixon Four could prevail over Nixon One for reasons entirely human. Shylock spoke for the Jewish race. He might as well have spoken for Nixon when he said, "Hath not a Jew eyes? Hath not a Jew hands, organs, dimensions, senses, affections, passions? Fed with the same food, hurt with the same weapons, subject to the same diseases, healed by the same means, warmed and cooled by the same winter and summer, as a Christian is? If you prick us, do we not bleed? If you tickle us, do we not laugh? If you poison us, do we not die?"

And—the final line—"and if you wrong us, shall we not revenge?"

Nixon Four is visible walking the sands of San Clemente and riding economy class in the little jet and answering questions about did he deduct $1.24 for finance charges from Garfinckel's. When Nixon Four and Nixon Three, espying a joint opportunity, fuse their vision, then Nixon will resign, not only with honor, but with pleasure.

Senator Buckley's Proposal

April 1, 1974

EVEN THE water buffalo and the springbok in Africa were talking about the startling recommendation of the tormented junior Senator from New York, that Richard Nixon resign the Presidency *pro bono publico*. Returning from abroad, and examining the response to his suggestion, one is struck by a number of misunderstandings which appear to have become institutionalized in American thought, not only among conservatives, but among liberals as well.

Most of them, in my judgment, are explicitly or inexplicitly incorporated in a two-sentence statement by a Republican Congressman from Tennessee, Mr. Dan Kuykendall. He is quoted as saying: "Senator Buckley's proposal is most dangerous as it would affect the Republic in its operations. His willingness to see a man forced out of office without proof of impeachable conduct shows a lack of understanding as to how this Republic was formed and how it operates."

If Mr. Nixon were to resign, would he in fact have been forced out of office? To answer in the affirmative, it is required that the word "forced" be used metaphorically. Because—obviously—there is no way to "force" Mr. Nixon out of office other than to impeach him and convict him. Inasmuch as Senator Buckley looks with horror at that prospect, the first part of which is by all accounts imminent, then the point to make is that Senator Buckley desires very much that Nixon should *not* be "forced" out of office.

If Mr. Kuykendall is using the word figuratively, then the question to ask is: Are we really committed to the proposition that the people should not express themselves concerning that which they desire? Here again, a distinction is necessary. If Senator Buckley had said that every time the American people desire a President to resign he should do so, he would have thrown in his lot with the plebiscitarians—with whom, as a conservative, he desires no affiliation. But he is not saying that. Nowhere in his profound statement is there a hint of it. He did not say that Mr. Nixon should resign because the majority of the American people would rather have another President. He said he should resign because the alternatives—for America—are less desirable. The alternatives being (a) the probability of impeachment and the possibility of conviction; (b) a presumptive suspicion of Presidential policies reflecting the loss of confidence in Mr. Nixon; and (c) an Executive weakened as an institution by tormentors who, in their anxiety to get Nixon, are likely to move further than is good for the institution of the Presidency.

Charles de Gaulle participated in a coup d'état, in effect, one of the principal purposes of which was to establish a strong Presidency. Even so, at a certain point, General de Gaulle, surveying the situation about him—resigned. He did not do so in order to inaugurate the plebiscitary government he replaced when he overthrew the Fourth Republic. He did it because the signals suggested France would be better off without him. Edward VIII, King of England, was not "forced" to resign: he elected to do so, and there are very few Englishmen—conservative as regards the monarchy in a sense unknowable to American republicans—who now believe that he did other than the statesmanlike thing. Very recently the governor of New York State, elected in a landslide, resigned. His motives were complicated. But even his critics do not believe that he did anything venal by resigning, or that he betrayed his mandate. Any more than Richard Nixon would betray his mandate, if he decided to turn over the reins of government to his own appointed successor, Gerald Ford. Mr. Nixon has time and again stressed that he was elected in order to carry out certain programs. Does he recognize that he is saying, in effect, that these programs would not be carried out under his successor, Gerald Ford? If that is the case, why did he appoint Mr. Ford?

I understand Senator Buckley to have asked the President to perform an act of noblesse oblige. That is to say, to put his country's interests above his own. That is not, surely, to misunderstand republican government, but to express the highest faith in it. Those who are hell bent to impeach Mr. Nixon rather than to urge his resignation are the bloodlusters, hiding under the skirts of constitutional formalism. Maybe Senator Buckley's recommendations are misguided. Certainly they are not outside the spirit of the Constitution, which three times mentions Presidential resignation as a possibility.

The Paralysis of Mr. Nixon

April 11, 1974

MR. NIXON is in a hell of a mess, and never mind for a minute the question what share of the responsibility he deserves for it. It has now come to the point of apparently serious discussion whether he can take his dogs on Air Force One to California without reimbursing the United States government. As has been pointed out, when this kind of thing was tried on Franklin Delano Roosevelt, he turned it around with withering skill and almost got the best of Westbrook Pegler. I say almost, because where FDR was concerned, the charge was that special trips were authorized exclusively for the sake of Fala. It has not been alleged that Air Force One was specially dispatched for the sake of picking up King Timahoe. Merely that the setter rode in the airplane. I do not believe Cotton Mather would have found anything immoral in this, but Nixon's critics, having tuned up, find it easier to bay through the night than to use restraint in anything involving Nixon.

There is a Congressman on the Judiciary Committee—a "hardliner" is how the morning paper identifies him. He is angry at what he considers the contumacious conduct of President Nixon. What is it this time? Well, Nixon wants until April 22 to hand over the tapes requested by the committee. Nixon's lawyer says, mind you, that he is making no commitment to hand over all those tapes at that time. The commitment, rather, is to hand over those tapes which Nixon feels relate directly to the Watergate controversy. If Nixon were prepared to hand over the tapes without any qualification, obviously there would be no point in waiting until April 22. He could, as well hand them over this morning. What the Congressman is saying, in other words, is that the White House has no right to pass independent judgment on whether these tapes refer in any way to Watergate. Mind you, it is always possible that, having found that a particular tape does refer to Watergate, and that it does so in a damaging way,

that tape will be withheld; or that the President will attempt
to withhold it. Still, the attitude of presumptive distrust is
very nearly poisonous.

Nixon goes to France, to attend the memorial services for
Georges Pompidou. And while he is there, he occupies himself with meetings with the heads of state assembled there.
He spends time with everyone, possibly excluding the elev-
en-year-old son of King Hussein. Everyone agrees that our
relations with Europe are in disrepair. Everyone agrees that
it is a matter of the highest priority that we should do something about it. But all of a sudden a critical community which
is not known for the accent it puts on showing reverence for
the remains of Georges Pompidou, may he rest in peace,
finds it profane that Nixon should take the opportunity to
talk about the problems of the living. I cannot imagine that
this criticism would have been leveled at Dwight Eisenhower,
or John Kennedy, or even Lyndon Johnson. The tone, on
the contrary, would have been altogether approving: President at Pompidou Rites/Seeks European Accord. And lots of
approving editorials.

Take the Russian trip. Everyone is ready to criticize it. I am
ready to criticize it, but, so help me, I was just as ready before
Watergate, because it is my conviction that we have been
morally fleeced by the Communist world during Nixon's
reign. But the people who were elated at Nixon's discovery
of the joys of life under Chairman Mao, and who con-
gratulated Nixon most heartily for his conclusion of the
SALT accords wherein we agreed like little gentlemen to military inferiority, are now putting Nixon in a position where
he literally can't win. If he drives a bargain that is good for
America, the Soviet Union will balk: and Nixon's critics will
say that the Soviet Union can't do business with Nixon because he is playing, in the fleeted phrase of Senator Javits,
"impeachment politics." He is being tough on the Soviet
Union—they will say—to impress the guys back home. On
the other hand, if he does make a deal with the Soviet Union,
they will say that he is so anxious to score, he is ready to give
the Soviet Union the U.S. Marine Corps Band, so as to be
able to come back victorious.

The tragedy is that there is no apparent escape from this

rut. The position of the critics is too nearly adamant, and Nixon has made too many political and psychological mistakes. It is a reason why men of true vision are less concerned now with individual justice than with the well-being of the Republic.

Destroy the Tapes

May 6, 1974

IT WAS back when Harry Truman was resisting Congressional committees in 1949. A Justice Department official named Herman Wolkinson drafted memorandums under the general title "Demands of Congressional Committees for Executive Papers." These became, when a few years later President Eisenhower was resisting the demands of Senator McCarthy's investigating committee, the authoritative source for all arguments exempting the executive from certain kinds of cooperation with the legislature, and the term "executive privilege" was born. The trouble is the legal memorandums were, on the whole, historical flapdoodle, as Professor Raoul Berger points out in his book *Executive Privilege.*

The guns are trained now, and every time Mr. Nixon opens his mouth to say something about the sacred Presidential precedents he is observing, he is quickly and, sad to say, most conclusively shot down. It turns out not that every President since Washington has taken the position that his papers are immune to inspection by Congressional committees looking into possible grounds for impeachment—but exactly the opposite from that. Every President before whom the subject has arisen has laid claim to certain kinds of confidentiality *except* when the question of impeachment has arisen. Professor Berger challenges even some of the accepted doctrines of confidentiality. But he treats with great scorn the notion that any form of confidentiality extends to matters relating to impeachment.

It seems to me that left out of public consideration is the

special characteristic of the evidence we are here mostly talking about. It is only in the last generation that technology gave us the tape recorder. Whether, if a tape recorder had existed in the nineteenth century, the Presidents then would have gone to the narcissistic excesses of recording every expletive uttered in the privacy of their quarters for the titillation of future historians, one simply cannot guess. But it is not too much to say, with some confidence, that men as keen-minded as, say, Jefferson and Madison, would have drawn a distinction between their obligation to furnish all documentary evidence necessary to deliberate the question of impeachment and such evidence as we now have before us: the stuttered musings of a President, in association with his closest associates, who is seen shuffling the cards over and over again trying to deal out an orderly deck. Permit me the thought that it was monstrous to ask that Mr. Nixon's tapes be made public. And that it was monstrous for Mr. Nixon to make them public. The assault on the private man is not worth it.

What none of the arguments has stressed—so far as one can tell—is the difference between conversation and documents. The lawyers use what they call the "best evidence" rule. It is required that the President turn over to the prosecution the "best evidence" available against him. The unfurrowed point surely is the extraneous importance of certain people's conversation. If, the courts having authorized it, a district attorney bugs the telephone of a Mafia czar in search of evidence that he is the head of a dope ring or whatever, the underworlder's mode of thought, habit of speech, his use of the vernacular, his way of canvassing alternatives, are of no general interest save possibly to sociologists interested in kinky human habits.

Where a President of the United States is concerned, there is a terrible imbalance between that which is revealed in the taped conversation, and that which is sought out. I have found much more discussion given over, in the assessment of the tapes revealed by Mr. Nixon, to how he speaks and how he cants moral and ethical issues and what is the "feel" of Presidential conversation, than to the raw question: What did he know about Watergate, and when did he know it?

When a conversation is reduced to a document, it has been

transmuted into something substantially different from what it once was. Professor John Kenneth Galbraith refuses to preserve even the first draft of his books, a solicitude for posterity one might hope he would extend into the final draft of his books. But he makes the point that there is such a great difference between first drafts and completed drafts that he would not endure anyone's looking over his shoulder to trace his analytical and stylistic progress.

Such is the general exaltation, I am waiting to hear it said now by an inflamed Presidential prosecutor that henceforth it should be required that Presidents tape all their conversations—so that future committees on impeachment can satisfy themselves, should the question arise, that Presidential consideration of this or another problem was conducted according to standards deemed seemly by Congress.

Now that we have the technology for recording Presidential conversations why has it not occurred to anyone to suggest that Mr. Nixon take a lie detector test? Presumably Professor Berger, consulting the seventeenth century, will find nothing there in the history of the formalization of legislative power that would argue against establishing scientifically whether an executive is lying. They talk about the "best evidence" rule: is there better evidence than the subjective intention of the President? If we are willing to tape his conversations, why not his mind?

Mr. Anthony Lewis, probably the premier prosecutor of Richard Nixon in the world of journalism, would of course run into his own tracks going the other way on this invitation to the violation of privacy. Richard Nixon is his Moby Dick, and my own guess is that if Captain Ahab had disposed of nuclear weapons, he'd have stuck one in his harpoon and fired it off at the white whale without a moment's hesitation. But then, of course, Captain Ahab didn't have to reveal the tracery of his thought three times a week before a very large audience: when in a pinch he could just set his jaw and look out, philosophically, over the poop deck. Mr. Lewis doesn't do that except perhaps on his summer vacation, during which the batteries of American iniquity furtively charge up again.

The direction to take, surely, is the opposite one: back toward the restoration of a degree of Presidential privacy. To tape Presidential conversations should be made a felony if done by someone other than the President; and if done by him, an impeachable offense. And all tapes should be destroyed, like poison gas, and chemical warfare pellets—with which the tapes are aptly compared.

The Jesuitical Benediction: Too Much

May 11, 1974

Is THERE no limit to the weapons Richard Nixon is prepared to use to defend himself? He began by telling us that the tapes would speak for themselves, and would fully exonerate him. A week later he has propped up a Jesuit theologian to pronounce the tapes as fine examples of Christian morality, and to describe their principal author as the embodiment of Christian virtue and high statesmanship.

Here is what I would like someone please to explain to me. Why is Mr. Nixon's judgment so awry these days? I write within minutes of reading the remarks of the Reverend John McLaughlin, Jesuit priest and Presidential aide, and I—who ran for public office only once, and achieved 13 percent of the vote—know as certainly as I know that the sun will rise tomorrow that this venture will bring yet further discredit to President Nixon—and discredit to Father McLaughlin. And, I might add, *should* do so, even as we dishonor those tame priests who have been trotted out in history by emperors and princes to baptize their grimy deeds. Mr. Nixon will succeed in arousing the anger of many who care deeply that we should not trifle with men of God, and who will recall that Mr. Nixon has at least a passive weakness for that kind of thing. For many years, Billy Graham was always there to suggest however faintly that God is a middle-class Republican. And when Mr. Nixon went to a church service in Key Biscayne to give thanks for the cease-fire in South Vietnam, he suffered himself to be described by the local pastor in terms that would have embarrassed St. John of the Cross.

The Presidential presence is said to be altogether over-awing. But Father McLaughlin is not a country preacher. To become a Jesuit requires thirteen years of hard study in the seminary. (Father McLaughlin should have taken the four-teenth year.) And after that, he served as an editor of the Jes-uit weekly *America,* which for a while was given to loosing thunderbolts at any Catholic who expressed any reservation over any papal inflection given in the least encyclical. During the sixties, many Jesuits, far from toiling in the vineyards of ultramontanism, became self-consciously, not to say obstrep-erously, independent, the hero of the group in question be-ing of course their fellow Jesuit Father Daniel Berrigan. Fa-ther McLaughlin then ran for Senator from Rhode Island against John Pastore, which suggests his inclination to lost causes; and now one detects the accents of yore, the only dif-ference being that Richard Nixon is taking the place of the Pope; in which respect, there is, once again, the old credibili-ty gap.

Father McLaughlin appealed to the virtue of charity, and of course he is correct—we should be guided by charity. But charity does not require the Congress of the United States and the American people to maintain Richard Nixon as Pres-ident of the United States. In my judgment charity might properly have been invoked against disbarring Spiro Agnew once he was removed from the Vice Presidency; but charity has nothing to do with keeping us from giving to the tran-scripts the kind of attention that Mr. Nixon *asked* us to give to them—from dwelling on the contradictions, remarking the selfishness of their concern, expressing a not uncosmopoli-tan dismay at the quality of the discourse. The only thing that charity absolutely requires is that no further analysis be made of the remarks of Father McLaughlin.

What is Mr. Nixon, the shrewd political analyst, saying to himself, as he drops bomb, after bomb, after bomb? Did he believe that a paid consultant wearing a Roman collar could transubstantiate the tapes from barracks-room discussions about how to lay the Statue of Liberty, into sacrosanct delib-erations of a man identified by Father McLaughlin as "the greatest moral leader of the last third of this century"?

What is finally surprising about it is that Nixon *isn't* really that bad. The *transcripts* are not really that bad. What *is* bad is that the transcripts should have been released at all, and what is bad is that Mr. Nixon actually believed they would lighten his burden. And, now, that either Mr. Nixon believes what Father McLaughlin says, in which case he has completely lost touch with reality; or else he doesn't believe it, but he thinks it will work, in which case he has—completely lost touch with reality. And if he has indeed lost touch, what is the most charitable thing the American people could hope for?

Meanwhile, Questioning Gerald Ford

July 1, 1974

GERALD FORD is one of those strange, strange men about whom it can be said with some conviction that he appears to have nothing to hide. Let's put it this way, to dispose of the cynics: sure, he probably would like to be President. But so would Prince Charles probably like to be king, which doesn't mean that he would slip a little ratsbane into his mother's soup, the way some of his ancestors did.

It is not reasonable to suppose that when Dwight Eisenhower was struck down in Denver, in 1955, it should have failed to cross the mind of Richard Nixon that if the angels and the saints desired to summon the compliant spirit of their servant, Dwight David, there and then, he Richard, accepting destiny, would take up the duties of the President with fortitude. By the same token, Gerald Ford, if something were to happen to Richard Nixon, would unquestionably undertake to do his duty with resignation, and a little furtive exhilaration.

But meanwhile, he is acting as dutifully as the Prince of Wales, who, when he sings "Long Live the Queen," does so with that facial commitment that would defy the most inquisitive lens ever invented. The question is—is he overdoing it? That is to say, does the pull of Ford's attachment to the individual cause of Richard Nixon blind him to some of the political problems by which he and Nixon are inextricably attached?

Consider this question, put to the Vice President last week. Suppose (I said) that it became clear that the House was going to vote to impeach the President. Would it not then make sense for President Nixon to ask the House Republicans to go along with the majority? His motives would be quite frankly political, but in the best sense.

Mr. Nixon is not *obliged* to do his best to make it hard for Republican Congressmen to be reelected. If, it having been made clear by the vote of the Judiciary Committee and by the private poll-taking that the majority of the House was going to vote to impeach, the President could with considerable dignity insist that the principal point to be transacted by the Senate had to do with Presidential authority, and that since the House was already determined to send the question on over to the Senate, it might as well do so unanimously. This would have the effect of permitting individual Republican Congressmen to face their constituencies and satisfy both camps: those in favor of impeachment, and those opposed.

Mr. Ford takes the position that individual Congressmen should make up their own minds on the subject—that indeed they are committed to do so by their oaths of office. In fact, it is not that clear. Because if the Richard Nixon case goes over to the Senate with the attention focused primarily on his refusal to give up the tapes to the Judiciary Committee, you will have here something of a clean constitutional question: as you did in the case of Andrew Johnson. And a Congressman is entitled to take the position that he has no transcendent right to consult only his own passions and convictions in settling the issue: that the issue is better settled decisively—like the issue of Presidential authority over federal appointments which was settled in the Johnson case and subsequently corroborated by the Supreme Court—in the Senate chamber.

Mr. Ford could not sympathize with this line of reasoning, and one suspects that he is unwittingly influenced by the suspicion that even to speak contingently about impeachment by the House might blur in the public mind as advocating impeachment. All of which is very honorable, except that meanwhile fifty or a hundred Republican Congressmen might lose their seats on account of it.

Mr. Ford is a truly amiable man, of intelligence and loyalty, so that it proved impossible to get him to talk about whether, if he became President, he might find it statesmanlike to grant amnesty to the Watergate Ten Thousand. Once again, it is a little like asking Prince Charles to say what he would do if he were king. Which means that all conversations with Gerald Ford, perforce, tell us something about him, and not very much about public policy in any administration headed by him.

The Senators Prepare for a Trial

July 28, 1974

NOTWITHSTANDING that the vote against Mr. Nixon by the Judiciary Committee was formally bipartisan, the cluster of nays was Republican, and everyone who speaks about the forthcoming event in the Senate speaks about "Republican stalwarts" or "Southern Democratic conservatives" as making up the hard core of "Nixon loyalists." It is of course too bad that, despite serious efforts, the question of whether Mr. Nixon should be impeached slits up as a partisan affair. Young liberals (at one of the antipodes) are in favor of conviction. Old conservatives (at the other) are opposed.

And of course it is, in a profound sense, a political question rather than a juridical question. By this I mean that scholars equally learned could disagree endlessly on whether Mr. Nixon should be impeached, though as the factual evidence mounts against him, the burden increases on the nonimpeachment scholars.

But nonscholars and nonlawyers are in a position to say that their view of the country's interests transcends the kind of discussions about what was or was not said on March 21,

1973 in the Oval Office. I could understand, and respect, a Senator who took the position that he would not vote to convict the President in the absence of the clear necessity to get him the hell out of the White House because his conduct showed that he had gone off his rocker, that he thought he was Napoleon or FDR or somebody. And I could respect a Senator who takes the strictest view of the conduct of the White House and concludes that this is a historical opportunity to reorient the Presidency toward the high road. Such a Senator upon being asked whether other Presidents might not have been impeached if subjected to such rigorous standards might reply: "Yes and probably many of them should have been. If we had impeached Andrew Jackson and maybe one or two since then, the problem of executive arrogance we suffer from now would not afflict us."

How proper is it for a Senator to be influenced, in choosing among the alternative courses of action, by his own constituency? That is a truly vexing problem, because there is that enduring historical ambiguity in the role of the representative in a republic. The House managers of the impeachment proceedings don't have the burden of persuading the people of Nebraska that Nixon has committed an impeachable offense. They have the burden of persuading Senator Curtis and Senator Hruska that Nixon has committed an impeachable offense. Let us assume—for purposes of illustration—that Senators Hruska and Curtis believed Nixon should be ousted, but that the voters of Nebraska were adamantly opposed to his ouster: how should they vote? There are two schools of thought, one of them plebiscitarian, the other the correct one. Nixon will be tried, and should be, by Senators who have been elected not to transcribe the will of the people, but to serve the people according to the Senators' best lights. If the people then desire to punish a Senator as they punished Senator Ross for casting the deciding vote for Andrew Johnson, that is the people's privilege, but it ought not to be confused with the privilege to put pressure on individual Senators.

I should think it prudent, accordingly, for each Senator to get up something of a personal statement concerning his own feelings on these questions and perhaps specifying procedures. He might say—for instance—that he will take into account what he believes to be the entire national question: Are we bent on regicide of sorts? And can we know what the consequences of it are? And is there a Cromwell in the shadows?

And, the Senator may say: I have instructed my staff to keep from my desk any communication urging upon me a course of action. On the other hand, I have asked my staff to cull arguments unusually stated or arrestingly arranged which might help me crystallize my position. But these arguments will be abstracted from letters, telegrams, telephone messages, etc. and put on my desk unattached to the name of the sender.

When one sits down to make not only a judicial but a moral judgment, one takes special care, or should, that one has taken the spiritual exercises appropriate to equip one to play that role.

Going Down

August 4, 1974

THE HEADLINES are that Mr. Nixon has gathered his staff about him, and they are hard at work elaborating a strategy of survival. Inevitably one thinks of the staff meetings called by Hitler in his bunker, as the Russians came closer and closer, with the precision and inexorability of an Aeschylean drama. Little by little it becomes clearer and clearer to all the staff that, in fact, there is nothing to be done: no stratagem left over; no secret weapon unfired. What you get then is the synthetic optimism of the generals and the admirals who dare not tell the leader the truth. The truth is: Mr. Nixon is going down.

These few words are not directed to the question of right or wrong, but to the shape of things to come. The erosion in Mr. Nixon's position during the past fortnight is extraordinary, and in fact was not foreseen by Nixon or his lieutenants. The critical moment came, we now know, when the

chief counsel for the House Judiciary Committee, Mr. John
Doar, suddenly evolved as prosecutor. He had spent months
and months assimilating the data, and now he recognized
what he saw as a pattern; and he felt it his obligation to advocate the impeachment of Richard Nixon, and his removal
from office.

His advocacy would not have been decisive except that
there were ten members of the Judiciary Committee, conservative Democrats and centrist Republicans, who listened. It
turns out that they were particularly disposed to listen after
the ranking Republican blurted out at a caucus of Republican members his belief that no Republican could in good
conscience vote for impeachment. This extraordinary and
subversive emission had the opposite effect of that intended:
a half dozen Republican Congressmen forced themselves all
the more diligently to come into mortal embrace with the
facts. And they arrived at conclusions adverse to Mr. Nixon.

The poll this morning shows that now two-thirds of the
American people believe that Richard Nixon should be impeached. Surely there was never a verdict given more reluctantly. A year ago the American people were solidly opposed
to impeachment—even though a similar majority did not believe that he was telling the truth about Watergate. Those
who oppose impeachment on the grounds alone that it
would prove to be a plebiscitary lubricant, encouraging Presidents in the future to come and go according to the whim
of the people, can hardly adduce the history of this impeachment proceeding, which demonstrates not how easy it is to be
impeached, but how hard it is to be impeached.

Let Him Go

August 7, 1974

SENATOR ROBERT BYRD is quoted as saying that he sees no
reason at all why Richard Nixon shouldn't go to jail if guilty.
It is fortunate that the people, in their treatment of Senator

Byrd, are more forgiving than Senator Byrd is prepared to be toward Mr. Nixon. Mr. Byrd's past indiscretion wasn't a cover-up. He merely joined the Ku Klux Klan. Come to think of it, my memory is that Senator Byrd then proceeded to try to cover up his relations with the Klan.

Richard Nixon's real crime isn't, in my judgment, the kind of thing you bump into on the statute books. It is a cliché that no man is above the law. Like many clichés, one must avoid a parsing of it. The fact of the matter is that most Presidents are above many laws, and if they weren't, they wouldn't be able to function in the way we expect them to function. The law Nixon violated—the cover-up—is not intrinsically important, viewed at a Presidential perspective. Mr. Nixon made it important by his denials and by the incredible mismanagement of his case.

A prominent New York accountant said privately last week that he thought the offenses for which Mr. Nixon will now be removed from the office were relatively trivial. "He should be impeached, instead, for being a horse's ass." I have, as a matter of delicacy, preferred the euphemism to the term he actually used, which is the term Mr. Nixon used, as revealed in Monday's tapes, to describe Gordon Liddy: the single character in this extraordinary drama who has not been caught telling a lie, in return for which he has been sentenced to go to jail more or less permanently.

It was Mr. Nixon who gave importance to Watergate. Discovering a little scandal in his household—the ill-conceived and ill-executed burglary—he reacted in a way not commendable, but entirely human: he tried to keep the knowledge of the involvement of his associates from becoming a major public issue. He was wrong to do that, but Presidents of the United States play for high stakes, and it is understandable that, when running for reelection, they tend to put their own interests foremost. But Mr. Nixon proceeded not only to take a certain course of action, but to denounce that course of action publicly. He got up there several times before the television cameras and deplored in stentorian tones the cover-up. He teased the Puritan conscience of America and loosed the hounds that finally arrived at his door. He demanded loudly that Congress and the Judiciary investigate and track down criminality to its lair. He was giving the public orders for his own execution.

Even then, he'd have got away with it except for—the tapes. So help me God, I'd have removed myself to St. Helena rather than permit the public to examine such conversations. Lyndon Johnson revolted television viewers of sensibility by showing his stomach scar. Nixon has revolted the public by letting them view his table manners in the Oval Office.

But assuming that everyone has the right to seek out diligently his own extinction, why do it to your friends and associates? Why permit, as long as he had physical custody over them, the release of tapes wherein he spoke disparagingly about old friends, about people whom he sent to the Supreme Court, and others he will now send to jail?

He should have taken those tapes, plumped them down on the lawn of the White House, and set a torch to them. "This is my property," he might have said, "and you can do what you want to me, but you're not going to have access to it." If they had decided to impeach and convict him for that, at least they'd have done it over a constitutional point. Now he will be thrown out with the chicken thieves.

But the notion that he should be sent to jail is not merely cruel, it fails to understand the moral character of the problem. To remove Mr. Nixon from office must now be done. To send him on to jail is not merely superfluity, it is sadism. And it would contaminate us much more than it would hurt him. It would be an act at once uncivilized and humiliating. Let the man go decently.

Julie at Bat

October 9, 1974

How to put it? Richard Nixon has been spared very few things, but at least, so far, his daughter Julie has not been publicly denounced. Whether this is a tribute to American political chivalry, or something less than that, related to the conviction that to criticize a biological appendage of Mr. Nixon is both degrading and unnecessary, we cannot say. Julie Nixon, as an instrument of Richard Nixon the monster, is—in the view of those I talk about—nothing more than a tentacle; soft, unmuscled, capable of nothing more than emitting a little squidlike stuff that clouds the vision not at all. So why go after her?

I hope the situation remains so, but I fear it will not, and therein lies a story.

I went recently to Philadelphia, on an utterly professional mission, to talk about my experience with the United Nations as a United States delegate, for the vulgar purpose of persuading people to take notice of a book I have written on the subject. Perhaps—to make a more general point—I have made my mission more unattractive than I should, since authors in fact write books for other than purely commercial reasons. They seek also to persuade, impress, or even to satisfy their vanity.

Well, I arrive in Philadelphia and there is not only Mr. Mike Douglas, the host of the television show that bears his name and one of the world's most amiable men, but also—Julie Nixon Eisenhower. She, I have been informed, is to serve during the entire week as the co-host of the program. I receive the news, to tell the truth, with some discomfort, because I know that Mrs. Eisenhower has not been retained by top management of the *Mike Douglas Show* to talk about my experiences in the United Nations, fascinating though they were.

And, sure enough, it is obvious from the very beginning of the program what Mrs. Eisenhower has been hired for. To talk about her father. And what he does in San Clemente. About his illness. About his mood. About the role Julie played in the final decision to resign. Inasmuch as the whole business of a loyal daughter's relation to her father on being kicked out of the White House is necessarily delicate, I sat glumly in what they call the Green Room—that is where, before you go on yourself, you watch over the monitor, along with other scheduled guests, the show as it is proceeding. I hoped that the limits of tastelessness would be reached before my own appearance in the third segment. The answer to that question is that said limits are unreachable on American television. I give you the following. One segment of the program was devoted to: What did Julie Nixon, freshly married to David Eisenhower, do when Richard Nixon, freshly inaugurated as President of the United States, announced on the telephone that he intended to fly up to Smith College on Air Force One to have dinner with Julie and David on Julie's birthday? Well, said Julie in the best manner of Blondie-being-asked-suddenly-to-prepare-for-the-boss, she called someone in California and got a recipe, because, you see, she had never cooked anything before. So they re-created—the host, and the hostess, and a couple of extras—on screen, the preparation of the chicken dinner for Richard Nixon. At which point one of the extras, who had been told to add a little salt, or garlic, or whatever, to the blend, objected: "Are you sure this won't give me phlebitis?"

What can the most genteel audience in the world do, under the strain of such a wisecrack, the day after Richard Nixon was wheeled out of the hospital with an infirmity that may prove mortal? What would 400 (the approximate size of the audience) daughters of Queen Victoria have done? I think they'd have done what this audience did. They laughed. So did Julie. Is that what it means to be a trouper? I'd have loved it if Julie had taken the chicken, *with* the spinach *and* the noodles *and* the garlic *and* the cheese, and smashed it in the face of the phlebitis-guy, and told him maybe the recipe didn't have any historical connection with phlebitis, as far as she knew, but that it here and now had a historical connection with such jokes.

But Julie laughed too. As, one supposes, Marie Antoinette would have laughed, if she had signed on as a bit player for the Comédie Française, doing a skit on the last days of Louis XVI's court at Versailles.

How desperately can the Nixons misunderstand the exigencies of the situation. Sending Julie to fricassee chicken and receive cracks about phlebitis, just so she can have an opportunity to stress her father's innocence, any success in which line of endeavor merely hardens the public misgiving

about Jerry Ford's act of pardon. . . . What is the matter
with the Nixons, that they cannot understand? Or with the
American public, that it should stand by, and laugh? That,
my friends, not the lousy oil shortage, was the great moment
for the argument against American commercialism.

Nixon in Perspective

March 20, 1975

Los Angeles—In San Clemente country one hears a good
deal about Richard Nixon and his tatterdemalion life, the
weekly attritions on his professional staff, his personal staff,
the overgrown ivy, the weedy tennis court, the languishing
lawn, the mysterious nonappearance of Mrs. Nixon's personal belongings, packed late on the night of August 8, 1974. It
is as if all of nature were concerting to do to Nixon what five
years of the barren, wet, cold isolation of St. Helena did to
Napoleon. And every day there are fresh wounds. This
morning we are vouchsafed a posthumous report on Nixon
made by former Chief Justice Earl Warren shortly before his
death, which came the month before Nixon's resignation.

"Tricky"—thus did His Honor refer to the President of the
United States—"is perhaps the most despicable President
this nation has ever had. He was a cheat, a liar, and a crook,
and he brought my country, which I love, into disrepute.
Even worse than abusing his office, he abused the American
people."

Intemperate words these, and inflamed, one is required to
conclude, by personal animosity rather than historical perspective. Nixon was proved to be a chicken thief of sorts, but
such abuses of his office as he was responsible for were of a
very low order by contrast with those that can reasonably be
imputed to the Chief Justice of the Supreme Court of the
United States.

One hears routinely about the "Warren Revolution"—

meaning an entirely new set of constructions placed on the Constitution of the United States. You don't hear much about any Nixon Revolution, and it pays to remember that the House of Representatives Judiciary Committee elected, finally, *not* to vote to impeach Nixon on the grounds that he had abused *his* constitutional powers. But then perhaps Earl Warren was in a crotchet of sorts, because on the same day he told the reporters that Warren's successor, Chief Justice Burger, was a "horse's ass"—which is Warrenese for anybody who, on reading the Constitution, interprets it more or less as the Founding Fathers did, rather than as Earl Warren did. Madison, Hamilton, and Jay were archetypal horses' asses.

It will be a very long time before there is a final perspective on the Nixon administration, and indeed on Nixon. But surely that perspective has been greatly accelerated by the publication (in *Playboy*) of excerpts from a new book by Benjamin Bradlee, executive editor of the Washington *Post,* who was an intimate friend of President John F. Kennedy.

President Kennedy is more or less accepted as the other end of the social, intellectual, and moral spectrum from Richard Nixon. He is accepted as the kind of man Boy Scouts should be encouraged to dream about as Chief Executive; while Richard Nixon is the man who becomes President in the world of Charles Addams, where all the dreams are nightmares, all the jokes macabre, all reactions sick. The world revealed, in brief, by the famous Nixon tapes.

A year ago the big joke was White House profanity. "Expletive deleted" became such a commonplace, in twenty-four hours it was a cliché. Mr. Bradlee begins his notes by describing a young Harvard Senator calmly telling a group of skeptical New Yorkers that he seriously intends to run in the forthcoming primaries to get the Democratic nomination. They smile, and ask how he plans to go about doing that.

"Well, I'm going to [expletive deleted] well take Ohio, for openers."

But—Mr. Bradlee's smile comes through the pages—"that line never appeared in print." There were no tapes, and no federal courts demanding testimony from Mr. Bradlee. "The press generally protected Kennedy," as Bradlee admits, "as it protected all candidates from [Kennedy's] excesses of language, and his blunt, often disparaging characterizations of other politicians."

Nixon was always being criticized for having selected Spiro Agnew as Vice President. Kennedy, we now learn, referred to the man *he* selected as Vice President as a "riverboat gambler." When the Bobby Baker scandal came up, JFK was as undisturbed as Nixon when the Watergate burglary first came up.

"Kennedy was unwilling to knock Baker, saying 'I thought of him primarily as a rogue, not a crook. He was always telling me where he could get me the cutest little girls, but he never did.'"

But what about his own Vice President? Unlike Nixon, who stuck by his associates, surely Kennedy would have moved to divest himself of the embarrassment of Johnson. . . .

Are you kidding?

"On the question of his Vice President . . . the President said he felt sure Johnson had not been 'on the take since he was elected.' [Neither was Agnew.] Before that, Kennedy said, 'I'm not so sure.' As for dumping Johnson from the ticket in 1964, the President said, 'That's preposterous on the face of it. We've got to carry Texas in '64, and maybe Georgia.'"

Kennedy, Bradlee reveals, was intolerant of other politicians. Nixon he thought "sick sick sick." "'Nobody could talk like that'"—like Nixon after his defeat in California in 1962—"'and be normal.'"

Normal psychologically, that is. Political normality is something else. When, in the 1960 election, the vote proved so close that everything appeared to hang on Illinois, Kennedy got a telephone call from Mayor Daley of Chicago, from whose lips he apparently heard for the first time, directed to himself, those elating words, "Mr. President"—"with a little bit of luck and the help of a few close friends, you're going to carry Illinois." Nixon's close friends went to jail. Kennedy's keep getting reelected mayor of Chicago.

Nixon is thought to have had a singular, pathological interest in the press. But here we find President Kennedy suggesting to Bradlee who might be hired by *Newsweek* (with which Bradlee was then associated) and why. Why not take Tom Wicker away from the New York *Times*? Wicker, said Kennedy, had written wonderful stories, by which, in context, is meant flattering to Kennedy. "It would be a hell of a coup for you to stick the *Times* by getting him." About another journalist being considered, Kennedy said that he was "a bit of a [expletive deleted] but I like him and I'd hire him."

None of the tapes I have seen show Nixon to have been more directly engaged in trying to use the press to cut down the political opposition than Kennedy was. "You ought to cut Rocky's ass open a little this week," he once suggested to Bradlee, "you" meaning *Newsweek*. Segretti went around dropping dirty stories about potential rivals of Nixon. JFK apparently sought to make *Newsweek* his Segretti:

"The President asked if we were going to take a look at Rockefeller's war record. It is interesting how often Kennedy referred to the war records of political opponents. He had often mentioned Eddie McCormack and Hubert Humphrey in this connection, and here he was at it again with Rockefeller. 'Where was old Nelson when you and I were dodging bullets in the Solomon Islands?' he wondered aloud. 'How old was he? He must have been 31 or 32. Why don't you look into that?'"

Nixon, who was sick, sick, sick, managed an entire political campaign against Hubert Humphrey without once bringing up Humphrey's war record.

The story about JFK vs. the steel companies is revealing, not to say robust. Bradlee variously quotes Kennedy: "Are we supposed to sit there and take a cold, deliberate [expletive deleted]? . . . They [expletive deleted] us and we've got to try to [expletive deleted] them. . . . We're going to give it to them and screw 'em."

And, as noted, the press was always getting him down. There was all that talk of a Kennedy dynasty, which JFK thought "unfair" and became the subject of heated discussion at a Kennedy party. JFK led off with a toast. I quote Bradlee: "He wanted to make a toast to the Attorney General, he said, and went on to describe how he had been talking that afternoon with Tom Patton, president of Republic Steel. 'I was telling Patton what a son of a bitch he was,' the President said with a smile.

"He waited with that truly professional sense of timing so instinctive to the best comedians [Nero must have had it], and went on. 'And he was proving it.' Patton asked me, 'Why is it that all the telephones of all the steel executives in the country are being tapped?' And I told him that I thought he was being wholly unfair to the Attorney General and that I was sure that it wasn't true. And he asked me, 'Why is it that all the income tax returns of all the steel executives in the country are being scrutinized?' And I told him that, too, was wholly unfair, that the Attorney General wouldn't do any such thing.

"And then I called the Attorney General and asked him why he was tapping the telephones of all the steel executives and examining the tax returns of all the steel executives. . . . And the Attorney General told me that was 'wholly untrue and unfair.' And then another Stanislavsky pause. 'And, of course, Patton was right.' "

And so it turns out that boys will be boys, even in Camelot.

IV.

Travels . . . Complaints, Impressions

Fiddlestix

April 24, 1972

A VERY prominent American Senator, whose defense of the free marketplace has been as steadfast as anybody this side of Milton Friedman, confessed to me privately a few months ago that he greatly fears that the old ethos is gone. He told me, for instance, that he was about to give up on American automobiles, after a decade of increasing trouble with the fancy models that develop difficulty after difficulty, which the garages, at great cost, fail to fix. His is a symbolic contribution to that general welling of resentment and despair, which transmutes, among the most severely affected, into the general disillusion which—mark my words—is the psychological basis of the popularity of George McGovern and George Wallace.

Everyone has his own particular case histories, and they are sometimes grand in scale. But it is the *trivial* complaints which, somehow, matter—because they are the least excusable.

A week ago, in Washington, D.C., I was holed up with my typewriter in the swanky hotel suite the American Society of Newspaper Editors warmheartedly reserves for its guest speakers.

We are all prisoners of the telephone, and to my astonishment I discovered that at this expensive Washington hotel, it was impossible to sit down in the living room and use the telephone. You see, the telephone cord was only four feet long, but was six feet away from the couch where you work. So that every time the phone rings, or every time you need to ring out on it, you have to stand up, and tightrope your way into the corridor toward the sinewy telephone stand on which the phone perches. From that position, however, you could not take notes on the conversation or write down the research you were hunting down; indeed, if you had to come

171

up with an explanation for it, you could only suppose that the telephone was placed where it was for the convenience of somebody who wanted to murmur an assignation out of earshot of the guests. So—FLASH!—I dialed the assistant manager, whose number sat staring me in the face because it was one of those hotel telephones that have everything written on the dial except Funeral Director.

And I said: "Look, something is obviously wrong. The telephone lineman obviously made a mistake. There is no reason why your telephone should fail to extend to where people would sit down to use the telephone. Could you please do something about it?"

I waited three hours, during which of course nothing happened, and then I dialed the assistant manager again: No answer. I could not afford to wait there in the solitary confinement of the telephone chamber for very long, so I dialed Western Union and to my great surprise reached it, and sent the message to the assistant manager, full rate, WHEN YOU RESUME TELEPHONE SERVICE WOULD APPRECIATE YOUR CALLING ME AT ROOM #269 IN RE CONTINUING PROBLEM.

That was about noon, but of course, like Ralph Nader, I am a romantic, supposing that Washington Western Union can reach a Washington hotel in time to effect, well, anything at all. I should report that shortly before midnight a young man did call, announced that he was *not* the assistant manager, who had retired, and divulged that he had just received a perplexing telegram. . . . Never mind, I said. And the next morning an editor who introduced a panel discussion made a minor animadversion on the service in the hotel in which we were quartered and got from his fellow editors that spontaneous, raucous, hysterical approval which recalls the startling reception given at San Francisco to General Eisenhower in 1964 when he dropped a crack about the media's bias against Barry Goldwater. Who—let the suspense terminate—happens to be the prominent American Senator whose complaints ignited this essay. To him I made a pledge to add my own testimony to others, on the assumption that it is the little things which, when people cease to care about them, discredit whole systems, like the free enterprise system, which the managers of a certain hotel in Washington would surely know more about if their telephones were within reach.

French Summer

July 19, 1972

NICE, FRANCE. There are things they don't tell you in the travel posters, which if you knew 'em, you might have stayed at home. Traveling in Europe in midsummer is a mixed treat, but it is safe to assume that the fun begins after (a) you have gotten off your Air France flight; and (b) the nightmare of it has worn off. Say a week.

Ten years ago, approximately, President Charles de Gaulle made a tour of Latin America. He got himself a Boeing 707 and flew to Martinique. Then quickly, while no one was looking except, as it happened, AP, UPI and Reuters, he sneaked onto a Caravelle, which is the French jet. The idea was to take a jet that would get him safely across the Atlantic Ocean; and then to appear, in Latin America, in a French-made airplane, in a Buy French sort of mood, much as his successor, M. Pompidou, appeared grandly at the Azores last fall for his meeting with Mr. Nixon in a Concorde, the French-made supersonic jet. It is not at this moment known what will be the future of the French (and British) Concorde, which is said to have room in it for only 110 passengers. No doubt the economic problems will be solved by Air France doing to it what Air France is currently doing to the Caravelles. When President de Gaulle stepped into his, one assumes it was designed to permit him to stretch out his presidential legs. If he had attempted to do so in the Caravelle Air France now uses, he'd have been arrested for molesting the lady four seats in front of him.

I do not exaggerate. Gasping for air, I asked the stewardess how could I make the seat recline, and she answered that there was no way in which I could make the seat recline, because the seat does not recline. I tried insinuating my legs under the seat in front, only to run into a barrier designed by a French engineer who has profited from the mistakes of M. Maginot. No way. I was asked, did I want lunch? I replied I could not possibly let down the tray in front of me until after my amputation. I tried to smoke, but reaching the ashtray required moving your hand left, but stopping short of the lady's thigh, and that required precise calibration. Then down, under her tray, back again then, flying blind, straight ahead, homing in on the ashtray by dead reckoning. Nothing like Marlboro Country. I tried to doze, but your chair tilts *forward;* not a chance.

The captain cruised back, and I raised a schoolboy's hand. Sir, I said, I have a suggestion. All smiles, he asked me what it was. Well, I said, instead of flying steadily at 30,000 feet, with everybody uncomfortable all the time, why not dive down to sea level, then begin a gra-a-dual ascent back to 30,000 feet? Then when you get there, dive on back to sea level, and begin again. That way, I explained, the passengers would be uncomfortable only during the dive down to sea level, which could be accomplished quickly if he would go down more or less vertically, like a dive bomber. But on the way up, the seats would tilt back comfortably, and you could be as comfortable as, say, on a bus! He promised nervously to relay the suggestion to Air France, but I am not sure that he took me seriously, even when I assured him that he was talking to *l'homme moyen gâté.*

Another thing. Although they know months ahead of time what gate your flight is likely to leave from, the people at the airport appear to enjoy the suspense of not giving you the information until fifteen minutes before departure time. So you are likely to dawdle, at a restaurant, or bar, or postcard counter, or whatever, until the sign twinkles. Then you find that between you and the emigration authorities lies about one hour's worth of people. So that you have to make a terrible fuss, which is awfully unpleasant, and doesn't always work. At Athens, there were five passport officials for about 500 passengers, and people were missing their flights right and left, never mind that they had arrived in plenty of time at the airport. That's the bad news. The good news is that they might have succeeded in missing a flight on one of Air France's Sardine Specials.

On the other hand, the people are very nice. The captain, the stewards, the stewardesses, the ticket agents. There is no word in French for *empathy,* but that, clearly, is what they feel for the poor people who get involved in their national, nationalized, airline. The overwhelming justification for the extravagance of the Concorde is that it will cut travel time on Air France in half.

An American Exhibit in Russia

September 21, 1972

Moscow. If you happen to be in the Ukraine, you should not fail to visit the city of Donetsk, a clean and orderly coal-mining center. In the center of Donetsk, occupying a couple of acres of space in an indoor track gym, are 25 young Americans, aged in their very early twenties. Beginning at ten in the morning, and ending at eight in the evening, the Americans are on duty. Two hours on, one hour off. When they are on duty, they are talking to the 10,000 Russians per day who pass through the United States Information Agency's current exhibit, called "Research and Development U.S.A." They are called "guides," and they have in common their incredible mastery of the Russian language, and their extraordinary charm.

A few of them came by Russian at their Russian mothers' knees, mothers who had emigrated from their homeland. But most got their Russian from American college courses, supplemented by study in the Soviet Union. All of them applied for work as guides, a grueling three-month exposure of five or six hours' daily discourse with Russian peasants, bureaucrats, artisans, and intellectuals who file by the exhibit ogling at the Pinto sportscar, squinting at the oscilloscopes, running their fingers over the Apollo 10 capsule that circled the moon thirty times, thumbing through the volumes in the technical library, chortling at the scientific *trompe l'oeil* that has you reaching to pick up an exposed coin which under the benevolent protection of trick mirrors evanesces from your grasp—it is all too much, and the conversation tumbles from Russian mouths as if they had been taking vodka all day long.

What do they say? There is very little that doesn't get said, in the course of a four-week exhibit. Probably the conversational favorite has to do with the automobiles which, in Russia as almost everywhere else among the emerging nations, are the distillate of Everyman's fantasy. "How much does it cost?" I heard a young Russian ask, a little breathlessly. Twenty-five hundred rubles, the coed smiles prettily. You leave the Russian dumbstruck, because he has to pay *seven thousand rubles* for an automobile which could only be described as a 1953 Chevrolet manque. And he can only get it by waiting for seven years, that being the waiting time, in Russia, for automobiles, breakfast, telephone calls, and just about everything except intercontinental ballistic missiles.

Soviet officials put up with the annual U.S. exhibits, the most renowned of which provided the backdrop for the kitchen debate between Nikita Khrushchev and Richard Nixon in 1959, only because it is their obligation, under the cultural exchange agreement which is renewed every couple of years, to put up with them. That agreement gives the Soviet Union identical privileges to mount its exhibits in the United States and also grants the Communists (and this is what they primarily want) the right to send a few dozen students every year to the United States, to mooch on U.S. technology.

The hospitality of the Soviet hosts is to say the least erratic. It reflects, however unsteadily, the temperature of official Soviet policy toward the United States. That temperature ranges from below freezing to just above freezing, and of course there are Soviet meteorologists who stake out their careers, not to say their lives, on forecasting the temperature, and suggesting appropriate dress. The U.S. exhibitors quite naturally do everything in their power to advertise their presence. But in Russia there is no advertising space in newspapers, or radio, or television. Therefore they rely on such posters as the host city will agree to display, and on the notices given in the local press.

At the afternoon opening in Donetsk on Thursday (September 14) of last week American officials were tremendously heartened by the splendid diplomatic and municipal representation, by the movie and television cameras, and the three newspaper reporters scribbling away on their pads like court stenographers catching every word of the dignitaries' speeches. Their combined efforts resulted in the following story in *one* of Friday's newspapers:

"Yesterday in the Donetsk Park of Culture and Recreation, named after Sherkob, the exhibition 'Research and Development in the U.S.A.' opened."

The exhibit director, Mr. William Davis, an effervescent, omnicompetent black USIA polyglot (German, French, Japanese, and Russian) who loves to whip out a photograph of his $50,000 home in Potomac, Maryland, in whose two-door garage he keeps *his* Mercedes and his *wife's* Chevrolet ("I tell 'em: 'Why does my wife have her own car? Because she *wants* her own car, that's why she has her own car!'"), the three morning newspapers piled on his lap in the car, finally finds the little notice in one of them—and he is alive with delight. We made it! he says triumphantly, as if Clive Barnes had just published a full-page rave. Now he is confident that word of mouth will bring even more Russians into his exhibit, in Donetsk, than he could *possibly* have hoped for!

The bare bones of it are: about 2,000,000 Russians, in six cities, over a six-month period, spending an hour or two in an American exhibit. There they view advanced American technological contrivances. And there they converse with superb American human productions. The cost to the United States comes down to about $1 per Soviet visitor. I cannot imagine a better leveraged dollar.

What do the Russians ask about, in the technological Disneyland? The expected things—cars, as I say, in particular. But many of them move quickly into ideological matters. Some of those who do so are readily detected as *agents provocateurs*. These come with their set speeches of denunciation of American practices international and domestic. The kids cope with them with extraordinary dexterity. But it isn't easy, because they are not permitted to make cracks at the host country. (One young man told me that he is frequently taxed by Russian visitors over the use of firearms in the United States for acts of violence. I suggested to him that he might reply that at least in the United States the use of firearms for acts of violence is illegal. But of course that won't do, won't do at all.) The ripostes must be nonpolemical, nonpersonal, and maybe even a little oblique.

What do the Russians mostly tax us with? Well, a current favorite is Angela Davis, whose picture and strictures have appeared almost every day in the Soviet press, featuring her critique of America. Miss Davis has been diligently shielded, while in Russia, from the Western press, some of whose members have desired to ask her why she has not inveighed against the exclusion of the press from the trial of the political dissidents in Czechoslovakia. The young Americans are not beyond gently splicing this datum into their replies.

Vietnam remains big in the Soviet press. The Soviet press is best defined as a daily anti-Western spitball in four or six pages. In the biggest tourist hotels, the only English-written newspaper you can buy is yesterday's London *Daily Worker*. As well ask for a hand grenade as for the Paris *Herald Tribune*. The American guides proffer explanations. Not answers, but explanations. Several of the guides wear McGovern buttons on their lapels, and routinely profess their own disagreements with administration policies in Vietnam. The effect on the Russian interrogators is stunning. The guides tell me that many of the Russian visitors come back sometimes a half dozen times. I can only assume that in some cases the purpose of the return visit is to discover whether the young bearded guide with the McGovern button has been vaporized, replaced with a Sears, Roebuck Nixonite. Not at all. It surpasses their understanding.

Even as Russia surpasses our understanding. Madame Furtseva is the cultural czar of Russia, a lady of striking beauty and charm who is the principal public agent for the enforcement of the dominant Soviet cultural paradox. She manages to maintain the position that in order to be pro-

Russian, it is necessary to be anti-Solzhenitsyn. I said to the lady: "Will you permit into the Soviet Union any American writer?" "Yes," she said, expansively; coquettishly, even. She then took the initiative. Why were we not spending more time looking into Soviet culture? My friend replied that we had hoped to get tickets to the Bolshoi's *Anna Karenina,* but the house was sold out. Madame Furtseva picked up the telephone and winked, "I am not Minister of Culture for nothing." It was too much, but sure enough midnight descended, as clear and as black as for Cinderella. "You must write a novel," she said as we got up to leave. "Okay," I said, "if you promise to publish it in Russia." "Of course," she beamed, "—just so long as you write the truth."

Midsummer Mexican Notes

July 30, 1973

THE PLANE was late taking off from Mexico City, so the latest edition of the paper was on board. The headline stretching across eight columns read: LOS ANGELES-BOUND JET CRASHES, ALL KILLED. It occurred to me on reading it that I was at that moment on a Los Angeles-bound jet and thus far unkilled, though I suffered from a Mexican stomach (Lomotil, two immediately, then one every four hours).

The crash, it transpired, was off Tahiti, and when a few hours later the captain intoned over the loudspeaker that there would be no delay in landing in Los Angeles, my son, mimicking the voice from the cockpit, added "because of diminished traffic coming in from Tahiti." I reminded him that the tragedies aside, plane travel still gets safer and safer every year, and he said yeah, so do the moon shots.

It had been a long day, beginning with the stomach seizure at 3 A.M. at Guadalajara, whose Autonomous University is a great venture in nonradical education where they occasionally mount guards with machine guns at the gates to discourage marauding bands from the neighborhood university and, while they are at it, to adjust the length of the students' hair, which is Regulation 1950's. The occasion was a convention of journalists and educators to ruminate on the theme of "educative journalism."

I began my lecture with a jocular reference to my father's having been exiled from Mexico in the early 1920's for having "involved" himself in Mexican affairs. Accordingly, I had been raised in the tradition of noninvolvement. But I said, ho ho, noninvolvement can be overdone. For instance, there was the professor in Czechoslovakia last summer who said that Czechoslovakia is the most noninvolved country in the world: "We don't even involve ourselves in Czechoslovakian affairs." I broke up. Unfortunately, nobody else did. The rumor went about that I was sicker than I really looked. I asked my son how I sounded on the simultaneous translation earphones they were mostly wearing. "Like Donald Duck," he said. I comforted myself by recalling that someone said that Walt Disney has been the best instrument of inter-American understanding in this century.

We rushed to catch the plane, Guadalajara to Mexico City, so as to catch the plane from Mexico City to Los Angeles. At the airport I focused on the geography, and realized that it was like rushing to catch a plane from Washington to Boston so as to catch the plane from Boston to Miami. Nobody had told me you could fly from Guadalajara to Los Angeles.

The plane was late. Why—*why?*—don't they give you the reason? More and more the American airlines do. But I do not think it has ever occurred to Aereo Mexicana to do so—though it would be more appropriate in their case to apologize for punctuality than for lateness. I was in one of those moods, so I actually asked the ticket clerk why the plane was late?

I know now the expression on the Beadle's face when Oliver Twist approached him and asked for more. Stupefaction, graduating to hostility, graduating to a resolve to seek revenge. I tried giving him a helpful hint, a sort of verbal multiple choice, check one. Had they run out of gas? Was the plane hijacked? Had the pilot forgotten to put his watch on Daylight Saving Time? The clerk retaliated by painstakingly scrutinizing my ticket, as though it might somehow betray my imposture, or contain in the fine print something about the plane's being late.

Mexico is flourishing. It is a melancholy commentary that this seems to be the case wherever there is political stability. Melancholy because wherever there is political stability in Latin America there is usually a one-party state. Mexico is wonderfully skilled at giving the illusion of democracy. The cynics call it *la democracia dirigida,* a programmed democracy. But every five years they conduct elections as though they were the real thing, and the opposition is permitted not the handful of votes they go in for behind the Iron Curtain, but 10 or 11 percent, and the press makes it sound like a hairbreadth victory. It is a fascinating country, and I shall continue to visit it often, and I promise never to involve myself in its domestic affairs.

There'll Always Be an England

August 7, 1973

IT IS IMPORTANT to remember about the English that they are the most charming people in the world precisely because they are (a) wonderfully adventurous, (b) superbly humorous, and (c) absolutely the world's top confidence men. G. K. Chesterton wrote that the upper class in England were tolerable precisely because, when all is said and done, they don't really take themselves seriously. The best indication of G.K.'s point is the glorious profiteering done by august, not to say egregious, representatives of the class.

I give you His Grace, the Duke of Leinster. I have a communication from His Grace, and so, probably, do you. How do I know it's from him? Blazoned across the top of the page is: *"From His Grace the Duke of Leinster."* This is in case the majesty of the provenance of this form letter should miss you. It is signed "Leinster," which is the approved way for

Their Graces to announce themselves. No one in America has ever gone in for that kind of thing except (curiously) William Faulkner, who went through a period of signing himself "Faulkner."

Anyway, His Grace is inviting us to buy a piece of his property. Listen to the pitch. "Anderita is the site of some of the most momentous events in English history. The Romans were here, the Saxons fought here, and it was at Anderita that William the Conqueror landed to conquer a turbulent land and establish a line of monarchy that runs through 29 generations to the reign of our present Queen Elizabeth the Second." His Grace is giving us a chance to buy into that land. You can buy 25 square feet for $675. That comes to $1,176,120 per acre. But hurry! "We are inviting participation," warns His Grace in those confidential accents made famous by IBM lithograph, "only from those families who are sufficiently aware of their heritage to want to buy part of it." Well, there are those of us who are sufficiently aware of our heritage to recall that we got our acreage from England at something less than a million bucks per acre.

Otherwise, the concerns of the English are as usual catholic. Mr. Malcolm Muggeridge's memoirs are being serialized, and they are not surpassed, perhaps not even equaled, in quality and interest. He has done everything, known everyone, and when he was born a star was assigned to him which has followed him about ever since, through all his enthusiasms, disillusionments, and rediscoveries, shedding its light on him and providing him the supreme blessing: Muggeridge has never been dull. He could rewrite the opera of the Fabian Society, and make them joyous to read.

Prince Andrew, thirteen, wishes, according to the front page of the *Express,* that "Mummy would sometimes say 'no.'" The incident grew out of the queen's reviewing some color guard or other yesterday, and being asked the ritual permission after the ceremony to break ranks. Her son was heard to whisper his yearning to his accompanying colonel, or nanny, or whomever, and one's heart goes out to him, particularly since the photographed expression on Her Majesty's face suggests that she will be practicing saying no in the moments immediately ahead of her on returning to the castle.

Also on the front page there is a call from the president of the football league, after surveying the damage done to the railroad cars by the young fans who had come to the game, to "bring back the birch," by which he means bring back the caning of youthful offenders who are not, one gathers, disciplined effectively by fines. Someone instantly objected that the damage done to the cars is done only by the "unruly minority," and the reader is left supposing that the president of the football league proposed birching the orderly majority, though that was not, I think, his intention.

Mr. Bernard Levin, a splendid writer and journalist of the antihumbug school, warns against having the Olympic Games in Moscow in 1980, reminding us all of the fiasco of 1936 when Hitler turned the Berlin Games into an Aryan paean. Actually, I think this time Mr. Levin is wrong. Nineteen eighty is only seven years off, and I cannot imagine how the Russians could simultaneously prepare (a) to receive, house, and feed 50,000 people for the Olympic Games, and (b) prepare for a world war. Anybody who has ever lined up for a cup of tea and a sandwich in Moscow will understand what I mean.

And—then—there is the English zoologist who has just now written to a correspondent in California to say that—he desires to emigrate to California. He isn't protesting the monarchy, or the likes of Leinster, or even the Labor Party. He just likes America, and finds that California is, well, 110 percent American. "There is a British commercial which shows a character in various stimulating situations who remarks, 'I'm only here for the beer.' What strikes me about California is that it is at grips with the cardinal problems of our time—reconciling technology with conservation, freedom with planning, revolution with stability and liberty, and, in particular, thinking with feeling.

"Emigration takes time," says the British scientist, "and I have yet to persuade you that I am a desirable or acceptable fly to have on your wall. I hope to do this, but if not, the exposure I have had to California already has given me a kind of intellectual tan for which I'm duly grateful. All traffic is two-way even when it is unequal. I was raised on an English classical education. As with the marriage Isadora Duncan proposed to Bernard Shaw, it will be interesting to see whose brains and whose beauty the progeny exhibit. Meanwhile I am packing my bags in hope." I welcome him as a compatriot, even as I would open my arms to that old commercial rake, His Humbug the Duke of Leinster, who could help with our balance of payments.

Getting About in Italy

September 1, 1973

PORTO ERCOLE, ITALY. It is generally accepted as an act of divine intervention that planetary order should have come out of the universal chaos. It is no less a miracle that one can travel in a mere seven hours the 200 miles from the Isle of Capri to Porto Ercole. With changes in Naples and Rome. But the odyssey is eventful, instructive, and expensive, and one concludes not only that in Italy every other laborer is a baggage porter, but that the porters are the bedrock of the capitalist class.

There were three of us, with eight bags, and it cost us $60 in tips. At that we were left feeling misanthropic, the genius of the Italian porter who sets out to rob you. You ask him how much for toting eight bags in his cart from one train to another leaving an hour and a half later. "Seven dollars is the tariff . . ." he will tell you, the final word pitched high, the Italians having learned the art of aposiopesis from the Greeks 2,000 years ago. It is rather as if, cracking open the safe in the bank, you turn to the manacled, gagged manager and say to him reproachfully, "Do you realize that after all the trouble I have taken, you have here only a lousy one hundred thousand in cash?"

My friend coaxed the taxi driver at Naples up to the quay where the hydrofoil disgorged the passengers after the forty-five-minute run from Capri. For some reason, the native population separated from us as if we had the plague. Quite. As we drove off, the driver explained in an ebullient English—he had spent a month in "Yonkers-New-York" as a drummer with a jazz band—that when he had been asked to come shipside to pick us up because the lady had a *gamba mala,* which was the nearest we could come in Italian to describing my wife's twisted knee, he inflected *mala* in such a way as to suggest to the milling crowd that he was proceeding to pick up a lady with a diseased leg; and since the disease-du-jour in Naples is cholera, we found ourselves with the leper's right-of-way.

The driver rejoiced over his gentle duplicity, talking all the way, braking to frenzied stops every few blocks to wave at fellow drivers and friends, giving us a running narrative about the Germans during the war, when he was a boy of fourteen, and, arriving at the station, all but embracing us good-bye.

Unfortunately it was the wrong station. Back went the bags, after tipping prodigiously the three porters who took the bags off the taxi only to put them back onto the taxi after telling us the train left from the *other* station. The driver was enchanted at the prospect of another few minutes with us and promised he would make the connection.

There followed a ten-minute drive that will remain in memory. When I say it was a drive that paralyzed my wife into silence, I mean such drives are truly paralyzing. My wife will complain of recklessness at the wheel at twenty-five mph, but would be stoical perched on top of Saturn II during the countdown. The driver reenacted the chase in *The French Connection,* hurtling through Naples around trucks and buses and applecarts, ricocheting through tunnels, and singing lustily the songs he learned at Yonkers-New-York, especially favoring "I Luff Noo Yohk Eeen Choon" and we arrived with ten minutes to spare.

Four porters grabbed two bags each and forced us to run as best we could keeping pace with one diseased leg, and we made it to the baggage car. The four porters desired 2,000 lire each, or $3.50 for the two-minute run. Our traveling companion, whose day it was to act as purser, resisted. Whereupon two other parties joined us, listened gravely to the contending parties, and rendered their judicious verdict that the porters were correct in the price they requested.

At this point, the train about to pull away, we capitulated, and just then the taxi driver rematerialized. He had forgotten to give us his card. "You feela free to write me *any* time!" he said exultantly, and we said, thanks, we certainly would, as the door closed on us and we could see the porters cheerfully chatting until, the train beginning to move, they saw that we were looking at them, whereupon their expressions changed, as if Arturo Toscanini himself had trained them, into a harmonized despondency over the human condition which our miserliness had jolted them into reconsidering.

Overweight?

September 17, 1973

Pursuant to my resolution occasionally to write about airline travel, hoping to make it ever safer, and more agreeable, I contribute a recent experience and a few observations.

It was Rome, a week or two ago, and I was checking into a TWA flight to New York, with five bags. The passenger agent verified my ticket, told me the flight would be two hours late, looked down at the scale and said I had some overweight. Then, speaking in Italian sotto voce, he whispered to the supervisor, whose grunt instantly communicated to me that TWA's decision was to get full ransom for my excess baggage. "You will have to pay us for overweight," the agent said. "How much do you pay me for being two hours late?" I asked playfully, handing over my credit card.

A moment later he gave me the voucher to sign and I saw that it was proposed to charge me $220. Two hundred and twenty dollars! I told him never mind, just cancel my reservation. I got a porter, collected my luggage, and walked across to Pan American. There the lady whispered to me as she wrote out the boarding pass that they would need to charge me because TWA's supervisor had shot down the word that I was overweight, and a sense of corporate solidarity required PAA to be as unforgiving as TWA. I whispered back that I understood her plight completely, that for the moment I cared not about paying the overweight, nor even about the unnecessary stopover in Paris, that my cup was spilling over with satisfaction at having denied the predator over at TWA not merely the $220 for the baggage, but the $500 for the canceled airplane seat. I was rather sorry to do this to TWA, because they are lovely people, except for that avaricious creature in Rome.

But I began to muse on the question, and have done a little arithmetic on the great overweight swindle, and I invite Ralph Nader, the Legion of Decency, and the World Council of Churches to look at the figures.

The overweight charge, Rome–New York, is *$2.50 per pound*. Now the airline will fly you Rome–New York in the off-season for as little as $155 each way. Let us say you weigh 155 pounds. They are therefore charging you $1 per pound to fly you to Rome, but they are charging your luggage $2.50 per pound. Since they give you two meals, wine, a movie, (some) leg room, lavatories, and even a little lounge, the question is raised. In a rational society, why do the airlines charge more for luggage than for passengers? In such a situation, you are better off getting a piece of luggage made in the shape of a (comely) human being, buying an extra ticket, and strapping your luggage into the seat next to you, and consuming all of its free champagne.

Now those who believe that the tax is by design punitive rather than revenue-raising are quite simply wrong. The modern jet airplanes, unlike the little planes of yesteryear, have tremendous holds which are seldom filled by passenger baggage. There was a day, again in another aeronautical age, when the cost of fuel per pound carried was an important economic item—no longer. The cost of kerosene, compared to the cost of high-octane gasoline, is minimal, and the extra cost of fuel in a jumbo as a result of passenger overweight is simply exiguous.

No one should resent paying overweight. It is the paying of overweight at the current preposterous scale that boils the blood of free men, and I for one pledge not to patronize any airline that is literal-minded about overweight. They will tell you that they have no alternative, the rates are pressed on them by IATA or the CAB, or whomever.

But where is the airline lobby pressing for reform? The

full-page ad by TWA deploring the overweight tariff? Perhaps they are all content to suppose that the seigneurial instincts of their agents will cause them to overlook overweight. But this they cannot count on, cannot count even on their agents disdaining from tippy-toeing over to Pan American to report the haughty American loose in the building with 30 kilos of overweight.

There are a lot of airline associations around that are mostly useless. One of them ought to pass around a rating geared to those lines that are sensible about overweight and those that are not. The word would spread very quickly.

Post Office Collapse

November 27, 1973

AN EYE DOCTOR, preparing his patient for a serious operation on cataracts, sent her instructions on how to prepare for the surgery, what blood tests and what-have-you she needed to go through, and what diet she should adhere to. The letter was posted in New York City and addressed to Sharon, Connecticut, 100 miles away. The letter arrived nine days later, two days before the operation.

A New Yorker with a country home filled out a petition for a variance. The law requires that he furnish the zoning board with a registered letter dated at least two weeks before the hearing date. Accordingly, he sent the forms allowing seven days leeway for them to reach Stamford, Connecticut, 35 miles away. The letter arrived nineteen days later.

An investor, filling out a form instructing his broker on the handling of a highly volatile stock, put it in the mail. The broker received it six days later. The broker's office is less than one mile away.

As the saying goes, something ought to be done about it. Nothing is more infuriating, in the present climate, than to see those bureaucratic reminders by the Post Office enjoining us to use the zip code. Presumably without the zip, a letter from New York to Stamford would take thirty-eight days, instead of a mere nineteen. The only instruction I would take seriously from the Post Office these days is the recommendation that I deliver my own mail.

One wonders: why is it so much worse even than it used to be? As usual, there have been inquiries by Congressional committees, reports from the Rand Foundation, and articles in the *Reader's Digest*. But it gets worse. It was anticipated that the Post Office reorganization would succeed in taking the politics out of the Post Office. Perhaps it has, and it may be that, just as Mayor John Lindsay took bossism away from New York, resulting in a uniform deterioration of New York services, it is so with the Post Office as well. It defies the natural order of things, but could it be that by making the mayor's sister-in-law the postmistress, you get better service than by putting someone in there from the meritocracy?

Or is it—and it is this I suspect—a true collapse in morale? I do not tire of calling attention to Walker Percy's novel, *Love in the Ruins*. It is, apart from the splendor of the imagination and the brilliance of the wit, a morphological report on a society—our own—that breaks down. A society in which the faucets don't quite close, the hoses leak, the sidewalks are weedy, the telephone operators don't answer: and, of course, the mail strays in nonchalantly, without reasonable or consistent reference to when or whence it was dispatched.

It must require studied inattention for a letter to take nineteen days to go 35 miles, at a rate of speed much less than it would require if the postman who delivered it had walked all the way. The old motto of the Post Office, about delivering under the worst circumstances, appears now as a period piece, this being an age in which firemen strike, and teachers, and subwaymen, and hospital workers. No inefficiency can be so abjectly offensive: it has got to be demoralization. For which, eschewing the drastic antidemocratic cure, there is only one tonic, and that is, of course, competition.

It is simply unjustified to permit the Post Office to continue to monopolize the handling of first-class mail. Privately run package delivery services already exist, and their performance, by contrast with that of the Post Office, is exemplary.

They get it there faster, with less breakage, and cheaper. It is time now for Congress to accost the mail situation, and to prepare legislation that would permit anybody who desires to do so, to collect and deliver mail: using Post Office facilities where convenient, for a nominal rental. And it is time for an enterprising organization to come forward with a plan. If one doesn't come up soon, I'll fill the breach.

So Much for 1974

December 24, 1974

HOW DID *you* spend Christmas Eve? Better than I, I hope, because the spirit of Scrooge never left my side, and now I know why people will say unpleasant things about 1974 for years and years to come.

I tend to, uh, put things off, things like renewing things. For instance, my license to carry a pistol. Every now and then, beginning when I ran for public office in New York City, people advise me, by various means, that they intend to do their bit for a better world by bumping me off. After a few of these I decided to buy, or rather to import from my house in the country, a small but very deadly weapon, so as to leave my assassin with my calling card.

Now the bureaucratic burden in New York City for someone who wants to carry around a pistol is heavy. But at least, once you got the permit, they used to leave you alone. Nowadays, every other year you are required to appear *personally* at Police Headquarters with the relevant paraphernalia. In my case, it went like this:

"Your three photographs, please."

I presented them.

"They are too large." But good-naturedly, the lieutenant told me he would use last year's, which were on file.

He asked me then for the application form, which I presented.

"You forgot to have it notarized." I was on a tight schedule, and obviously looked crestfallen; so the lieutenant's assistant escorted me to a nearby drugstore where a notary dwelled.

I returned, and the lieutenant asked me for my pistol. I had forgotten it. He turned the other way.

"Now your personal check for twenty dollars." *Personal check?* There it was written on the form. . . .

"Can't I pay cash?" No. . . . The lieutenant produced from his own pocket a money order for $20, which every year he sends as a Christmas present to his uncle in Ireland. He would procure another one, he said; meanwhile, I could have it. I thanked him, my thanks by this time grown to a crescendo that began to attract crowds. I reached into my wallet to reimburse him the $20. I had a total of $4. We stared at each other.

I could tell that by this time he readily understood why people threatened my life. I told him I would *send* him the money. He sighed, and asked for my old license, which he is required to put into the file. I didn't have it. You see, I said, it burned, in a fire. It was a couple of years ago in Switzerland . . . everything burned . . . everything I owned.

I found that I had been led to the door, gently but firmly, and I wished Lieutenant Patrick Gallagher a Merry Christmas.

I have a telephone in my car (indispensable). And it was ringing. I must telephone an associate in Florida, *right away,* my office said; and I did; and he told me that my schooner headed for Nassau to pick up a charterer had—gone aground. Off Grand Bahama. The Coast Guard can only get within six miles of the boat. The charterers, stranded in Nassau, have no place to spend the night. What could I suggest? I made a feeble rally, and do not at this writing know where the poor family spent the night, or whether my beloved schooner floats.

We were nearing my apartment, and the telephone rang again. My lawyer. He had just received a telegram from the Supreme Court. It had ruled against us. I.e., it declined to hear our arguments about why we should not have to pay dues to any union in order to appear on television for the purpose of expressing our opinions. The Supreme Court upheld the court of appeals, which tragically, and misguidedly, overruled the district court, which had, only two years ago, ruled in our favor. What should we do? Appeal. To whom does one appeal from a ruling from the Supreme Court?

To one's banker. He was there, waiting for me, to lunch together. I told him the odyssey I had traveled that morning, and wondered whether he would prove to be the fit ending for that morning.

He smiled, and I was suddenly warmed, thinking that that probably was the nicest thing that had happened to me in 1974.

And a Happy New Year to you.

Travel Notes at Christmas

December 1973

IT BEING the season to be jolly, one forces one's thoughts away from the world of getting and spending and plea bargaining. And this means, as usual, traveling, concerning which a few recent notes.

There is a gentleman attached to the Metroliner train who, if his name were known, would fill any cars he services, booked years in advance. He was on duty this morning, on the train from Washington to New York, stops at Baltimore, Wilmington, Philadelphia's Thirtieth Street Station—"the only stop we make in Philadelphia, ladies and gentlemen, so take advantage of it—I mean, if you want to go to Philadelphia"—Newark, and New York.

On the whole, one wants to watch out for the ho-ho-hearty types, for instance the occasional airline captain who is a frustrated geologist and will not take you from Los Angeles to New York without instructing you on the glacial ages, and their impact on the geography of America. But the Metroliner conductor, who is W. C. Fields, aged about forty-five, is irresistible. "Please leave the car from the rear, if that is convenient." *If that is convenient!* To hear such words from someone connected with the railroads is, as the kids used to say during the late unpleasantness, mind-blowing.

When he takes your ticket, he thanks you heartily, and wonders whether your seat is tilted back at a satisfactory angle. "Here, try it at this angle—it's my favorite and maybe it will appeal to you." He appeals to me, and who knows, maybe he is that way because he read about the new bill in Congress that would pump in at least $4 billion into the railroads. But I suspect he was born happy, and nonbureaucratic-minded, and I would put him in charge of a great big school, wherein the dramatic story would unfold over the course of the semester about good nature triumphing over technology and the bureaucracy.

The bureaucracy. I have had, surely, the ultimate encounter with it. So I am flying to New Orleans and am offered at lunch a wine which must be from the same vineyard Professor Hugh Kenner drank from during his honeymoon. His description of it is graven in my memory. "It was a New York State Rosé, which tasted as if a few drops of Coca-Cola had been mixed with old battery acid."

But that night the manager of the hotel was so thoughtful as to provide me and my wife with a plateful of cheese and crackers and a half bottle of sound-looking St. Emilion. This we did not consume, and I thought to put it into my briefcase. And sure enough, returning to New York, the smiling stewardess offered us another draft of Professor Kenner's potion. Triumphantly, I produced my half bottle of St. Emilion and asked her please would she let me have the use of her corkscrew. She paused, then, sadly, shook her head. "We can only let you drink, according to the regulations, our own beverages." "Very well," I said brightly, "I will present Delta with this bottle, so it will be yours." She was puzzled. "I'm sorry, sir, but we are not allowed to accept gratuities."

I thought to tell her about Abraham Lincoln, but I was discouraged. It was a receiving line, in the White House, and a bumptious lady plunked a huge bundle of flowers in the President's hands, causing instant social paralysis. "Are these really mine?" he smiled ingenuously at her. "Yes!" she whinnied. "In that case," he said grandly, "I can think of nothing I'd rather do than present them to you."

Ah well, the stewardess was very charming, and in the Watergate age, one doesn't want to break the rules. What would the Special Prosecutor say if she had accepted the bottle for the purpose of opening it and serving it to me? She would not have been living up to the Spirit of the Laws.

And this morning at eight, before my encounter with the euphoric conductor, the telephone rang. "This is Allegheny Airlines. The flight you were going to take to New York at 9:10 has been canceled because of a problem with the equipment. We have you on a flight at 12:30 if that's not too late." I thanked her. Much more perfunctorily than I was disposed to do. I was disposed to tell her that I and the whole American public loved her for her thoughtfulness, and consideration, and that I would never criticize Allegheny ever, for anything. And then, of course, it was on account of her that I met Santa Claus on Amtrak.

V.

The Mideast

Israel and American Policy

July 21, 1972

IN 1967, when Israel was threatened and the Six Day War resulted, prominent American liberals paused in their clamor to get us *out* of the Southeast Asian imbroglio, to clamor, in a highly publicized declaration, for getting us *into* the Mideast imbroglio, causing Professor John Roche of Brandeis to remark wryly that their manifesto should have been labeled "Doves for War." They got quite sore at Professor Roche, fussily insisting on the distinction between independence for the people of South Vietnam and independence for the people of Israel.

What it came down to was pure and simple: where Israel is concerned, the encroaching demands for a reticent American international profile do not apply. John Kenneth Galbraith, a leading philosopher of neo-isolationism, confronting the paradox on television in Miami Beach during the McGovern Convention said, simply and honestly, "I confess I have a special affection for Israel."

Indeed, a lot of us do. Not only for reasons of compassion that reach into history, ancient and horribly contemporary. But because there is so much in the behavior of the leaders of the modern state of Israel that we need to learn from. Israel long ago took the measure of her security requirements and—acted accordingly. The United Nations counts it a day lost that it does not pass a resolution of censure against Israel; and Israel simply does not care.

Interestingly, but not surprisingly, she is not on that account either ostracized or disdained by other nations of the world (the Arab states obviously excepted). Neither would the United States be—it is my conjecture—if we had behaved, for instance in Indochina, as decisively as Israel would have done. If General Dayan had managed our war against Hanoi, that too would have been a six-day war.

197

Senator McGovern now advances the contradiction quite formally, by proposing a total American commitment to Israeli independence alongside an all but uniform disparagement of United States commitments to other countries, most particularly South Vietnam, to which we have for years made quite fervent commitments. McGovern likes to point to Israeli democracy as his justification, but this of course is disingenuous. After all, he is quoted as desiring to recognize the "legitimate" government of China—while angrily disavowing the government of South Vietnam.

The problem is to reason from the legitimacy of Mao Tsetung's government, on over to the illegitimacy of President Thieu's. Never mind. Better to be straightforward like Galbraith, and say simply that Israel occupies a "special" place in the American heart.

While you are at it, be even more straightforward than Galbraith. Recognize that on top of that special affection, a U.S. pledge to Israeli independence is for the time being necessary for anyone who aspires to be President, for the simple reason that the strategically situated Jewish community is for the most part very generous in backing political causes, and very insistent on the matter of Israeli independence.

Even so, and notwithstanding Senator McGovern's protestations of fidelity to the cause of Israel, many Jewish leaders have confessed their concern. They do so for quite obvious reasons. One of them is that the preceding leader of the Democratic Party, Mr. Lyndon Johnson, wrote into policy his entire dedication to the survival of South Vietnam. So did his coadjutor, Hubert Humphrey. In due course, however, Hubert Humphrey, running for the Presidency, not only renounced that pledge, he went so far as to say that if he were elected President he would not authorize a dollar's worth of military aid for South Vietnam.

As it has gone for South Vietnam among the leadership of the Democratic Party, so might it go for Israel. Why not? The fear among prominent Jewish leaders in America, and in Israel, is that the logic of George McGovern's foreign policy and his insistence on military retrenchment point to an eventual Vietnamization of all our commitments.

Professor Galbraith's heart is admittedly large, but it is not necessarily coextensive with the heart of Middle America, and it is just possible that Senator McGovern's glamorous rhetoric about the end of the Cold War, and about the necessity to reduce our international commitments, will in due course strike the majority of Americans as a mandate to get the hell out of the Mideast and let Israel worry about her own sovereignty. What holds for Saigon today holds, *mutatis mutandis*, for Tel Aviv tomorrow.

My feeling is that the contradiction cannot hope to survive indefinitely. The Jewish community in Israel, and indeed in the United States, cannot reasonably suppose that an American public, finally persuaded by George McGovern that we should consider the Cold War ended, will fail to act on the consequences of that assumption. We will have no grounds for maintaining a formidable military establishment geared to international responsibilities. Inevitably, the implications of retrenchment are bound to hit the American people as demanding, evenhandedly, a withdrawal from any commitment to sustain Israel, at the risk of reigniting the Cold War or participating in a regional war.

Unless, of course, we see in our relationship to Israel something truly unique, something that should be cemented against the vagaries of public passion.

Count me as among those who do. The creation of the state of Israel, for all that I acknowledge the enormous vitality and dedication of the settlers themselves, could not have been accomplished without the sanction of the United States government. The survival of the fledgling state of Israel could not have been achieved without the assistance of the American government and a community of generous Americans totally devoted to the cause of Israel. The survival of Israel in the 1967 war, once again acknowledging the bravery and ingenuity of the Israeli army, could not have been effected save for the neutralization of the Soviet Union by armed American military might.

It would appear sensible, under the circumstances, to regularize—to institutionalize—what appears to be a de facto relationship between the United States and the state of Israel.

As things stand, we suffer most of the disadvantages, and enjoy none of the advantages, of separate nationhood. Why should we not propose to Israel annexation, as the fifty-first American state?

What would we have to lose?

If we are in any case committed to Israeli survival, as most political parties insist we are, pending that change in public attitude we speak of, then we would go to war in any case if Israel's sovereignty were threatened.

Israel is geographically remote? It isn't any further from Washington than Alaska and Hawaii. And anyway, when we incorporated Alaska and Hawaii, we recognized that geographical contiguity, in the jet age, has become irrelevant.

A language barrier? Ask Switzerland how insupportable that is. Anyway, Senator Robert Kennedy insisted, and won his point, that Spanish-speaking New Yorkers should be permitted to vote. Why not Hebrew-speaking Americans?

If Israel's foreign policy were written in Washington, the Arab countries' fear of Israeli expansionism would end. We could begin by giving back to Egypt, and to Jordan, most of the terrorities conquered during the 1967 war, and retained by Israel, as Israeli officials have repeatedly assured us, for reasons of military defense only. If Israel becomes a part of the United States, there is no further question of attacking the state of Israel—as well attack the city of Chicago.

The net result would be the introduction of a genuine state of serenity to the Arab region. That would all but eliminate tensions in the area, making Soviet efforts to finance and provision anti-Israeli expeditions fruitless, and incidentally providing us, at the eastern point of the Mediterranean, naval and military facilities as truly our own as the Norfolk Naval Base and the SAC base in Omaha.

Would Israel object? Some Israelis unquestionably would, though not all by any means, provided we affirmed our dedication to states' rights, and pledged a constitutional amendment to modify the harsh restrictions against the public practice of religion improvised by the Warren Court. In any case, the people of Israel should consider the proposal. And meanwhile Americans should be asked, by the two candidates for President in the forthcoming election, to declare themselves on a fifty-first state. An annexation resolution should be introduced in Congress, and a national debate should begin. Put me down in favor.

The Uses of Blackmail

November 7, 1973

IT IS SAID, here and there openly but for the most part in whispers, that the disadvantages of our Mideast position are gravely damaging to us, and that as the results of the oil embargo begin to hit us, the public will rise in wrath against the foreign policy that brought it all on. And what—they say—of our allies? How can we justify what we are doing to them? What will be the cost to us of the loss of friendship?

In that reasoning, it would appear to me, is implicit much of the weakness of the American position over the past years. It is a weakness that shows up in the defensive character not only of our deeds, but of our attitudes.

Begin, for instance, with the matter of our allies in Western Europe. Why do we think of them as our allies, when it is more accurate to think of ourselves as their allies? A learned strategist recently asked, "What has Israel ever done for us?" Posed just that way, it is hard to come up with the name of a single nation in Western Europe that has "done anything for us" in this century. Consider England—long may she wave, and while I am at it I wish Princess Anne great happiness— what has she done for the United States? The question is historically naïve. The most obvious favor done in this century by one great country for another is the intercession by the United States in the Second World War, without which intercession Hitler would probably be giving away the bride at Westminster Abbey. Yet that intercession is also explainable in terms of self-interest: the prospect of a Hitler-dominated Europe was frightening to us.

But in the current situation, our allies surely need the United States more than the United States needs them? They need our investments, our products, our tourists, our navy, and above all our nuclear umbrella. West Europe is far gone in the enchantments of what its leaders are pleased to call practical diplomacy. "Even if Russia were presided over by Stalin, I would seek *Ostpolitik*," Willy Brandt is quoted as saying, exaltedly. Détente is pleasing to the Europeans, whose concerns these days are primarily economic; and it is not plain how they would inconvenience themselves merely in order to accommodate the United States.

The Arab powers, however, are punishing Western Europe for America's role in the Mideast as principal supplier to Israel, the perennial target of a military machine deployed by the Soviet Union in Arabia. Everyone seeks nowadays to impose pressure through intermediaries. The question arises why the intermediaries do not assert themselves. It mystifies me that Western Europe should think of itself as defenseless against the Arabs' use of blackmail.

To deprive a country of that which it absolutely needs in order to survive is quite simply an act of war. It is both a moral question and a legal question whether the Arab embargo has reached the point of asphyxiation that warrants belligerent reprisals. But the talk is that it is headed toward that, and the question arises: Why should Western Europe tolerate it?

The most extreme response to which the Europeans would be driven is: war against the oil-producing states. If an abundance of oil can unite Syria and Saudi Arabia, the lack of oil can unite Italy and Scandinavia. A military expedition aimed not at taking over Arab territory, but forcing the Arabs to export their oil at the market price, would be justified, under extreme circumstances, by the laws of nations.

But there are lesser sanctions, and it is not too early to talk about them. I mean a total embargo. No food to Arab ports, no automobiles, no manufactured goods, no tourists, no airplanes. Let the Arabs attempt, for a couple of months, to get from the Soviet Union what it now imports from the United States and Western Europe. The Soviet Union doesn't have enough surplus to export to Greater Moscow, let alone to 100,000,000 Arabs.

These are unpleasant recourses. But why must we be so defensive in our reflexes? The United States is determined to assure the survival of the state of Israel—reduced in size, to be sure, from its bloated postwar dimensions. There are strategic and moral reasons for our decision, and no need to swerve from it under the intimidation of a boycott which could be made to hurt the aggressor far more than the intended victims.

Talking Back to the Oil Monopolists

November 8, 1974

HEREWITH MY long-awaited solution to the oil crisis.

First, a little perspective. As recently as 1970, producers were paying the Persian Gulf states about $1 a barrel for oil. By 1973, before the embargo, this had risen, in response to what one might call natural economic forces, to $1.75. At that point came first the embargo, then the huge administered rise—to the present level of about $9.50.

Meanwhile, on the home front, there is what they call "old oil" and new oil. The old oil was discovered before the embargo, and the price of it was controlled at $5.25, to which it had recently risen from $4. Figure a buck to transport a barrel from the Persian Gulf to the east coast of the United States, and you note that U.S. crude was about $1 a barrel more expensive than Persian Gulf crude before all the excitement. That differential was owing to import controls. These were justified on the grounds that for the sake of national defense, we had to encourage local production. Those controls, needless to say, have been anachronized. Now we charge a flat 18 cents per barrel on imported oil, a trifle.

It is, under the circumstances, reasonable to assume that in the absence of political manipulation, crude would be selling for about $5 a barrel. Let us accept that figure for the sake of analysis.

Congress should proceed to levy a tax on imported oil as follows. For every $1 an American importer pays *in excess of the $5 per barrel,* a tax should be levied of $1. Thus, an importer paying the price currently charged by Saudi Arabia, which is $11.25 per barrel, would have to pay a tax of $6.25 per barrel. This means that Saudi Arabian oil would cost American importers $17.50 per barrel, which means that they would search frantically for cheaper oil. And that, of course, is the purpose of the exercise: to break down the cartel by exaggerating the cartelized price—by doing one's best to price it out of the market. The objective, obviously, is to put a premium on cheapness. Those exporting countries that desire a large share of the American market will in effect have to bid for it. At the same time, the tax, which will be passed on—necessarily—to the consumer, discourages the profligate consumption of oil.

Ninety-five percent of our imported oil comes from the following countries at the following rate. From Canada, 25 percent (about 300,000,000 barrels per year). From Nigeria, 20 percent. From Iran, 20 percent. From Indonesia, 9 percent. From Saudi Arabia, 9 percent. From Venezuela, 8 percent. From Algeria, 5 percent. Canada is not a member of OPEC.

The point need not be elaborated. To the extent that the consuming public absolutely has to have the oil, it will pay the increased price for it. But the demand will slacken, and when that happens, you will find Canada reducing its export tax. And you will find Nigeria's representative meeting a big American buyer on a park bench and whispering out a proposed deal. . . .

The best way to combat a cartel is to force it to go beyond the economic limit it is itself careful not to traverse. And supply a quick inducement to those who will break away from it in order to maximize income.

There isn't an alternative that combines the effectiveness, and the sense of fairness, of this one. By now we have come to terms with our extra-military incapacity to solve the problem. The suggestion that we should embargo the shipment of grain to the Arab states breaks down under scrutiny: they don't need that much, and could get what they want easily, paying hard cash, from a fugitive exporter. No embargo of machine goods is likely to bind the West: someone will trade. Moreover, although it would be all the more effective if England and France and Italy and Japan joined us in adopting the identical approach, it is unnecessary that they should do so in order to make it effective: we import over a billion barrels of oil per year, so we are ourselves big enough to have an effect.

As usual, the market system provides an elegant reply— even to the pressures of oligopoly.

VI.

African Sojourn

Johannesburg

THIS IS NOT the ideal moment to interrogate John Vorster, the Prime Minister of the Republic of South Africa, because on April 24 there will be an election, and between now and April 24 Mr. Vorster, manifestly, does not desire to say the kind of thing that might upset his diehard wing (I use this designation in preference to "his right wing").

If you were to say to Mr. Vorster, a big smile on your face, "Why, Mr. Prime Minister, relations in South Africa between the races have greatly improved in the last few years!"—he would probably feel he had to answer: "Oh? Have they?" Because to admit that they have improved would suggest to the Bilbo wing of the Nationalist Party that Mr. Vorster is making concessions to miscegenation which will end by destroying the purity of the white race.

What he has done, in fact, is to make—slowly, easily, sometimes unnoticeably—concessions in the direction of easing the awful Jim Crow that has been a part of the South African ideological ethos for over a generation. But it is the kind of progress it isn't good politics to report.

Alan Paton, whose sublime, poetic voice has filtered out of South Africa for thirty years, may be a poor politician, an abstractionist in search of Utopia. But he has lately been writing pretty practical things. He says that what will bring relative freedom to the South African black is less the elaborate system of Bantustans (the separate black state) than the requirements of a highly industrialized society. These have put such a premium on skilled labor as to advance the technical training of the black South African, and his compensation on the marketplace.

Forget dreamy political reforms, says Paton, and concentrate instead on economic upward mobility. Therein the solution. And Chief Mangope, an influential black leader, says much the same thing. "If a mutually acceptable formula for economic partnership is found, then it is distinctly possible to improvise, on that basis, acceptable solutions for the social and political needs in the emerging pattern of coexistence. Where economic partnership is not achieved, all the finest theories and ideologies aimed at regulating the social and political spheres will be completely futile and useless."

It is, no doubt, under the influence of such analysis that American black leaders, like Roy Wilkins, have come out strongly against economic boycotts of South Africa, aware that these would hurt most the South African blacks, whose gradual economic vitalization is the key to political parity. It is a pity that these black leaders do not apply the same criteria in formulating a position on the advisability of boycotts against Rhodesia.

Meanwhile there are ugly features in South African life which do not relate to the race question. There is the awesome institution by which the Minister of Justice can "ban" an individual, i.e., confine him to his home, prevent him from writing, or being written to.

I asked the Prime Minister whether this was subject to appeal in the courts (which are a vigorous and thoroughly independent South African institution, like the press). He replied, yes. I asked, had the courts ever sustained a defendant? He replied, no. Why? I asked. It turns out that in order to be successful, you have to prove to the court that the provisions of the law were arbitrarily or maliciously visited upon you. But in fact the law is itself so arbitrary, it is almost impossible arbitrarily to apply it.

I asked a government senator, "Do you have to prove that someone is a Communist in order to ban him?" Well, no: "You have to prove that what he says plays into the hands of the Communists." "Well," I said, "by that token you could theoretically find yourself banning Henry Kissinger." "That would be frivolous," he said; and of course I agreed, though I am not in a position to say that the law hasn't been used in South Africa to ban, frivolously, mere nuisances to the government.

For all of which I was repaid a day later by a telephone call from a reporter from a prominent South African newspaper, who asked me to expand on "the charge" I had made at

Johannesburg that "Henry Kissinger is a Communist." I told him, through the operator, to go jump in a lake, but I am not in a position to report on whether my recommendation on this, or on other matters, has been followed.

Salisbury

March 20, 1974

THEY WILL TELL you in Rhodesia that the terrorists are under control, and that there is nothing to fear. In fact they are not under control, and the situation threatens to get worse, as why should it not with the Soviet Union beginning to compete with Red China in sending arms to the terrorists, and with assorted Protestant bishops standing by more or less to baptize a movement that is becoming as fashionable as the Black Panthers and the Vietcong. The casualties of the Mau Mau have been exaggerated in the popular historical imagination, like those of the Jacobins during the Reign of Terror. There were thirty-two white settlers killed by the Mau Mau over a period of four years. Double that number have been killed by the Rhodesian terrorists in eighteen months.

But overwhelmingly the black population of Rhodesia is antiterrorist. There are complicated reasons for this. The first (and least obvious) is that black leaders do not share the revolutionary turn of mind of the terrorists and their backers. They see no advantage whatever in exchanging rule by a white elitist government headed by Ian Smith for a black ideological government headed by Peking or Moscow or its surrogates. For another, while they desire—indeed demand—change, they have not, yet, abandoned hope that orderly change will come under the nonviolent pressure of the predominantly (95 percent) black population.

But this, I am led to believe, must come soon. Drastically compressed, here is the chronology of events, which are racing to a conclusion of sorts.

In 1965, the Rhodesians declared their independence of

Britain. Almost immediately, the United Nations voted sanctions, which got progressively more stringent after supplementary resolutions in 1966 and 1968. In 1969, Prime Minister Ian Smith promulgated a constitution which would in effect have guaranteed white supremacy through the century and beyond. In 1971, Smith and British Foreign Minister Sir Alec Douglas-Home initialed an agreement calling for constitutional reform and additional opportunities for black political power. The agreement was subject to ratification by the black community which, in the finding of the so-called Pearce Commission the following spring, said no.

Probably it was a mistake not to implement the agreement anyway, for strategic reasons. But this was the electric political moment in Rhodesia when the blacks would see the papers' headline: BLACK RHODESIANS VETO WESTMINSTER PACT. Things would never be the same again.

Gradually it has dawned on the white community that the critical man in their midst is a mild-mannered Methodist bishop, in his early forties, called Abel Muzorewa. He is said to be relatively without guile, and that's not all good—he is a procrastinator, an ambiguist, inexperienced in the unholy ideological ambitions of many of of his fellow liberationists. On the other hand, no one suspects him of corruption of any kind, and I accept it as true that he has for the moment the singular power to prevent universal bloodshed in Rhodesia.

For how long? That is the dark question. There are secret negotiations going on at this moment between the bishop and Ian Smith. Smith is a man of quite extraordinary personal valor, who has become the symbol of white supremacy. Actually he is no more a white supremacist than George Wallace proved to be, when the social attitude changed. He is a good politician, but it is feared that at this moment he underestimates the resolve of the black majority to effect substantial change. And it is above all feared that if the bishop does not succeed in budging Smith, others—who would then declare impatiently their independence of Muzorewa—will embark on violent action. This would destroy Rhodesia. Smith tells his lieutenants that it would be political suicide for him to yield too much. So the question arises: Is Smith statesman enough to avoid political suicide—by leading the white intransigents toward reconciliation and organic progress? The betting is that he could not persuade his own ministers to conciliate. But that if he went to the white voters, he would earn their support.

One hopes so. Not only in order to avoid catastrophe, but to indulge a valid social experiment. If a country 95 percent black is willing to give the advanced white 5 percent the major creative political and educational role for a specified period of time, so as to ascertain whether greater progress might not thereby be made than under the lash of the black nationalism of some of Rhodesia's neighbors, then a quality of moderation might make its way into African affairs which would be instructive not only for the black population in Rhodesia, but everywhere. And it is in any case difficult for a visitor to Rhodesia to count lightly the benefit of reconciliation for the white population, men and women of extraordinary charm and apparent good will.

Nairobi

March 28, 1974

WELL, NOW, I have a tale to tell. There I was at the studio in Nairobi, waiting for the Foreign Minister to do an hour's television on the theme, "Black Africa Looks at White Africa." Dr. Njeroge Mungai (he is a medical doctor, licensed to practice after completing studies at Stanford, California, and internship in New York City) had said he wanted to talk to me briefly before the tape began to roll, and I said sure.

He was a half hour late, having met with the President—his boss, his personal patient, and Kenya's God—and he sat down easily and smilingly in the waiting room, and we exchanged pleasantries. What, I said finally, looking a little apprehensively at the clock, did you want to discuss in advance of the program? Well, he said, as Foreign Minister I would be very embarrassed if you were to get into the subject of

Nixon and Watergate. No problem, I said. Anything else? Well, he said, as Foreign Minister I couldn't criticize any other African state or its leaders or its policies.

We were there, of course, to criticize white Africa, which is to say South Africa, Rhodesia, Mozambique, and Angola. "Those are not states," Dr. Mungai corrected me: "they are colonies—white colonies." All right, I said, but the argument against these states is that their policies are racist in foundation, but this requires us to probe definitions, and in order to do that, it becomes necessary to probe the policies of other African states that might be called racist in character.

But he declined. Declined even to decline during the televised exchange to answer such questions: such questions were simply not to be *put* to him. "Well," I said sadly, "it's your country. But it's my program." So I scrubbed the show.

Bright idea. Could he suggest a prominent Kenyan journalist or academician who would be able to discuss freely the policies of other African countries? Nobody in Kenya—Dr. Mungai smiled, but there was a touch of steel there—would be willing to criticize another African country. I got the picture and exchanged a glance with my producer. We were, after all, sitting in government studios. And we had been told, in almost as many words, that nobody in Kenya would, from that studio, criticize another government in Africa. I have made inquiries, and here is a more precise way of putting it. You can find, in Kenya, black intellectuals and black journalists who will criticize, say, the expulsion of the Asian minority by Amin in Uganda. But you can't find a black intellectual or a black journalist who will criticize the government of Kenya for failure to criticize the government of Uganda for expelling the Asians. What would happen to someone if he did criticize the government, I asked? Oh, it depends who it was, I was told. Maybe he would lose his work permit, maybe they'd just find a way of putting him in jail. Dr. Mungai likes to talk about the "fascist policies" of Rhodesia, South Africa, and Portugal.

Things here in Nairobi are, to be sure, unusually touchy just now. Yesterday the Kenya Parliament, whose members are all Kenyatta's men—there is no parliamentary opposition—struck out against a television profile shown the day before in Britain of Jomo Kenyatta. The profile was done by Lord Chalfont, a former Labor Minister, who criticized in language entirely moderate the imperial habits to which President Kenyatta increasingly is given. "Worship of *Mzee* (the Father) [has become] a national habit and even receives legislative sanction. Any disrespect for his person has been made an offense, and any settler found guilty of it, even in the form of a joke, was liable to be expelled from Kenya."

And Lord Chalfont went on, "*Harambee,* which can be roughly translated as 'we'll all pull together,' but which has no other connection with the Eton boating song, has become Kenya's national slogan, and although it is demonstrably a less sinister slogan than *Sieg Heil,* its effect on a crowd of hero-worshiping followers is not to be underestimated."

From all of which one deduces that a public discussion inquiring into why the President of Kenya does not criticize racist policies committed by black men could be interpreted as, well, disparaging of the leadership of *Mzee.* In Parliament yesterday, an assistant minister demanded that the local BBC facility should be closed down "until the BBC comes down on its knees, begging for it to be reopened." And Vice President Moi said that foreigners "have nothing to teach Kenyans. . . . In fact, if anything, Kenya can teach them many lessons. Contrary to what some people try to make us believe, the African way of civilization is the best." He was talking about the streaking craze. "These foreigners go 'streaking,' running naked everywhere," he said scornfully, to which I suppose Lord Chalfont might have responded that the streakers are only going about in what many Africans consider their native dress.

But that would sound invidious, and it is important to recall that Lord Chalfont said that it is his opinion that Kenyatta is a good man, perhaps even a great man. But that Kenya is slipping, perhaps unconsciously, into the habit of dictatorship.

VII.

Sports

Reflections on the Phenomenon

[An Introductory Essay to *Esquire*'s "Super Sports Issue," October 1974]

IT WAS midmorning, at the break for milk and cookies, when James came through carrying groceries for the lunch he would serve us in his impeccable white jacket. He stopped to chat on the way to the kitchen and mentioned that he had seen him, crossing the street just now, on his way into the Langham Hotel. I froze, but I knew without hesitation where I would be five minutes from now. I whispered to my younger sister to provide me cover, walked out of the schoolroom nonchalantly as though on the way to the bathroom, which I slipped past, and walked-ran the two blocks down Portland Place to the small lobby of the little residential hotel. After looking in at the empty dining room and the barbershop, I sat down self-consciously, as if waiting for my father, avoiding the eye of the receptionist when its beam shone at me. In due course the elevator door opened, and he came out, talking animatedly with a companion. It did not occur to me to accost him—had he *ever* spoken to a thirteen-year-old? I wondered—and I'd as soon have slipped a pad and pencil in front of him for an autograph as to a pitcher midway through his windup at the crucial moment of a World Series. I just followed him, numbly, out. A car was waiting, and he drove off: and I rushed back, elated, and told my sisters, and the forgiving tutor, that I had been, just then, and for several moments, within feet—inches, I corrected myself—of Arturo Toscanini.

Arturo Toscanini, I feel obliged to explain, having read the contents of this special issue of *Esquire*, was not a baseball player. I say this as a gesture, a complementary admission of my own feeling of ignorance, having read the names of the athletic superstars of my generation listed in a feature here, and failed to recognize more than ten of them. Dan Wakefield says, as if it were the shared experience of American writers, that he began by covering sports for an Indiana newspaper. I "began" by reviewing the Gordon String Quartet concerts at Music Mountain (I hope and believe that Wakefield's sports was better than my music). Roger Kahn (how marvelously he writes) passes it along as the universal experience of his boyhood that the stars were baseball players, and illustrates by incanting the names of baseball players I, a contemporary of Kahn's, never experienced until just now. When I read about this mystique, the sports mystique— which, full-disclosurewise, I tend to do only when I am paid to—I find myself being pitched outside the one real world, without any suggestion that my own is inhabited by people who, any more than the Jew of Venice, are also capable of feeling pleasure and pain. So I am driven, as I expect all of us are who are trying to understand other people's enthusiasms, to reach for analogous experiences. The only human being I worshiped at thirteen was Toscanini, though I would also have played hooky to gaze at Kirsten Flagstad. I assume the sensations are identical. That these sensations tell us more about what is extrinsic to the hero worshiped, than intrinsic to him. Just remember—we are reminded in this issue of Jimmy Cannon's deflating words—that they are just little boys playing baseball. As much might be said, in the same iconoclastic mode, about Toscanini, or Flagstad. He was just a little man waving a stick in the air and giving his boys the right beat; and she a great big woman warbling as in a shower stall. Reductionism, the enemy of romance! Immanuel Kant said that marriage consists in the mutual monopolization of genitalia. So much for reductionists.

The hero-worshipers are to be preferred, but one does wonder why so many of them, in America and elsewhere, visit their adoration on ladies and gentlemen who practice sport. Is there a difference in the intensity of *their* feeling toward *their* heroes? Are they feelings that are more frequently stimulated? Joe DiMaggio is up at bat not necessarily more often than Toscanini, but the results are easier to chart, and they appear in the next morning's newspapers and the next year's almanacs. DiMaggio's home runs were discreetly recorded; Toscanini's merely accumulated a little more density in the aurora borealis that hovered over his name. And we have all hit home runs at some level of competition, in Little League or in stickball or one-on-one against the little sister's knuckle curve: these small successes can be magnified, the crack of the bat simulated by a popping tongue, the home-run follow-through held, frozen, like "Discobolus'" sculpted approach. Few of us, on the other hand, have conducted even a kid sister's chorus. Is it that? In part.

Is it because there are more people who would like to be successful athletes than would like to be, say, successful musicians?—or poets, or writers, or politicians? Is it because the notion is popular that the great athlete is, but for the capricious working of the stars, really what you and I might have been, if it had happened that our lungs had been a little stronger, our limbs better coordinated, or our resolution more iron; whereas the great musicians and poets, and even the actors and writers, are a species apart, minted in Olympia by artisans who would be all thumbs if asked to produce a shortstop? Do they feel that DiMaggio was just that little critical step better than Johnny, who concededly is not a member of the same human family that produced Einstein or Freud? Is that it? Again, in part.

In part, too, it is the means by which achievement—heroism?—is authenticated. At age thirteen, my faith in Toscanini was—a matter of faith, really. He had no batting average, awarded by statisticians incorruptible only because their figures are audited by tens of thousands of exuberant and sharp-eyed monitors in the stadiums of the world. That Ezra Pound writes fine poetry is something we can say with confidence mostly because we are told by people who write lesser and more apprehensible poetry that he writes fine poetry, and because we know about the tributes of the critical community. Though even then there is fluctuating fashion: tomorrow they will tell you that Hemingway was a punk, that Fitzgerald was really the great figure: come to think of it, tomorrow was yesterday. In sports, fashion plays a role but not so decisively. It is harder, I think, to become a John Updike than it is to become a Larry Csonka: the impact of a great short story registers in negative figures on the Richter scale, whereas a great forty-yard touchdown run, even at the college level, is awarded radio and local TV exposure. Concomitantly, though, it is harder to stop being John Updike than it is to stop being Larry Csonka. There is nothing in literature that resembles, for its career-ending finality, a destroyed knee ligament. And a novelist's waning powers cannot be graphed statistically.

Athletes, and for that matter horses, have their individual traits which are or are not endearing: but they are judged finally by whether they are winners. Silky Sullivan was briefly a great national enthusiasm because we loved it how at the stretch he would come up from behind. But when he took to sweeping up from behind but not quite making it to the front, he was quickly forgotten. Pete Rose speaks proudly in this issue about how he makes headlines when he strikes out, even as he makes headlines when he hits. But he makes the former because he strikes out less frequently than he hits. In the course of convincing himself that he is headline copy under any circumstances he convinces one of exactly the opposite. During July and August, he observes, when most of the other players begin to wear out, he comes on strong: so that he can afford a poorer batting average in the spring—by midsummer it will have begun to climb. That has got to happen to the Joe DiMaggios, or else—or else it is left for them to marry Marilyn Monroe, and get written about by Gay Talese, and discover the Bowery Savings Bank? No. That is only for the statistically exiguous few, that life after death. Mostly, for those who begin to lose, it is just plain death. Can you imagine Mark Spitz making out if he had not been a half second faster than the other guy?

Itself a haunting qualification. We were about to conclude that the reason sports heroes are real heroes is that the game they play is incorruptible. But that isn't really the way to put it. It is presumed to be incorruptibly the case that that man's batting average is .400 while the other man's is .375, and that that girl beat the other girl playing tennis, and that Mark Spitz is the fastest swimmer in the world. Those achievements you cannot take from them. That they then go on to advertise banks and perfumes and electric razors which, for all we know, they have never patronized, smelled, or owned is corruption, but of another order. And Roger Kahn touches on it when he suggests that the hero in sports is headed down because of television. Now all his secrets are known, and the intimacy makes the batting average more a statistic, less a romantic event. We'll have to wait and see on that, as we belabor the question: Why the universal appeal?

Nobody is making any effort of any consequence to relate the appetite for sport, or the tendency to lionize athletic superstars, to the bourgeois constitution of our culture. I have wondered why capitalism has not been blamed for competitiveness in sport, or for the delirious quality of the public's participation in organized sport. The ideologists of the left are too canny to try it, one supposes. With a few exceptions, notably Paul Hoch's recent book *Rip Off the Big Game*. For one thing there is the obstacle of the Olympics, about which roughly everybody knows roughly everything, like how the managers behind the Iron Curtain turn them into agitprop, which is the left equivalent of big business. Hoch handles this nasty objection by ignoring it. Sure—as is illustrated in this issue—we are doing something analogous, for instance to professional football, which the year after next, at the rate we are going, will be a subdivision of General Motors. But ours is straightforward commercialization, theirs is not; our professional teams play against each other, while in international events the Soviet Union's professional teams play against our (mostly) amateur teams. No. Competitive sports isn't a useful springboard for socialist polemics; so they tend to leave the subject alone.

But what about the human appetite for competition? Is it something that will disappear with the Marxist historical evolution toward community and brotherhood? Competition is not permitted in the marketplace in the maturity of Marxist China, but it is certainly permitted in sports. I was never more attracted to Maoism than on the evening I spent at the huge arena in Peking, crowded by Mao-men and Mao-women, dressed mostly in the standard dark-blue Chinese mufti, but with here and there a touch of color in the ladies' shawls, furtive little blossoms creeping up from the hibernation of the Cultural Revolution. There would be gymnastic events first, and then championship badminton and table-tennis matches. The American press walked in, eighty of us virtually unnoticed, during one of the acrobatic preliminaries. Then the brass: Chou En-lai et al., escorting President Nixon and Mrs. Nixon, and Henry Kissinger, and the rest of the Presidential party. The fans applauded. Politely. Perhaps, we mused, Chairman Mao has delivered a Thought on the subject of the permissible volume and duration of the people's applause. But not three minutes later, one of the champion Ping-Pongers came in to take his station, and the crowd spent itself in delight. Nothing like Brooklyn, or Houston, or Los Angeles—but still very loud, and with sustained applause, in startling contrast to the perfunctory reception given to their own Premier and our own President, the cool reception of whom could not alas be attributed to the general Oriental disgust over Watergate, which, in February 1972, had not quite yet happened. We know of course that Mao-man is infinitely malleable, and that, properly instructed and coordinated, the same audience would have thrown itself onto a pyre for Nixon, or—preferably—thrown Nixon onto the pyre. But uninstructed, they registered in their own unambiguous way their relative enthusiasm for their Premier and his foreign guests, and their athletes.

This would appear to touch universality, would it not? Because it is everywhere. Sure, there are exceptions. During the height of a Presidential political campaign in America, for instance. Or when a lesser politician attends a stadium clearly for the purpose of testing the water—in which case the crowd will wire him instantly into the competitive circuit and, cheered by his supporters and booed by his opponents, he will know how he is doing. Out of season, visiting American Presidents and English queens get applauded, but more or less routinely, as the Chinese applauded Chou. Not to be compared with the applause for the athletes. At Ascot, Queen Elizabeth's horse is more popular than its owner.

The exact comparison is between the enthusiasm of the fan for the athletes at the sports event, and the enthusiasm of the partisans for the candidate at the political rally. That enthusiasm will reach a very high pitch in certain circumstances. It is helpful if the country is headed toward a nominating convention, or a national election. It helps if the candidate is the representative of an enthusiastic and ideological minority (McGovern and Goldwater regularly got greater hands than Nixon and Johnson). Or, if he is the majority's candidate, it helps—before selected audiences—if he is threatened. Threatened by either deposition (Johnson pre-Chicago), or by unusual disparagement (Nixon addressing the POWs). But what we then have is, substantially—competition. An enthusiasm for a political candidate not terribly different in quality from the enthusiasm one feels for one athlete confronting another.

In China, we have no way of knowing exactly how general political enthusiasm is contrived, because China has not yielded us a Solzhenitsyn. We learned only very recently from him why during the tensest years, the applause was so very prolonged after a speech by an official representative of Stalin. No one dared to stop applauding first. On one occasion, when after a ludicrous interval someone finally did so—stopped clapping and sat down—he was singled out, arrested, and sent off to a concentration camp for ten years. In China the devotion to Mao may be altogether spontaneous, like the street applause for Queen Victoria, or Ivan the Terrible. But it is not—apparently—automatically inherited by the People's Ministers—not by Chou En-lai, in any case; not by contrast with the enthusiasm shown for the People's Ping-Pong Players. The genuine enthusiasm—in China, in Russia, in Greece and in Spain, in France and in America—is for something that involves: competition. Often there are great consequences riding on who wins a political election. See the movie Z. But most often the line is so long and elusive and unpredictable between a particular candidate's election and a felt change in national policy, one suspects that the public fires that burn are mostly—competitive fires. "Will it be Nixon or McGovern who wins the election?" becomes more vibrant than "What will happen after the election if Nixon, or McGovern, wins?"

But the competition isn't all. It helps to associate oneself, however tenuously, with one contestant or another. I sense that it is missing in me that I truly do not care whether Yale wins or loses at football. But I know that though I will not bother on Sunday morning to notice in the paper whether Yale won yesterday or didn't, if I were physically present I would cheer lustily for the Yale team. And since this isn't, so far as I am able to judge, a matter of affectation, I must assume that the tribal fires, though they are mostly banked inside me, will flame up and perform in response to the lightest foreplay. I found a companion actually betting on a horse because the dam was Irish. It is expected that residents of Brooklyn should be enthusiastic about the Brooklyn Dodgers, and that Catholics should root for Notre Dame. But the dam's *birthplace?* How about the dam's birthplace, if there is no more obvious connection?

I bumped into the phenomenon early—once again James figured, only this time he was the principal. He was my father's colored butler, a man of great discrimination and ardent opinions, a fine athlete, and devout Catholic. It was a special treat when he would take me to the lake to swim—I thought him the best swimmer in the world, but then the only other strong swimmer I had ever heard of was Buster Crabbe. As he steered the car one summer afternoon he talked excitedly about the fight that evening between Joe Louis and the champion, Jim Braddock. "I hope Braddock wins!" I said impulsively. "Why?" he asked, visibly crestfallen. The thought of hurting James was impermissible. "Because he is a Catholic," I groped. I looked out of the corner of my eyes at James' confusion. I had scored a polemical checkmate. He would not permit himself to superordinate racial over religious loyalty. The Braddock-Louis fight, like the Schmeling-Louis fight, was more than just sport, but sport was the maieutic agent in that stride toward racial parity.

Many years later I was chagrined to note that I would be addressing a convention of women brought together by the Cincinnati *Enquirer* at exactly the moment when Bobby Riggs would be playing against Billie Jean King. Reaching for an appropriate reference to the simultaneous event, I said to the ladies that they had been summoned at this hour by the Cincinnati *Enquirer* no doubt in order to reduce the total number of women available to witness the forthcoming humiliation of their sex at Houston. Before my speech was ended, the results of that match had reached the audience, who were good-natured about my chauvinist exposure, but palpably exhilarated by the liberating news.

In the finally atomized society, where every man is Howard Roark, sports would undoubtedly suffer the loss of those natural, animating allegiances of the group. Whom would one presumptively root for in the wholly rational order? The home team? *Where's home?* The college team? *That's for male animals.* The national team? *Chauvinist.* The Catholic, or Jewish team? *Cabalistic.* The blackman or ms.? *Old-fashioned.* The poor boy? *Antimeritocratic.* The loner? *Antisocial.* The woman? *That was years ago.*

Will there then be no magnetic fields around the natural polarities of which the fans can gather? Tribal loyalties survive, but they are not intellectually fashionable—for reasons that could, theoretically, affect the future of sport. It is permissible for individual athletes to put winning above every other value, and even for teams to do so. But not for philosophers of sport, really. Vince Lombardi was very recently admired for saying that winning was everything, but nowadays his name comes up on the atavistic side of the ledger. Richard Nixon's use of sports metaphor is elsewhere remarked. He wasn't using a metaphor when he said at the height of the Vietnam War that he was not going to be the first President of the United States to lose a war. By putting it this way, he gave not-losing a bad name. If, having run out of empires to manage, countries exhaust their chauvinism in soccer, the intellectuals will find here something on the order of sublimation.

But the general disdain of achievement *at any cost* comes out, necessarily, as a disdain of achievement. The case against an ever-increasing GNP is, one supposes, also the case against an ever-faster mile. William Shockley might in due course turn his attention to genetic means of increasing the speed of not only four-legged, but two-legged animals. The limitations of economic cost assert themselves quite naturally. Before the war, contenders for the America's Cup were 130 feet long, now they are one-half the size. At the old size, you would need $10,000,000 to mount a challenger. But there is no money to be won in the America's Cup, so that contributions to a contender must come not from the nickels and dimes of millions of fans, but the $100 bills of millionaires: and the size of the boat diminishes. There are year-round schools now to which boys and girls can go if they wish to concentrate exclusively on the problem of diminishing by a full second the speed at which they travel down the mountainside.

But skiing is another nonprofessional sport, except for the very few who triumph, and go on to give their names to a ski wax or whatever. In the wholly commercial sports like football, the money is there, but a ceiling begins to suggest itself, to be penetrated only by the superstars, the Frank Sinatras of football, who know their own value, and can single-handedly attract the reluctant fan. The great Manolete was the first Spanish bullfighter to travel to Mexico after the Civil War. His managers extracted from the promoter the price of $15,000 per bullfight, and accordingly the price of tickets doubled. At the airport the reporters were bristling with the resentment fed up by the fans, and the senior reporter spoke the first question. "Matador, do you really propose to charge fifteen thousand dollars for killing two bulls?" "I don't charge to kill the bulls," Manolete spoke with his habitual chill. "I charge to fill the plazas."

Which, at twice the price, had not an empty seat during the heady days that Manolete fought. But arrangements between Manolete and the fans, like those between Frank Sinatra and the fans, are matters of public policy only insofar as legislators decide how much of the boodle to confiscate. It is when the community becomes officially involved that the resistance begins to crystallize. Should Congress appropriate money to finance the Olympics? How much are the alumni expected to give in order to provide competitive scholarships for high school basketball stars? Is it really only the business of the managers of the Indianapolis 500, and the drivers, whether they shall be permitted to risk their lives? By extension, will the community continue to reward the young man who rises at dawn to run five miles before breakfast in preparation for the grueling competition at the track? Or will he˙ one day, having broken the tape and set a new world's record, turn, like the hero back from Vietnam, to find the fans not only indifferent to his achievement, but disdainful of the sacrifice that went into it?

It required the Renaissance to rouse the individual's artistic, spiritual, and intellectual energies. I cannot say that, through dark ages to come, unnoticed men will improve on the fleetness of foot, or on the distance the discus will be hurled, but I assume it. I assume that directed physical exertion can proceed thoughtlessly, without the philosophical benediction of a culture otherwise torpid, shiftless, and prideless. And that if it does, straining for excellence for its own sake, we will know that though the pulse is very low, it continues to beat, and to tap out a stimulus that is ultimately more exciting than the second hand of a stopwatch or a locomotive cheer on the crowded sidelines.

On Being Rescued by the Coast Guard

February 1973

THE WIND would not budge from the east, but having powered for seven endless hours from Miami to Cat Cay and waited here a whole (pleasant) day for a change in the wind, so that we might turn off the motor and sail in the general direction of Nassau, we decided what the hell, let's accept the wind's obstinacy and move north to Grand Bahama, which we could do under sail, and *then* work our way, again under sail, southeast to the Berry Islands, and on into Nassau, which we didn't have to reach until Thursday, this being only Saturday—all the time in the world to complete a leisurely detour. But Grand Bahama is a good stretch from Cat Cay so we resolved, in late afternoon, to get a leg up on the northerly trip by coasting there and then, before nightfall, the eight miles to Bimini, in order to overnight there.

It was the kind of afternoon, with which the Bahamas are so frequently touched, which causes the heart and the memory to flutter: a steady balmy breeze, lengthening shadows on sugarbeaches, ten shades of blue and green between my schooner *Cyrano* and the entrance to the little harbor, only forty yards away. We were on the leeward side of the dock, tied up alongside, and so we had only to release the lines to the pilings, float clear of the Hatteras behind us and the Hatteras ahead of us, back gently under power out into the channel, then hard right rudder, a lazy 90-degree turn and on out by the inland passage to Bimini. We slid smoothly away from the dock and in due course I eased the gear stick into reverse and quickened the throttle by a few hundred rpm, and in seconds I found myself dreaming the dream where you are trying desperately to run away from the monster who is chasing you, only your legs, though they go furiously through the motions, fail to propel you. My beautiful 60-foot schooner was proceeding slowly, majestically, toward the stone jetty, twenty yards downwind.

Only once before had I geared in and gotten zero response. The experience occupied an instant and secure place in my repertory of nightmares. It was Newport, the day before *Dame Pattie* would begin the first race in her competition for the America's Cup. Newport was crowded with sportsmen, sportswriters, and other lay and professional enthusiasts and celebrants. I was bound for Nantucket on my steel cutter, *The Panic,* and proposed to my friends that before leaving the harbor we might have a look at the challenger. We powered into the U-shaped pier basin, slid slowly, closely, by the pier opposite *Dame Pattie,* and turned sharp left pointing my chubby steel bowsprit directly at the soft underbelly of *Dame Pattie.* Five or six seconds of that and I would be perfectly situated to slide into reverse, turn left again, and cruise quietly back out into the channel after enjoying a long lascivious look at *Dame Pattie.* I moved the gearshift back. Nothing happened. Fifteen tons of *The Panic* were sliding without room for maneuver, smack into the challenger at about five knots. Then seconds later, at the speed we were going, we'd have precipitated the withdrawal of Australia from SEATO. Four or five young crewmen were relax-

edly, adoringly, lying about their beloved *Dame Pattie*'s deck
in the midday sun, eating sandwiches, when suddenly they
noticed the dagger approaching slowly but ineluctably the
heart of their vessel. As if programmed by Balanchine, five
bodies went into pandemoniac motion which climaxed with
ten frozen hands interlaced over the side, each pair holding a
fender or seat cushion, piled one on top of the other at the
point in *Dame Pattie*'s midriff toward which our juggernaut
was lumbering. It occurred to me to throw myself into the
water and plead later, at the war-crimes trial, that I had suffered a heart attack when—suddenly, unaccountably, providentially—the propeller engaged.

At the exhaustive postmortem I was told cheerily by an expert that a collapsible propeller sometimes disdains to engage immediately in reverse gear at low rpm speeds. (I got
myself a noncollapsible propeller.) At Cat Cay, Danny Merritt was following us in the whaler under his own power, so as
to be out of the way of our stern when we backed down. With
the whaler as tug, in a few seconds we were laced back along
the pier, and discovered that the drive shaft had disengaged
from the coupling.

For those as ignorant of mechanical arrangements as I,
this means that the rod to which the propeller is affixed,
which rod must (obviously) itself be turned by something,
had come loose from what turns it, namely, the engine.
Frank Warren, the young professional captain of *Cyrano*,
had had this difficulty under tame circumstances a few weeks
earlier, whereupon he took the boat to a great shipyard in
Miami which put it in drydock, aligned the engine, tested the
shaft, repaired the coupling, for all I know prayed over it,
and wished us happy cruising.

We examined the shaft and found that a stainless-steel
through-pin binding the shaft to the engine had sheared,
and that moreover the liberated member had rocketed aft,
imbedding the propeller in the sternpost forward of the rudder. A local mechanic meditated laconically on the situation
and in three hours, during which I had laboriously devised a
beaching program so that we could at low tide hammer the
shaft into position, pronounced it repaired. He used a gal-

vanized pin and suggested that we exchange it for another stainless-steel pin, the collapsed one having been clearly defective, eventually, when the boat got back to Miami. The next day, approaching Lucayan Beach in Grand Bahama, we had the identical experience.

This time the local mechanic pronounced oracularly on the sources of our difficulty. The pin, he said, is not nearly strong enough to carry the load of the revolving drive shaft. The shaft should *to begin with* engage positively a key in the engine. This key had worn. We needed a new key. He would have one made up at the machine shop—perhaps that very Sunday afternoon!

Thirty hours and $125 later, he pronounced us totally fit. Not only had he put in a fresh key, and a fresh pin, he had capped in three set screws. There was no *way* for the drive shaft to give us any more trouble.

It was early afternoon, and the wind now was oscillating from south to southwest, in a dirtying sky, barometer, however, steady (at 30.02). It seemed reasonable, since we were edgy to move on, to sail the thirty-seven miles to the end of Grand Bahama, beyond which is the bight wherein Deep Water Cay beckons. The *Yachtsman's Guide to the Bahamas* describes it as "an anchorage [which will] carry 6 ft. at L.W. while 4 ft. can be taken in over the bar. The Deep Water Cay Club . . . [is] an attractive fishing camp with space for four boats, gas and diesel fuels, electricity, water and ice in small quantities. . . .The bone fishing is considered among the best in the Bahamas. There is a 2,200-ft. grass airstrip, but buzz the Club and make contact . . . before landing as it might be soft." Would that we had been airborne.

Chart 26320 shows the shallow water along the southern coast of Grand Bahama tapering off decisively ten or twelve miles before the entrance to Deep Water Cay, with glorious depths of not less than thirty feet (we draw only five feet) right up to the beaches approaching the bight.

Six hours later the wind was stiffening, so we pulled down the fisherman. I noticed then that two (of the seventeen) lugs that slide up the groove in the aluminum mast, holding the luffline of the mainsail to the mast, had pulled out. Strange, they have never done that before. They are tough, one-inch by half-inch, hard plastic. My son Christopher tightens the halyard with all his strength, another half inch, to take the strain off the remaining members, but within minutes the rest of them have ripped out and the mainsail is now sloppy and in the whippy wind very nearly intractable. Turning on the engine, sliding the gear forward, and turning the wheel to windward, I order the mainsail hauled down.

I do not know what happened, in the all but total absence of stress—we had used the engine only to get out of Lucayan Harbor—to the beautiful new key; to the set screws; to the stainless-steel pin, but I was accosted by the distinctive purr of an engine in neutral. We were still three or four miles from the bight, but with less than an hour of daylight, and we needed to make way. I gave instructions to fasten on the storm trysail. As we wrestled with it, Peter Starr, having peered forward, rushed back quickly to the wheel. I have known him since he was a boy, and have sailed with him 100,00 miles. His voice had the imperative ring to which one pays very special attention. We are, he said quietly, about 300 yards from a reef, breaking in the sea and stretching right out along our course. I look up from the trysail operation. There it is, clear as pitch. A mile south of the shoreline, as far as the eye can see, exactly where the chart indicates a freeway. To the right of us is upwind. To the left, land. We rush forward, fasten the sixty-pound Danforth, let down the headsails, pay out 150 feet of chain, and hold our breath. The waves and wind pound against us, and our twelve-foot bowsprit rises and plunges like a bronco. But the anchor holds. On the whaler, Danny takes out a second anchor, the plow, attached to one-inch nylon, out about the same distance, forty or fifty feet to the right of the Danforth. Frank Warren dives down to alert the Bahaman Air Sea Rescue station at Freeport, forty miles west, and reports that thus far we are not dragging, that we are a mile from the beach, that the mainsail is inoperative. Freeport replies that inasmuch as we are not in any apparent physical danger, they will not send out their rescue vessel, which in any event is busy right now with other emergency duty. I dispatch Danny and Warren in the whaler into the womb of Deep Water Cay to request a fishing boat to come to us to take the ladies—my wife and sister-in-law—to the club, there to take refuge from what I knew would be a tossy, emetic, nerve-bruising night, manacled as we were in the way of a raucous wind and boisterous sea. The boys returned, three hours later, tatterdemalion, announcing that the alleged channel through which we proposed to pass had, even at high tide, scratched the whaler's eighteen-inch propeller shaft a half dozen times. That the club was inoperative. That there were no boats anywhere in the vicinity. That they had hitchhiked twenty miles to the nearest telephone, whence they had called Freeport once again giving more exact details on our position. This much we had known. We were guarding 2182 and Freeport had called in to report that the boys were safe, and would spend the night ashore. Instead they elected to make their way back to *Cyrano*, where they now huddled, wet and exhausted. We sprawled about the huge cockpit, covered by canvas, looking past six squat candles smug in their colored chimneys, gazing through the large windshields at the wind and the sea and the rain.

During the long night our position didn't change. The anchor watch reported not a detectable foot of drag. The boat's motion made sleep difficult. The gusts, though specially strident in our fixed circumstances, probably didn't reach more than thirty knots. We were not shipping water, and the reserve anchor, to judge from the tests we put it through on the forward winch, was itself nicely kedged. If it had happened that both our anchors had slipped, *Cyrano* would have floated toward the shore, on the safe side of the vicious reef, there either to be battered or, if we were lucky to get there at high tide, which would come just after midnight, and not again until noon the next day, to be lumpily beached, in whatever chaotic way (she is thirty-five tons). We could briefly hold the boat away from the beach by pulling it with the whaler (and its 40 hp outboard); but in this sea, this would not have worked for more than long enough to try one time or perhaps two to resituate the anchor. We had on board two six-man emergency life rafts, which would have drifted our crew and passengers, a total of eight people, safely to the beach. We had repaired the mainsail by pulling the runners out of the trysail and stitching them in. The halyards were poised ready to lift all sails. We needed a windshift, though not much of one. Forty-five degrees west and we could sail away from the reef on a starboard tack. Twenty-five degrees east, and we could sail back toward Freeport at a safe distance from the shore. Schooners are not designed to tack out of an acute angle.

But the wind held. Then, unaccountably, just after dawn as I was listening gloomily to a weather forecast that gave no indication of a prospective change in wind or weather, a cutter approached us over the horizon, slowly, sniffily. Through the wind I could hear the bagpipes! But it was so much unexpected, I found myself waving my cap, lest the cutter should ignore us or continue east. At least I could warn them that if they wished to bone-fish in Cat Cay, they would need to portage their cutter into the harbor. . . .

Within a few minutes we could see the Coast Guard cutter *Cape Shoalwater*, which soon came within hailing distance. Moments later two men in a powered rubber life raft approached us, Chief Green, an engineer, and Seaman First Class Mike Harvey. They required, first, to inspect our documentation and our safety equipment. We passed triumphantly. It transpired that at about 10 P.M. Freeport, without our knowledge, had called over to Fort Lauderdale to request assistance in our behalf. Within one hour, the cutter *Shoalwater* had collected its standby crew of twelve men, under the charge of Lieutenant Bowersox, and started out on the 120-mile journey. Pretty damned good show.

Chief Green inspected our drive shaft, and in an incredible forty-five minutes had it reconnected—a dazzling feat of virtuosity, which had required him single-handedly to slide the entire shaft forward with only the tools at hand. (Alas, it slipped out again twenty minutes later.) Captain Warren, outside my earshot, had meanwhile asked, wistfully I assume, if the cutter might tow us all the way to Miami, instead of merely to Freeport, since in any case the cutter was bound eventually to Fort Lauderdale. Within minutes, the portable telephone relayed the request to the cutter, the cutter relayed it to Fort Lauderdale, and the request was approved. A very long hawser was slipped out over the *Shoalwater*'s stern, bound to our samson post forward, and we were off on a sixteen-hour trip to Miami, with Mike Harvey aboard to relay necessary signals on his radio. Sixteen hours later, averaging just under ten knots (we do ten and one-half maximum under sail) we reached Government Cut at Miami, and there a small tender took us over.

As the tender pulled us through the cut, we heard from behind a strangled cry from Danny, who at my instruction had leaped into the whaler as was our mode coming into port. We could not see in the dark what had happened to him; we attempted to get the tender to go back and fetch him, but were told that would come later—first came the job of depositing *Cyrano* a mile down the line at the marina. As we drew into the dock, Danny was getting out of a car, right in front of us. The huge outboard, the fastenings loosed by the long haul, had jumped up over the transom of the whaler and purred away under water for a minute or so, gurgling finally into silence. Danny, who is as resourceful as Robinson Crusoe and as buoyant as styrofoam, used the water skis to paddle to one side of the cut, and bounded up to flag a passing car. The driver instantly obliged. It developed that he was working on his twentieth can of beer, and asked Danny where he lived. Danny replied Stamford, Connecticut, whereupon the driver looked blearily at his map for the most direct route to Stamford. . . . No, no, Danny said. Miamarina, Fifth and Biscayne, would do just fine, and that was only twenty blocks away. At the dock there were reporters and a couple of cameras. Evidently Dick Cavett had heard the news and observed brightly on his program that he hoped I had not run my yacht off the edge of the world. I was too tired to riposte that if the edge of the world had happened to be located in the Bahamas, the detail would have escaped the attention of the man who drew chart 26320. The Miami *Herald* was already out with a report taken from Freeport radio, which was quoted as observing: "They either had no sail aboard or no one who knows how to sail." Peter Starr and I could not work up the strength to be indignant. Somehow, I mused, it would never occur to a newspaper to write: "Apparently no one in the Caribbean area knows how to connect a drive shaft." We settled for professing our gratitude to the Coast Guard. That gratitude is keen. How best to express it? By passing along the word. . . .

One continues to learn. One learns and relearns of course the conventional things. For instance, that piloting in the Bahamas is a continuing act of brinkmanship, and that unless you have on board someone who knows the waters personally, you are best off being skeptical of everything you read, doubting every reassurance you get, and treating all charts the way Little Red Riding Hood should have treated her unconvincing grandmother. You relearn for the dozenth time the critical importance of super-rugged anchors and anchor lines, ready to go at very quick notice (it took us a couple of minutes: the chain was twisted the wrong way around the windlass). That kind of thing.

At another level, you meditate on larger themes. I wrote exasperatedly fifteen years ago on the theme that nautical expertise (I define *expertise* very narrowly as *the body of operative knowledge* available in any given field) is highly limited. I was angrier at the Miami shipyard after the first failure than after the fourth. If the mechanic at Cat Cay had fixed the drive shaft so that it held, I'd have been totally unforgiving about Miami. Again, if the meticulous mechanic at Lucayan had fixed it, I'd have been irreconcilably critical of Miami. If Chief Green, after a few minutes of tinkering, had made it hold, I'd have dismissed the lot of them as incompetent. Back in Miami, I met eyeball to eyeball with the head of the shipyard and his chief foreman. I heard the foreman say: *"I never did like that arrangement for the drive shaft."* Question: Why did he not register his skepticism about it? To whom did he speak of it? To his priest? Why did he not recommend a different arrangement? Boat fixers are presumably not more evil as a class than, say, car mechanics, and probably less so than, say, newspaper columnists. The trouble is their failures magnify a problem most critically. Let the drive shaft fail in an automobile, and you miss your appointment. Let it fail coming in, say, to Cat Cay, and you are on the rocks. Last year a young man perched down on *Cyrano*'s lifeline in the

Hudson River, talking with two friends. One minute later the line parted and he was in the water. One minute after that he was dead of drowning—he did not know how to swim. The rigger had not, according to the surveyor, properly crimped on the lifeline cable to the shackle fitting. If you like, another coupling had failed.

My local boatyard (in Stamford, Connecticut) has now upped its basic hourly charge for work done on your boat, no matter how routine, to $15 per hour. I do not believe it is engaged in profiteering. The city of Stamford, foraging about like all taxing authorities for insufficiently bled sources, pounced on the boatyards, without regard—to say the least—for the guidelines suggested by any of Mr. Nixon's various price boards.The effect on the marginal user of the yard is not yet known. It is bound to be substantial. It is bound to increase the desirability of yachts that are relatively maintenance-free, and increase the amount of home-tending by boat owners. But how is an amateur supposed to instruct a professional on such matters as how, soritically, to assure the linkage of a propeller all the way to the engine? I know that there is no easy answer, any more than there is an answer, this side of a stony-faced jury that levies draconian penalties on the delinquent, to deficient motivation. But increasingly I am tempted to believe that no matter how little you, or your representative, know of a technical nature, it probably pays always always: to have someone there. An acute eye can detect indecision; certainly it can detect sloth; and often sloppiness. Beyond that, a human circuit is activated, and clearly such a circuit needs to be revived, between workman and boat owner. The nuts and bolts that occasionally get left behind in the jet engine probably wouldn't be, if the pilot had been there. His psychic presence doesn't appear to be enough. "I never *did* like that drive shaft assembly. . . ." And as a matter of practice, I wonder if, when its services are summoned, the Coast Guard shouldn't be encouraged to conduct quasijudicial investigations the purpose of which would be to censure ignorance, incompetence, or outright delinquency?

The water is the last area on earth where total spontaneity of movement is possible. The odds are benignly in favor of the sailor. But the odds build on certain assumptions, such as that workmen will competently use the expertise at their disposal, and advertise the case when the expertise does not pronounce reliably on the solution to a particular problem. Such as that if a chart indicates safe passage over a particular area, you may proceed. Certain of the sea's resources we cannot ever match—its occasional fitfulness, uncharted meannesses, occasional savagery. But the odds shouldn't close down against the sailor merely because those who are concerned with the sea become indifferent. There is a limit to how much the Coast Guard can be expected to take on, and I repeat, in behalf of my family and friends, our gratitude that last August 29 the Coast Guard had a little scope left over for us.

Strange Bedfellows

September 1972

THE STRANGE athletic inversions of the past fortnight raise questions about the stability of the universe beyond even the authority of Avery Brundage to resolve, though he is the catalyst of at least one of the great discontinuities, Russia over America in basketball. He had little to do with the second, Russia's successful challenge to Canadian hegemony in hockey, though his agents tried to abort the contest on the grounds that pitting Russian amateurs against Canadian professionals caused a fungible situation: now the amateurs would be thought professionals, and likewise their colleagues in other athletic disciplines. But he found himself arguing, in effect, the virginity of Zsa Zsa Gabor, which is always the chivalrous thing to do but does not any longer engage the public attention. So the show went on. Concerning the third, he had no role at all. What Bobby Fischer did to Boris Spassky was not exactly an athletic event—the rules were not laid down by an Olympic committee—but it is clearly a defeat the Soviet Union consoles itself over only by reminding itself that it is unlikely that the United States will make Bobby Fischer the head of our SALT II delegation.

One of the questions raised, of course, is: Is there a natural affinity for any single sport by any single nation, or is distinction purely a matter of tradition? Some of the answers come easily. Obviously where there is a lot of snow and ice, there will be a lot of the sports that require snow and ice. As I say, that one is easy.

But moving over, for instance, to basketball, what are the natural conditions auspicious to playing the sport? One thinks only of physical stature. But that, really, is unsatisfactory, inasmuch as there are at least enough very tall men to fill a nation's basketball teams in almost any medium-sized country, so it is not even worth inquiring into the relative median height of the American compared to the median height of the Russian; it is largely irrelevant to an inquiry into natural prowess.

One can talk knowingly about a "basketball culture," but not really surefootedly. One engages in sociological gamesmanship, a sport that has its own gold-medal winners, but the rules are inscrutable and the talk endless and pointless.

And then chess. We are now encouraged to call it a sport, and one of the reasons why is that it apparently requires a keen physical condition to play championship chess. Boris Spassky, it is said, does push-ups and lifts weights as diligently as if he were headed for the gymnasium rather than the chessboard. There are even those who say that the defeat of Spassky by Fischer was substantially a physical defeat of an older man by a younger man. I do not trust the constitution of that argument, and certainly not its implications, and will not be seduced by it into betting on the younger against the older computer. The morphology of championship chess is inscrutable, something that contributes to the game's fascination and edges it surreptitiously away from sport in the direction of art.

Still, it remains a fact that chess is traditionally a Russian monopoly, franchised to the colonies in Eastern Europe, even as hockey "belongs" to Canada and basketball to the United States, and we are best off examining the triple convulsion by examining the most conspicuous explanations for it.

Obviously a nation covets that which another country pre-eminently has. Not everything, else you'd find Russia covet-ing American freedom, which jealousy has never been in prospect—except, I suppose, America's freedom to covet, which the Soviet Union long ago surpassed. There was great enthusiasm in the United States over the victories of Fischer and Mark Spitz, but the victories of the Soviet Union in hock-ey and basketball were celebrated in Russia, one gathers, by condemned prisoners dancing together with their execution-ers. Unseating the champion is a universally satisfying thing to do, and if the theatrical circumstances combine a con-trolled titan and a bumptious challenger (Spassky vs. Fisch-er), or better still a supercilious defender and a poor-boy challenger (Canada vs. Russia), the satisfaction sweetens. It is in this sense obvious that a nation given to collective enter-prise, which notoriously the USSR is given to, spends more time plotting to occupy someone else's turf than to defend-ing its own. So much for motivation.

To get out of the way another point, let us acknowledge that the jury of appeals under whose patronage the Russians took the gold medal away from the American basketball team was, to say the least, highly obliging to the Russians. The lawyer William Kunstler is forever talking about Ameri-can justice being a juggernaut at the service of the Establish-ment, though to be sure he gives his thesis discreet leaves of absence for a week or so after American justice springs an Angela Davis or a Bobby Seale. But the quick and congested succession of decisions that resulted in giving the gold medal to the Russians is only explainable with reference to the ideas of transcendent justice, the labored explanation of which furnished the reputation of Professor Herbert Marcuse. I am clumsy at it, but it goes something like this. If an Ameri-can player knocks down a Soviet player, it is a foul because it is against the rules. But if a Soviet player knocks down an American player, to invoke the rules is to invoke the exten-sion of that entire mechanism of repression whose sole job it is to frustrate the emergence of proletarian reality. Concen-trate hard and you too will understand.

Anyway, there were five judges, representing Hungary, It-aly, Poland, Puerto Rico and Cuba. The vote in the con-troversial decision that gave Russia the medal was, it is said, three to two. As they would put it in the children's test, group together the two likely clusters of numbers: 1. . . . 47. . . . 2. . . . 48. . . . 3. Mr. Nixon is asking for another term in part in order to change finally the balance of power in the Supreme Court. The Olympic committee is not pledged to a similar reform.

So, then, they stole the basketball title, which is Russia's now as a result directly of the courtesy of the judges. But we must remember this, that hanky-panky aside, the teams were very nearly even at the end of the match, so that supremacy by the United States was substantively challenged. Most tight Olympic contests waged by individuals are won by the breadth of a split second, and that sliver confers upon a whole nation the sense of honest corporate achievement. It is different in some of the team sports when the score is very close. If you win a basketball game 50–30 (or a hockey game 7–3), you are the better team. If you win a basketball game 50–49, what you have is two evenly matched teams, one of which is lucky.

The Soviet Union's greatest natural advantage, to be sure, derives from the institutionalization of fraud. It has so often been pointed out that Russian athletes are professionals that it is tiresome even to repeat the point. Incidentally, this cultural characteristic is worth nothing, if only because its Olympic implications are also conclusive. Not only is it generally true that Communists do *not* tire of being the butt of criticism, it is also true that Westerners *do* tire of offering criticism. Thus you will not only not wear down the Soviet representatives of the Olympic committee by documenting the professional care and feeding of their competitors; you will simultaneously wear down the Americans who level the charges. This is a signal advantage, not only because it produces a salvific insensitivity as one learns to tune out criticism, but because by one's strategic indifference to it one discourages the critic. It is a commonplace in international affairs that the reason why it is joyous for foreigners to burn down, say, a USIS library is because America always reacts with horror and hurt. If you know ahead of time that to document that young Ivan, who approaches the basketball court as an amateur, has been training as a basketball player since he was six and a half years old, and that during the entire period of his training his father, mother, sisters, brothers, aunts, uncles, grandparents and bastard children have been given extra-socialist materialist consideration by the state, will arouse no more attention than the metronomic motion of a recording clerk's acknowledging the receipt of your brief—why, you tend to give up. And you say to yourself, in effect: well, the job at hand is for American amateurs—or, if you insist, demi-amateurs—to compete against Russian professionals. Well, let's see if we can't accomplish that. For years we did.

We are slipping now, and it is clearly not on account of a universal national flatulence. Athens eventually lost to Sparta, under the pressure of Spartan concentration and single-mindedness. We do not know what to do, assuming we elect to make glory at the Olympics a national enterprise. Nationalize the enterprise?

Moving away from the obvious, is it safe to generalize that free people will exert themselves more completely than enslaved people? That is the legend but perhaps it is also the myth. It is easily gainsaid by spot comparisons. The vaunted tenacity and nobility of the British people who stood by freedom during the awful early days of the Second World War are no more striking than the behavior of the inhabitants of Leningrad. Less so, I suppose it would be fair to say—even avoiding the polemically tempting observation that inhabitants of the Soviet Union are professionally trained in duress, while inhabitants of England are clearly amateurs. Freedom is the indispensable catalyst of a certain kind of greatness, and this is as indisputable as that any magnet tuned to search out literary genius in Soviet Russia would instantly home in on Solzhenitsyn, without a quiver's distraction in the direction of the time-serving Lenin Prizees who coo and chuckle and swoon over the detritus of Nikolai Lenin as schoolboy.

But a whole people are variously moved. And even as the inhabitants of Leningrad clearly preferred death from starvation or disease, as hundreds of thousands proved they did in the most convincing way, to surrender to the Nazis, the representatives of the Soviet Union in basketball, and in hockey, and in chess, will clearly do their best for their homeland. Their homeland, using the cant phrase, is a peculiar combination of tropisms, some of them nationalistic and patristic, some of them egotistic. The fact of the matter is that the typical Soviet athletic competitor does not pause halfway through the 400-meter sprint to denounce the treatment of Josif Brodsky by Soviet authorities.

Once again the mind turns to the uses of national subsidies. One can see it now, in a future political platform. . . . *We pledge to change the name to the Department of Health, Education, Welfare and Sport.* Federal feeder farms for shot-putters, discreet and not-so-discreet scholarships for the ice skaters and pole vaulters. That is one direction, the other being a total reconstitution of the Olympic Games, which is unlikely in an age in which the projection of the graph shows that it is moving in a direction advantageous to the totalitarian communities. Though the collision of interests could cause the Games ultimately to come apart. America might find that adjustment to the ethic of Olympic victory requires a correlative adjustment of domestic values which we are not willing to tolerate, let alone subsidize.

Where, then, do we go next in inquiring into the recent convulsions? It is tempting to yield to the magnetic draw of political analogies. If Richard Nixon can go to Peking and adumbrate there the similarities between George Washington's revolution and Mao Tse-tung's, we have a *volte-face* at least the equivalent of the Soviet defeat of a Canadian hockey team, one would think. If the power-conscious Mr. Kissinger can endorse a SALT treaty which with lapidary relish relegates the United States to inferior status as a strategic nuclear power, then it should not so much surprise us that a Hungarian, a Pole and a Cuban together outwitted and outnumbered—enjoying advantages cultivated and ontological—an Italian and Puerto Rican at a critical moment in an athletic contest between Us and Them. Mr. Arthur Daley of the New York *Times*, who is renowned for his good manners, meditated a day or two later on the spectacular refusal of the United States team to accept the second-place silver medal. Very bad show by the conventional criteria. But, he found, under the galling circumstances, that their refusal was—OK. I am reminded that Henry Kissinger, describing for the first time to the American press the terms of the SALT treaty, excused it on the grounds that such was the momentum of the Soviet lead, the United States was not left at the bargaining table in a position of doing better than it did. Mr. Kissinger also refused the silver medal, not because the United States didn't deserve it—as the second nuclear strategic power we clearly do. But because Mr. Kissinger for reasons of tact declined to fix the responsibility for our having slipped in four years from No. 1 to No. 2. The irony is that the culprits in this instance weren't anything like the equivalent of Soviet satellite judges. The White House proved more respectful of Congress than our Olympic team did of the satellite judges.

Christopher Dawson, the historian, remarked a dozen years ago on the movement of world revolution. It is, he said, toward the West, not away from it, and deep historical conclusions can be drawn from will-o'-the-wisps like Nikita Khrushchev's arriving at Geneva for the first postwar summit conference wearing a fedora. We are used to resentments. Twenty years ago they started, in France, to protest against the Coca-Colonization of their culture. In the turbulent sixties anything surprising could happen and most things did, but the one rock on which Gallic certitude was founded was that Charles de Gaulle would never lapse into Franglais, never mind what the former McCarthyite Richard Nixon was destined to say, in Peking, about our identification with the Long March or, in Moscow a few months later, about the bona fides of the Soviet leadership. The pull of Western ways was terribly obvious to Christopher Dawson, but the pull turns out to be rather more bilateral than unilateral. They say that the Soviet Union in programming the hockey team that upset Canada was wonderfully guileful— not at all in the traditional pose of blunderbuss Bolshevism. The twenty-year-old Russian goalie (or so the story goes) in his initial exposures was all over the lot in clumsiness, as if Stepin Fetchit had been mistakenly conscripted to serve. At the real thing in Montreal, he turned out to be devastating, better by far than the Maginot Line. Aw shucks, he said, when confronted with the disparity of this with his earlier performances: the Americans watched me play a match the day before my wedding, and needless to say my mind was on other things.

Now that is pure Yankee—charming, jumping-frog disingenuousness. Meanwhile, only a few weeks earlier in Reykjavik (Reykjavik!—I mean, it is too much!), Bobby Fischer was treating Borississimo Spassky the way old Iron Butt Molotov treated the Western powers over nearly a generation. No. No. No. No. No! The square was too square, the circle too round, the line too straight. Fischer did not lack the confidence our diplomats lacked (during those crucial years when the gold medals hung sloppily around our necks)—he made his demands and discovered (what others have less conspicuously discovered) that when one wishes to prevail against the Soviet Union, the best way to do it is to assert oneself. The movement of world revolution, like one of those playful hurricanes that do a twirl or two, gyrating back on their course in a lazy circle, is all over the place, and the students of gamesmanship are going to spend many hours, or in any case should, on what happened in Montreal, and in Reykjavik, and in Munich.

Reflections on Skiing

October 1972

GSTAAD. Having been invited by the editors of this journal to discuss, opposite John Kenneth Galbraith, a subject concerning which I know less than almost anybody, more only than, say, Professor Galbraith, I begin by that Full Disclosure which is among the reforms of the New Deal most generally celebrated.

(1) I am not a very good skier. If you were to rank skiing ability on a scale of 1–20, I would rank approximately 12. Those who want a personalized application of that standard

should think in terms of ski teachers at 20, a first-day novice at 1, Galbraith at 8.

(2) The aptitude for learning how to ski is something which is primarily a function of age. By this I mean: if you are five years old and learning how to ski, you will almost surely, by the time you are six, ski better than I can ski, having begun at age thirty, and persevered to the age of forty-six.

(3) The older you are, the more necessary it becomes to intellectualize skiing. For instance there are those who, very early, discover that to lean uphill in order to avoid going downhill doesn't work, and they tend therefore to do the right thing instinctively. Older debutantes (as the European ski teachers persist in calling us) need to knead this datum (forgive the homonym: in fact it should cause the reader to knit his brow in contemplation of the point, even as we middle-aged skiers need to concentrate on the delicate distinctions we are handed down by our instructors). The young skiers simply take it for granted, and lean downhill quite naturally after the first day or two.

(4) The ski teachers are always ahead of you intellectually. So that even if you develop instantaneous docility, such as to cause you to do exactly what the teacher tells you to do, you tend to founder on: paradox.

For instance, they are nowadays telling you that it is extremely important to make your turns *slowly*. My teacher has a sexy way of saying this. *Caressez la neige*. She takes her ski pole and, leeringly, moves it in front of you down the fall line and e-v-e-r so gradually, to the right, or of course to the left, if that is the direction in which you want to turn, assuming you are so mature a skier as actually to command such great decisions. And then the teacher tells you that you must never be ambiguous on the point of where your weight is. In other words, you must move your weight *decisively*. Now, how to move your weight decisively, when at the same time you are engaged in so subtly seducing your skis across the fall line into the new direction, becomes one of those philosophical problems about which you meditate long into the evening. You find yourself having very highfalutin thoughts about such philosophical concepts as complementarity, which thoughts, typically, are unresolved when you find yourself, the next morning, instructing your muscles in contradictory imperatives which are abstractly warring against each other in your sleepless mind.

(5) Skiing is a capitalist's paradise, and I do not mean the cost of ski lifts and hamburgers and motels. The sport is so much the object of a great many people's passion, that they are always finding out new ways to improve you, and this means (a) ever-different equipment, and (b) ever-different techniques.

Concerning (a), I remember that for the first six years I skied, my instructor would look at me the first day of the season, behold my ski poles, look up despairingly at the sky, then down to my shriven face, and say condescendingly: "Who told you to buy ski poles that are six centimeters too short for you?" You would mumble something about last year's instructor, and then go buy ski poles six centimeters longer. Next season. "Who—who conceivably?—recommended ski poles six centimeters longer than they should be?" After six years it doesn't much matter, because you own a full inventory of ski poles, and merely bring out the reanointed pair.

Concerning (b), the problem is much more difficult. When I first "learned," I was told by my teacher that when I made a turn, I should suppose in my mind that I was picking up a pail of water from my left side and moving it to my right side. I just managed to perfect that discipline when it was discovered (I think they called it the Austrian system) that it was *exactly* wrong; that when you turn you should keep your shoulders *facing downhill,* rather than moving them from left to right, or right to left. Okay. I was once young and resilient. Now—now, they tell me that shoulder-down-hill, down-knees, up-knees, is *quite wrong,* that you should be structurally immobile, only the ankles moving, the weight way-way back on the skis—and I find myself telling my instructor that I have given up aspiring to qualify for Olympic perfection. I found that, on saying so, I came close to hurting her feelings, so I reached for a way to say it satisfactorily, which way I here divulge for the first time.

Look, I said to Anita, the science people have discovered a

way to resituate the keys on the typewriter so as to speed up one's typing by 30 percent. But do you understand my declining to relearn how to use the typewriter? She agrees to understand, though I know that when I face downhill bravely and bob down before each turn, and up, triumphantly, after completing the turn, on those happy occasions when I succeed in completing a turn, she is a little embarrassed, looking around at the fancy company that is witness to her pupil's recidivism.

(6) Skiing is becoming very expensive, particularly in America, and I suppose it won't be too long before the Democratic National Committee decides that the only thing to do is to nationalize the sport. Professor Galbraith, no doubt, could be got to write a touching declaration to that effect.

Besides (7), skiing manages, somehow, to retain a sense of privacy notwithstanding that it is the fastest growing sport in the world. And it has economic and hedonistic advantages over, say, ocean racing. Ocean racing, a bitter participant once wrote, "is like standing under an ice-cold shower, tearing up thousand-dollar bills." Skiing is less expensive than that, and—as a rule—less painful. Sure, sometimes skiing manages to be sublimely sadistic. I think of my friend, the publisher, who rounding a turn a few years ago took a forward fall that left him immobilized, rear end skyward, at which point a swinger zapped around the bend managing to slice his ski edge (the uphill edge, let the purists relax) right across both of my friend's Achilles' tendons, severing them as neatly as a surgeon would have done at an exhibition, the whole freshman class looking on. The executioner, appalled, braked, climbed back to confront a victim whose morale was sustained only by vindictive passion, only to recognize one another as, respectively, the closest personal friend and personal lawyer (the tortfeasor), of the (legless) publisher.

Notwithstanding such experiences, skiing manages to be, primarily, a *private* preoccupation, sharply to be distinguished from all those Chinese, Russian and Nazi gymnasts who coordinate together in great public spectacles for the delectation of their slavemasters and visiting chiefs of state. It has to do, I think, with the natural rhythm of the sport, whose animating force is—gravity; which was there, free, even before the New Deal discovered it was a human right, even as the wind that propels the sailboat is the gift of nature, rather than of distributive justice, as also the thermal current that lifts the sailplane—the three great sports: natural, related, individualized, divine.

The Ocean Race of William Snaith

November 1973

THERE ARE sublime uses for the cliché. An example was Westbrook Pegler's, reminiscing about the fascist demagogues of the 1930's. He came to Gerald L. K. Smith. "It was Smith," Pegler wrote, "who said about Franklin Delano Roosevelt: 'That liar, that scoundrel, that thief!' " You could hear Pegler pausing on the page before going on to write, with a sigh, "I wish I had said that." It is a cliché that sunsets-at-sea-are-beautiful, that crossing the ocean in a small sailing boat is a dangerous and exhilarating experience, that the sea is the enemy but a seductive enemy. And there are many books about crossing the ocean in sailing boats, some of them as overindulgent as a banana split, some as telegraphically dull as the log of a Coast Guard cutter. Both extremes have however yielded classics in the literature, Joshua Slocum's at the Apollonian end, Joseph Conrad's at the other. William Snaith has here a classic. It combines the steadfast narrative energy of Slocum and the discursive verbal fecundity of Conrad. He hasn't Conrad's overlay of quiet tragedy, but he has its counterpart, a ribald, self-skewering sense of hilarity, and the result (for all that the writing is uneven) is the most exuberant reading experience of the season. (How I wish I could have written it!) If there is a human impulse it does not satisfy, that is an impulse to be veiled with shame. It nearly ruined Apollo XI for me when I overheard someone say, "Imagine how many housing projects might have been built instead!"

Yes yes. And William Snaith, president of (I guess) the most famous industrial designing firm in the world, might have used his money to plant more soybeans. Instead this liberal Democrat subsidizes his recreational passion: ocean racing yachts. On the occasion here recorded he slipped his boat out of Bermuda and headed it, against a competitive field of a dozen and a half other boats, toward Skagen Light Ship off Sweden, 3,500 miles away. He had with him his oldest son and six experienced friends younger and older, each of them marvelously integrated into the engrossing narrative. Under him, a forty-six-foot yawl designed by the restlessly perfectionist team of Sparkman & Stephens, but altered and burnished and fussed over by Snaith with a consummation that brings to mind the demi-lifetimes highly-strung men have spent on single enterprises, great and small. Snaith is a scientist who can read the lines of a hull as Henry Ford read the lineaments of an automobile engine. He is also an architect and artist, whose eye for line and color has got his work hung in New York galleries. He is also the most infuriating, exacting, hedonistic, sadistic, competitive, engaging captain in the Atlantic fleet, and I can imagine that if a huge wave were to carry him overboard, any member of his crew would first hesitate for a luxurious, fugitive moment, and only then throw himself ardently overboard to rescue him at any cost. True devotion, in contrast to automatic heroism, requires, when risking one's life for another, that split second of hesitation.

You are at sea, the conditions are grandly awful. Only yesterday the crew discovered that an eccentric leak had voided the tanks of all but a few gallons of drinking water. But there are 3,000 miles of open ocean yet to go. The grim decision (one of the few collective decisions reached aboard the autocratic *Figaro*) was to go ahead—to add dehydration to the risks of dismasting, knockdown, fire, man-overboard, not to enumerate the routine discomforts of racing at sea, which need to be experienced, to be believed.

There is a supreme pleasure on such passages, and it is—sleep. It is the obligation of someone going off duty to awaken those who are going on duty; and the only civilized way to do it is with a dry, matter-of-fact, faintly compassionate resignation, lint-free, God help us, of bonhomie. Here is Snaith performing this function:

"I call the off-watch with a rousing solo, an *a capella* selection from the Cantata 'Sleepers Awake' which I think not only beautiful but apt. As always any attempt to keep the cultural level of this voyage up to the mark is greeted with complaint. I am disheartened. It is disheartening for one who believes in the uplifting and healing properties of art to find such a level of response from grumpy, disheveled auditors. They quench all thought of evangelism as they stagger about in their baggy-kneed long johns. In their unfeeling responses they are concerned with niggling plaints of being done out of five more minutes of sleep. These are difficult companions at times, but my very own."

The crew, in particular the younger members, show just the right blend of dutifulness and irreverence, and during the endless hours on deck, when the skipper is below, they play at awarding themselves points as the helmsman succeeds in tilting the boat in just such a way as to cause a torrent of water to tear down the lee deck to serve sometimes a useful purpose, such as washing the dishes, but most often malevolent purposes. The highest score registered by midpassage was 50 points. The captain, after presiding over a body- and spirit-breaking watch in ice-cold and tumultuous weather, requiring untold changes in rig, hours of sail patching, trips to the masthead, public séances on inscrutable meteorological developments, is finally off duty, exhausted, and dead asleep. When,

" . . . by some freak of timing *Figaro,* rolled to leeward at the moment of meeting a wave, took on a boarding sea which came roaring up the waterway, hit the cabin house like a breaker hitting a cliff, broke high in the air, poured over the cabin house, and shot down the companionway. Most incredibly it found me in my *bunk*, some distance from the opening. It came over me like a firehose. The shock was indescribable. The gasp which normally comes with a sudden cold immersion was choked off by water in my nose and mouth. I coughed and sputtered. I could hardly grasp what had happened. But the cause of that spreading wet and cold was not long in making itself known. All peace and contentment gave way to rage. I crawled from the berth, mad as a wet captain, shouting my wrath, trying in some way to release the outrage that flooded my being, only to hear my first-born, Cleody, my son, carrier of my name, the staff and rod to comfort me in my declining years, shouting, '*I get a thousand points! I get a thousand points!*'"

William Snaith's complex understanding of such an episode as this race across the Atlantic is suggestive in every relevant field. He has a literary gift for technical description I do not see equaled this side (curiously) of the critic Hugh Kenner, who can describe a solenoid with an airborne precision Sir Isaac Newton would have envied. The spinnaker halyard suddenly gives way. "The trouble and its cause were simple enough. The fitting was made of bronze when it should have been made of stainless steel. In the two days' wear of go-go swiveling, added to earlier erosion, the soft flange at the bottom of the spindle had worn down until it slipped through the barrel of the cylinder like bath soap through a wet hand." Is this the engineer talking, or the artist?

Or the sailor? It is all three who execute Snaith's unparalleled description (pages 121-122) of the helmsman's role in maneuvering the ship in a following wind, or his analysis of the circumstances that probably produced the lowering menace slowly catching his little yawl in midpassage. "Now the horizon was black, Dylan Thomas' Bible-black. It arched up [and] joined the gray in knife-edged resolution. Underneath, the gray sea took on a pale ophidian flecking without shine. The flat highlighting of the breaking wave tops was dull and lusterless. . . ."

Figaro survived that one, and worse, and in between the crises there was hilarity, a doggedly voluptuous cuisine, fitful, blurted-out confidences, during the long night watches, by young men of their secret cares, fears, and ambitions; musings by the author on old romances and tribulations, but all of it under the metronomic lash of the competition: they meant, in this pretty, stalwart, silly little boat, to finish the race, to survive sleet and storm and calm and fog and maelstroms off the Orkney Islands: and to win. They did win, but the trophy is this numinous book, so vibrant with adventure and spirit and beauty.

VIII.

Freedom—Backing Away

AFTRA Backs Down

June 9, 1972

Two NIGHTS ago I sat in the television makeup room scanning my notes. A few minutes later I would be discussing, as I had been asked to do, my reservations about the SALT Treaty. A pleasant middle-aged man approached me, begged my pardon for the interruption, and asked me to sign the form on his clipboard. He very kindly consented to let me read it first, which, for an agent of the American Federation of Television and Radio Artists (AFTRA), is a quite extraordinary concession. AFTRA is not accustomed to permitting its members any liberty whatsoever, insofar as AFTRA's interests are concerned: you have to join the union, you have to pay your dues, you have to sign a form agreeing to do what the union tells you to do, you have to strike when they tell you to strike, you have to refuse to cross any picket line they tell you to refuse to cross.

So I read the form, wondering what would be AFTRA's latest amendment to the First Amendment to the Constitution of the United States which says that Congress shall make no law abridging the freedom of speech. Congress can't keep you from speaking, AFTRA's position boils down to, but it can authorize AFTRA to do so, and the question that is now working its way slowly up the court system is precisely: Is the Act of Congress which purports to authorize AFTRA to compel membership or the payment of dues as a condition of going on the air a violation of the First Amendment? So I read on. The form authorized Dick Cavett to send $75 of my fee (of $200-odd) directly to AFTRA. How come, I asked AFTRA's muscleman, how come you are docking me right here on the program? He replied that my office had neglected to send in the check for my dues for the month of May. In other words, I was apparently five weeks behind. If I hadn't signed that form, AFTRA was in a position to go right then and there to ABC, which is Cavett's sponsor, and demand that I not be permitted to go on the air to give my views on a treaty which the President of the United States has hailed as perhaps the most important in the history of organized efforts to make peace.

By total coincidence I had on my clipboard at the time, apart from my notes on SALT, a memorandum of quite startling significance put together by my attorney, who with the help of the National Right to Work Committee has been pressing in behalf of me and a few other analysts and news commentators for our rights as guaranteed by said First Amendment. Therein I found twenty (20) instances, dating back to 1964, and as recently as this very year, in which officials of AFTRA had stated that I (and others like me) am obliged to *join* AFTRA, to be a "member" of AFTRA. Being a member of AFTRA requires not only that you pay dues but that you obey AFTRA's instructions, on strikes, crossing picket lines, the whole bit.

Now, without a sound, coming in on little cat feet, arrives the legal brief of AFTRA, contesting my position. And what do you know, my lawyer informs me: there is not a *single* mention made in it of any insistence by AFTRA that I should belong to the union. They talk now only of paying dues to the union.

This, in my judgment, they have no right under the Constitution to do. But the victory is startling. Suddenly AFTRA has given up the requirement that one become a member of that union. It will settle for dues. By extension, no newspaperman would need to join the union. Which means he could not be punished for crossing picket lines. Which means that you may just see the day ahead when crippling citywide newspaper strikes called by unions can be successfully resisted by newspaper employees without fear of losing their jobs.

AFTRA has come a long way under legal pressure; and needless to say it didn't issue any press release, or send out any communication to its membership telling it that henceforward it need only pay dues, not, as it has unflinchingly insisted up until now, join, and be servile to its orders.

The final victory remains to be won. But an important one has already been won. Let the word go out: news analysts and commentators of America—you need no longer join AF-TRA in order to appear on radio and TV.

CBS on the Line

November 20, 1972

I HAVE HERE a communication, just received from the American Federation of Television and Radio Artists. It is struck in the Napoleonic mode: "You and all AFTRA members are hereby ordered, pursuant to the resolution of the AFTRA National Board, to respect the picket lines of the International Brotherhood of Electrical Workers at CBS, and members are ordered to refrain from performing any broadcast or pre-broadcast services for CBS. This order is effective Tuesday, November 21, 1972, at 6 P.M. You are advised that any member who violates an order of the AFTRA National Board may be found guilty of conduct unbecoming an AFTRA member and shall be subject to disciplinary action."

As we know, at this writing the key analysts and news commentators of CBS have announced that, reluctantly, they will adhere to the instructions of AFTRA. CBS meanwhile groans under the burden of conflicting, confused and confusing legal opinion, while the house theologians weigh the moral questions. Eric Sevareid, on Tuesday night, was tough as nails on the unions, though a little less so on himself and his colleagues. "Union loyalty," he said, "is made to supersede a journalist's loyalty to his employers, his profession, and his concept of his duties to the public. . . . The present mess has reached the point where flying picket squads interfere with the filming of news events. . . . In other words, striking technicians are presuming to decide what news the American people shall receive, at least via this network."

In fact, it transpires, the CBS-AFTRA contract lapsed last week, so that the CBS newmen could resign their "membership" from AFTRA without any apparent difficulty. It is, moreover, most clearly asserted by the courts (see, e.g., *Lewis v. AFTRA,* 1972) that although the union shop is a legal device, "membership" in a union can reduce to simply paying one's dues. "If an employee in a union shop unit refuses to respect any union-imposed obligations other than the duty to pay dues and fees," said the court in *NLRB* v. *General Motors Corp.* (373 U.S. 734), "and membership in the union is therefore denied or terminated, the condition of 'membership' . . . is nevertheless satisfied and the employee may not be discharged for non-membership even though he is not a formal member." Judge Quinn put it in his own language last spring: "As long as plaintiff pays his dues, his employment cannot be compromised."

So what is the remaining reason for the walkout of the CBS newsmen? Mr. Walter Cronkite divulges that the luminaries in the CBS news staff fear two things, (1) a reckless discontinuation of pension and medical plans in the event of their precipitate resignation as "members"; and (2) the effects on lesser employees of resignation en masse. I.e., although AFTRA is hardly in a position to do anything of material consequence to such as Walter Cronkite and Eric Sevareid, what would happen, if their resignations broke AFTRA's back, to men and women whose income depends substantially on the bargaining power of the union?

These are legitimate personal considerations, the first self-concerned, the second fraternal. But these are not the reasons being publicly ventilated. The facts are as stated: there is no legal obligation for Cronkite et al. to walk out. There is a very real professional and public obligation to stay on, all the more so since they publicly disdain the cause of the strike by the technicians. Mr. Sevareid concluded his statement by saying, "This is profoundly embarrassing to broadcasters like this one, who have worried aloud about governmental threats to the free flow of information. At the moment tyranny from below smells as bad as tyranny from above."

Surely the clearest way to dissipate suspicion about the tyranny threatened from above would be for the Attorney General's office to side with plaintiffs (myself among them) who question the constitutionality of AFTRA's arrogation of the

National Labor Relations Act as permitting a union shop for people engaged in reporting or analyzing the news. Settle that point once and for all, and we will know, when we hear the lucubrations of Mr. Sevareid, that when he walks out it's because he chooses to walk out: that it has nothing to do with any contractual obligation to walk out.

A Post-Watergate President

September 28, 1974

IT IS EVERYWHERE said that with the withdrawal of Senator Edward Kennedy from the Presidential race, the Watergate drama has come to a complete cycle, crushing, with the same juggernaut that crushed Richard Nixon, the GOP's principal contender for the Presidency, Edward Kennedy. You cannot, we are told, remove the Republican Nixon for his failure, among other things, to come clean about his misbehavior—and then elect the Democrat Kennedy notwithstanding his failure, among other things, to come clean about *his* misbehavior. Richard Nixon's public declaration to the effect that he deeply regrets his mistaken judgments greatly annoyed people who wanted him to appear in sackcloth and ashes, regretting the day that he was born. In fact, politicians use euphemisms, wherever possible. When Edward Kennedy renounced the race for the Presidency, he talked not about Chappaquiddick, but about his obligations to his family. I don't doubt that he feels sincerely his obligations to his family. But then I don't doubt, either, that Richard Nixon feels quite sincerely his regret at his mistaken judgments. After all, when you attempt to obstruct justice and fail to do so, among other things, you have been mistaken in your judgment.

I wish that we would take the opportunity at this point to reflect less on the need of an American President to have been born without sin—pre partu, in partu, and post par-

tum, as the theologians say—than to have been born with
outstanding qualifications to serve as President of the United
States. I do not mean to be naïve. Back around 1967, *Esquire*
magazine published a charming essay on who should be
President of the United States. It turned out to be some Indiana industrialist, if memory serves, who relaxed by reading
Greek poetry in the original, and whose avocation was
stuffing money into John Lindsay's pocket. He sounded like
a very nice man, and I don't doubt that he should be more
prominent than in fact he is. But, presumably, a republic has
very little choice than to select a candidate from among people who are substantially involved in public life. And the
question arises: How come Richard Nixon was considered
the top Republican in the country, and how come Edward
Kennedy was considered the top Democrat in the country?

It is easier to answer the second question than the first.
Senator Kennedy is the surviving brother of a publicly illustrious brood, and the martyr's blood one longs to avenge
runs only in his veins. That in itself would substantially account for his popularity, and you then add, of course, his
good looks and his youth. I hear it said, incidentally, that he
has developed into a fine public speaker. But his popularity
was secure before that happened.

In the case of Richard Nixon, he got to where he got by a
combination of extraordinary luck (the need of Dwight Eisenhower to capture the California delegation in 1952), and
dogged and intelligent perseverance: 10,000,000 town hall
appearances for local candidates over a period of twenty
years. But Mr. Nixon never distinguished himself as a man
of extraordinary gifts, or capacity. If his dealings with the
Watergate prosecutors, and with Internal Revenue, and with
Bebe Rebozo, were as chaste as those of Snow White with the
Seven Dwarfs, would he therefore have loomed as a man
more august than he is seen now to be? Isn't it clear that his
shortcomings, those that greatly matter, were of an extra-
venal character?

Here is the trouble with the Presidency. People are
laughed at for merely mentioning as a possible President

someone who is not heavily steeped in a ritual which tends rather to vulgarize than to ennoble. It is safe nowadays to say, for instance, that you think Senator Jackson should be President. But it is ludicrous to say that you think Frank Stanton should be President. Why? This has nothing to do with any question of sharing or not sharing Jackson's or Stanton's views on public policy. But a wall lifts up, as impenetrable as Berlin's, between the two categories of men. Stanton's executive experience is far greater than Jackson's. His general attraction to left domestic policies is about the same. His views on all matters are very well known. His position on foreign policy is not very different. He is neither much more or much less effective than Jackson as a public speaker.

Surely this is a direction we should consciously turn to: increasing the list of Americans who should be considered for the Presidency. The mere mention of someone as a possible President has the effect of getting his name thought about. But it should be more than that. Committees should examine men from different professions. They should be written about, listened to. And the old mold should be destroyed: the one that says you have got to stick to a governor or a Senator or a Congressman, however obscure. Watergate should liberate us from something more than merely the lack of candor.

The Consequences of Disestablishment

October 2, 1974

THERE WAS a time when the Establishment referred to a New York-based congeries of businessmen, politicians and academicians who had a pretty tight hold on the policies of America, and were quite satisfied to run things their way. The term, used in England for generations, was introduced into

America (as it happens) by *National Review* to refer to the crowd that put Eisenhower in office and deprived the Republican Party (and the nation) of the services of Senator Robert Taft.

The ideology of the Establishment was what one nowadays calls Eastern Seaboard Liberalism. In domestic policy, it was all aflutter over the discoveries of Lord Keynes. As regards welfare, the Establishment was paternalistic—eager to get on with America's version of the Beveridge plan of cradle-to-grave security. In foreign affairs it was internationalist and, for a while, taken with the doctrine of containment. I.e., Soviet imperialism and Red Chinese imperialism should go no further than it reached by about 1949.

Then, during the sixties, the Establishment became, suddenly, not the enemy of the American conservatives, who distrusted Keynesian economics, shrank from the centralization of power in the bureaucracy and in the Presidency, and thought that the doctrine of containment didn't answer the strategic threat posed by a Soviet Russia busy developing hydrogen bombs and intercontinental missiles. The American Establishment became the enemy of the kids who smoked pot and read the exciting serialization in the *New York Review of Books* on how the United States government is run by a military-industrial complex that wants to keep us fighting unnecessary foreign wars, and sending poor and preferably black American boys to fight them.

The head of the Establishment was suddenly Lyndon B. Johnson, and there was a fleeting sense in which he became the head of the conservative camp in America. I.e., he was defending due process and constitutional order against the antinomianism of the radicals, against the street people who were burning up buildings, and the Kunstlers who were debauching the law. The title passed from Johnson to Nixon, but the Establishment was beginning to show signs of strain. The old institutional loyalties were wearing very thin. Probably history will agree that the Ellsberg case showed how very thin it was.

I mean, everybody defended Ellsberg: or, almost everybody. Every now and then, in the late period of the thirties and into the early years of the war, a newspaperman or a Republican politician would come upon a document unflattering to the secret diplomacy of the President of the United States. Most often, in deference to the national security, these documents were suppressed from public view. In those days, a general—one thinks of George Marshall, advising forty reporters in great detail about the forthcoming invasion of Pantelleria—could disclose national plans with a sense of total security. That a Congressman would reveal the secret testimony of the head of a national intelligence agency was simply unthinkable.

In other words, the quarrels in America were over the public policies of the Establishment. But there was hardly a quarrel over the necessity that an Establishment should survive, and indeed—in a sense—prosper. Decisions about public policy, even wrong decisions, needed to be made, and competent administrators were needed to administer them. Some of what had to be done had to be done confidentially, and the notion that one could stick one's spy into National Security Council meetings and report out in the paper the next day what one overheard there—and win the Pulitzer Prize for doing so—was, well, once again unthinkable. And since government cannot easily defend itself against a total disorganization of restraint, what happens is that it resorts to unpleasant ways and means of doing business. One hardly needs to illustrate, at this point.

So now Congress, while expecting the President and the Secretary of State to help to keep equilibrium in the world, is doing things like deciding how much wheat should be sent to Chile, or arms to Turkey, or credit to South Vietnam. A general assertiveness by Congress is overdue. But to assert control in such a way as to disestablishmentarianize the government of the United States is to invite chaos. I propose a modification to the oath of office, which should now read: "I do solemnly swear to defend the Constitution of the United States, and I herein depose that I have read the book *Love in the Ruins* by Walker Percy." It is all there in that book. I mean, what is happening to us, and the directions we are taking.

Are You Against the Handicapped?

April 7, 1973

THE REACTION to Richard Nixon's veto of the aid-to-the-handicapped bill brilliantly illustrates a difference between the Democratic and the Republican modes of operation; indeed, a difference between the always elusive "liberal" and "conservative" ways of looking at things.

Never mind for a moment any structural defect in the proposed law. Consider it simply as a means of helping the handicapped by voting federal dollars for their use.

Senator Hubert Humphrey emerged as the best, i.e., the quintessential, spokesman for the Democratic approach to such questions. For Senator Humphrey it was very simply this: Do you or do you not believe in helping handicapped children? Pure and simple. The Senator went so far as to personalize the argument, going even beyond his abstract identification with the cause of the handicapped. He spoke his rage over Nixon's veto on the floor of the Senate, saying, "I am the grandfather of a mentally retarded child. Our family can afford to take care of that child, but many families can't. I ask every Senator here to search his own conscience. I don't believe the President of the United States knew what he was doing. If he did, he ought to be ashamed of himself." Such language is highly volatile. It spreads like wildfire through the college campuses.

From such an onslaught the conservative reels. If the critic will listen, the conservatives can patiently ask a few questions.

(1) Do the Democrats believe that there is as much public money available as there are worthy causes in the world on which it might be spent?

No one, on reflection—not even Teddy Kennedy—would answer that question with a categorical yes.

(2) Do the Democrats acknowledge that we have at this moment in American history strained the safe level of government spending?

No one, on reflection, can safely say that we have not. To

do so would mean to interrupt his own criticism of the high price of meat for one thing.

All Democrats deplore the effects of inflation, and all Democrats recognize that the dollar's humiliation in the money markets abroad is the direct result of inflation at home.

(3) Did the Democrats suggest that the $1 billion aid-to-the-handicapped bill take the place of $1 billion already appropriated for another social service? Did Senator Humphrey propose that Congress reduce by $1 billion appropriations for medical aid to the elderly? For education for the young? For the purification of our water and our air?

We nudge up against the argument that we should commensurately reduce the military budget.

(4) As a matter of fact, the military budget has been reduced. In constant dollars we would need to spend $105 billion to maintain the same level of spending the Democratic Congress judged necessary when Mr. Nixon assumed office, subtracting the cost of the Vietnamese operation. Now, spending on defense is what a society, resolved to maintain its sovereignty, begins with, even as you begin a house by building a foundation. To economize by pouring more sand and less concrete into the cement is to be compared with economizing by offering the sick man a half million units of penicillin when the doctor has prescribed one million.

(5) Since approximately one-half of the states of the Union pay more money for social expenditures to Washington than they receive for social expenditures from Washington, what is to keep these states from appropriating their own funds for the help of the handicapped? Senator Javits, for instance, who voted to override President Nixon's veto, comes from a state that sends to Washington $1.60 for every dollar it gets back. Why doesn't Senator Javits satisfy himself to recommend to New York State that it look after its own handicapped?

In his classic book, *Economics in One Lesson,* the economist Mr. Henry Hazlitt remarks that it is distinctively the conservative who looks beyond the immediate effect of any particular expenditure; that the liberal foreshortens his perspective, so that he is able to talk only in terms of: Are you or aren't you in favor of helping invalids? It is an onerous responsibility that the conservative needs to bear under the pressure of such demagogy, and we can only be grateful that Mr. Nixon and a few Senators have had the courage to think in strategic terms.

The End of the GOP?

January 26, 1974

AT LUNCH the other day I was startled to hear an American specialist in Republican Party affairs give it as his judgment that not inconceivably the Republican Party would die in about three years. "Here's what would do it," he explained to his two guests. "First, a tremendous defeat in the Congressional elections this fall. Next, in 1976, a catastrophic defeat at every level—Presidential, Congressional, and local." After that, he said, in the ruins of 1977, the commanding position of the organized party would be lost, and ambitious conservatives would look for another label. It would be not unlike the end of the Whig Party in the mid-1850s.

As an obliging Providence so often arranges things, not an hour after hearing this analysis my eyes ran over the latest issue of the official Republican Fight Sheet called *First Monday*. The central message was from Congressman John Rhodes, the minority leader of the U.S. House of Representatives. Mr. Rhodes is on Cloud Nine. He grants, looking ahead to the elections of this fall, that there are things out there to worry about, mostly on account of Watergate. But, he tells us, there isn't all that much to be worried about, for two reasons. The first is that the GOP was in no way responsible for Watergate. So the public won't blame the Republicans in general.

And then, "secondly, I am of the opinion that our Watergate-inspired difficulties will actually make us stronger as a party in the long run. That is because Watergate has caused many of us to reexamine our party's great principles." I shall try it. I shall walk the streets, and accost the first pensive face I see. "Sir, excuse me, but could it be that Watergate is causing you to reexamine your party's great principles?"

Poor Mr. Rhodes, playing Knute Rockne to the Republican Party. The trouble is that, in the forward inertia of his pep talk, he *has* to go on. Who says A, must say B. Who says that we are fondling our party's great principles, has to say what they are. Here is how he copes with the problem:

"We recall that it was the GOP that helped provide America with a sense of racial justice through the wisdom of Abraham Lincoln. We recall that the GOP helped to provide America with a sense of global purpose at the turn of the century through the vision and energy of Theodore Roosevelt. We recall that the GOP helped provide America with a sense of balance and security through the leadership of Dwight Eisenhower. From Taft, to Dirksen, to Goldwater, the Republican Party has supplied the nation with sensible and effective direction at key points in our history."

Somehow, one cannot quite conceive these words coming from the mouth of Henry V and stirring the troops to prodigies at Agincourt. They are unlikely to stir the voters at the polling places.

The fact of the matter is that in recent years—and this goes back to General Eisenhower—the Republican Party insofar as it is a party that causes the political blood to heat up with excitement, and voters to swear fidelity to it by their grandmother's grave, is the party that is there to defeat a George McGovern from time to time.

In between, it behaves as though it should apologize to the voters for having done so. Free health, huge deficits, inflation, kissing conferences abroad with the Communists, military weakness, subsidies for string quartets, revenue sharing in place of tax reduction. . . .

If my friend's predictions come to pass, they will blame it on Watergate. But Watergate was a transfusion of sick blood into anemic blood, and if we go down, the pathologists will tell us, in the course of time, that it was the latter condition that did it, not that silly little infection which a healthy body could have thrown off laughingly in weeks.

Ford and the Impossible

January 20, 1975

THERE IS A lot of talk, some of it loose, about President Ford and the conservatives, and how he has lost them, once and for all, by his economic program. Concerning which, a few observations:

(1) To say that one knows how a bad situation might have been prevented, or even to say that one knows how a bad situation might be set right, is not to say that an American Chief Executive can, or even should, attempt the logical plan. An example would be the stalemate in South Vietnam back in 1965-66. There were competent generals then saying: You can't win this war in this way. The alternative was the devastation of Hanoi, cutting off the Ho Chi Minh trail in Laos, and blockading Haiphong. As the months went on and we didn't do this, it became progressively harder to do; and, finally, psychologically and even militarily unthinkable.

It was so with the Berlin Wall. It might have been struck down as illegal on the day after it was erected in 1961. What wouldn't have worked is for President Kennedy to announce that each day the United States Marines would dislodge one (1) brick, leaving Berlin without a trace of the wall on the twenty-fifth anniversary of its erection. It is so with the economic mess brought on by four Democratic Congresses, one Democratic President, one Republican President, and a generation of liberal economists.

(2) But it does pay, however unthinkable it may be to make the appropriate recommendations, to remind ourselves of what would in *fact* work. The atomization of Hanoi would in *fact* have worked to end North Vietnamese obduracy. It isn't something we would have done or should, at that point, have done. But the term "unthinkable" here is best used as a metaphor. We should precisely force ourselves to *think* what exactly it is that would cure a situation, however disposed we are to reject that cure. It would cure the evils we now suffer from if we inflicted upon ourselves a commensurate austerity. I say commensurate, because there is some relation— these are figures entered as much in the ledger books of the

saints as in those of the statisticians—between overindul-. gence, and the requisite underindulgence. If, for eight years, a people have voted themselves a couple of hundred billion dollars of services which they didn't pay for, then—using rough figures—they owe themselves a couple of hundred billion dollars of austerity.

(3) How is austerity here defined? Let us be entirely direct about it, not at the expense of oversimplification, but in quest of oversimplification. If the budget were slashed by, say, $50 billion per year, four years from now we'd be back in the registrar's good books. But what would be the means of doing this, and the tactical effect?

(4) The federal government would have to withdraw substantially from its role as subsidizer of social services. This it should do in respect of the thirty-one states of the Union whose own resources are above the national average. Pull out of education, health, construction: let such subsidizing as needs to be done be done in behalf of the nineteen poorer states.

(5) Now this will cause widespread unemployment without offsetting compensation. Benefits would need to be raised locally, by the individual states, and the cost of them would be palpable, because local taxes always are. The result would be a great crack in the wage-price structure. People would be willing to go back to work for a dollar and a half an hour, but lo! they would discover very quickly that they were earning a living wage.

That all this should sound like a parable is a measure of how far we have slouched toward the superstition that the universal enjoyment of plenty is primarily a problem in political-economic manipulation. For Gerald Ford to come forward and recommend what actually should be done would be as shocking as if a voice from the heavens were suddenly to startle the world by voicing the Ten Commandments, and promising hellfire for those who failed to heed them, or failed to repent that failure. A generation of mankind would be swept away.

And that, children, is why Gerald Ford cannot be expected to commit orthodoxy. He would be committing suicide.

The Decline of Patriotism

October 15, 1972

IT IS A cliché that patriotism has become a dirty word. There are two reasons for it, one of them understandable. It is true that the invocation of the love of country is often associated with someone who is really engaged in shilling an audience into a nefarious enterprise. This was done on a grand scale during America's brief adventure in jingoism. And it is done by individual charlatans when they seek to distract attention from what it is they are actually up to.

But the more recent assaults on patriotism aren't based on a posteriori indictments, reasoning from the obnoxious character of the America booster on over to the obnoxious character of what it is that he is boosting. The attack, led as usual by the intellectuals, is both on the concept of patriotism, and on the qualifications of the United States to be loved. The internationalists have for quite a while now confused patriotism with nationalism, and they therefore despise patriotism as the fuel of imperialism and isolationism. Others simply say that America isn't worth it—isn't worth the devotion of its subjects. Edmund Burke said that a country to be loved must be lovely. That isn't in fact true. There are people who love Uganda and South Africa. But it is worth exploring, in an age when people are pretty mobile, whether America is straining the bonds that attach people to her. I think it is happening, though not for the reasons most generally adduced.

Garry Wills reiterates the irreplaceable phrase to describe that which makes society cohere, "the bond of social affections." Our bond of social affections is weakening for some of the best reasons, secular and nonsecular.

Concerning the former, it is increasingly true that the attitude of the people who run the government is that Americans are in all economic matters the wards of the state. I do not think it ever occurred to George McGovern, for instance—and it doesn't occur to Nixon all that often—that it is an awful presumption for the state to reach into the life of the average citizen in the way generally sanctioned by the socialist communities. The average American spends forty hours a week working. During that time he accumulates his pittance, or his millions. Some of it needs perforce to be taxed to run corporate enterprises that only the state can feasibly administer.

But the arguments generally accepted in Congress these days do not acknowledge the presumption against taking money from the people for purposes wildly unrelated to the survival of society. George McGovern talks about people's earnings as though the earnings were ours at his sufferance. In an age in which the liberty a typical man exercises is primarily economic, the impositions of the socialists necessarily weaken the fundamental attachments of a citizen to his country.

There is something more important even than this that is straining the bonds of common affection. The final commitments of the human species are always eschatological, commitments to end purposes in life. To love of family, to redemption, to transcendence. There is a special kind of impiety abroad, and the top of the iceberg is the antireligious joke. A magazine features a blasphemous, altogether vile caricature of the Incarnation by which the Christian community is guided, and inspired. I wrote once that no one should be permitted to stage a musical on the theme of Buchenwald, that to do something that insensitive at the expense of the Jewish people is to cut bonds of affection to one another in so decisive a way as to make us strangers to ourselves.

By the same token, sacrilegious assaults on each other wound perhaps irreparably. In this connection, the Supreme Court recently ruled against a California expedient which would have allowed the state to return their money to individual parents for their use in schools of their choice for their children. All in the name of the separation of church and state. Well, if church and state are to be separated to that extent, then the society that asks us for patriotic attachments to it has singularly less appeal than once it had. Surely a generous gesture by everyone involved would be a constitutional amendment restoring the right of people to patronize religious schools. But, above all, the spirit of generosity, of rec-

ognizing the central place of the individual and his transso-
cial affections, is needed. To strengthen the kind of patriotism which does cause countries to be lovely.

To America with Love

October 31, 1972

BRUSSELS. THE LEAD time on Vietnam analysis being what it
is, I take leave of the cosmic imperative. The terms of the
proposed cease-fire continually reify, like the photographs in
Mr. Land's new camera, which however will give us in fifty
seconds what, respecting Vietnam, it will take fifty hours or
days—or months?—to perceive distinctly enough to evaluate.

Pending this I should like to report that as of this afternoon the Minnewater Canal in Bruges (Belgium)—as en-
chanting a town as exists in all of Europe—is a dirty, stinking
mess. What should America do about it? Nothing; but it
brings to mind that Mr. Nixon recently vetoed a $24 billion
anti-water pollution bill rushed through Congress in the hectic final hours of its life.

Mr. McGovern will no doubt reveal that this clearly means
that Richard Nixon would rather napalm civilians than clear
rivers; but soon now Mr. McGovern will cease to distract.
And although one can appreciate Mr. Nixon's preeminent
concern for a sound dollar, still one thinks wistfully about
clear water, and it occurs to me that the bicentennial celebra-
tion committee has really failed to come up with anything exciting with which to celebrate the 200th anniversary of the
founding of the Republic.

Why not propose to the American people that they make a
present to themselves of—clear water. Clear lakes, clear rivers, clear streams.

Congress should empower a bicentennial committee to sell
ten-year tax deductible bonds at just-under prevailing interest rates, the proceeds of which would begin instantly to be

used to launch the great enterprise. Twenty billion dollars is, as they say, a great deal of money, though it is just less than we spent at the urging of President Kennedy who in 1961 called on the Congress to finance through taxation America's determination to reach the moon. In a half dozen years we had it made and for a while there was a great corporate exultation. This in due course evaporated, in part because the landings became routine, in part because in the nature of the thing landing on the moon, like exploding an atom bomb, doesn't give the kind of resonant satisfaction one gets from, say, discovering the cure for polio; or for polluted water.

I see here several opportunities. One is to summon the nation to a corporate enterprise on a comparatively voluntary basis. I.e., to the extent that the money is raised, the job gets done. During the Second World War bonds were sold not so much because the revenue was necessary to finance the Normandy invasion, but because the selling of the bonds was a means of involving the public in the national enterprise; and a means, also, of withdrawing, however temporarily, funds that otherwise would fuel inflationary pressures.

This time around, Congress might say simply: Put up the money to clean the water, or let the waters remain fetid. Every community, every category of American, could sponsor the sale of the bicentennial bonds. All of them from John Wayne to Jane Fonda, from Noam Chomsky to Milton Friedman, from George Meany to Barry Goldwater, could put aside their differences and ask their constituencies to: Buy the Bicentennial Bonds.

It would be for an economist to analyze the indirect consequences of $20 billion invested in the Bicentennial Bonds. They are not exactly dollars removed from circulation, because they would need to be spent, in some form or other, to promulgate the myriad programs of pollution control. Still, much of the money would not be poured raw into the economic bloodstream. Subtle inducements and regulations, carrot and stick, designed to rearrange waste habits of manufacturers is a part of it. Research into sewage disposal is a part of it. Regulation of routine disposal habits by individuals is not necessarily costly, if the regulators are in any case on the public payroll. But the $20 billion that now are spent on other things will not be available to those who have mortgaged $20 billion to that end. In due course there is a reckoning, but that can be gradually amortized, particularly with the tax-deductible feature of the plan.

They ask for participatory government. Here surely is the stuff of it. Granted, eventually the investors will be repaid, even as the war bondholders were repaid. But the interest is not glamorous, the return is in inflated dollars. And on July 4, 1976, removing the bandage from our eyes, we might look down into the water, and see a clear reflection of ourselves: the face of a smiling America.

IX.

The War on Business and Property

Down the Businessman

May 5, 1972

MR. ROBERT TOWNSEND, who is the author of the spirited tract *Up the Organization,* gives a hero's welcome to a new book called *In the Name of Profit,* published by the respected house of Doubleday and Company, in the hope of profit. Mr. Townsend is more the advocate than the judge, and he recognizes intuitively that he had better insist right away that the American system is thoroughly, pervasively corrupt, or else he is left merely with the task of praising six authors who blame six companies for six discrete acts of wrongdoing.

That is not a particularly profitable pursuit, not because companies that are guilty of wrongdoing oughtn't to be criticized, but because it is one thing to review a book that tells you about My Lai, another to review a book that says My Lai is the rule, not the exception.

Like so many of the enthusiastic critics of the American way, Mr. Townsend is anxious that we believe that *the whole* of American society is That Way. He tells us, "If you think that Dita Beard, Harold Geneen and the other weasely wafflers in the ITT affair are somehow unusual, read this book. Here are six well-documented cases of corporate conspiracy against the public good, and together they give us a picture of misbehavior that is more the rule today than the exception."

In passing along the indictments dug up by the authors of this book I do not pass judgment. For all I know, each one of them is a corporate Dreyfus. But here the authors allege that one major automobile company deliberately decided to cheapen a bus, so as to make it dangerously obsolescent and, in due course, increase the company's profits by selling more buses.

They talk about a chemical company that manufactures napalm, and about its principal official, who, they say, affects

277

to know nothing about foreign or military policy for the sole purpose of relieving himself of the burden of needing to talk about the uses to which the product is put which makes profits for his shareholders.

They talk about a pipeline company which contrived to persuade an oil company to bribe certain officials in Woodbridge, New Jersey, so as to secure particular commercial advantages.

About a rubber company that "cooked the figures" in a qualification report so as to deliver an unsafe air brake on time to a new Air Force plane.

And about a company that "doctored its research" in order to sell an anticholesterol drug, even though that drug had the effect of causing human hair to fall out, and cataracts to spring up in the eye.

From these sins, grave indeed if they are correctly described, Mr. Townsend, like so many other critics of American institutions, draws categorical conclusions. They are not revolutionary in the formal sense. That is to say, they do not call for replacing American institutions with Soviet or whatever, never mind that that might be the logical extension of what they advocate. But rather Mr. Townsend seeks dramatic legal and political interventions, and since he was formerly an advertising specialist, he does not lose the opportunity to suggest that candidate George McGovern is the providential vessel for such reforms. Never mind exactly what he proposes, though that is itself interesting. Even as it is interesting that the fever against capitalist enterprise mounts for reasons not exactly incandescent.

This morning the news carries the confession of an executioner who was paid to murder a man and his wife and their daughter by the competition: no, not Ford moving against General Motors, or Post Toasties against Corn Flakes; but a labor union team which, seeking to discourage the competition, did so—by the simple expedient of hiring people to kill them. We have not heard, however, cries against the practices of labor unions from George McGovern—or Robert Townsend—notwithstanding that we can consider it safe to assume that both Mr. Townsend and Senator McGovern *are* against killing: at least if the killing is done in Vietnam.

No, business is the new butt of the political and intellectual season. We have seen it before, but the wrinkle now is not only the greed and corruption that made Upton Sinclair famous. The attack, though fueled emotionally by Sinclair-type exposés, perches on a sophisticated technical scaffolding of which John K. Galbraith is the principal architect. It will be big this season, you watch. And, as so often, the wreckers' instrument will be the taxing power.

Professor Galbraith's *China Passage*

April 1973

THERE IS ONLY one thing John Kenneth Galbraith found in China that truly disturbed him. Goddammit, the Chinese smoke too many cigarettes, which are bad for the health. Beyond this nagging reservation, one has the feeling, after reading this easygoing little book, that Mr. Galbraith is reporting on the economic organization of an ant colony, and it is of no particular concern to him that very recently the big ants ate up or subdued tens of millions of little ants ("I am not especially well read on Chinese history," Mr. Galbraith says in the preface, and proceeds to write as if he had not heard about the Cultural Revolution). Oh well, ants will be ants.

The traces of skepticism Galbraith shows are temperamental, not iconoclastic. They are hardly intended to induce an organic or principled rejection in the reader of modern Chinese society, the most advanced totalitarian society in the world. "The retirement age is not completely clear: It is described at fifty for women and sixty for men at 70 per cent of the last pay. But apparently healthy workers can and are encouraged to continue in the labor force. *This, obviously, could mean many things.*"

Or: "I doubt that Hsu Hong is a wholly typical commune. *There is a tendency in such matters to mislead.*"

Galbraith would insinuate as much about the Democratic platform of George McGovern, for whose election he worked so enthusiastically. A meiotic cynicism is a part of his literary and analytical style, and he takes it with him everywhere he goes. It is not here used subtly to impale Chinese society upon reality.

On the contrary, so routinely and un-self-consciously is the reader nudged away from any chance meditation on historical reality that the least nexus between modern China and the West is garlanded with ideological fancy. Thus, in Peking, Galbraith comes upon Frank Coe, "who supported my interpretation of the vegetable market."

Frank Coe. . . . A familiar ring. He is briefly introduced as "a Treasury friend of New Deal days, expatriated by McCarthyism." What Professor Galbraith doesn't mean for us to recall is that when it transpired (Joe McCarthy had nothing to do with it) that Frank Coe had been a Communist agent, Coe elected to sneak out of the country and advance the revolution at Mao's side. Perhaps Mr. Galbraith will undertake a Russia Passage, on reading about which we will run the risk of: "I happened on Kim Philby, an old Foreign Office friend, who was expatriated by John Bullism." Mr. Galbraith observes merely that these are *happy* and well-fed ants, that a modus vivendi has been reached by which the powerful ants get what they want from the little ants with a kind of—let's call it *Oriental*—grace, and that their way of doing things is altogether pleasing to a man of gentle disposition, who would rather know about problems of discipline only in the abstract. "(Dissidents [his, pained, parentheses] are brought firmly into line in China, but, one suspects, with great politeness.) It is a firmly authoritarian society in which those in charge smile and say please." On reading this book, Mao Tse-tung emerges as the Rector of Justin.

Whittaker Chambers wrote twenty years ago that the ways of the West and the ways of the Communists would one day melt together, "like two balls of wax into a single tallow." The job has already been done by our intellectuals, insofar as they trivialize the differences. This they have done most conspicuously in their reaction to Communist China. They neglect to make the main point—the only point, in nontechnical books—which is that China is as it is in virtue of the exuberant elimination of the individual. Authoritarianism (as Mr. Galbraith calls it, mindful ever of the uglier inflection of totalitarianism) can indeed work marvels, as the ever wistful former head of the Office of Price Administration discerns. "In any other country the difference between urban and rural incomes . . . would set in motion a large movement of people to the cities, and in China it once did. This is not now happening. The reason is straightforward. The Chinese are assigned to jobs and remain where they are assigned."

But what about the vegetable market we slipped by, in our haste to arrive at Frank Coe? After all, Professor Galbraith is an economist, and although most of the book is composed of travelogue and impressions, charming and humorous and exquisitely readable, Mr. Galbraith is traveling to China with his two predecessor presidents of the American Economics Association, and tucked into the book is an account of how the Chinese economy actually works. Much that Mr. Galbraith says is extremely illuminating. But I treasure in particular what comes when the great economist has stripped for action, and becomes all-professional, like Charles Darwin whipping out his magnifying glass. . . .
 "While higher authority decides what prices are to be," says Professor Galbraith about the working of a municipal marketplace, "such authority is intelligently susceptible to suggestions as to when abundance requires reduction and scarcity an increase. The keeper of the apple stall, whom I consulted informally, told me that of course apples were reduced in price as the autumn advanced and the supply became more abundant." LEAPING LIZARDS! STOP THE PRESSES!! Reduce the price of apples when they are abundant, increase it when apples are scarce! So *that's* how they do it, in the inscrutable, revolutionary People's Republic of China! Score another Thought for Chairman Mao.
 Granted, Higher Authority isn't always finely tuned to the vagaries of nature, and harvest yields, and fluctuating tastes, and reallocations of still Higher Authority, and when the

Highest Authority makes wrong decisions, well—
"[Professor] Tobin [a traveling companion of Mr. Galbraith]
observes that there are no dogs or cats in China. The reason
is presumably economic; if food has been scarce and ra-
tioned, affection for a participating pet must diminish. This
seems especially probable if the pet is itself edible."

But let me tell you something, Professor. The reason for
eating one's pet *isn't* economic. It is biological. And it is to
such biological extremes that the ants are driven by Higher
Authority—routinely, as they accept their lot. And when the
Higher Authority, putting the mantle of the marketplace
upon itself, makes miscalculations so serious that not even
Great Politeness serves to bring dissidents into line, why then
the muzzle of a gun becomes the only relevant article in the
marketplace, and the supply of guns in China *never* fluctu-
ates with the seasons.

But by that time Mr. Galbraith has finished his brief passage in China, and is back in America, preaching the anach-
ronism of the free marketplace and the price system, and
dealing with his own dissidents, not *always* with great politeness.

Economic Damnation

December 15, 1973

I HAVE HERE, addressed "An Open Letter to Mr. Buckley," a
communication reminding me that, in this imperfect world, I
am not everybody's favorite analyst. The gentleman in question, who is from New York, says that once upon a time he
admired me. "No more. God damn you, Buckley, and your
goddamn friends, Schultz and Nixon, and your whole goddamn arrogant 'elitist' club of very fat cats. I want some gas
for my 1965 Falcon, so I can get to work, do the shopping,
take my kids to the games they play, ride out to the beach be-

fore the oil slicks move in. By forcing the price of gas up to perhaps a dollar or more a gallon, the rich and powerful will price the rest of us out of the market, leaving just enough gas for the rich and powerful. God damn you all."

One can only hope, in the heat of so categorical an anathema, that there is an energy crisis in hell. And wonder, sadly, at the sad estate of economic understanding.

Here, I would judge, are the salient figures, and the irreducible minimum in economic analysis.

(1) Nobody believes that that which is scarce can, by the process of rationing, be made plentiful. Even John Kenneth Galbraith, the principal enthusiast for wage and price controls, gives up at this level. "Controls," he says, "should not be used where price increases are caused by an excess in aggregate demand or a shortage in the specific supply."

(2) Although rationing is clearly justified when there is a dire physical shortage of an essential commodity, that is not now in prospect. In the first quarter of 1974, petroleum supplies are expected to fall by about 3,000,000 barrels a day short of the projected demand of 19,700,000 barrels. That is still 2,000,000 barrels per day more than the average use throughout 1970. The population of the United States has not risen significantly since 1970. So that at worst, we are facing a situation in which we would have to get along with a little more than we got along with in 1970 when there was no pinch whatever.

(3) The average American family spends 22 percent of its budget on food. When food became scarce last spring, there was no serious lobby for rationing—because of the universal experience with rationing as a useless, and counterproductive, means of coping with scarcity. Besides, the farming community is not an easy villain. Food prices were allowed to rise, and did so—by a huge one-fifth. However, the inducement to producers was such that, quickly, the supply increased and now there is a downward pressure on food prices.

By contrast, the average family spends about 2.7 percent on gasoline—about one-tenth what it spends on food. A rise in the price of gasoline by the same amount as the rise in the

price of food will make much much less of an economic difference to the typical American family than what it sustained
last spring. And consider, now, the figures. . . .

(4) Professor Philip Gramm of Texas A&M has collected a
set of projections. "Estimates of how much the demand for
energy sources would decline in a period less than one year,
if prices rose by one per cent, range from roughly 0.2 per
cent to 1.2 per cent. Estimates of how much the quantity supplied would rise in the same period, if prices rose by one per
cent, vary from roughly 0.6 per cent to 2 per cent." What this
means is that even if "demand exceeds supply by 20 per cent
at the current price, we might expect a price rise of less than
10 per cent." This would suggest that gasoline selling for 40
cents would need to rise no higher than to 46 cents simultaneously to reduce the demand and increase the supply to
the point where they would meet. Gasoline would then be
selling at less than one-half the price paid for it all over Europe for lo these many years.

(5) Like steak, plumbing, and ballet teachers, the price of
gasoline is a function of supply and demand—*ad aestima-
tionem fori*. Apparently there are those who do not know this,
and while not wishing that they be damned, one hopes they
will not propel Congress or the Executive into economic ab-
surdity.

The Economics of a New York Assemblyman

October 21, 1973

Mr. Andrew Stein is a young New York assemblyman of
considerable ambition and uncertain taste. He is devoted to
fashionable causes, preferably in fashionable settings. A few
years ago he presided over a party in Southampton for the
benefit of Cesar Chavez's union. At that party he served
champagne, which is harvested by Frenchmen who are paid

50 cents per hour, and urged the socialites in attendance to boycott grapes, harvested by Americans who are paid $2 per hour.

Now Mr. Stein has sent a furious letter to Senator James L. Buckley, protesting his position on school lunch money. As one would expect, the sainted junior Senator from New York does not reply to apoplectic communications. But Assemblyman Stein sent a copy of his letter—one has a paralyzing suspicion that he thinks it clever—to me; and we workhorses of this world have to acknowledge our mail, so here we go.

Mr. Stein advises Senator Buckley that "malnutrition of children" is an inappropriate "weapon against inflation." He says that Mr. Buckley should have voted for the disputed $200,000,000 increase in federal subsidies for school breakfast and lunch programs because "after all, these children are not responsible for the Vietnam War and its impact on the national budget and on inflation." He then reminds Senator Buckley—I kid you not—of Dean Swift's Modest Proposal for reducing Irish hunger by eating children—a brilliant parody which however was overused by the time, approximately, of the American Revolution. Mr. Stein has evidently rediscovered it, and suggests that Senator Buckley's indifference to the fate of American children "lacks the grace and humanity of Dean Swift's earlier proposal."

Now. In 1968, the federal government was contributing $500,000,000 for school lunches.

In 1973, the Nixon Administration recommended an appropriation of $1.5 billion for school lunches. That is, three times as much as under the last Democratic administration, under the prodigious spender Lyndon Johnson. One would think that if with $1.5 billion Mr. Stein's children would die rachitically before arriving at the trenches of a future Vietnam, then with only one-third that sum, they'd have disappeared four years ago.

But the story is not even then complete. The House of Representatives took Mr. Nixon's request for $1.5 billion, and added $149,000,000. That bill arrives in the Senate, and the Senate adds $108,000,000. Along comes Senator Humphrey, who wants to add $83,000,000 to the Senate's $108,000,000 to the House's $149,000,000 to the President's $1.5 billion. Senator Buckley at this point raises his voice to point out that the subsidy has by now outpaced the increase in the cost of food by something like 43 percent, he supports one-half of Senator Humphrey's projected raise, and he urges the House to reject the second half. Those figures, processed by Mr. Stein, become a call for children's malnutrition.

Mr. Stein then quotes a New York welfare official as saying: "If reimbursement rates are not increased there will be general price increases to students and many programs throughout the state will terminate." Presumably Mr. Stein believes this, though it is perhaps uncharitable to suggest that Mr. Stein really believes anything he says. But why then doesn't he address his letters to Albany, and to his colleagues in the New York Assembly? Why do New Yorkers—the richest people in the entire world—need to go to Washington to raise money for New York schoolchildren?

The answer is they don't need to at all. All the money flows out of the citizens' pockets to begin with. But blaming it on Washington is the course of the simpleminded, and of the demagogues who, if they persist in writing letters, should not send me copies of them.

Galbraith and Inflation

August 20, 1974

EXPERIENCING Professor John Kenneth Galbraith is always a personal pleasure, though one must be on one's guard, and the Republic is wise to steel itself to resist his seductive nostrums. Most recently I met with him to discuss on the *Today* show the disappearance of Richard Nixon. He took huge delight, in a telephone conversation the day before, telling me how much he had enjoyed the newsy column I wrote that day about deteriorating airline service. Mr. Galbraith's sarcasm is never obscure, and his point was that while Nixon was resigning, I was writing about airline food, and so would he be doing if he had been so retarded as to have backed Nixon in other days. I expected he would bring up the subject on television and am somewhat disappointed he did not, as I was prepared to tell him that there are those of us who, when avoiding vigorous thought, write about the airlines, while others write economic textbooks. But the subject did not arise, and before going on we sat for a minute or two in the little antechamber listening to a lady theologian. I do not doubt that during those two minutes Professor Galbraith doubled his knowledge of theology.

And then it began. Strangely, the subject of Mr. Nixon's perfidies did not wholly occupy Mr. Galbraith, a man of personal generosity not always visible through his polemics. His generosity is most pronounced, come to think of it, when dispensing other people's money (he calls it public money) hither and yon, to improve on the works of nature, and nature's God. And in a matter of moments he was agreeing with *Today's* attractive new host Mr. Jim Hartz who was agreeing with President Gerald Ford that the country's most urgent problem is inflation. The formulation usually has it: "The Number One Problem."

Professor Galbraith then said that everybody knows what it is that should be done about inflation. The only problem, he says, is to develop the Will. As a matter of fact, this is not correct. Most economists will agree that certain measures would be deflationary in their impact, but by no means could one get most economists to agree on the stresses that are properly put on one as against another anti-inflation measure.

Here, highly compressed, would be Mr. Galbraith's recommendations: (1) Raise taxes immediately, particularly on persons earning $20,000 or more per year, and on corporations. (2) Use the money on public works projects. (3) Impose wage and price controls on critical industries. (4) Stand by to target a lot of help to groups that are afflicted in the course of shaking off the inflationary fat, provided these groups aren't held together by corporations. For instance, be prepared to help out Lockheed employees, but not Lockheed. If you want to keep Lockheed alive, nationalize it.

This is something one might call classical-1930s-liberal. I fear it is very full of holes. Obviously of a political and social character; but even of an economic character; and, of course, there isn't time, ever, to get deeply into the subject. It is perhaps easiest to observe that there are many countries in the world suffering from inflation even though dominated by one man, or a group of men. Lenin used to say that revolution plus electricity would bring Communism. Will plus expertise won't bring deflation: not in the absence of government restraint.

It is, of course, the government that is responsible for inflation. Mr. Nixon, during his years in office, spent $70 billion more than he raised in taxes. The difference between a dollar spent by Washington and a dollar spent by the taxpayer isn't the difference between one more maple tree at Yellowstone Park and one less empty beer can at the roadside, as Mr. Galbraith likes to leave us thinking. It is the difference between a dollar spent or invested with airy notions of where the common good is or ought to be, and dollars spent with very clear notions of individual preference. These last have a more resonant effect: in causing homes to be built, or skyscrapers, or hospitals—or schools.

The public dollar, beloved of the socialists, is both difficult to target (60,000,000 Americans can now qualify for food stamps), and difficult to restrain (a conservative President overspends by $70 billion). Inflation is indeed the number one domestic problem, and indeed it is true that marshaling the Will is required to contain it. But the will to do what? One fears that Professor Galbraith and other centralizers look on the current mess, which resulted from an overindulgence in their own nostrums, as an ideal opportunity to proceed with their vision of a socialized economy.

Economics via TV

January 21, 1974

THE OTHER night on CBS News they were talking, as usual, about the energy crisis. There followed a sequence that went roughly as follows:

Anchorman: In Washington today, Representative John Axelrod from Massachusetts interrogated Mr. Stanley Lifeless from the Petroleum Institute.

Rep. Axelrod: What worries me, Mr. Lifeless, isn't the profits of the oil companies. As far as I am concerned, you oil people are sitting pretty and taking advantage of the current crisis. What I'm worried about is the little people. The people who need to get to work in the morning and can't find gasoline for their cars. The old couple who are sitting in a cold house because they can't afford to pay double for the fuel oil they're buying. That's who I'm worried about, Mr. Lifeless, not corporate profits.

Anchorman (focusing the camera on Mr. Lifeless): Mr. Lifeless explained to the committee the position of the oil companies and denied that profits were excessive. . . . In Miami today, the Dolphins beat the Aquaducks by a surprising score of. . . .

I have made it a point not to look at a transcript of the exchange I have just finished reproducing, because what is primarily important is the impact of it, rather than exactly the words spoken. It is the impact of television journalism, and there isn't anyone in the United States who denies its importance, primarily in establishing a public mood. It is, by the requirement of the medium, antithought. It is at the service of those who express readily communicable attitudes and emotions: indignation, despair, joy, skepticism, hatred. In any colloquy in question we have a politician saying the obvious things, but those things that he was saying stir the resentments, latent and matured, of everyone who deplores (a) paying more for gas or fuel, or (b) finding it hard to get gas or fuel. Roughly, everybody. By contrast, the oil executive is speaking about such abstractions as demand, supply, costs, controls, allocations: so that the anchorman gives him very short shrift. Who cares to waste valuable network time in explaining the causes of unpleasant economic developments?

What can one assume a responsible executive could say, should Walter Cronkite vouchsafe him, say, one whole minute to reply to the Congressman?

It isn't easy. Really, it isn't easy, and it is one of the exasperating things about television that it is expected that you should be able to say things, no matter how complicated, in seconds of time. I was once asked, when running for mayor of New York, to explain my position on rent controls—"You have thirty seconds, Mr. Buckley." "In thirty seconds," I said—icily, I hope—"I cannot explain my position on rent controls." So it is on the seven o'clock news. Particularly in answering someone whose formulations, like Congressman Whatsisname's, are arrantly demagogic.

What is there to say? About profits, for instance? Well, you can say that the oil industry last year ranked seven out of ten as a profit maker, among the major industries in America. You can try to put the thing in perspective by pointing out that Mobil Oil made slightly less than 2 cents per gallon of gas last year, so that if all the profits were removed, it wouldn't substantially affect the price of oil and fuel. You might point out that the New York City subways, which threaten a 60-cent fare, up 400 percent over 1965, make no profits at all, because they are municipalized, which by the way is one of the reasons why subways have risen in price so many times the rate of gasoline. You can point out that the tax now paid on gasoline is many times as high as the profit made by the producers. You can explain that matters are demonstrably worse now than they might have been, precisely because thoughtless Congressmen egged on the President to institute wage and price controls and generally to screw things up.

But in the last analysis you need to count on the viewers' knowledge of some of the basic axioms of economics, about supply and demand, and resource allocation, and the function of price rises. These, alas, are harder to grasp. Harder still to grasp is the cynical exploitation of ignorance by demagogic Congressmen. A society that tolerates demagogy is unlikely to penetrate economics. A pity. And a pity that such as Mr. Cronkite do not even attempt to mediate.

A Congressman Objects

February 20, 1974

A FORTNIGHT ago I commented on a demagogic appearance on television by a Congressman who dumped on the oil industry for the benefit of those of his constituents who are particularly ignorant, manifestly the majority since he is, after all, their chosen representative. I judged, however, that no purpose would be served by identifying the gentleman, and so I gave him an assumed name. But now he writes me in high dudgeon demanding a reply, which under the circumstances I am forced to make.

He is Mr. Silvio O. Conte, a Republican from the First District in Massachusetts, and though I have never met him, he addresses me as "Dear Bill," which is, alas, his only contribution to conviviality. He begins by saying that he takes "exception" to my "shrill ode to Triassic cerebrations." I don't know what that means, but cannot assume it matters.

He says it is fortunate I do not represent the people of the First District of Massachusetts. "Otherwise, they would have frozen or moved out long ago under the sponsorship of the oil import quota program." I am, once again, not sure what he means by that, except perhaps to suggest I have over the years favored oil import quotas, which I have always opposed.

"If you have a reasonable solution for alleviating the plight of the thousands of New England families on fixed incomes who suddenly, within the space of three months, have to find some way to pay $500 more for heat this winter, I would be pleased to hear it. In the meantime, you cannot expect me to complacently watch corporate greed sap the economic vigor of my constituency."

And he concludes, "Allow me to return the ad hominem. In light of the egregiously excessive profits reported this week by Exxon and the other corporate fiefdoms, tell me, how did the Buckley oil barons fare in 1973?"

Well.

(1) Inasmuch as fuel oil in Boston has risen an average of 25 percent, a family forced to pay an extra $500 was already paying $2,000. Anyone paying $2,000 for his winter supply of fuel who was living on a fixed income, I worry about not at all. Since the fuel bill of the average family represents approximately 2 percent of its income—and that is for an entire year, not just for the winter—then the family paying $2,000 for fuel is earning about $100,000 per year.

(2) The profit of the oil companies on fuel is approximately 2 cents per gallon. The tax by the government on fuel is, depending on where you live, somewhere between 8 and 12 cents per gallon. So that the answer to Mr. Conte—excuse me, to Silvio—is: If you want to help these people, get off their backs—lower their taxes.

(3) Silvio refers to the crisis that took place "within the space of three months." The only crisis that took place within the space of three months was a political crisis. Political crises are made by politicians, not businessmen. If Mr. Conte is displeased with the crisis in the Middle East, let him by all means do something about it. But to blame American oil producers for it is, well, a politician's diversion. Like worrying about the plight of someone living on a fixed income after voting for inflationary budgets year after year.

(4) The principal reason for the rise in oil company profits in 1973 compared to 1972 is that they were too low in 1972 for the health of the industry. And that was because of the silly and dangerous wage and price controls implemented by Mr. Nixon pursuant to authority given to him by Congress and voted for by Silvio.

(5) Concerning my own situation, I regret to divulge the news that my holdings in oil in 1950 were worth more than my holdings in 1973. Alas, too many dry holes in between.

And to reveal, further, that the oil stock in which I am predominantly interested was selling at $30 per share three months ago and is selling at $21 today.

And finally,

(6) I reflect on my relative freedom to speak my mind. Whatever I say or write about oil affects my income by not a penny. By contrast, Silvio's income is 100 percent dependent on whether he flatters his constituency, which, alas, he finds it easier to do by stimulating ignorance, than by telling such liberating truths as I specialize in communicating.

Oil and the Demagogues

May 25, 1974

MR. ALAN REYNOLDS of *National Review*, a young man who was born to understand economics even as Vladimir Horowitz was born to play the piano, has lately made it a hobby to probe some of the stuff the snake doctors are selling on the matter of oil. His findings are too good to husband even for an elite readership, so I pass along a few items.

(1) In a recent issue, *Time* magazine referred to the profits of Occidental Petroleum as having risen "a stunning 718 percent." That's the kind of figure that bounces about the country, feeding the demagogues—which reminds me, I haven't heard lately from Silvio—and causing people like economist Robert Lekachman to wonder whether we shouldn't nationalize oil, thus settling our problem for good and all, the way England settled hers by nationalizing coal. But back to Occidental.

It turns out that the Occidental Petroleum Company is a major *coal* producer, and the rise in the price of coal has gone up far more rapidly than even that of domestic crude oil. Moreover, only 2 percent of the crude oil Occidental sold here came in from its domestic wells. Last year Occidental did extremely well: on the sales of chemicals, fertilizer, and gold. Now: profits from Occidental's oil and gas divisions rose 54 percent internationally. But sales were up far more in proportion. So that, actually, profits *per dollar of sales* went down—from 3.7 to 2.5 percent. In 1971, Occidental suffered a sizable loss. In 1972, the return to the stockholder was a pathetic 1.3 percent. Then last year, the stockholder got 9 percent—which is what caused *Time* magazine to ooh and ah.

One sees how easy it is to achieve the desired effect. If the editors of *Time* magazine had reflected on the profits of Occidental from 1970 to 1974, they would have been required to comment that the profits were down 56 percent. So: the fact of the matter is that Occidental's profits were 9 percent, in an extraordinary year in which the price of oil zoomed as a result of the Mideast crisis. Well, during the same year the New York *Times* brought in a return of 14 percent (why not nationalize the New York *Times*?) and the Washington *Post* came through with 14.7. In turn, chicken feed, compared to CBS's 18.5 percent. So it goes.

(2) Mr. Reynolds notes that Senator Kennedy in last year's returns claimed a depletion allowance on some oil revenue. Nothing scandalous about that. But one asks: Did he buy his oil stock because of the depletion benefit? You see, the stock market instantly discounts the depletion benefit. In that way tax breaks are quickly dissipated: the price of oil land and equipment is bid up, and the stock market builds any remaining advantage into a stock price which is higher than otherwise.

But now Congress, substantially at the prodding of Senator Kennedy, is preparing to change the rules of the game—retroactively. In other words, it is proposed to eliminate the depletion allowance even on old wells. People who invested in oil at a price that reflected the tax advantage are now scheduled to suffer windfall losses. Will Senator Kennedy now move his investments into something more profitable? Like the news media? How many people will act as he will, assuming he is more prudent as an investor than as a legislator?

(3) The notion that government interference is going to help the consumer is, well, a laugh. A very expensive laugh. Over the past five years, domestic taxes on oil products went

up by $1.3 billion. During the same period, profits went up
by $0.4 billion. And the notion that a federal agency is going
to protect the consumer is another, forced laugh. The agencies invariably act to help the inefficient, to protect them
from low prices. The Federal Trade Commission has issued
at least eight complaints against major oil companies. Guess
what for? Price gouging? No. For reducing the price of gasoline.

(4) Now Venezuela is expropriating the oil, paying the
owners about 20 cents on the dollar. Well, we'll see what happens to the flow of investment dollars into Venezuela in the
next period. Or will all investment dollars in the next period
be government dollars, notoriously attracted to profligate
waste?

Middle-Class Poverty

February 11, 1974

THERE IS A professor at Temple University named John
Raines, a theologian who teaches courses in social ethics and
religion, and is given nowadays to making pronouncements
about the plight of the American middle class which, if I may
say so, are on the order of someone breaking into a faculty
meeting of MIT with the breathless news that he had discovered that the world is round. Professor Raines has discovered that people in the middle class in America are having a
tough time.

In particular, he has discovered that it is extremely costly
to send a child to college, but that it is especially expected of
middle-class Americans that they should send their children
to college; and that parents with incomes of more than
$12,800 per year are not eligible for federally guaranteed
loans. Though the figure varies, neither are students eligible
for college loans and scholarships if their parents earn more
than a particular figure—irrespective of how many brothers
and sisters there are to help eat up that income.

I know an industrious toiler in the vineyards of the middle class. His annual income, at $38,000, is almost exactly four times the median family income in America. He has three children of college age, and they cost him each $5,000 per year. Two of them will go to professional school. His school bills for the three children will total approximately $170,000. After taxes, food, rent, clothes, and maybe a cigarette every now and then, he figures he will have paid back the bank for his children's schooling by the time he reaches, approximately, age sixty. Moreover, the net rise in the actual purchasing power of the average American family, Professor Raines has discovered, increased in the decade of the 1960s by only $1,160 per year, or $96 per month. "How much upward mobility does that represent?" asks Professor Raines. Well, by the world's standards, a hell of a lot. But by American standards, it's tough going.

And then Professor Raines, with that unerring academic eye for the false solution, tells us what *he* would do. What he would do is tax the top 1 percent *more*. He cannot understand it that the American middle class hasn't directed their "social anger and frustration at the top 1 percent of the economic scale, where I think it belongs."

One wonders why full professors can't pick up the Statistical Abstract, or even the World Almanac, to keep from saying foolish things. In 1970 (I round off the figures) there were 59,000,000 taxpayers. One percent of 59,000,000 is 590,000. Now if you took everybody in America whose gross income was in excess of $50,000, you would come up with 428,230 people. In other words, fewer than 1 percent of all Americans make over $50,000. Now these people are paying a tax of $12.270 billion—on taxable income of $29.382 billion. That leaves them with approximately $17 billion. And that's less, by one-quarter, than $50,000 apiece. In other words, about $39,960 apiece if you take not a penny more in tax.

When will the professors learn that the money doesn't exist up in those high brackets to run a rapid transit system, let alone bring relief to the middle class? What the American middle-class member suffers from is the high overhead of life. And the principal load on his shoulders is: government, for which he works approximately eighteen weeks per year. You talk about lifting the burden on the middle class. If you take away 100 percent of the income of everyone making $1,000,000 a year, you have got yourself $624,000,000. If the government increases its dependent exemption by $100, it takes $4 billion off the backs of the taxpayers.

I hate to think of adding to the burdens of the old man, but I wish he had treated young John to a course in economics before sending him on to theology school.

Palm Coast and the Knee Jerks

November 27, 1974

ITT HAS A development project going in Florida, in a place called Palm Coast, near Daytona. Anything wrong so far? Well, one can assume that some of the sports who live in the area aren't pleased, but what else is new? The Indians no doubt were displeased when Peter Stuyvesant started building frame houses in their old hunting grounds on Manhattan Island. As far as ITT is concerned, a development is an OK thing to do, under the law. Indeed, the expenditure of capital for construction means employing people, and that is, nowadays in particular, an especially commendable thing to do.

The ITT people decide they want to bring attention to the area they are developing. So what do they do? Hire Jackie Gleason to preside over a golf tournament? Entice Richard Burton and Elizabeth Taylor to stroll the beach and become reconciled? No, they decide to stage a highbrow extravaganza, to which end they approach a distinguished professor of sociology from Princeton, and ask him to round up a dozen or so well-known names for four seminars to last over the weekend. Professor Melvin Tumin does his ingenious best, and comes up with big-name scientists and Nobel sociologists (e.g., James Watson, Gunnar Myrdal), famous writers (Tru-

man Capote, Saul Bellow), philosophers and critics (Sidney
Hook, Leslie Fiedler) and even the requisite freaks, a woman
libber (Kate Millett) and a conservative (me). The experiment was conducted before an enthusiastic audience of Florida educators.

The conference has suddenly become a cause célèbre. Not
because of any of the speeches given, or insights discussed.
But because the intellectuals were, or such is the fancy, dancing to the tune of ITT.

The current issue of *People* magazine, for instance, heaps
great scorn on the enterprise, suggesting that the tycoons really put one over on the intellectuals. Professor Arthur
Schlesinger is quoted as having accounted for his presence at
the conference by saying, "The more you can rip off ITT,
the better." After which, the reporter tells us, "he laughed."

A few observations:

(1) American corporations are always being told that they
should spend more of their time and money sponsoring the
life of the mind. Why should they be reproached when they
do so at Palm Coast, Florida?

(2) The planted assumption of the critics is that the intellectuals who attended the conference were doing something
they would not normally do. In point of fact it would have
been pleasant, not to say sensational, if, at the conference,
Gunnar Myrdal had blurted out that all of a sudden he had
come to recognize that American capitalism is the hope of
the world. Or if Arthur Schlesinger had delivered a solemn
lecture (he is expert at it) explaining the overarching justification for ITT's opposition to the government of Allende.
Or if Kate Millett had said that, upon profound research into
the question, she now knew that it was right that at ITT the
women do the secretarial work, while the men are the executives.

As a matter of fact, these conversions were not effected:
Myrdal sounded like Myrdal, Kate Millett acted like Kate
Millett, and Arthur Schlesinger sounded like Arthur Schlesinger. If Mr. Schlesinger had really wanted to rip off ITT, he
could have gone down there and said something sensible.

One wonders how else Mr. Schlesinger thinks we should

rip off ITT. By pouring ketchup on the carpets of ITT-owned hotels?

(3) Most of the distinguished gentlemen who attended the conference and gave thoughtful speeches are affiliated with universities. Most of these universities are endowed by funds accumulated by American capitalism. In what sense is it improper for a professor to travel to Florida to discuss physics, but proper for him to occupy, say, the Thomas B. Watson Chair at Harvard University? As that stock flourishes, so will the colleges' resources, and the professors' salaries. For all they know, the future security of a half dozen young scholars now hard at work learning an academic discipline will be paid out of earnings flowing from a development at Palm Coast, Florida.

The cynics prove nothing more than that their carping is ignorant, and their manners bad. The panelists apart, only ITT—and Professor Tumin and most of his guests—came out of all this with honor: the treatment of their guests was exemplary, there was never a hint of what should be said; there were no taboos. There was just the problem of the profiteers and exhibitionists.

X.

Notes and Asides

•Hon. (?) James L. Buckley
Washington, D.C.
Sir:
Now that my nausea has subsided after accidentally observing your appearance on *Laugh-In* last evening, I, as one of your constituents and former admirers, am constrained to comment.

Your silly grin as the inane and vulgar questions were asked and your equally inane replies were less than worthy of a Senator of the United States.

The fact that you appeared on that program at all was an insult to the decent people whom you represent.

The disgusting episode in which you freely participated and apparently enjoyed as an accomplice in lending your position to a disgraceful program is an affront to the dignity of the Senate, to your family, to your church, and to your constituency. I trust that your acting the clown insured the support of the addicts of the program who undoubtedly enjoy its indecencies. I trust, too, that they are in the minority.

Yours,
Robert Hitchcock
Buffalo, New York

Mr. Robert Hitchcock
Sir: I have forwarded your letter to my brother the columnist—William F. Buckley Jr. It was he, not I, who appeared on *Laugh-In*. I can't help but be curious as to why you consented to watch a program of which you so strongly disapprove.

Sincerely,
James L. Buckley

United States Senate Memorandum

Dear Priscilla:
A sample of the fan mail we receive. I look forward to reading Bill's reply. Cheers,

Jackie (Sec. to Sen. James L. Buckley)

Robert M. Hitchcock

Dear Mr. Hitchcock: It is typical of my brother to attempt to deceive his constituents. It was, of course, he, not I, who appeared on *Laugh-In,* just as you suspected. On the other hand, you need not worry about it. His greatest deception is as yet undiscovered. It was *I,* not *he,* who was elected to the Senate. So you see, you have nothing to worry about. You are represented in the Senate by a responsible, truthful man.

Yours,
Wm. F. Buckley, Jr.

●Arthur Schlesinger, Jr., Esq.

January 15, 1970

Dear Arthur:

I hope that Mr. Steibel [the producer of *Firing Line*] inaccurately reported a conversation with you concerning a proposed appearance on *Firing Line.* He told me that you declined to appear on the program because you do not want to "help" my program, and you do not want to increase my influence, although to be sure you "hope" that the program "survives." It seems to me that the latter desire is by definition vitiated by the initial commitment. If all the liberals who have appeared on *Firing Line* reasoned similarly, it would necessarily follow that the program would cease to exist—or is it your position that other liberals *should* appear on the program, but that *you* should not? And I should have thought it would follow from your general convictions that a public exchange with me would diminish, rather than increase, my influence. And anyway, the general public aside, shouldn't you search out opportunities to expose yourself to my rhetoric and wit? How else will you fulfill your lifelong dream of emulating them?

Yours cordially,
Bill

March 2, 1970

Dear Bill:

I do not see the *National Enquirer* or *National Review* or whatever it is called; but I understand that you ran your silly letter of January 15 to me in your issue of February 10. I gather also that in neither this nor the succeeding issue did you run my reply of January 30, though it had obviously been in your hands in plenty of time. In a better world I might have hoped that you would have had the elementary fairness, or guts, to provide equal time; but, alas, wrong again.

Sincerely yours,
Arthur Schlesinger, Jr.

March 12, 1970

Dear Arthur:

I should have thought you would be used to being wrong. But to business. . . . Now, suppose I had begun this letter, "Dear Arthur, or Dear Barfer, or whatever you call yourself"? Would I do that? No; and not merely because it's childish, but because it isn't *funny*. The reason I did not publish your reply to my original letter is that I thought it embarrassingly feeble and it did not come to me with your permission to publish it. But, of course, now that you have relieved me of responsibility, I shall proceed to release it [see below].

One night, two or three years ago, you leaned over to me during a television broadcast when Lyndon Johnson was speaking about conservation, and whispered, "Better redwoods than deadwoods." I granted you, on the strength of that, a plenary indulgence. But the crack must have worked hell on your batteries, and it is obviously going to take a few years before they are capable of another successful discharge. Meanwhile I beg you, visit not your wit on me. Manifestly, it hurts you more than it hurts me.

Yours faithfully,
Bill

[Mr. Schlesinger's reply to WFB's letter in *NR* February 10]

Dear Bill:

Can it be that you are getting a little tetchy in your declining years? Nothing would give me greater pleasure than debating you on neutral ground; you are quite right in detecting my feeling that such public exchanges would diminish rather than decrease your influence. But is it really *lèse majesté* to suggest that I am under no obligation to promote

your program? As for others, let them make their own decision. Don't tell me that you have stopped believing in freedom of individual choice!

You remind me of my other favorite correspondent,
Noam Chomsky.

Best regards,
Arthur Schlesinger, Jr.

Dear Bill:

It should have been obvious even to you, I would have
thought, that the reason one confuses the *National Enquirer*
and the *National Review* is because they have comparable
standards of wit, taste, intelligence and reliability. I am interested to see you so sensitive on this point.

As for your decision to excommunicate me (again), I fear
that this is a weightier matter from your viewpoint than from
mine. The notion that the withdrawal of your approval must,
of course, bring your adversaries immediately to their knees
could commend itself only to an egomaniac. And, lest you
are in doubt, you have my permission to publish this letter
too.

Sincerely yours,
Arthur Schlesinger, Jr.

Dear Arthur:

It is obvious to me that only someone who had difficulty in
distinguishing between the *National Enquirer* and *National
Review* could have written such works of history as you have
written. Nor have I intended to suggest that I have driven
you to your knees, merely that you should spend more time
on them before presuming to challenge.

Your patient nemesis,
Wm. F. (Envy His Rhetoric) Buckley, Jr.

●Dear Mr. Buckley,

Perhaps it has never occurred to you, but most people do
not tune in to *Firing Line* to hear your inane opinions and tedious talk, but, rather, we tune in to hear your guests. You
do, as a rule, have some extraordinarily interesting guests.

We all look forward to the times you realize you are out-classed and are content to be quiet and listen. I want to pro-test your boorish behavior toward Miss Jessica Mitford in your last show. You interrupted her every time she tried to develop a line of thought, badgered her over trivia, and left me with a feeling of annoyance at you and sympathy for her.

Sincerely,
Henry F. Schwarz III
Columbus, Ohio

Dear Mr. Schwarz: (1) A secret poll, recently conducted by a joint team of Gallup, Harris, and Yankelovich, reveals that 94 percent of the American people are *wild* about my opin-ions, and 91 percent *fascinated* by my talk. That poll suggests that dissenters are outside the mainstream of American opinion. (2) I did not try to interfere with the development of Miss Mitford's line of thought, but to midwife a line of thought. Alas, her line of thought on prison reform proves to be stillborn. But do not despair. My efforts, and your an-noyance, might serve to refertilize her mind, leaving us to worry, tomorrow, only about you.

Yours cordially,
—WFB

●Mr. Charles Lam Markmann
New York City
Dear Charles:
That was an impressive collection of Buckley prides and prejudices [*The Buckleys—A Family Examined*]. The old *elan vital* came through clearly and I learned a little more about the elements that so often make their views dogmatic and one-dimensional.

I do, however, want to register an objection to a reference to my views on page 140. You say, "Like Emerson . . . Yoakum regards the Buckleys' propaganda for their version of freedom as essentially a call for Fascism; and, again like Emerson, he challenges the chicaneries to which they are ready to descend in debate whether formal or infor-mal, as well as the club of the threat to sue for libel."

The last portion of that sentence does reflect my views and

I consider my sixty-inch letter to the *Lakeville Journal* a definitive condensed work on the subject. But I do not believe that Buckley propaganda is essentially a call for Fascism and have *never* said so. (I've just reviewed the transcript of our talk and the word Fascism doesn't even enter it.)

They *are* authoritarian. They are quite willing to push for laws that tell me what books I can read and what films I can see—laws that result in greater state supervision of my private life, including, of all things, my sex habits.

My heroes are Jefferson, Madison, the Adamses, Paine, and Franklin, so of course I am suspicious of all those who are so sure they are right that they are willing to restrict the freedoms of others.

These antifreedom absolutists exist at both political extremes. As I have said for years, once my freedoms are gone—once Big Brother can tap my phone, bug my room, sabotage my political party, tell me what I may read or view—it doesn't matter to me whether those freedoms were lost to the Far Right or the Far Left.

The Buckleys are at least aware of the problem, and they occasionally modify their absolutism in ways that upset the way-out right. Now and then, as a matter of fact, they actually do or say something that does increase individual liberties.

Best,
Robert Yoakum

cc: John W. Buckley
    William F. Buckley, Jr.

John W. Buckley
Lakeville, Connecticut
Dear John

I have here a copy of a letter from your neighbor Robert H. Yoakum, addressed to Charles Lam Markmann.

John, it seems to me indicated by Yoakum's general approach to public issues that he is entirely misguided. Accordingly, I wish you would undertake an investigation of his reading habits. Specifically, what books and magazines does he read? Whose lectures does he attend? I think we ought to draw up a curriculum designed for his improvement. We should begin by advising the local librarian not to make available to him those titles that would only add to his confusion.

On the matter of Yoakum's sex habits, you and I have of course spoken. I think it would be wise, in your instructions to the State Police, to specify Remedy S-130. Needless to say, we should follow our usual discretion in the matter.

John, I want you to know that my heroes are Savonarola, Mitchell Palmer, Joe McCarthy, and John Ashbrook. If any one of these gentlemen ever wanted to tap my phone, I'd be there to help them splice the wire. My only regret is that I have only one telephone to give to my country.

Let me know when you are done with Yoakum. There are others. It is important for us to maximize our incumbency.

As ever, affectionately,

Bill

●Dear Mr. Buckley:
You make me sick! I've never heard a person I'd like to shut up as much as I would you. If you saw yourself, as many do, your leer, sneer and malicious grin, if you had any sense, you'd take yourself off TV.

Didn't your nanny tell you as a child not to interrupt someone that is talking? Do you ever listen? Do you ever let anyone finish a statement without pushing your obnoxious self in? You are really a perfect example of a spoiled creature of the rich and inbred.

If it wasn't for the great guests you have, for sure you wouldn't have a program. If you would listen more to people like Ellsberg, Galbraith, etc., you could learn a lot and be of greater service and utilize your time on TV for better things.

Take some of your excess money and buy yourself a TV station. Respectfully,

Jean Rosenberg
Farmington, Mich.

Dear Miss Rosenberg:
I've done that. What shall I do next?

Cordially,
—WFB

●Dear Bill:
Three cheers to Dr. Ross Terrill. He slashed you to bits as

you have been doing to yourself for the past year. Cancel my
subscription.

Wm. W. Morris
Green Valley, Arizona

Dear Mr. Morris:
Cancel your own goddamn subscription.

Cordially,
—WFB

●Dear Mr. Buckley:
I am a sixteen-year-old High School Junior who is going,
slowly but inexorably, out of his mind. I have come to the
conclusion that you are the only person on the face of the
earth who can save my sanity.

My problem, briefly, is this: for the past year I have been
trying, without avail, to discover just what, in God's name,
the phrase "to immanentize the eschaton" means.

I heard you speak the phrase once on *Firing Line* and immediately made a valiant attempt to look it up. Upon discovering that my dictionary did not list the words I instantly resolved to ask one of my teachers in the morning.

When I tried this course I drew another blank. I would ask
a teacher the question, whereupon he would have me repeat
it a dozen or so times and then plead ignorance. I would then
be asked: "Where'd you hear it?" When I informed him that
you had used it the night before he would generally give me
a forlorn look, mumble something like, "Oh *him* eh?," and
express his innermost convictions, i.e., that you had probably
invented the words. I'm sure you'll be thrilled to know, Mr.
Buckley, that I had faith in you. I *knew* you hadn't invented
those words. And, sure enough, when I was reading your
book *The Unmaking of a Mayor* I came across a passage which
revealed a Mr. Eric Voegelin as the author of the phrase. Ju-
bilant, I raced to our school library and asked the librarian
for everything written by Mr. Voegelin. "Never heard of
him," the woman answered. As I left, ruminating upon the
intrinsic failings of the public schools, I encountered the
teacher to whom I had put the original question. When I explained the matter to him he expressed the conviction that,

not only did you make up the phrase, but that you also contrived Mr. Voegelin!

Now, Mr. Buckley, more than anything else in the world I would like to know what that phrase means. I really think you should tell me because: (1) I have watched every one of your TV shows and have read all of your newspaper columns ever since I first heard of you. And (2) I've read all of your books (save only the last one, *The Jeweler's Eye*, which, curse my parsimonious soul, costs a small fortune. I'll wait 'til it comes out in paperback). Also (3) I subscribe to the *National Review* and even *read* all of those silly renewal notices I keep getting.

Thanking you for your time in reading this I remain

Sincerely yours,
Edward H. Vazquez
Old Bridge, New Jersey

Dear Edward:

Eschaton means, roughly, the final things in the order of time; immanentize means, roughly, to cause to inhere in time. So that to immanentize the eschaton is to cause to inhere in the worldly experience and subject to human dominion that which is beyond time and therefore extra-worldly. To attempt such a thing is to deny transcendence: to deny God; to assume that utopia is for this world. All of these things Professor Voegelin draws out of the Gnostic heresy of yesteryear. His phrase, far from being a contrivance of mine, is so famous that buttons actually exist, one of which I am sending you pinned into a copy of *The Jeweler's Eye*, that bear the legend, "Don't let THEM immanentize the eschaton!" Tell your teachers they have a great deal to learn, not least the impeccable use of the English which you are manifestly equipped to teach them.

Yours,
Wm. F. Buckley, Jr.

●Dear Mr. Buckley:

The "theme" upon which Chaucer's Pardoner preaches ["Notes and Asides," November 9] is *radix malorum est cupiditas,* which is derived from St. Paul's first epistle to Timothy,

Chapter 6, vv. 9-10: *"Nam qui volunt divites fieri, incidunt in tentationem, et in laqueum diaboli, et desideria multa inutilia et nociva, quae mergunt homines in interitum et perditionem. Radix enim omnium malorum est cupiditas: quidam appetentes erraverunt a fide, et inseruerunt se doloribus multis."* Your comment, "As a matter of fact, cupidity isn't the root of all evil" seems to me a bit tasteless coming from a man of your pretensions. It might be helpful to recall also that St. Augustine maintained that "Scripture teaches nothing but charity, nor condemns anything except cupidity, and in this way shapes the minds of men." It may be argued that *cupidity* did not mean quite the same thing to St. Paul and to St. Augustine that it does to the "modern reader." Nevertheless, you did the quoting.

D. W. Robertson, Jr.
Princeton, New Jersey

Dear Mr. Robertson:
Well well. What *are* we talking about? (a) I quoted Chaucer correctly except that I assigned to the legend in the Pardoner's Tale the qualifier "all" which Chaucer didn't use. St. Paul, on the other hand, did: which means that (b) either Chaucer shouldn't have edited St. Paul so as to change Paul's meaning, or that I shouldn't have edited Chaucer so as to restore Paul's meaning. So whose "tastelessness"—what an *odd* word, you should have tried the Latin—is your quarrel with? (c) Inasmuch as the Latin does not indicate whether the definite or the indefinite article is appropriate, "radix" can mean either "a root" or "the root." *The* root is comprehensive, *a* root is partial. Now, King James said "the root," whereas Monsignor Knox uses "a root." Since Chaucer came before King James, who came before Knox, we cannot know whether Chaucer thought "root" to have been intended by St. Paul as meaning "the root" or "a root," since Chaucer evidently relied on the Latin. King James's crowd did not lean at all on the Vulgate, but on the Greek and Hebrew. If you wanted to throw light on whether St. Paul intended to say that cupidity is a root of "every kind of evil" (Knox) or "the root of all evil" (King James) then you should have come through with Greek or Hebrew leads as to which of the two is authentic. As a matter of fact, Robertson, I don't usually spend this much

time on people who can't read Greek or Hebrew. And no, (d) it isn't helpful at all to recall what St. Augustine said. In the first place, when he says "Scripture teaches nothing but charity" he clearly meant to communicate that "Scripture *stresses* nothing *more* than charity," and when he says "nor condemns anything except cupidity," he means "nor condemns anything *more strongly than* cupidity." After all, Scripture condemns pride too, and pride doesn't have much to do with cupidity. And anyway, the older meaning of cupidity—namely, an inordinate longing—isn't flatly condemned by Scripture. It's okay to have an inordinate longing for God. And something only just a little less than that for *National Review.* How are things at Princeton?

Regards.
—WFB

Dear Mr. Buckley:

Please allow me, for the benefit of your good readers, to set you straight about St. Augustine's conception of cupidity ("Notes and Asides," December 7), and to come to the defense of Geoffrey Chaucer. I promise neither to question your good taste again nor to comment on your apparent confidence that doctrinal matters will eventually be settled by philologists. In this connection I should note, however, that you failed to mention that the Douay-Rheims Bible, which refreshed many English-speaking parishioners until recently, omits the word *cupidity* from 2 Tim. 6. 10, saying simply, "For the desire of money is the root of all evils," with which the Jerusalem Bible agrees except that it uses "love of" instead of "desire of." We should not, of course, contend in words, for as St. Paul says (Rheims), "it is to no profit but the subverting of the hearers."

To return to St. Augustine, I can assure you that he meant exactly what he said when he observed that "Scripture teaches nothing but charity, nor condemns anything except cupidity." He went on to explain, "I call 'charity' the motion of the soul toward God for His own sake, and the enjoyment of one's self and of one's neighbor for the sake of God; but 'cupidity' is the motion of the soul toward the enjoyment of one's self, one's neighbor, or any corporal thing for the sake of something other than God." Because of St. Augustine's enormous influence, these definitions became commonplace for about 1,200 years, and it is still quite possible to accord them a certain respect.

You will notice that the definition of *cupiditas* is broad enough to include all of what later came to be known as the seven principal vices; and, indeed, medieval representations of or descriptions of the "tree" of the vices often show *cupiditas* as the "root" of a "tree" whose "fruits" are the vices themselves. This doctrine was found to be pleasantly and perhaps Providentially harmonious with Ovid's description of the evils of the Iron Age dominated by *amor sceleratus habendi,* which found an echo in that favorite book among our Christian ancestors, *The Consolation of Philosophy* of Boethius, revered and translated by King Alfred, Queen Elizabeth I, and Geoffrey Chaucer, to mention only a few.

It is not surprising, therefore, that Chaucer's Parson quotes 2 Tim. 6. 10 by saying "the roote of alle harmes is Coveitise," and there can be little doubt that *radix malorum est cupiditas* conveyed to Chaucer and to his audience the idea that *cupiditas* is *the* root of all evils. The Pardoner is an extremely reprehensible character. He openly subjects himself to cupidity while he preaches against it, professing a determination to gain "moneie, wolle, chese, and whete," not to mention wine and "a joly wenche in every toune," the last being something a certain misfortune prevented him from enjoying fully. Moreover, he leads others to be cupidinous so that he can sell the pretended benefits of his false relics. However, his use of a slightly abbreviated form of the verse from St. Paul simply reflects a common practice in the formulation of "themes" for sermons that did not, in the context of his times, deserve censure.

Finally, I do not think that one should regard *National Review* cupidinously. As I contemplate the copy before me, I can not bring myself to think of it as a significant increment to my worldly goods, to be ranged along with money, wool, cheese, wheat, wine, and jolly wenches. Rather, I believe, its value is more intangible, residing in any "wit and goodness," as Chaucer would say, provided by the Good Lord to you so that you may pass it on to your readers.

Princeton, Mr. Buckley, if you mean the University, is not

an exclusively political institution, and in many ways things are splendid there.

Sincerely yours,
D. W. Robertson, Jr.
Princeton, New Jersey

Dear Mr. Robertson:
Thanks. The matter rests.

Cordially,
—WFB

•Dear Mr. Buckley:
Tch-tch . . . you'll never learn.

I don't really mind your dipping into your pathetic little treasury of Shakespeare quotes . . . the effect is nice and you don't overdo it. But, please . . . get them right.

On page 622 of *NR* [June 8], you reply to a letter from reader S. Manning with the most threadbare of your quotes stock thus: "Dear Mrs. Manning: That would be gilding the lily. Yrs. Cordially, etc.," and that rumbling sound you've been hearing ever since is ol' Bill Shakespeare spinning like a top. Ol' Bill *never* said anything about gilding the lily, and were you playing hooky during the term they taught *King John?*

Act IV, Scene 2, Earl of Salisbury in reply to Earl of Pembroke:

Therefore, to be possessed with double pomp,
To guard a title that was rich before,
To gild refined gold, *to paint the lily,*
To throw a perfume on the violet,
To smooth the ice, or add another hue
Unto the rainbow, or with taper light
To seek the beauteous eye of heaven to garnish,
Is wasteful and ridiculous excess.

Did you get any other letters on this? Or am I the only Shakespearean hawkeye among your readers? Cordially,
Saul Glemby
New York, New York

Dear Mr. Glemby:

(1) To call to the attention of anyone over 14 that Shakespeare didn't say gilding the lily is like calling to the attention of anyone over ten that Voltaire didn't say the one about how he would fight to the death for your right to say it. Come to think of it, I doubt very much that Voltaire would fight to the death for the right of anyone to remind anyone that Shakespeare didn't himself use the phrase gild the lily. (2) The phrase gild the lily, and a number of other phrases, can be used even though Shakespeare did not originate them. (3) When we use a cliché around these parts, boy we mean to use a cliché, understand, Glemby? (4) Of the four editors of *National Review,* one used to teach Shakespeare, one still does, and, when I retire, I intend to.

Cordially,
—WFB

●Clay Felker
Editor, *New York* Magazine
Dear Clay: Ideology launches a thousand ships every day, I know: but in civilized places, at least the effort is made to look honest about it. In your issue of September 15, your editors list the books of the forthcoming season, with comments, and divide them into two categories, Worth While and Worth Little. Under Worth Little I see: "*Odyssey of a Friend: Whittaker Chambers' Letters to William F. Buckley Jr., 1954–1961* (Putnam). What can one say?" What one can say is not a goddamn thing. Because the ideologized impostor who put the book in that category had not even seen the book, not a single review copy having been sent out (the existing edition is privately printed). I do believe we have here the *locus classicus* of book-burning, liberal style. Do you agree?

Yours faithfully,
Bill

P.S. Mr. Felker's answer will be published just as soon as it comes in, but remember, the mails are very slow.

—WFB

Dear Bill:

New York Magazine is planning a special year-end issue with a selection of short contributions from influential people, and I hope you will want to participate.

I am asking each person to write fifty to two hundred words on the following question:

"If you had the power, what is the one change you would make immediately in New York City?"

The deadline for your answer is November 24, and we pay an honorarium of $50.

Sincerely,
Clay Felker
Editor

Dear Sirs:

In answer to your recent query, if I had plenipotentiary power in New York City I would decree that Mr. Clay Felker should be required to answer his mail.

Yours faithfully,
WFB

●To the Editor,
The Washington *Post*

In re your man Ungar (Sanford J., Washington *Post* , July 21).

(1) It is obvious that he did not trouble to read *Did You Ever See a Dream Walking?*; which is just as well, inasmuch as it is by no means clear that he'd have understood it if he had. One thing. He mentions three of the (two dozen) contributors to the book, only one of whom he pauses to characterize. He refers to "the old reliable Whittaker Chambers." I do not know what he means by "reliable," although it is obvious that he doesn't use the word in the sense, say, in which you and I would use it about the Coast Guard. If he means that Chambers was reliably an evangelist for this or that position in the sense that, say, Billy Graham and Robert Ingersoll were, then he knows nothing at all about Chambers' intellectual peregrinations, which is too bad. If he meant to use the word professionally, then I think I must record that Chambers was

the most "unreliable" writer in modern journalism—forever missing deadlines. I do not see exactly how one can call "the old reliable" someone who over a period of thirteen years (1948–1961) wrote one book, and maybe ten articles. It is rather like referring to "the old reliable Katherine Anne Porter."

(2) Mr. Ungar complains (?) that my book *The Governor Listeth* contains my "minor speeches." Pray, where does he think I publish my major speeches?

(3) Mr. Ungar says of me, "He wants very much to be a public figure." That is like saying, "The Washington *Post* wants very much to be a newspaper." I think he meant to say that I want to be admired as what I am, even as, presumably, the *Post* does.

(4) He says that I had "some encounters with black militants which he will apparently never stop talking about." I wrote about the incident when it happened, and never again alluded to it. What *is* it with Ungar?

And, finally, (5) "His philosophies are dubiously [as opposed to unequivocally?] two-faced. Civil disobedience, for example, is always bad, except when it occurs behind the Iron Curtain, on the other side of which resides all that is evil in the world, including, of all things, Polish ham." I have never championed civil obedience in any totalitarian country. As for the Polish ham bit (I eat them regularly, and with pleasure), I am reminded by Mr. Ungar of a line from Guy Davenport: "Sometimes, on reading Goethe, I have a paralyzing suspicion that he is trying to be funny."

Yours faithfully,
Wm. F. Buckley, Jr.

•To the Editor
The Washington *Post*
Dear Sir:

I had no intention of intruding into the quarrel, and as a matter of fact I disagree with the totality of my colleague George Will's rejection of Norman Mailer, but alas Mr. Michael Olmert in taking issue with Mr. Will went on and on at my expense, which is okay, and much of it good boiler plate. But he made a curious factual point about my public contacts with Mailer. Mr. Olmert wrote:

"There are many who still remember his [my] travels on the debating circuit with a man named Norman Mailer, two barnstorming wrestlers whose first duty was to entertain us. Their philosophical struggles were covered thoroughly by the media, while we watched weekly (it seems) for the familiar litany of ideological leitmotifs and codas. At times, the entire debate format seemed to be on the brink of physical violence, and we thrilled to the possibility of their status as wrestlers becoming the stuff of reality rather than just another metaphor."

Mr. Olmert has a vivid imagination. I debated with Norman Mailer for the first time in Chicago in 1962 before a live audience: i.e., it was not broadcast or televised. Subsequently we appeared together once on David Susskind's program, and once (briefly) on Les Crane's television program. Years later he appeared (once) on *Firing Line*. I can only assume that Mr. Olmert's television set stuck and repeated one of those programs week after week in Mr. Olmert's living room, driving him crazy. Clearly he has not recovered.

Yours cordially,
Wm. F. Buckley, Jr.

June 1, 1971

●To the Editor,
The New York *Times:*

In your issue of April 27, on the Op-Ed page, you published a piece on "The Catholic Resistance," wherein the authors, Mr. and Mrs. Thomas Melville, write that I "called" Pope John's *Mater et Magistra* "warmed-over Communism."

(1) M & M isn't warmed-over Communism, it is other things. (2) I would never use the cliché. (3) I didn't say it. (4) You shouldn't have printed it.

Wm. F. Buckley, Jr.

To the Editor,
The New York *Times*
Dear Sir:

You write (May 27): "There is something repugnant in the enthusiastic publicity-seeking of Senator James L. Buckley of New York in participating in a whaling expedition by the hunters of an Alaskan village."

Now I have seen everything. So my brother is visiting, once again, the Arctic circle. It is his fourth trip, not even counting his trip to the Antarctic. He has a thing about Arctic circles. He first went to the Arctic circle way before he went to the Senate, and he will go to the Arctic circle after he is out of the Senate, assuming the inconceivable, that he and the voters should tire of one another before death do them part. On this particular trip a New York *Times* reporter *asked* to go with him. Jim said okay, but only if the Eskimos say okay. Those who know my brother know that the prospect of a reporter traveling to the Arctic with him for the purpose of recording the Senator's movements, far from overjoying him, was a tribulation he bore gracefully only because he will bear the pains of purgatory gracefully. A New York *Times* editor then decides to put the New York *Times* reporter's story on the visit on the front page, whereupon a New York *Times* editorial writer gives my brother hell for publicity-seeking! Your reference to his "gleeful pursuit" of a whale is both gratuitous and ignorant, inasmuch as my brother, a naturalist, has himself always declined to shoot or hunt down any living creature. What was he supposed to do while his hosts were shooting the whale? Cock his eyes heavenward and recite the *De Profundis*? I do not doubt the integrity of his concern for endangered species, though I confess that my own is qualified as I meditate a world without the species that writes New York *Times* editorials. Yours faithfully,

Wm. F. Buckley, Jr.

•Editor,
The Travel Section,
The New York *Times*
Dear Sir:

I have only just now seen your spread of August 12, under

the heading "Some of the Best People Are Afraid of Flying," and featuring a gallery of faces including what I hope is the most poltroonish photograph of me ever taken. The writer includes me in the roster of the fearful with the sentence, "William F. Buckley says in his typical fashion that flying is 'committing an egregious effrontery upon the laws of nature' and recommends 'a little of the grape.'"

I have great respect and sympathy for those who fear to fly, but it happens I have never been one of them. The snippets quoted by the author are from a column of advice to the airlines for the benefit of those who fear to fly, and the recommended poultice is of course pleasant not only for them but for others.

My problem (since you are apparently interested) has been in the other direction. As a student at Yale, I, along with a law student who came to be the sainted junior Senator from New York, and one or two others, purchased a secondhand airplane. I found it so exultantly easy to fly that after a single forty-five-minute lesson, I volunteered in a moment of characteristic compassion to fly a fellow student to Boston the more quickly to unite him with his lady love. I managed to take off all right, and to land, but on the way back to New Haven I quickly deduced that I had forgotten to account for the previous night's return to Eastern Standard Time, leaving me short of light by one hour. I ended by flying one hundred feet above the ground over the NYNH & Hartford railway, which brushed by the airfield at New London, mercifully lit: and I effected my first solo landing, and hitchhiked back to school. Since then I have patrolled the DMZ in a light plane, engaged in a night mission over Laos in a low-flying DC-3, chased kangaroos in Darwin in a helicopter, flown upside down in a Phantom II at twice the speed of sound, taken the controls of a helicopter to do a pas de deux with Barry Goldwater, Jr., over the Antarctic, glided serenely in a sailplane over the presidential palace of Salvador Allende, and suffered the rebuke of the pilot for trying to take the controls while landing on an aircraft carrier in the Gulf of Tonkin. My observation is correct, that the laws of gravity are offended by flight, but what else is new? The laws of truth and beauty are likewise offended by the First Amendment's guarantee of freedom of the press, and who would compare, unfavorably to the airplane, the disaster record of the airplane, over against, let us say, that of the New York *Times* editorial page?

Yours cordially,
Wm. F. Buckley, Jr.

*   *   *

●   John Kenneth Galbraith
Harvard University
Cambridge

June 6, 1969

Dear Bill:

I wonder if you would allow a friendly, puzzled note? Can I assure you I have nothing more in mind. I would think this libel suit [you have filed against Gore Vidal] would be costly and most unwise. Most judges are going to come rather reluctantly to your side. This is not for ideological reasons—although there are liberal judges—but because you are at least thought to describe others with a certain candor and vigor. However unfair the reference, you start with a handicap.

Additionally, don't you have a stake—as I do—in the feeling that there is much one can say without fear of the courts? Maybe it is worth a bad word now and then.

Do you have some deep design here I do not grasp? Otherwise I would foresee much grief to slight result. Yours faithfully.

Ken

June 26, 1969

Dear Kenneth;

Believe me. I do very much appreciate your letter on the inadvisability of suing Vidal. It raises implicitly two points, the one, Ought anyone to sue for libel; the second, Is the Vidal suit, assuming the answer is yes, to be one of them?

On the first point I am reminded of that electric moment in the Nivens' cellar four years ago when you and I were discussing my impending departure to battle with Linus Pauling. You sat back and said, "Isn't it possible that Hugo Black is correct, that we shouldn't have *any* libel laws?" Jackie Kennedy interrupted her conversation with David to say, "Oh no, Ken. You have to have the laws. Otherwise people begin saying things, and before you know, IT happens, and little children clap their hands in school." That isn't sufficient explanation for JFK's assassination, and in any case there are fallacies in the line of reasoning a-plenty, but I think the lady's intuition is correct: you have got to have libel laws, or else IT can happen.

Now, on the second point, the inside story. I wrote a (non-libelous, by everyone's admission) piece on the whole Vidal episode, which I shall be sending you in a few weeks (it will appear in August's *Esquire*). Vidal went into a high pitch of fagwrath and responded with a piece of such filth and venom as would have persuaded the average reader that where I belonged was in the dock at Nuremberg. *Esquire* of course declined to print it, and he howled off announcing he would print it elsewhere. That is when I moved. I sued, and wrote to prominent publishers informing them that I should be given an opportunity to confute such charges as were being spread about by V against me and my family, before they published them. The legal reference was directed to *Butts* v. *Satevepost*, in which the Supreme Court ruled that precisely the *SEP*'s failure to permit Butts to give evidence on his side, even after Butts requested the opportunity to give it, deprived the editors of the protections of *Sullivan* v. *New York Times*; i.e., here was proof that by going ahead with the story, the editors proceeded in reckless disregard of the available facts.

At a more general level, one doesn't give up the resources of the law when (this will sound stuffy) one's case is in some way symbolic. If it can be said of me that I am a crypto-Nazi, then as much can be said about every vigorous American conservative. Add to it, also, that Vidal sought to revive ancient and slanderous charges against my family, never mind that they had nothing whatever to do with me. So that is how it is. I hope that after reading my article, you will understand more fully the human element of the thing.

Tell me, why do you people put up with V?

And finally, my piece will be worth reading if only because it will give wider currency to the imperishable judgment of the reviewer for *TLS* who wrote that *Myra Breckenridge* was obviously intended as allegory, but that after finishing it one concludes that it is less *Paradise Lost,* than *The Golden Ass* penetrated.

I am grateful to you.

Yours faithfully,
Bill

August 12, 1969

Dear Bill:

I should say that I do not know Gore Vidal especially well. I thought his book on Washington was on the whole better than the reviews and my few encounters with him have been interesting. He was sharp in repartee and otherwise pleasant.

Your *Esquire* piece, as always, is lively, with great aptness of reference and research. And in spite of the incredible length, it is very interesting. But it lacks plausibility for reasons that I have previously mentioned at least in part. You are talking about a staged row between two highly experienced controversialists. If you had encountered Vidal at either of the conventions and had fallen into a quarrel, political, personal, or otherwise, you could persuasively seek support for your case. And even though you initiated hostilities, which to a surprising number of people would seem plausible, you would be listened to with interest and possibly even concern.

But this was a *staged* battle. That was ABC's intention when they engaged you. And there is a *further* and devastating weakness in your case when you concede that you first *refused* and then accepted Vidal. Obviously you accepted a risk of which you were aware. You are in the position of a man who sees the warning signs at the crossing, drives in front of the train and then complains about the locomotive. No amount of literary skill can evoke support. You do well but not well enough.

None of this is excessively encouraging. But it forces me to urge my point. As entertainment you perhaps could pursue this controversy. As an issue of justice you simply cannot. That holds especially for the courts. I am reacting, needless

to say, in purely practical terms. Were you the literary cyno-
sure of the SDS my advice would not be different except as I
might suppose your instinct for self-preservation to be less
developed.

Yours faithfully,
Ken

August 25, 1969
Dear Ken:
How strange to hear from your lips so dogmatically stated
the old bourgeois maxim, *caveat emptor.* Your analogy of the
locomotive is strained. Here is one that suits the situation. If
I have reason to suspect that a casino is crooked but nevertheless patronize it and lose my shirt, is it then inconsistent
that I should go to the courts and complain of the casino's
practices? Obviously not. And anyway, lifting the thing out
of the legal point, what am I to make of people of fastidious
standards reading what I documented about the behavior of
Vidal, and continuing to tolerate him? When you happen on
an answer to that one, let me have it, as I find myself short,
and have never doubted you are more resourceful than I in
such a matter as this, as in so many others.

As ever,
Bill

September 3, 1969
Dear Bill:
Many thanks for yours of August 25. I am willing to accept
your analogy. The courts are certain to be less sympathetic to
a gambler who gets cheated than an ordinary citizen who
loses his shirt in the course of honest employment. And so it
is with a professional polemicist. I am concerned with this,
not on any political grounds, and certainly not to defend
Gore Vidal. I urge you only as a friend—one who differs politically but is not, I think, inexpert in handling matters of
this kind. It is the kind of issue which will take a great deal of
time, quite possibly involve you in much anguish, require
money if that is important, and for a very narrow recom-
pense if any at all.
As to Gore Vidal's rebuttal, which I have read, I must say I
did not like it. I especially cringed at the stuff at the end. As

to my indulging Gore Vidal it is hardly, to use your phrase, a blood brotherhood. I have not seen him for something over a year. But I think I will continue to adhere to the rule of indulging almost everyone who indulges me. And if that sounds a bit pompous, as it undoubtedly does, it is nonetheless easier that way.

Yours faithfully,
Ken

P.S. I wrote the above before reading your telling account of the incident in the current *NR*. The letter is persuasive enough to give me a second thought. But I would still plead against—for your sake. The courts are not for those who live by the pen but use it as a sword.

September 10, 1969

Dear Ken:

Well now, we are making progress. If one is a professional gambler—mind you, an honest professional gambler in the analogy we are so painstakingly constructing—does he lose his right to protest against the rigged casino? Clearly not. I think what you are saying is that a jury will prove less sympathetic to such a man, which point I cede you, provided I have from you in return the concession that whatever risks I run at the hands of a jury drawn from the lists of New York County, that risk I ought not to run when being judged by a jury of my peers. I am prepared to proceed through life unembittered if, let us say, the jury grants me ten dollars' damage, I having run up a lawyer's fee in six figures. I will not forget it however if the clerisy indulge themselves in the excuse that they cannot bother with it since after all we are dealing with two controversialists. I have demonstrated that, at least in his dealings with me, Vidal has proved himself contemptible, a dogged liar, a foul human being. And I think you may yet be surprised by what the jury does. Just possibly. I have working against me one thing, I grant. It is that three years hence when the trial takes place, the word "Nazi" may have become totally etiolated, causing the jury to wonder that anyone should particularly care about having been so designated. If that is the case I shall be left with nothing more than an expensive footnote in my autobiography, pointing to the irony that it was a conservative who struggled to regulate the use of a word so as to immure within it some sense of the hideousness of Hitler. You have been very generous with your time in discussing this affair, so don't read this letter as demanding an answer.

As ever,
Bill

September 29, 1969
Dear Bill:
Your last letter puts a slightly different color on the matter. I have a natural aversion to the courts. And for me the mental even more than the financial anguish would be strongly adverse. You are obviously more nearly immune on both counts—and as one with a compulsive and reprehensible addiction to principle, I can hardly take exception to your defending a principle. So I end up wishing you well.

Yours faithfully,
Ken

September 25, 1972
STATEMENT BY WM. F. BUCKLEY JR. CONCERNING DISPOSITION OF LIBEL SUITS AGAINST ESQUIRE INC. AND GORE VIDAL.
Mr. William F. Buckley Jr. issued the following statement in New York City this afternoon:
In September 1969, *Esquire* published a libelous article about me written by Gore Vidal, notwithstanding repeated warnings that if it did so, I would proceed against *Esquire* in the courts.
I proceeded to file suit in the federal court for the Southern District of New York against *Esquire,* as I had done against Vidal. Vidal in turn filed suit against me.
The court has dismissed Vidal's suit against me as being without merit.
The same court has now sustained my suit against *Esquire* and correlatively against Vidal, by ruling that, notwithstanding recent Supreme Court decisions, Vidal's article was defamatory, and the case would have to go to trial.
Having lost its motion, *Esquire* has agreed to publish in its November issue a full statement totally disavowing the views of Vidal. And has agreed to compensate me for the legal ex-

penses involved in bringing about a judicial determination satisfactory to me. One hundred and fifteen thousand dollars is the cash value of the settlement.

Having disposed of Vidal's lawsuit against me, I am instructing my attorneys to take the necessary steps to discontinue my action against him, to avoid the time and expense of a trial. In the long period between the publication of the libel and the disavowal of it by *Esquire,* I have learned that Vidal's opinions of me are of little concern to the public. *A fortiori,* they should be of little concern to me now that the publishers have disavowed them. Let his own unreimbursed legal expenses, estimated at seventy-five thousand dollars, teach him to observe the laws of libel. I hope it will not prove necessary to renew the discipline in future years. There are limits even to my charity.

—WFB

•Lawrence K. Miller, Editor
The Berkshire *Eagle*
Pittsfield, Massachusetts
Dear Mr. Miller:

I should have thought that you put a high enough value on your readers to protect them against columns written by a "notorious antisemite." In the event that that isn't the case, you are less fastidious than I am. Because I would not want to be associated with any newspaper disposed to tolerate among its regular writers a notorious antisemite. Under the circumstances, (a) you should fire me because you believe the characterization of me by [the columnist] George Connelly (your issue of October 6, 1969) to be true; or (b) you will disavow the charge and apologize for having printed the libel, and perhaps take the opportunity to say what is your policy towards columnists who pass their libels through your pages; or (c) I shall—just to begin with—instruct my syndicate to withdraw my column effective immediately.

Yours faithfully,
Wm. F. Buckley, Jr.

Dear Mr. Buckley:

Thank you for your letter of October 13 addressed to Lawrence K. Miller. In response thereto, the marked item en-

closed was appended to the October 20 column of Professor
George G. Connelly.

Yours obediently,
Robert B. Kimball
Assistant to the Editor

Enclosure: "Apology. Prof. Connelly, in a column of Oct. 6
based in part on an article by Gore Vidal in the September issue of *Esquire,* imputed antisemitism to William F. Buckley
Jr. Upon examination of all available evidence . . . an apology is tendered Mr. Buckley on behalf of our columnist and
this newspaper.—Ed."

Lawrence K. Miller, Editor
The Berkshire *Eagle*
Dear Mr. Miller:

I note that not only are you too busy to prevent your columnists from submitting libels, you are also too busy to take
the time personally to apologize to the victim for publishing
them. I note also that the normally verbose Mr. Connelly is
suddenly struck dumb, leaving it to others to apologize to me
on his behalf.

I am not disposed to have dealings with such people: not
even professional dealings. On the other hand I do not wish
to satisfy myself at the expense of such of your readers as desire to read my column. Under the circumstances, I shall
continue to send you my column on the regular basis, on the
understanding that you will not henceforward pay any
money for it. I shall myself absorb the cost of mailing. Perhaps you and Mr. Connelly can meet and giggle together at
this demonstration that crime can, after all, pay.

Wm. F. Buckley, Jr.

●*Remarks by Wm. F. Buckley, Jr., New York Conservative Party
Dinner, October 15, 1973*

Ladies and gentlemen, I sometimes have the feeling that to
me the balance of the year is nothing more than an interruption of the continuing speech I deliver to the Conservative
Party at its annual dinner. Worse still, I sometimes feel that

this is the way many of you surely look upon it. I have no doubt that some of you have whispered to yourselves: "God, I wish Buckley would take a bribe. We need a new face." I would not blame you, though I hope you would blame me, concerning which point more in just a minute.

It was eight years ago that you nominated me to run for mayor of New York. The punishment visited upon the city for its failure to heed your advice has been draconian. I think we can say not merely that there will be better days ahead, but that there are bound to be better days ahead. It was said recently that Abe Beame wouldn't know how to find a Broadway theater. Well, he could always ask the vice squad for directions. Four years ago you nominated John Marchi, and it was he who was the instrument for demonstrating that the majority of Republicans did not think of John Lindsay as one of them. This demonstration ended by driving Mr. Lindsay from the ranks of the Republican Party, though to be sure in due course he discovered, in Florida, that the majority of Democrats do not believe him to be one of them. There is nothing to be ashamed of here. John Lindsay's ideas occupy a unique place in American politics, and there is no room for a following. Mr. Lindsay is his own man, and I desire for his views a genuine exclusivity.

I mentioned that you nominated John Marchi four years ago. Please believe me that I intend to say nothing Florentine when I say that having pledged myself to John Marchi in 1969, and having campaigned for him in 1969, I was so much struck by your wisdom in nominating him, and so much struck by his talents, and devotion to duty, that I made a subjective commitment to endorse him if he ran again, and this commitment I made to him over a year ago. John Marchi, as some of you are aware in contemplating his late decision to run, is not the most punctual of men. Rosemary Gunning, who is the most diplomatic lady in the world, once said about him that he is "sometimes a few minutes late." A more accurate way to put it is that he is sometimes a few minutes late for yesterday's speech. I hope he wins, and in case he does, I suggest the committee that will escort him to his inaugural should prepare for its duties soon.

A year ago our guest of honor was Spiro Agnew. I gather, from listening to the President's speech the other night, that

Mr. Agnew's name will not again cross Presidential lips. This is what Mr. Nixon must mean when he deplores what he calls our "obsession" with the past.

One wishes that his instinct—to treat Spiro Agnew the other night as an unperson—was merely an act of chivalry. One fears it is something more than that. My own feeling is that it is an unkindness to Mr. Agnew, as his speech tonight on network television itself indicates, to proceed as though he had never existed. I say this intending to make a human point, and a social point as well. Charles Van Doren was permitted twenty years ago to slip into oblivion, and many centuries have gone by since it was prescribed that guilty men be exposed at regular intervals for public castigation. But there was much to learn from the episode involving Charles Van Doren, and there is much to learn from the tragic career of Spiro Agnew. It did not require the experience of Agnew to teach us the dangers of greed. A tale of Chaucer began with the legend: *"Cupiditas radix omnium malorum":* Cupidity is the root of all evil. As a matter of fact, cupidity isn't the root of all evil, but of much evil. Certainly it was a factor in what we have come to think of as the great betrayal of Spiro Agnew.

The fault was substantially his. But the consequences of his weaknesses are substantially ours. We go to such lengths to identify positions with people that we find it hard to detach those positions from those people when it becomes convenient to do so. So comprehensively did Agnew emerge on the political scene as the incarnation of law, order, probity, and inflexible ethics, that now that he has fallen, we are made to feel that the case for law, order, probity, and inflexible ethics has somehow fallen too: that ethics is itself subject to bribe and delinquency. This tendency to anthropomorphize our ideals is an American habit that can get us, indeed has just now gotten us, into deep trouble.

The conservative community was outraged when, twenty years ago, Dean Acheson said following the conviction of Alger Hiss that he would not turn his back on Alger Hiss. It was felt then that Acheson was not saying merely that he would stand by, in his hour of need, an old friend—even one who had lied and lied and lied, and who had worked for a foreign dictator, and who had attempted (indeed still does) to bring down an innocent man in order to save his own skin—Acheson was saying not merely that he would stand by that man, but that, in effect, he doubted the processes of justice that found that man guilty. That was why we were outraged.

And we have a right to be outraged against those who, for old times' sake, and in veneration of their ideals as so trenchantly defended by Vice President Agnew, will say now: *I'm standing behind Agnew—Agnew was framed.* Mr. Agnew, reaching for self-justification tonight, is no more plausible than Alger Hiss. He lost his plausibility after looking the ladies of California in the eye and telling them that he would not resign under any circumstances, only to do so a fortnight later, pleading guilty to one felony, and acquiescing in the publication of a dossier of data about his activities which, if it is a tissue of lies, permits us to believe that the Justice Department and the FBI and the Judiciary conspired together to frame Alger Hiss. I do not see that it is a part of our creed to suggest that no one who believes in our creed can succumb to temptation. Rather our political creed is substantially built upon the need to advertise the lures of temptation: government, we believe, is presumptively guilty of self-enhancement at the expense of the people's liberty, and although the definition of a crime is often capricious, and can even be a reflection of idiosyncratic cultural traditions, making it for instance perfectly OK to promise to make someone a judge when you come to power, or even a Vice President, it is in fact wrong for money to pass hands. What you cannot tolerate, in politics, is precisely what is required in law: a consideration. Mr. Agnew knew all this, and it really would not affect one's judgment of what he did if he could prove that while governor he had in fact selected among all the bidders and awarded the contract to paint the ceiling of the Sistine Chapel to Michelangelo. He looked us all in the eyes and said he was not guilty, had done nothing wrong, was being persecuted by the Justice Department, would not resign: And we believed him. I think it right that we should have believed him. But I think it wrong because we have over several years now treated Mr. Agnew and the ideas Mr. Agnew is associated with as inseparable, that we should, in order to attempt to salvage those ideas, attempt to salvage Mr. Agnew. The temptation—our temptation—is, really, to salvage our own pride. The temptation is to say, as so many said to themselves about Alger Hiss: The man I trust is therefore trustworthy.

I began by saying that it is the highest tribute to Mr. Agnew to take his ideals so seriously as to apply them to Agnew himself. To say that the guilty should be removed from power, however great the sacrifice to those of us who are bereft. That we are mature enough to make moral decisions and abide by the consequences. That we are so gravely committed to high standards of behavior that we are willing to renounce those who stray from those high standards—even if they are our friends and heroes.

It is a terrible irony that at the moment in history when liberalism is sputtering in confusion, empty of resources, we should be plagued as we are by weak and devious men. The terrible sadness of Spiro Agnew's existence touches everything we do today: our manifestos, our analyses, our hymns, and our laughter. Through our participation in this adversity we must seek strength, such strength as we derive from knowing that Mr. Agnew was profoundly right about many of the causes of our decline, that though he proved to be a physician who could not heal himself, in his words as uttered over four years there were the rocks of truth, and to these truths, however dazed and saddened, we rededicate ourselves, without hesitation, with faith, with hope, and with charity.

* * *

•Dear Uncle Bill:

My guess is that you will have heard about what my mother did to that woman last Wednesday. My father told us on the phone that it caused quite a stir. Poor mother. I think that the last thing she would want to do would be to get up and strike that woman. What comes to my mind is that if what that woman was saying was bad enough to make my mother mad enough to get up and slap her, I hope she slapped her hard.

Love,
Michael [Bozell]
El Escorial, Spain

—*Excerpts from remarks by Ti-Grace Atkinson at Notre Dame.* "I don't have any time for s— tonight. [The] church's chief source of income today is women's vaginas. [It would have been better if] the virgin had been knocked up. The Women's Movement will take responsibility for [the church's] destruction, because the mother-f—— belongs to us."

—*Excerpts from statement by Mrs. Patricia Buckley Bozell, to the press, March 12.* "I have been brought up to believe that intolerance of blasphemy is a Christian duty. The fact that I was attending the meeting as a reporter forced me to choose, when she began her defamation, between my responsibilities as a member of the press and my responsibilities as a Catholic. The choice was spontaneous, instant and easy."

Dear Bill:
. . . The publicity around here is really remarkable. Over one thousand letters, for instance. I haven't read them yet—glanced through some dozen only—but it intrigues me as to what caught the imagination of the public. Are there some things *really* still holy? When things calm down I will go through them and see if I come up with an answer.

All love,
Trish [Patricia Bozell]

—"The higher the stakes, the greater the temptation to lose your temper. We must not overvalue the relative harmlessness of the little, sensual, frivolous people. They are not above, but below, some temptations. If they had perceived, and felt as a man should feel, the diabolical wickedness which they were committing and then forgiven . . . they would have been saints. But not to perceive it at all—not even to be tempted to resentment—to accept it as the most ordinary thing in the world—argues a terrifying insensibility. Thus the absence of anger, especially that sort of anger which we call indignation, can in my opinion be a most alarming symptom. And the presence of indignation may be a good one. Even when that indignation passes into bitter personal vindictiveness, it may still be a good symptom, though bad in itself. It is a sin; but it at least shows those who commit it have not sunk below the level at which the temptation for that sin

exists—just as the sins (often quite appalling) of the great patriot or great reformer point to something in him above
mere self. If the Jews cursed more bitterly than the pagans,
this was, I think, at least in part because they took right and
wrong more seriously"—C. S. Lewis (as quoted by WFB in
"On Experiencing Gore Vidal," *Esquire,* August 1969).

●The Honorable James L. Buckley
Washington, D.C.
Dear James:
  Next month, I propose to pass through the ivory gates of
the Republic of Zambia for a twenty-one-day period—hope-
fully not my last twenty-one days.
  It has come to my attention that our brother Bill has been
declared persona non grata in that shining example of democracy; and it has further come to my attention that Bill
publicly allowed as how that, "on the whole, he would rather
be banned from Zambia than have to go there."
  Accordingly, on the off chance that our brother's unpopu-
larity with the authorities there might wash off on me, I appeal to you for your aid in securing me the full protection
which has been so gloriously granted by our State Department to vexed Americans wherever they may find themselves in trouble.
  Consequently, would you be kind enough to dust off your
Form Letter #3 and substitute for the sentence "one of our
most illustrious citizens" the words "one of our most powerful witch doctors"? Armed with this and with the seal of your
august office, I will dare to enter Zambia with my worries
confined to elephants and lions. Affectionately,
                                        John W. Buckley
                                        Sharon, Connecticut

●Sirs:
  Mr. William F. Buckley, Jr., in his column [see p. 1079]
makes the following offer:
  "If anyone can find me one vote by Sen. Kennedy in favor
of one measure designed to reduce government spending, I
will retire to the DMZ."

We would point to Senator Kennedy's vote against the ABM as evidence of his concern with wasteful government spending on war.

Would you be kind enough to inform us when Mr. Buckley is leaving for the DMZ so we may arrange an appropriate farewell party?

Richard D. Parker, Michael A. Heifer
Douglas Melamed
Harvard Law Review, Cambridge, Massachusetts

Dear Bill:

On September 19, 1967, I voted in favor of an amendment to reduce by $21 million the Independent Offices Appropriations Bill for fiscal year 1968. Included in this amendment was a sum of $1,177,000 for a new federal building for Springfield, Massachusetts.

Shortly after this vote, when I returned to Western Massachusetts, I learned that there is a lesson to be drawn from economy in government: When you are the senior Senator from Massachusetts, and you want to cut federal spending, don't start by voting against a post office in Springfield.

So I did want to point out that you haven't given me proper credit for keeping my eye on the federal budget. And I can assure you that the DMZ is not such a bad place since we reduced the bombing.

Best regards,
Ted

DMZ
Dear Ted:

You may resume bombing when ready. Now, at last, you have a sufficient motivation.

Best,
—WFB

●Dear Mr. Buckley:

I find it odd that you have failed to quote in *National Review* a passage uniquely useful, though it was written fifteen years ago, about Richard Nixon. You have very little excuse, inasmuch as it was written to you, by Whittaker Chambers, and published in the book, *Odyssey of a Friend.* . . .

B. B.
New York

". . . Some words to update our telephone conversation about Mr. Nixon. My rule is never to mention to anyone my contacts with him. I'm going to break it this once, for a reason, but I wish you not to mention what I shall say. Not long ago, I had lunch with him. He asked us down on Sunday, and we had a long talk. What was said? Except for two minor points, I could not say. I came away with a most unhappy feeling, neither the reason for, nor the exact nature of which, I have been able to explain to myself. I suppose the sum of it was: we have really nothing to say to each other. While we talked, I felt crushed by the sense of the awful burden he was inviting in the office he wants. I felt dismay and gnawing pity, which is pointless and presumptuous, since he seeks the office. He is asking to assume the first post of danger at the moment of the most fearful and (at least) semifinal stages of the transition from the older age to the new. If he were a great, vital man, bursting with energy, ideas (however malapropos), sweeping grasp of the crisis, and (even) intolerant convictions, I think I should have felt: yes, he must have it, he must enact his fate, and ours. I did not have this feeling (I believe Ralph has it). So I came away with unhappiness for him, for all. Of course, no such man as I have suggested now exists? Apparently not. Mr. Nixon may do wonders; he may astonish us (and himself), a new *stupor mundi*. Then I shall have proved the man who, privileged to see the future close up, was purblind. I hope so. I hope, too, that he gets his chance, since that is his wish. But I could not help wondering too: suppose he misses it? I cannot imagine what such a defeat will do to him. Yet I cannot bring myself to believe that his victory is in the bag. In short: I believe he is the best there is; I am not sure that is enough, the odds being so great.

As always,
Whittaker

●(CULTURAL LAG IN THE SOVIET UNION DEPT.)
SOVIET PUBLISHES
PRO-STALIN WORK
Study in Youth Magazine
Encourages Adulation
Moscow, June 15—The most ardently sympathetic literary
portrait of Stalin to appear here in years is being given mass
national circulation in a literary magazine for young people.
—New York *Times,* June 16, 1974

"Directly behind Lenin's tomb is the simple slab beneath
which are the remains of Josef Stalin, removed from alongside Lenin soon after the anathematization in the late Fifties.
But Stalin is gradually rising from the dead. Only a month or
so after we dallied over his perfunctory slab, a bust sprouted
from the ground—an enterprise which could not have required less official attention than the launching of a Soyuz
moon landing. Just this year, the Soviets managed to publish
an official history of World War II without once mentioning
Stalin after 1945—one of those breathlessly humorless accomplishments of which they are so singularly capable, reminding us again and again and again of the undeniable vision of George Orwell. But the hagiolaters will not be forever
denied, as witness the unobtrusive rise, by the Kremlin wall,
of the likeness of Stalin, which like the beanstalk is likely now
to grow week by week back to full trinitarian status with
Marx and Lenin. For one reason because a mid-position on
Stalin is, historically and morally, like coming to rest in mid-
air between the diving board and the water; for another because Communism, or whatever you choose to call what it is
that they practice in Russia, cannot easily allow for a ruler
who, preaching Lenin, proceeded to misgovern for 25 years.
Irregular performances by bad popes well after the consolidation of the Church are one thing. But you cannot announce that Saint Paul was after all a liar, a thief, and a lech-
er, without subverting Christianity. So, in due course, they
will preach that Stalin the Prophet was despised only by the
despicable."—WFB, "A Thousand and One Nights in Soviet
Russia," 1970

•Dear Mr. Buckley,

I always very much enjoy your linguistic prancing showing your vast and deep cultural resources, like for instance "GE- NUS AMERICANUS," in your *National Review* of February 1 last, page 124 (seven lines from the bottom).

Now, I know that "genus" should be used with neuter gen- der, unless you kept "Americanus" to rime with it, making your ex cathedra definition smooth for the eyes of your ad- miring readers? Or perhaps you use Gallic vernacular?

Yours,

Argus

Dear Argus:

Our thought here was that *genus Americanum* sounds kind of faggy.

Cordially,

—WFB

•Dear Bill:

Here's an amusing letter I thought you might like to an- swer personally.

I didn't realize Nixon had kept those leftover JFK and LBJ fructs in the White House, but what can you expect from a guy who looks like a usucar salesman?

Yours,

William Attwood

Publisher, *Newsday*

Dear Mr. Buckley:

Now really what the hell kind of word is this to use in a col- umn directed to the average person with the average vocabu- lary. ["He likes being President. He likes the power, the usu- fructs of the Presidency . . ." *NR*, March 1.] It annoys me to run across any such ludicrous words that I'm supposed to leave my easy chair and dig out the old Funk—to find out what you are about. I realize you know what it means and probably a couple of other people on this planet like the professors of English at Oxford and a fop like Truman Ca- pote. But I'll tell you this, to the average American "usu- fructs" sounds like some Italian guy telling another guy what

kind of loving he enjoys. Really what a stupid word usage—
sometimes you are just too much.

Regards anyway.
Robert Moran
Wantagh, New York

Dear Mr. Moran:
What then would you do to the nursery rhyme,

Could eternal life afford
That tyranny should thus deduct
From this fair land
. . . A year of the sweet usufruct?

●Dear Bill:
The enclosed is for your attention.

—JKG

John Kenneth Galbraith
Cambridge, Mass.
Dear Mr. Galbraith:
I have been a fan of yours for quite some time and I agree
almost 100 percent with your liberal views. I particularly enjoy watching you chew up William F. Buckley during de-
bates.
I would like to ask a favor of you. I possess a hobby and
that is I collect autographs of people I admire. I would appreciate it very much if you would send me your autograph
and I will be very grateful. Thank you and best of luck to you
in the future.

Sincerely,
Mark Sheeran (Age 14)
New York

Dear Mark:
You are at the perfect age to be a fan of Professor Galbraith. He has a new book coming out, and with every copy
you get two popsicles. Watch for it.

Forgivingly,
—WFB

UNITED STATES
ADVISORY COMMISSION ON INFORMATION
WASHINGTON, D.C. 20547
OFFICE OF THE CHAIRMAN

November 15, 1972

Dear Bill:

A note from the Voice of America informs us that they provided you with a Nordmende receiver on a long-term loan basis when you first came aboard.

They have asked me to remind you that if you no longer use the set would you kindly return it to the Agency. Many thanks.

With best personal regards.

Sincerely,
Louis T. Olom

November 21, 1972

Dear Lou:

You advise me that Voice of America asks, do I still have the portable radio they presented me with during my residence as a Commissioner of your august institution, and if so, would I please return it; to which I reply. . . .

Anxious to do my duty, I took the radio on my trip to the Antarctic in January. You may or may not be aware that smack on the magnetic South Pole is a colony of twenty-seven Russians. They are there apparently conducting scientific experiments, pledged to reveal their findings impartially to the world's scientific community. I desired to establish whether the Voice of America has a program beamed to this important colony. On arriving there, together with Secretary Chafee, Senators Goldwater and Buckley, and lesser gentlemen such as myself, I lugged my radio into the underground shelter where the Russians live and work, and while pretending to toast to international comity with vodka and caviar, I surreptitiously twiddled the dial in search of a program beamed to the South Pole. I must confess that I did not succeed, although I cannot say that my investigation was exhaustive, because one of my Russian hosts, suspecting that my concern for my radio in the circumstances was extra-scientific, began singing the Song of the Volga Boatmen most raucously, making it impossible to pursue my search of a signal beamed to the South Pole.

On my return to McMurdo Station, I discovered that the insides of the radio had frozen solid. But I managed, in Hong Kong, to eviscerate the old, and usher in the new, so that by the time I reached New Delhi, the radio was in perfect order, and served me greatly in passing along the news of the day to Ambassador Keating, whose reliance on Jack Anderson for the thrust of American foreign policy normally required him to wait as much as one week for his Washington *Post* to arrive in the diplomatic pouch.

I next used the radio at the meeting of the commission in London, so attached had I become to it—rather to the concern of my colleagues who didn't feel it was a prudent use of my time to monitor the Voice in London while the commission was attempting to interrogate prominent English lords and journalists, but my notebook reports that the Voice reaches London with great assurance, no doubt explaining the amicable relations between our two great countries.

And from there, of course, I went with the President's party to Peking, with my radio in hand—by this time we had become absolutely inseparable. You may have read that a Chinese band played "Home on the Range" at that first banquet in the Great Hall of the People. Well, actually, you have the Voice to thank. Because I was showing it off to the conductor, and remarking on the fine reception in Peking, when he thought to nudge the radio up against the microphone, suddenly drowning the entire hall with the chorus of America's favorite Western song.

But this proved to be the final triumph of the radio. The next night, while my colleagues were listening to the *Red Detachment of Women,* I was instead, though sitting in the auditorium, happily monitoring the Voice—I had bought myself an earplug in Hong Kong, so that I could listen uninterruptedly, without disturbing my companions. Suddenly an Oriental, with a fixed smile on his face, beckoned to me, politely but firmly, just at the moment when, on stage, Ching-hua was being beaten by a running dog. I was taken to a little office and interrogated. What was I doing? I said I was listening to my radio. They said: that isn't your radio, that radio belongs to the Voice of America. I said listen, goddammit, that radio was given to me by the Voice of America, the better to perform my duties for the United States Information Service, and no running dog of a Communist can get away with the slur on my country that when the Voice of America gives a commissioner a radio, that radio still belongs to the government—we're not Communist yet, said I triumphantly. At this point they called in the Chief of the People's Security, who said abruptly: "Our operatives inform us that that radio is still considered to be the property of the United States government. Since it was made quite plain to all correspondents that they could bring to China only their personal property, your radio is herewith confiscated."

So you see, it wasn't my fault. If Voice had told me it was still government property after it was handed to me, I certainly wouldn't have exposed it to all those risks. Perhaps you can ask Henry Kissinger, on his next visit to Peking, to plead with the People's Security Service to return it?

With deepest apologies from your downcast friend,

Wm. F. Buckley, Jr.

*   *   *

●Mr. Melvin Lasky
Encounter Magazine,
London
Dear Mel:

Thank you for your invitation to comment on *Encounter*'s feature. Mr. Ball's amusing, and extravagantly comprehensive, essay on the differences between English-English and American-English fails, I fear, to do much more than document what we all know. I mean by that not that all of us knew the two forms in every given case ("pantechnicon" indeed! No wonder the lorry driver who came on was "articulated"); but that no one was surprised that, often, there are two forms. Even so, I think the problems are neither (a) practical (really, no American I can think of, lying on a British operating table, would balk at the prospect of "lint's" being applied to his open wound, unless he had reason to suspect that the medication in question was an exclusive creation of the Minister of Health. And the Englishman in New York innocently expressing a desire to stroke his hostess' pussy would surely not be misunderstood, always assuming the reasonably conspicuous presence of a cat). Nor, (b), literary. Perhaps there is an idiomatic literature being published in England the force of which I miss by reason of my ignorance of, or inattention to, the divergences Mr. Ball is worried about. But I am serene about it, even as I read American works of great verbal inventiveness, not to say licentiousness. These, however, more often propel me to the serene conviction that, well before the bondsman requites his mortal toil, the neologisms will have reduced to a metabolically reasonable level of assimilation, than to that weightless alienation that so frightens Mr. Ball, moving him to encourage the production of more glossaries. I hope these materialize; but mostly because, as a free market enthusiast, I believe there ought to be a market for philology. I fear, besides, that the alternative is that typical patrons of philology will turn their energies elsewhere, in which case they would do more harm to society than vernacularists are likely to do to language. Although as I say, these patrons are unlikely to get into trouble while visiting London or New York, philologists *can* keep them out of trouble by giving them glossaries and other diversions to wrestle with, occupying their time in intellectually energetic pursuits, and commensurately reducing the time available for devoting themselves to the dangerous business of seeking solutions for public problems.

Yours cordially,
Wm. F. Buckley, Jr.

Dear Bill:

On the way to Heathrow last evening, to catch Pan Am 001 to JFK, just before the Great West Road turns into the M4 motorway at the Hogarth roundabout, one of Berry's giant motor coaches, jammed full of schoolboys, passed my taxi. In the rear windows were three hand-lettered signs held slightly askew smack against the expanse of glass by several impish teenagers. The first one said "SMILE," the middle one said "IF YOU HAD IT" and the third "LAST NIGHT." The young girls in the following Ford Cortina were all giggling. And what appeared to be two young male instructors in the front of the bus were reading intently as we passed—to the right, naturally.

Frank Stanton
New York

Dear Bill:

Sent to the Waldorf, I didn't finish reading the galleys and didn't see "Notes and Asides" until . . . too late. I take no pleasure in predicting with absolute assurance that the pussy passage will offend more readers per square mile than anything of its kind, if ever there was anything of its kind, in *NR*'s history. Not only the word, but its juxtaposition with the superbly sensuous verb "stroke," and then that letter that follows it . . . but it's basically "pussy" that does it.

I think the letter is very funny, but shouldn't be in the magazine. It's like a bawdy joke, hilarious, but told too loud in a public place, and falling on the ears of those who had the right not to hear it, and no forewarning that they would. Even the people to whom it was directed are less amused than shocked at the discourtesy to others. So here: I was shocked. Dan was shocked. Kevin was shocked. ALAN REYNOLDS was shocked. In a ribald time, only the man of known refinement has the power to shock, and I have never seen such power so startlingly exercised as by you, in this case. It is not so much a breach as a laceration of manners, like a violent dissonance in some soft serenade. People will take it as a signal of contempt for their sensibilities, the way I take the incessant use of "motherfucker" by Negroes in buses and subways. You will get hate mail from some who stood by you through "goddamn" and "crap." (How will you explain it to Kuehnelt-Leddihn?)

I learned delicacy from you, Bill, and not only what it is but what its rationale is. Although I'm given to these heated sermons from time to time, I feel a little insolent at directing them at you, as if I were taking my own father over my knee. Forgive me. But I have never known you, of all people, so grossly to underestimate the power of a single word to disgust. And though the line is a good one to those who don't mind the obscenity, to those who do it must look strained, since I don't think any man would use the word "stroke" with reference to a cat as such; you "stroke" the fur, but you "pet" the cat; unless the British idiom is different from ours in this respect too, which I doubt; so that it looks as if you went out of your way to fetch a word of offensive potency. Which I take it is true, though I know the offense was not your intention.

Remember too, Bill, that people read *National Review* principally because they admire you, and they turn to your parts of the magazine almost at once. You must maintain a certain royalty of bearing. We buffoons of departments like Arts & Manners, who must chronicle the perversities of the day in their lewdest forms, may accordingly claim a certain license. Quod licet bovis, you might say.

It goes without saying that in my Utopia, the magistrates would seize every copy of this issue, and clap the lot of us in jail.

Joe Sobran

November 13, 1974

MEMORANDUM

TO: Miss Linda Bridges, Messrs. Dan Oliver and Joe Sobran, and The Legion of Decency.
FROM: Wm. F. Buckley, Jr.

I very much appreciate your candor in the matter of the alleged lapse in taste in the current *NR*. There are several objections, but the gravamen appears to be directed against the sentence in the letter to *Encounter;* nay, against the use of the one word conjoined with the verb "stroke." Indeed Joe is particularly offended because he believes that my use of it was so "strained" as to constitute the major offense, "since I don't think any man would use the word 'stroke' with reference to a cat as such; you 'stroke' the fur, but you 'pet' the cat."

Very informative; except a man *did* use the word, in just such a way—the Australian journalist, resident of Manhattan, who wrote the essay for *Encounter* on which I was asked to comment, Mr. Ian Ball. The gentleman, whose essay was very long and substantial, was here and there uninhibited, but it is not clear that he could otherwise have made his points: ". . . I shall long recall the parting words spoken to the guest-of-honor at a farewell party for an American journalist bound for a London posting: 'For chrissake, remember that *fanny* to them describes the vulva!' (In American-English, it means, cosily, simply the female bottom.) *Pussy* falls into the same category. An Englishman could encounter a strange Ms. holding a kitten in her lap and say to her, quite politely, 'May I see (or hold, or stroke) your pussy?' If he were to make the same remark to an American girl in a similar situation he would most likely—or used to—get his face slapped. On a similar level, Americans and Englishmen have to be fully briefed on the conflicts that arise on different sides of the water over the use of the term *knock up*. Legion are the number of English maidens who have retired red-faced for the evening after asking their American hosts to 'make sure you knock me up early in the morning.'"

So you see, dear friends, how much, in fact, I spared you? Now if you will study the construction of my letter to Lasky, you will note that I was engaged in listing some of the problems that allegedly arise from the different uses of the same word on the two sides of the continent. I began by using quotation marks (around "pantechnicon," and "articulated" and "lint"), because these are words Americans are not used to using in the British way. When I came to the last of the examples given by Ball, I dropped the quotation marks because both the verb and the noun were given in the American usage and did not need the arms'-length labeling. I could very well understand it if you had suggested that this punctuational nicety should have been waived—so as to make it especially plain to the reader that I was transcribing a vulgarity from *Encounter,* rather than coming up with one of my own.

What puzzles me is that it did not occur to you that I was quoting from *Encounter,* my own contribution being merely the business about the nearby cat. If in fact I am seen to do something so completely out of character, isn't it prudent to search for alternative explanations than my swift descent into vulgarity? I remind you that the passage wafted past Priscilla, and Elsie, and Barbara, without causing a wince. It remains to be seen whether the public will read it as you did, or as Priscilla et al. did. I make no predictions on this, I hasten to add: if I can be surprised by what my own colleagues read into a passage, I certainly can be surprised by what strangers who read the magazine will see in it, and it may yet prove that you will be surprised by joy. Although as a general point, I agree that future references to bulbocavernosi should, when they are necessary, be of the nonsniggering type.

In re the Frank Stanton story, a respectful disagreement. I checked: Neither James Burnham, nor Priscilla, nor I, was familiar with the jape. Obviously Frank Stanton wasn't, or he wouldn't have sent it around to his friends as an amusing anecdote. I think it safe to say, then, that readers over thirty will come upon it afresh, and will be refreshed by it. Schoolboy humor can be quite funny. Did you know the football chant of the Norfolk (Virginia) Junior High School? "We don't smoke/We don't drink/Nor-FOLK! Nor-FOLK!")? Hmm.

Now I don't much like scatalogical humor, and it works only when the oxymoronic impact outweighs the vulgarity—as in Bill Rickenbacker's legendary "Conservatives are organizing a paean to the Warren Court. They're going to go down to Warren's chambers and paean him." Wheeler's wasn't that good. But intending no offense, it was much better in the original than in the bowdlerized form. I don't need to remind you, dear Dan, what the effect was when they stroked over the private parts of Michelangelo's Sistine Chapel. Better, in situations like that one, to pull the paragraph (which I authorize you to do) and discuss it at a Taste-Session before the next mag, and we can decide whether (a) to run it; (b) to alter it; or (c) to can it.

I do not mean for this memo to sound contentious. I surround myself (my greatest luxury) with people I love and admire, and not least because they will call me to task, even when I don't deserve it.

●Dear Sirs:
NR has done it with the help of David Brudnoy [May 5]. You've elevated 'mother' to four-letter word status.

National Review has made clear its policy about obscenities—not to use 'those words' itself and to quote others' use with ———— (but give enough info so we all know what the words are).

NR seems something like the sweet young thing who talks about the birds and bees and all that stuff.

Are we conservatives so fragile that u, c, and k's will break our necks but dashes will not harm us?

R. D. Sommers
Berea, Ohio

Dear Mr. Sommers:

Our policy, as stated eighteen months ago, is to spell out the words when necessary, but otherwise, *pas de baissant autours.*

—WFB

●MEMO TO: WFB
FROM: Linda

Readers are beginning to write in asking what is the connection between the cover and the contents of *NR* in the last issue. What shall I tell them?

MEMO TO: Linda
FROM: WFB

Tell them that the connection is there, though it is sometimes elusive; and calls, to be sure, for a little cosmopolitan experience. In the last cover, as of course you know, dear Linda, the Chinese characters on either side of the picture of the nude lady say: *"Just as it is an unusual thing for a man to reach the age of 70, so it is unusual for a woman to have a perfectly shaped breast."* Now: that picture abutted one of Mao Tse-tung smiling, together with Richard Nixon. Mao Tse-tung, as you know, is not considered, in China, to be a mere man. He is more than a man. More in the divine sense, and more also in the sexual sense. You might say that he is an *androgynous god.* But you will have noticed that none of the portraits of Mao stressed his perfectly shaped breasts, quite possibly because he doesn't *have* perfectly shaped breasts. There he is in the picture, next to a smiling Nixon. But Nixon's smile, you will notice if you look at it carefully, is forced: like a lover's smile, after an unsuccessful wedding night. *That* takes you to the metaphor used in the lead story: "The Honeymoon That Wasn't," and back to the Chinese legend: that just as it is unusual for a man to reach the age of seventy, so it is unusual for a Chinese leader *with imperfectly shaped breasts* to have a successful honeymoon with the President of the United States. . . . The issue before, featuring the (clothed) backside of Gloria Steinem, would appear to speak for itself, as witness that the two lead articles were "The Market for Ideas" and "Inflation: The German Experience." Gloria Steinem is widely identified as the principal historian of the German inflation that led to the market for ideas.

●Is it true that you gave orders to your editors that the American Party ticket was not to be mentioned throughout the campaign, in the pages of *National Review*? If so how much did it monetarily profit you personally?

Anon.

Dear Anon:
    No, it isn't true. I have only given one order to the editors, see below.

December 18, 1972
MEMORANDUM
TO: Priscilla, JB, Jeff, Linda, Kevin, Alan, Joe, Pat, Carol, Chris, Barbara, and George Will
FROM: WFB

Two things. We are suffering at *NR* from an epidemic of exclamationitis. Two issues ago, in the review of Garry Wills' book, I was quite certain that Will Herberg would succumb from it, before finishing the review. It is a dreadful way to go. In the current issue, Mrs. Nena Ossa concludes her interesting essay on Chile, "That would be the moment to pack and leave!" "That would be the moment to pack and leave." I submit is a much tenser way of suggesting that that would be the moment to pack and leave. A few pages later, Herr Erik von Kuehnelt-Leddihn, discussing the economic situation in

Spain, remarks that "it is significant that workers who had gone abroad are now coming back in large numbers because wages (for the skilled!) have become quite attractive." Why!? (or, if you prefer, Why?!) The reader had nowhere been led to believe that Erik had constructed his argument in order to mock the superstition that unskilled wages were attractive in Spain. So why? I ASK YOU, WHY!

The other thing. A ukase. *Un*-negotiable. The only one I have issued in seventeen years. It goes: "John went to the store and bought some apples, oranges, and bananas." NOT: "John went to the store and bought some apples, oranges and bananas." I am told *National Review*'s Style Book stipulates the omission of the second comma. My comment: *National Review*'s Style Book *used* to stipulate the omission of the second comma. *National Review*'s Style Book, effective immediately, makes the omission of the second comma a capital offense!

Dear Priscilla:

I have read with dismay WFB's ukase on the serial comma. I can't do it. No way. It's just plain ugly. WFB says this is *un*-negotiable. You're his sister. . . . How serious is he? Can I arrange a dispensation?

Look . . . I'll compromise. There should be peace in the family. Instead of "John went to the store and bought some apples, oranges, and bananas . . ." How about if he just buys oranges and bananas? Or a head of nonunion lettuce. You see what this sort of restriction leads to. And they ask me why fiction is dying. Erich Segal, I bet, uses the serial comma.

You may tell WFB that, from now on and as ordered, I salute the red and white.

Sincerely,
D. Keith Mano
Blooming Grove, New York

P.S. However, the first ukase on exclamationitis was long overdue. The exclamation point may be used only in dialogue and then only if the person speaking has recently been disemboweled.

Dear Priscilla:

In re the serial comma controversy in the current *NR*, on *this* issue, amusing, as, your, comments, are, I agree 100 percent with Bill's ukase on this matter. "My coats are green, red, black and white" means something different from "My coats are green, red, black, and white," as a rather silly example. But in my book the serial comma is a *must*.

Corinna Marsh
New York, New York

Dear Mr. Buckley:

About your *un*-negotiable Style Book ukase: Fowler says the comma before the "and" is considered otiose (his word). Too many sections.

Seventeen years of silence, then the ukase labored and brought forth a comma, by caesuran section no doubt. That indeed is exclamationitis!

Yours,
Vox Dictionarius
c/o George Foster
Los Angeles, California

Dear Vox:

Otiose blotiose. *He dreamed of conquering Guatemala, Panama, San Salvador and Nicaragua?* Without the comma, San Salvador and Nicaragua appear positively zygotic. Is that what you want, Vox? Well, count me out!

—WFB

• Dear Mr. Buckley:

How do you square your "goddamns" with your Catholicism? Are you *really* blaspheming (which I tend to doubt), or is there some distinction between "goddamn" *(NR)* and "God damn" with which I'm not familiar? If so, I'd be interested to know how one makes this distinction in the *spoken* word; also, to have your definition and understanding of "goddamns," not in *my* dictionary.

Ann Jones
New York Hilton Hotel

Dear Miss Jones:

No, I am not really blaspheming, or in any case, do not mean to be blaspheming, blaspheming being one of those things I am against. "Goddamn" is nowadays a simple expletive, and intensifier. It is that by cultural use. In the most cloistered convent in Catholic Spain, you will hear from the venerable lips of an aged nun, "Jesus Mary and Joseph, I forgot my umbrella!" "I would pray hard to his Maker to save his soule notwithstanding all his God-damnes," a writer is quoted by the *Oxford English Dictionary* as saying in 1647, back when they were fighting religious wars. Three hundred years later, the *American Heritage Dictionary of the English Language* lists "God damn" and "goddam" as "a profane [i.e., a-religious] oath, once a strong one invoking God's curse, now a general exclamation . . . used as an intensive."

—WFB

●MEMO TO: Priscilla, Dan, Elsie, Barbara
CC: Library of Congress, Pope Paul, L. Brezhnev
FROM: WFB
RE: The Cover of *NR*, September 13.

We all know, here at the shop, something that our readers have no reason to know. Namely, that the formation of the cover of *National Review* is done in two entirely distinct editorial transactions. At the first, which happens two weeks before we go to press, we commit the cover except for the northeast corner. That we are permitted by the printers to supply two days before going to press.

On the cover in question, we feature an article by "WM. F. BUCKLEY JR." Okay. But then, on the corner, we feature another article—by "WM. F. BUCKLEY JR." Making me, I am morally certain, the only writer in the history of journalism whose name appears twice on the same cover of one magazine. Now this would be astonishing under any circumstances. Given that my name also appears inside as editor in chief, it is appalling. I know, I know, in selecting the last-minute title, the relevant editor forgot about the cover that had been set up a fortnight earlier. The result however has given me great mortification, inasmuch as it might suggest to our readers a certain immodesty in your editor in chief

WHICH YOU KNOW FROM PERSONAL EXPERIENCE TO BE UNTRUE!!
Kindly repent, and prevent recurrence.

•MEMO TO: My colleagues
FROM: WFB

As I hope most of you know, I surrendered a dozen years
ago to the iron requirements of flackery. My mentor Burnham has said of promotional copy that it is to be judged good
or bad by wholly instrumental standards. Accordingly,
though I continue to wince at seeing in *National Review* books
I wrote when barely out of adolescence referred to as masterpieces of literature, I have learned to turn quickly past the
offending page, which has the virtue of being framed on
both sides by contemporary masterpieces of opinion journalism. But now (*NR,* March 1) I see myself referred to as
"America's most literate spokesman for the conservative
point of view." To my great relief, this presumption is committed not by National Review Inc., over which I possess a
technical authority, but by my publishers, G. P. Putnam's
Sons, over whom God knows I exercise no authority at all. I
am reminded of one of WAR's stories concerning the governor of New Hampshire who boasted about his state that it
generated more kilowatts of power per resident senior citizen than any state in the Union: and, having said it, cau-
tioned the press to get it exactly right, otherwise it would be
wholly wrong. Alas, there are not enough qualifiers in G. P.
Putnam's description of me to plead the immunity of the
governor of New Hampshire. Accordingly, I disavow the title, in deference to a score of truly literate Americans. This is
not to be taken as an excuse for failing to buy and read *Four
Reforms.*

*   *   *

•Dear Mr. Buckley:

I am stranded here without my reference library for a couple of weeks, and have come across a sentence from Terence
used as an epigraph of sorts, which I am unable to translate.
Would you be so kind as to do so, and let me have it in the

enclosed envelope? It is: *"Bono animo es: tu cum illa te intus oblecta interim et lectulos iube sterni nobis et parari cetera."* Many thanks.

M. Patrick Glenville
Sun Valley, Idaho

Dear Mr. Glenville:

It defeats me, sorry, and also one or two of my colleagues. Normally, I would write to Garry Wills and ask him to translate it for me. However, I am so outraged by his recent *stupid, preposterous* column on the Shockley debate at Yale, I declared a ninety-day moratorium on any correspondence with him. There are still thirty-two days left. If you can hold out, I'll ask him then, and ship you out the translations to Sun Valley.

Yours cordially,
—WFB

●Dear Sirs:

Since Mr. Buckley has placed me under Interdict [August 2] I must translate for Mr. Glenville through your mediation: [*"Bono animo es: tu cum illa te intus oblecta interim et lectulos iube sterni nobis et parari cetera"*] "Relax. Amuse yourself inside, for a while, with her. Order the banquet couches spread and the other things prepared."

I cannot describe Mr. Buckley's [friend's] column on the Shockley debate as "stupid," since it was written by a student I gave an A to last term. It is just wrong. I would give it a B-minus.

Best,
Garry Wills
Baltimore, Maryland

●Dear Bill:

I completely forget if I have told you about the Jane Chord. It is a critical dowsing-rod invented by Jane Brakhage, wife to the poetic filmmaker Stan Brakhage, and it can be applied with profit to any book by any mortal. To obtain the Jane Chord you combine the first and last words of the book—inflected languages, where words are riveted together, occasionally require that you permit some article or pre-

356   EXECUTION EVE

position to tag along—and if it is a book worthy of human veneration these words combined will state the book's quality in a phrase. Thus the *Aeneid* catches the Virgilian chiaroscuro with "arma/sub umbras"; thus *Ulysses* yields "Stately/ yes"; thus in *The Pound Era,* to group small things with great, we perceive "Toward/labyrinth." I am told that it works also with the *Iliad* and *Odyssey,* but while I can remember the first words of these I cannot recall the last and have no texts here (remember that we cannot expect much of translators). I was once describing this precious principle to the novelist Edward Loomis, and his book *Heroic Love* being handy we inspected it and obtained "In/her." And the *Divine Comedy* yields "nel/stelle," in the stars. Later I discovered that Mallarmé seems to have arrived at this principle for himself and used it consciously to structure poems, leading them from an opening to a closing word in such wise as to expand and adorn that bracketing phrase. His most famous sonnet gives "Le vierge/cygne," and his Poe-poem, "Tel/futur."

At any rate, *Inveighing We Will Go* reverberates, all 160,000 words of it, between the members of surely the most resonant, most majestic, most scintillant Jane Chord of 1972, if not of—what doesn't sound too hyperbolical?—oh, say the Kissinger Epoch: "Herewith/light."

All the best,
Hugh Kenner
University of California

•Dear Bill:
Can you hum the *Die Meistersinger?*
How about the *Il Trovatore?*
Do you dine at the El Morocco?
Does your column run in the *Le Monde?*
No. Then don't say that Galbraith's theory of redistribution was originally discovered by *the* hoi polloi ("On the Right," July 16, 1972). Even with duplicated articles, I like your articles. Keep up the good work.

Sincerely,
Bob Hardwick
Fort Pierce, Florida

Dear Mr. Hardwick:

Nice. Thanks. And now, if I may, from Fowler: "**hoi pol-loi.** These Greek words for the majority, ordinary people, the man in the street, the common herd, etc., meaning literally 'the many,' are equally uncomfortable in English whether the *(= hoi)* is prefixed to them or not. The best solution is to eschew the phrase altogether." "**Pedantry** may be defined . . . as the saying of things in language so learned or so demonstratively accurate as to imply a slur upon the generality, who are not capable or not desirous of such displays. The term, then, is obviously a relative one; my pedantry is your scholarship, his reasonable accuracy, her irreducible minimum of education, and someone else's ignorance. It is therefore not very profitable to dogmatize . . . on the subject."

Cordially,
—WFB

●Dear Mr. Buckley:

One misty Saturday afternoon driving from Dromahair to Mullaghmore to get lobsters for Sunday lunch, I stopped at a small graveyard at the foot of Ben Bulben, and made several snapshots, one of which is enclosed. Yeats' epitaph was as enigmatic to me as it was to Gene Tunney, who asked you to explain the epitaph [see *Cruising Speed*]. Since that time, I have asked countless people if they knew the true meaning, and no one has known. I am delighted to know that, courtesy of Hugh Kenner, you can tell me.

Cordially,
Jay T. Saunders
Memphis, Tennessee

To: Gene Tunney
Dear Gene:

I asked my friend Hugh Kenner, the distinguished critic and scholar, and of course he had the answer you wanted:

Cast a cold eye
On life, on death.
Horseman, pass by.

In the eighteenth century it had become habitual to moralize in one's epitaph, especially to the effect that passersby should meditate on their mortality. The most typical formulation was, *Siste, Viator.* I.e., Stay, traveler: and consider your transience on earth.

But when Jonathan Swift came along, he decided to take the maxim one step further and invite passersby to meditate on the extraordinary accomplishments of Jonathan Swift: i.e., they should pause to consider not only their transience on earth, but also the good uses to which some people, notably J. Swift, had put their days on earth. So, his exhortation to the traveler was not to linger at the graveside, but to busy himself doing good deeds. *Abi, Viator, et imitare si poteris.* . . . Go, traveler, and imitate me.

Now William Butler Yeats, on his deathbed, musing on the evolution of the epitaph, decides that he will moralize to the effect that passersby shouldn't moralize: i.e., that they should be preoccupied neither by their transiency, nor by the meaning of life. However he concludes that it would be condescending to enjoin this lesson upon aristocrats; they know it already. "Horsemen" are aristocrats, in the old usage: i.e., those who could afford to come on horseback as opposed to on foot, or by chartered bus. Whence,

> Cast a cold eye
> On life, on death.
> Horseman, pass by.

He might appropriately have added:

> Translation available from
> Hugh Kenner, University of California
> Send one dollar
> Horsemen, half price.

> My best as ever,
> Bill

*   *   *

●Dear Mr. Buckley:
Many years ago, I remember hearing of an organization

called the Invisible Hand Society. Does such an organization really exist? If so, what does its emblem look like? And is it the sort of organization a thinking man like myself would want to have anything to do with? Is it affiliated with the Committee to Horsewhip Jack Anderson?

Sincerely,
Felix Tilley
Van Nuys, California

Dear Mr. Tilley:
The Invisible Hand Society most definitely does exist, but access to it is difficult, and possible only through: Commodore Donald Lipsett, Hillsdale College, Hillsdale, Michigan. It is one of the virtues of the Invisible Hand Society that it teaches you that, really, you don't *have* to think. . . . No, it was not affiliated with the other committee you have in mind. But get that one straight: it was: The Committee to Horsewhip *Drew Pearson.* Since the sins of the father should not be visited on the son, the committee disbanded when Jack Anderson took over. The old board convened when Jack Anderson published the National Security minutes during the Bangladesh war, but decided to give him a second chance.

—WFB

•Dear Mr. Buckley:
A mutual friend has suggested that we recognize your achievements by awarding you an honorary degree.

I have personally reviewed some of the factors submitted, and I feel that our Board of Trustees would react favorably to your application for an honorary doctorate in Philosophy (PhD) in Business Administration.

Since the number of degrees awarded annually must necessarily be limited, I suggest that you file your application as soon as possible.

I am enclosing the necessary forms. Most sincerely yours,
Milton K. Ozaki, Ms.D., Litt. D.
President, Colorado State Christian College

Dear Mr. Ozaki:
My business administration isn't so good, I mean *NR* is always broke, but at home where we used to have six goldfish, now we have eight!!! So how about an honorary doctorate in the Philosophy of Marine Biology? I can send you lots of references, and a picture of my goldfish.

Cordially,
—"Doc"

P.S. They're already calling me "Doc" here!

•Dear Sir:
Would appreciate very much receiving a word or two stating that you are *not* a member of the bloodstained Council on Foreign Relations. I will be happy to relay this on to some friends who believe differently.

Thank you.
Don Bennett
Elmhurst, Illinois

Dear Mr. Bennett:
No, I am not, but I was a member of the bloodstained United States Infantry.

Yours,
—WFB

•Dear Mr. Buckley:
Of late you have come under strong attack from the Washington *Observer* and a group which plans to try you as a war criminal, Youth Action.
The thrust of their attacks revolves around an allegation that you "advocated the American invasion of Libya and the mass genocidal forced expulsion of the Libyan population into the waterless deserts of North Africa." According to your detractors, it is because "he had his sights on the oil of Libya."
As an avid *NR* reader, I have often heard these accusations. Would you, at least for the sake of this sixteen-year-old

conservative, elucidate your readers upon this matter and set the record straight?

Cordially,
Peter Blackman
Malibu, California

P.S. I would very much appreciate it if you would publish this letter inasmuch as *NR* readers and other conservatives would be at last convinced as to where *you* stand on this issue. Thank you.

Dear Peter:

I reply to your letter only because you are sixteen years old.

A company in which my family has an interest and which operates mostly in Australia and New Zealand bought an option to acquire a share of an exploratory lease in Libya held by an unrelated company, but the option was never exercised and had been abandoned prior to the publication of the article to which the Washington *Observer* refers. I never heard of this option until I made an investigation after the Washington *Observer* asserted that the purpose of the article was to save me oil royalties in Libya. The suggestion that in order to help a Libyan exploration in which a company managed by members of my family had already decided not to invest I would (a) found a magazine, (b) corrupt its directors and editorial board so as (c) fifteen years later to publish an article by (d) a man I never met who (e) proposed military action against the government of Libya with the professed purpose of bringing order to the Middle East but with the true, hidden purpose of (f) facilitating an oil exploration in Libya in which members of my family had once shown an interest, an interest by then abandoned—is a causative sequence which Rube Goldberg would have rejected as a strain on the intelligence. Intelligence, however, is a disqualifying attribute for anyone who seeks to take seriously the commentary of the Washington *Observer,* a smut sheet whose only organizing principle is a full-witted antisemitism.

Yours faithfully,
—WFB

●To the Editor,
Newsday

I have just seen the letter you published by Mr. Louis Eackloff (April 23), wherein he found it "unbelievable that *Newsday* continues to carry the Buckley column. It persists in being full of fabrications, deceit and intentional distortions. His article on Chile is a complete distortion. . . . He completely forgets to mention his family's oil and mining interests in Chile." Not only did I forget to mention my family's oil and mining interests in Chile, my father forgot to tell us he had oil and mining interests in Chile. But since we forgot we had them, it hurts us less that they should now be taken from us without compensation. I wonder, by the way, why Mr. Eackloff forgot to mention that Allende is his father-in-law.

Yours cordially,
Wm. F. Buckley, Jr.

● British Embassy,
Washington, D.C.
7 July, 1970

Dear Mr. Buckley,

I have been asked to thank you for the telegram of congratulation which you sent to The Right Honourable Edward Heath after the General Election.

You kind thought was much appreciated.

Yours sincerely,
John Freeman

Dear Mr. Freeman:

(a) I did not send a telegram of congratulations to The Right Honourable Edward Heath, but (b) your letter thanking me for doing so reminds me how ill-mannered I was not to have done so, and (c) emphasizes a wonderful piquancy, that the former editor of the *New Statesman* should be thanking the editor of the *National Review* for congratulating the people of Great Britain for emancipating themselves from the influence of the *New Statesman*.

Life *can* be worth living.

My most cordial regards.
Wm. F. Buckley, Jr.

*   *   *

●Dear Mr. Buckley:
I read somewhere that you don't send out Christmas cards.
Okay—and you can whistle before I send you a Christmas
card. *Lex talionis,* as you would say.

Regards,
Ella F. Winter
Chicago, Illinois

Dear Miss Winter:
I am sorry; but I recognize the merit of your point. Merry
Christmas. By the way, the law you cite was replaced by the
gentleman whose birth your Christmas cards celebrate.

Cordially,
—WFB

●TU QUOQUE, ELEPHANTINE DEPT. OR LIFTING A VENDETTA OUT
OF PARENTHESES OR THE LONG AND SMOKY MEMORY OF JIMMY
BRESLIN
WFB (in *Esquire,* October 1969, "On Understanding the
Difficulties of Joe Namath"): ". . . (I sound like Jimmy Bres-
lin, God save me) . . . (alas, even Breslin writes like Bres-
lin)."
PENTHOUSE (Interview with Jimmy Breslin, February
1974): "What about William Buckley, do you think he could
have been a good writer if he weren't such a dilettante?
BRESLIN: "Well, Buckley don't write that good. He can't
ever get serious about writing because he really can't do it.
Nobody can follow his sentences."
NATIONAL REVIEW (Interview with WFB, current issue):
"What about Jimmy Breslin, do you think he could have
been a good writer if he pulled his sentences out of all that
beer?"

WFB: "I don't know. I don't think it ever occurred to him to try."

NATIONAL REVIEW: "Is that the *only* thing you don't know?"

WFB: "The only thing I can think of offhand.

—WFB

•Dear Mr. Buckley:
Your syntax is horrible.

Ron Kelly
Mattoon, Illinois

Dear Mr. Kelly:
If you had my syntax, you'd be rich.

Cordially,
—WFB

•Concluding passage from Class Dinner speech, by WFB, at Twentieth Reunion of Yale Class of 1950.

". . . It is by the exercise of reason that one discovers the errors of the particular idealism to which Bukharin remained faithful, and gave his life. But reason also reveals the symmetrical cogency of his final decision to repent, even as reason discloses the irresistible arguments for considering this impure nation of ours as the altogether proper vehicle for our hope, as a continuing source of our critical pride, as the deserving object of our devoted attentions. Surely Yale has failed to register these points, if indeed they are worth registering as we suppose them to be. And to note that Yale's failure is after all not greater than the failure of society at large is twice to obscure the question, because Yale's responsibilities are greater than the responsibilities of the Provinces, Point One; and, Point Two, in fact the Provinces seem to have done much better than Yale at registering the essential points. Mr. Agnew's suggestion that Mr. Brewster be replaced was certainly presumptuous, even as it would be presumptuous for Mr. Brewster to suggest that the Class of 1950 designate a different dinner speaker. But the provenance of a suggestion does not define the merit of it. And anyway, the replacement of an individual does not in and of itself assure that the politics one desires to replace will accordingly be replaced, which after all is the complaint we hear from those who understood themselves to be voting for Mr. Nixon in order to alter the policies of Mr. Johnson in Vietnam. Mr. Agnew's suggestion that Mr. Brewster's replacement would transform Yale is as romantic as Mr. Brewster's suggestion that abandoning Vietnam would compose Yale. Mr. Agnew's interest in the policies of Yale no doubt reflects his assessment of Yale's importance in the public polity, which assessment in no sense differs from that of Mr. Brewster, who also thinks of Yale as a great national institution. Mr. Brewster no doubt rues the fact of his living in a society governed by such as Mr. Agnew, even as Mr. Agnew rues the prospect of living in a society governed by those who are being taught by such as Mr. Brewster to be skeptical-about-the-ability of American institutions to behave justly. There are no ready resolutions to these problems, my very old friends, but I hope we can control at least the snobbish impulse to observe, as was indirectly done by one champion of Mr. Brewster at Yale, that a man with the limited educational background of Spiro Agnew isn't fit to advise so finished an educator as Mr. Brewster. Because, of course, that way Tu Quoque lies; and before you know it, you have Mr. Agnew observing that anyone who cannot control the Students for a Democratic Society on the campus at Yale ought not to instruct the President of the United States on how to control the Communist armies on the Asian continent. If you see what I mean.

"I do think this, that five years from now when we meet again, it will have become clear whether Yale will survive as a private institution devoted to her old ideals. I can only say in defense of my remarks, and others that I have made about Yale during the preceding twenty years, that I hope I have made it clear that I am, most resolutely, on the side of Yale's survival and, not incidentally, the country's survival, in recognizable form."

●*Remarks by WFB at the* Yale Daily News *banquet (May 4, 1973) in honor of* Yale Daily News *Advertising Director Francis Donahue, retiring after fifty years' service.*

Ladies and gentlemen, Mr. Brewster, Francis:

I remember eight years ago when I was running for mayor—an unrequited proposal to the voters of New York City—being informed by the press moments before my scheduled luncheon address to the Overseas Press Club, that at *his* lunch at the other end of Manhattan, Candidate John Lindsay had just uttered a witticism at my expense. "Buckley is such a bastard," Lindsay told his audience, "I sometimes wish he *would* be elected mayor of New York."

I replied with a story impossibly labored, yet splendidly rococo, which I had come across years before in the autobiography of G. K. Chesterton. It appears that at Chesterton's preparatory school, St. Peter's, the headmaster maintained the tradition of delivering a eulogy upon any departing member of the school staff. On this occasion the boys were duly assembled to hear him remark the virtues of a mathematics teacher who was leaving to join the staff at St. Paul's. Chesterton and his fellow students, having endured a dozen such tributes at the hands of an orator whose ponderousness was an institutional plague, settled down to daydream or to doodle. Fifteen minutes into his somnolence Chesterton sat up, having been elbowed by his desk-mate, and indeed the entire assembly was astir. *The headmaster had uttered a witticism!* He had said triumphantly that the boys had witnessed the very act of robbing Peter to pay Paul.

That night Chesterton and his roommate composed an extended fantasy, based on the assumption that the headmaster had devoted the entire sum of his life's wit to plotting a career that would make possible that afternoon's climax. He had studied to become a teacher, had pursued the headmastership of St. Peter's, had hired a young mathematics instructor only after prearranging with St. Paul's that he should in due course be hired away: And thus had he contrived his destiny and others' to make possible his witticism. Thus had I served John Lindsay—in 1965. I wonder now whether Francis hasn't contrived his fifty years so as to deliver me, as a captive audience, President Kingman Brewster, and the Reverend William Sloane Coffin, Jr.

Accordingly, I shall spend the first fifteen minutes in explaining prevalent misconceptions about constitutional law, the next fifteen minutes in discussing needed reforms in educational philosophy, the next fifteen minutes in explaining the background of the Vietnam War, and the final fifteen minutes in explaining the incompatibility of the New Testament and the collected works of the Reverend William Sloane Coffin, Jr.

Such, in any case, was my intention; but I fear that time is running out. Perhaps Jonathan Rose, who is here tonight from the White House, can arrange to supply Mr. Brewster and Mr. Coffin with a tape recording of my views on these matters.

I reach, on this occasion, to speak very briefly of matters that are not strained by factional attachment, or are weary to the ear of the weary. Though Hank Luce's suggestion a moment ago that it is *Republicans* and *conservatives* who have attempted to impose conformity upon American life reminds me of the great line in Sir Walter Scott: "Oh Geordie, jingling Geordie! It was grand to hear the baby Charles laying low the guilt of dissimulation, and Steenie lecturing on the turpitude of incontinence." A return to Yale, for most of those who are here for the occasion, is among other things a surcease from the strains of the world of power and commerce. On the other hand I hasten to reassure the members of the *Yale Daily News* that the temptation does not cross my mind to reminisce about the Yale I knew. The Yale I knew, after all, I memorialized in a volume I published a year after graduating, which sits at the bedside of President Brewster.

Let me say just this, that the experience of those of us who served on the *News* was very special. It is as it should be that you should manage the institution as you see fit. But it would be a pity if you did not know, because you did not happen to experience, such an organization as we knew. I am in no position to pass judgment on what changes you have effected or inherited, or on whether such changes were necessary in order to accommodate academic requirements or extra-academic and extra-journalistic distractions.

I do remember wondering, at least once during the period when I heeled the *News*—which term, I understand, is far-gone in desuetude, rejected alike for its singularity and ignominy—whether there was any justification for an effort so very time-consuming. I had been made aware by my brother Jim of the pleasure he got from the friends he made on the

News, but I did not know, beyond the general way in which one knows these things, very much about the quality of the experience, or the strategic impact of it. I came to realize that it grew out of a rather stern insistence upon excellence. I am not suggesting that excellence was achieved by paradigmatic standards. But that excellence was exacted to the extent that the reserves were actively or latently there. It mattered a great deal to the associate or senior editors that sentences should be lucid, that attention should ingeniously be given to detail, that the data should be accurate, that bias should be contained, that words should be carefully used, that headlines should neatly communicate. Having said as much I hasten to say this, that I know that I would be appalled to be confronted at this point by any stretch of prose for which I was responsible during the time I was here. I dwell on the point only in order to remark that, as I think back on it, the time we spent as heelers, and the time we subsequently spent as editors and as officers of the *News*, must have been given as ungrudgingly as it was because we felt that we were laboring usefully: on the one hand to produce a respectable product, on the other to train ourselves in a craft—as writers, to compose communicable prose; as businessmen, to learn something of the constituent parts of journalistic commerce.

I make the point tonight because during the last period of years, elsewhere and presumably also at Yale, the attitude became here and there fashionable that college journalism is a form of release. That it is justified largely as a means by which individuals can magnify the sound of their opinions, or indulge the scope of their petulances. We live, after all, in an age that is greatly tolerant of the notion that one communicates best by tactile contact and that knowledge is communicated by osmotic processes which it is vain to seek to understand, let alone to parse; in an age that flirts with the suggestion that it is an effrontery to suppose that there are standards to be observed; that there is life in form, let alone inspiration in it.

It may be that from the self-indulgent slouchiness of that movement there will be a residue of spontaneity that will enliven journalism, even as it has been enlivened by the New Journalism, out there, of Tom Wolfe, and Gay Talese, and Garry Wills. But see how these gentlemen are disciplined.

They could, each one of them, write you an anthologizable news story, before midnight, on a crisis in the department of garbage collection or in the department of sociology—indeed they can even manage to distinguish between the two.

I think it safe to say that there are two kinds of college newspapers. To reach for a convenient division, they are the papers whose achievement is measured simply by the raw manufacture and delivery of the paper, and the service done to the vanity of those whose names appear as by-lines and on the masthead; and those other papers which, however erratic their performance, are instantly recognizable as artifacts presented with passion, with pride, and with joy. It is a participation in such an enterprise that gives true satisfaction, bringing together people of sensitivity and depth. I wish you all the happiness that that experience brings.

Our host tonight, representing the 1973 Board, undertook, quite alone last summer, to right, single-handedly, an inadvertent negligence that might have resulted in an egregious injustice. Though still an undergraduate, he is the true patron of this evening. The venturesome good will of the chaplain of the university toward the guest of honor will lighten his burden in purgatory—he is perhaps the residual beneficiary of this occasion. The benevolent auspices that only the president of Yale can provide are particularly exhilarating tonight inasmuch as once he was the heeler, while the guest of honor was sovereign.

And then, of course . . . The last time I attended a banquet of the *Yale Daily News,* the guest of honor was the retiring president of Yale, and the speakers were five presidents of the principal colleges in the Ivy League. One of them, a year or two later, became President of the United States, and the others continued for many years to command the destinies of illustrious institutions.

The guest of honor tonight is not known outside the boundaries of Yale, or the memory of Yale graduates. But I recall at this moment the toast that President Kennedy gave at the White House on the evening that he had collected there all the writers and doctors and scientists who had won the Nobel Prize. The dining room of the White House, Mr. Kennedy remarked, had not been so greatly honored since Thomas Jefferson ate there alone. I know that you will agree with me when I suggest that our guest of honor tonight ranks first among all who have appeared at these banquets, in the affection and admiration of this company.

Excerpts, from Address by WFB to the Red Cross Convention, Vancouver, B.C., April 1972.

"I do not pretend that I am here only to register my enthusiasm for the Red Cross. I could after all have done that, accepting to be sure certain risks about its arrival, by Western Union. I am also here to celebrate my enthusiasm for Mrs. Taylor, and to register publicly my docility as her son-in-law. If you are inclined to wince at my mention of matters so personal, permit me to remind you that my devotion to my mother-in-law, far from being irrelevant to your annual meeting, contributes substantially to its solvency.

"Accordingly, I expect you to listen with great patience to any reminiscence I impose on you respecting Babe Taylor. I am, after all, forty-six years old, and this is the first time I have had an opportunity to speak in her presence without the risk that she will contradict me, change the subject of my discourse in mid-sentence, observe that the chair on which I am tilting is an irreplaceable antique, close the bar, or turn off the electricity.

"Babe Taylor has of course served the Red Cross for more years than I have served her. For all that she has accomplished prodigies as a civic servant, she has been first and foremost a wife, a mother, and a mother-in-law. She is a pillar of reliability not only in community relations, but also in family relations—where her authority is absolute, except when her sense of humor is provoked, and inasmuch as her sense of humor is more easily touched off than Bob Hope's, her family usually manages to navigate around her sense of order and rectitude by the simple expedient of making her laugh.

"I know of only one occasion when this failed. Her late husband, the formidable Austin C. Taylor, was a taciturn man, particularly touching his business affairs, concerning which his family notoriously knew nothing. On one occasion, many years ago, Babe came home bursting with organizational pride, and launched at lunch time into an extended account of her prowess in her capacity as chairman of the Vancouver Ladies Society in shepherding the society away from—let us call it the Brighton Hotel—where for years the society had had its headquarters at considerable profit to the Brighton Hotel—on over to the—let us call it the Piccadilly Hotel. Babe bubbled on about how she had finally won the fight, and had just that morning signed a ten-year lease in behalf of the Ladies Club with the Piccadilly Hotel. Austin Taylor was stirring his coffee wordlessly throughout the extended account by his wife of how she had maneuvered the club in the desired direction. At this point he spoke up. 'You know something, Baby'—as he called her—'you own the Piccadilly Hotel.'

"It is recorded that she did not speak to him for two weeks, and only then after forcing him to sell the hotel, preferably at a loss.

"Babe Taylor is a running welfare department of her own, providing to her friends and to her family an inexhaustible supply of affection, guidance, encouragement, loyalty, shelter, and peanut brittle. I know that those of you who know her personally will not take offense at my exceeding my authority in proposing a toast to her, gratefully and affectionately, from her friends and family."

KATHLEEN ELLIOTT TAYLOR
August 15, 1896–September 28, 1972

XI.

Taming the Kids

Generals and Kids at Yale

April 26, 1972

YOU WILL recall that early in the month General Westmoreland, who is the Chief of Staff of the Army, went to Yale at the invitation of the students' Political Union. They took him to dinner, and then began to propel him toward the auditorium. But at that point an aide to the general reported that the massive wall of shouters and hecklers made it impossible for Westmoreland to speak, unlikely that he could accomplish anything by trying to make his way to the podium, and just possible that he might be physically assaulted. So the general pulled out of his pocket a politely worded statement declining to go ahead with his speech, and inviting student leaders of the anti-free speech movement to visit him "in peace and dignity" in Washington, where he would receive them and communicate his message.

The president of Yale, Mr. Kingman Brewster, pulled some boys-will-be-boys boilerplate from his bookshelf, spliced it with a little lard on the general subject of academic freedom, and went back to worrying about how hard it is for a black man to get a fair hearing in New Haven. The student newspaper, frightened at being censorious, did a perfunctory editorial, and published a regular columnist, a young man of exquisite discernment who announced, "I think that Westmoreland is a war criminal," and argued that depriving Westmoreland of a platform had been not a theoretical or philosophical or constitutional deprivation, but a tactical blunder, because it prevented a Yale audience from acquiring firsthand knowledge of Westmoreland's criminal mentality.

All this proved to be too much for Eugene Rostow, professor of law, former undersecretary of state for political affairs, and former dean of the Yale Law School. He addressed an open letter to the president of Yale and the fellows of Yale

375

University. He might as well have addressed it to his wife, for all the publicity it received. To be sure, the New Haven press gave it notice. But the *Yale Daily News* (as of this writing) seems to be taking the position not only that Yale students shouldn't hear Westmoreland, but that Yale students shouldn't hear distinguished professors who believe that Yale students should hear Westmoreland.

Mr. Rostow began: "In my considerable experience at Yale, I have never before known a situation that justified a direct appeal to the Corporation by students and by members of the Faculty." He went on to cite the commitment of the university to academic freedom, and criticized the president's statement as being inadequate because it "did not order an independent investigation to determine whether disciplinary proceedings against the students involved should be brought, or criminal charges preferred against those who, through the use of force, deliberately made it impossible to hold the meeting at which General Westmoreland was scheduled to speak."

Mr. Rostow then reminded Yale's officials that the student newspaper had carried notices that students would try to break up the meeting, and even so, adequate preparations were not taken; and that no apology had been extended to General Westmoreland. "The weakness of your statement invites worse trouble. But it is to be deplored for a deeper reason. It does not begin to meet your responsibility to the laws of this community, and especially to the laws protecting academic freedom."

Unofficial Yale is taking the line that, after all, Westmoreland didn't try *physically* to speak, and therefore, *in a sense,* his rejection was *platonic.* After all, isn't it true, one worldly professor with a copious memory points out, that Adlai Stevenson was heckled in 1956 by the students to the point where he couldn't speak, but after all, he tried for about ten minutes. . . . Yes, it is true, and it is also true that the students should have been disciplined at that time, if indeed they were not. What is wrong about the current situation is most cogently singled out by Eugene Rostow. It is less that students can behave like Nazi youth squads, it is that there is something less than a universality of disapproval of those that do. Name one person who came to the defense of the hecklers of Adlai Stevenson.

Perhaps it isn't so bad elsewhere. A freshman profile published in the *Yale Daily News* reveals that it is further left than most American universities. Sixty percent of the freshman class considers itself "liberal," 14 percent "far left"—as compared to 41 percent and 3 percent for the rest of the country. Twenty percent of the freshmen think of themselves as "middle of the road," 6 percent as "conservative"—compared with 42 percent and 14 percent nationwide. Somebody ought to write a book about the left-mindedness at Yale University. The trouble is nobody would believe him.

Secretary Fonda

July 27, 1972

No DOUBT about it, if George McGovern is elected President, he will name as his Secretary of State Miss Jane Fonda. She is already practicing for the role, and indeed it is widely conjectured that she hasn't been informed that she isn't yet the Secretary of State. If that is so, that is just one of the things she hasn't been informed about, a lack of information having plagued Miss Fonda during much of her life.

You see, she turned rather earlier than most people to her career, leaving Vassar College prematurely and turning enthusiastically to ecdysiasm, and on into formal acting. A few years ago, when she hit young middle-age, she discovered social conscience, and has been playing it, using the Method approach, ever since. One commentator, after a Fonda performance, observed that "being socially involved may be the mating call of the 1970s. Like knowing how to dance the tango in the Thirties." Miss Fonda goes tirelessly about the college circuit and grunts out her views on international policies, which views are always at the expense of United States policy. She donates the proceeds of her lectures to an organization in Washington staffed by Mark Lane, the lawyer who a few years ago concluded, as I remember, that it was Allen Dulles who shot John Kennedy, not Lee Harvey Oswald.

Nor is there any danger, after the Vietnam War is over, that Miss Fonda will run out of causes. She has been greatly fired up about women's liberation, Indians, Cesar Chavez, grapes, lettuce, the Dutch elm disease, and poison ivy. "She may well be the only revolutionary with her own PR man," *Life* magazine once commented, adding with chivalrous understatement that Miss Fonda's "command of facts and complexities is unconvincing." But, of course, ignorance is an instrument of oppression deployed by the bourgeois classes, and Miss Fonda, who last week termed Richard Nixon "a very serious traitor," will not surrender her vast investment in it. She is Miss Grim, walking about the world hectoring American institutions with what one writer has characterized as her "solemn, Red Guard face," never smiling, never laughing, never, obviously, looking into the mirror.

Her most recent report has been to the effect that American prisoners in Hanoi whom she interviewed desire to see the defeat of Richard Nixon and the election of George McGovern. Now to begin with, Miss Fonda is so easily deceived, we cannot know for certain whether she actually was in Hanoi. Maybe she was in Tokyo, and didn't know the difference. And maybe the "prisoners" she interviewed, dressed in those funny costumes, were actually McGovern delegates from Massachusetts, telling her what she wanted to hear. But assuming it was as represented, there is genuine pathos behind the uses the North Vietnamese have made of the poor dumb American actress. When Commander Bucher was in prison in North Korea, being tortured every day, he did in fact get a letter through to his wife. It was the summer of 1968, and he told her that if he were home, he would vote for Richard Nixon. He felt that Lyndon Johnson had let him down by not authorizing instant action to prevent the *Pueblo*'s capture.

But Commander Bucher, reviewing the matter in his book a year or two later, recognized what is, on reflection, obvious, namely that the prisoner of war quite naturally thinks exclu-

sively of his own concern, which is to reach home. Those who
do otherwise are martyrs and heroes, and they are not only
uncommon these days, but unfashionable. The return of the
American prisoners of war is a concern of the United States.
But it cannot be the *only* concern of the United States. If it
were, there would be no prisoners in the first instance. If
peace were the only concern, there would be no bombs.

But we venture outside Miss Fonda's command of facts
and complexities. She thinks like a calliope programmed at
the Lenin Institute. "Men like [Nixon and Agnew] are war
criminals under every international law," is one of hers (she
has been secretly studying every international law). "But,"
she adds magnanimously, after sentencing Agnew, "I would
not like to see him executed." He should simply be put away,
to devote himself, one supposes, to a lifetime study of the
thoughts of Jane Fonda.

The Students: What Is Their Problem?

December 24, 1972

I SPOTTED the scholarly and irrepressible Anthony Burgess,
the English novelist-essayist-fantasist (author of *A Clockwork
Orange,* among other things), giving advice publicly to his
students (he is visiting America, teaching at the City College
of New York). And what he said to the students, among other things, was: "I would ask you only to expand your vocabu-
laries, develop a minimal grace of style, think harder, and
learn who Helen of Troy and Nausicaä were. And for God's
sake, stop talking about relevance. All we have is the past."

Mr. Burgess was musing about the college students he
comes in contact with at a university that practices an open
admissions policy. Mr. Burgess was tactful about the whole
thing, but he gave away his meaning, which is that the adul-
teration of education results in phony education. And when
that happens, what you develop is new universities. When

egalitarian ideology overtakes these, then "super-universities will be built"; and after that, "super-super-universities . . . This can go on forever. Ultimately, the gods of learning are not mocked. The term 'university' may be rich in noble connotation, but it means only what we want it to mean."

Professor Burgess gave an example of a student essay on *Macbeth* to which soon he must give a pass mark: "Lady Mackbet says she had a kid not in so many words but she says she remembers what it was like when a kid sucked her tit so I reckon she was a mother some time and the kid must have died but we dont hear no more about it which is really careless of Shakesper because the real reason why Mcbeth and his wife are kind of restless and ambitious is because they did not have a baby that lived and perhaps this is all they realy want and S. says notin about it."

Mr. Burgess provokes us by juxtaposing against that passage one from another student, presumably in the same class, whose grade—one assumes—is going to be indistinguishable from that of the young man who penetrated to the heart of Mr. and Mrs. Macbeth's difficulty. The other student wrote: "The weakly placed negatives in Dr. Faustus' penultimate line—'Ugly hell, gape not, come not, Lucifer'—may conceivably be taken as expressive of a desire, not implausible in a Renaissance scholar, to dare even the ultimate horrors for the sake of adding to his store of knowledge."

Now hang onto the point for a minute, please, and reflect on one of the recommendations of Mr. Burgess. He believes that "the division between a scientific discipline and a humanistic laxness is already manifesting itself in undergraduate lifestyles. The banner-waving students who hold protest meetings are merely indulged. They will, regrettably perhaps, never rule America; America will be controlled by the hard-eyed technicians who have no time for protest."

We should shrug off those intimations of that passage that fuel the superstition that we are being managed by a military-industrial complex. (It would appear plain that this is not the case.) But one hears plaintively the call of Mr. Burgess to his students to "expand" their vocabulary. I note, among the Christmas advertisements lying around, one for a new radio receiver: "There's 150 watts IHF power, a loudness compensating switch, power output/heat sinks, IF/FM/ multiplex decoder, FM muting, FM Stereo."

Now, the advertising agency that wrote those words is not putting on the dawg. It is, as they say, "communicating." It is communicating, one supposes, not only to the "hard-eyed technicians" who are getting educated in the colleges, but to students in general. It is not afraid to use words and terms which are demanding—I, for instance, deficient in the appropriate education, do not have the least idea what the manufacturer is talking about—"power output/heat sinks" indeed! Lady Macbeth was never so inscrutable.

The moral is that the resistance to a rich vocabulary is inconsistently exercised. When the talk is of scientific or mechanical things. the public is altogether acquiescent to strange and minutely differentiated terms. Is this what Mr. Burgess is saying, namely that the difficulty of making distinctions in human and social affairs leads people to Tarzan-talk in the classroom, the same people who can talk to the hi-fi people with maximum scientific sophistication? Worth musing upon during the holidays.

Crisis in Princeton

December 2, 1972

THERE IS A most amusing, and not uninstructive, hassle going on in Princeton, and here is the narrative.

A young man called T. Harding Jones, freshly graduated last spring, agreed to serve as editor of a modest publication called *Prospect* magazine, financed by a few Princeton alumni who are concerned about the direction of Princeton education. They are conservatives who feel that in recent years Princeton has become unbalanced politically and ideologically, rather a center for liberal and radical indoctrination than for orderly and dispassionate study. There are lots of ways of looking into such questions. The easiest being to ask professors whom they voted for, particularly in this last election, since the differences between Nixon and McGovern are symbolically decisive. Accordingly, Jones decided to take a poll.

A poll had been taken four years earlier, by the *Daily Princetonian,* the student newspaper. That poll resulted in 71 percent for Humphrey, 7 percent for Nixon and 7 percent for Dick Gregory. That last passes for humor in the faculty lounges of the Ivy League, but let it pass. Jones was eager to see what, among the learned community of Princeton, had been the movement of opinion as regards Nixon between 1968, when faced with a liberal-moderate, and 1972, when faced with a liberal-radical.

To his dismay, he learned that the *Princetonian,* for reasons unknown, did not plan to take a poll this year. So Jones, who is more enterprising than Colonel Sanders, called the president of the Whig-Clio Society, a debate and public discussion group, and asked him if Whig-Clio, a plausible sponsor for such a poll, would agree to address the ballot to members of the faculty. Jones agreed to pick up the cost of printing and mailing the ballots, and the president of Whig-Clio went along. The ballots went out to 500 members of the faculty.

When they came back, the preliminary tabulation revealed that McGovern was the favorite of the Princeton faculty by 82 percent, Nixon running second with 7 percent, and Doctor Spock, Shirley Chisholm, and Mickey Mouse running way behind. In other words, while the country went for Nixon up from 44 percent in '68 to 61 percent in 1972, the Princeton faculty stayed, unmoved, at 7 percent for Nixon, and gave Dick Gregory's old votes to McGovern. Even so, young Mr. Jones pronounced himself as very encouraged, because this time he counted three members of the Social Science and Humanities departments voting for Nixon whereas last time there had been none.

It is perhaps on account of this embarrassment that rumbles began to be heard from the faculty, and before long it transpired that the poll had not in fact been initiated by Whig-Clio, but instead by young Jones, acting for *Prospect* magazine. The council of Whig-Clio thundered against the deception as did members of the faculty . Jones replied that he had no apologies to make, that he simply assumed that any political poll sponsored by an ideologically uncommitted body would elicit more accurate replies. "You wouldn't expect the Young Republicans or the SDS to be ideal sponsors of such a poll," he said.

One professor of politics, Edward R. Tufte, said that the poll's results couldn't be trusted because, among other things, you couldn't trust the response rate. But in fact over 40 percent of the faculty replied to the poll. Relying on a very small fraction of 1 percent Gallup was able to predict the outcome of the last presidential election to within a single point. It was Professor Knapp of the English Department who really said what the faculty protesters had in mind when he questioned "whether the faculty should ever be polled on anything."

What strange immunities, these faculty members want. *Time* magazine pollsters published, shortly before election day, detailed breakdowns based on polls of old men, old women, young men, young women, students, nonstudents, engineers, doctors, Negroes, Jews, Catholics, Adventists, lesbians, vegetarians. Why shouldn't the faculty of Princeton University divulge their views on their political preferences? No one suggests that answering Whig-Clio's postcards was obligatory, and nobody can cogently maintain that it was a substantive deception for Jones to desire the same information routinely elicited only four years ago by the college newspaper.

It is curious how so many of those who are constantly talking about the free flow of information should recoil from contributing to that free flow of information. Well, the faculty succeeded in intimidating the poor students of Whig-Clio. They have pledged to write letters of apology to all the faculty members polled. I recommend to Mr. Jones that after ascertaining the final count, he leak the figures to Mr. Dan Ellsberg who can in turn give them out to the Associated Press. That would silence the Princeton faculty: and who could object to that?

Sex and Ideology at Princeton

April 2, 1973

So THE Sex Education, Counseling, and Health Clinic at Princeton University, for reasons compelling as will be noted, decided to distribute to all Princeton students a "Birth Control Handbook"—presumably, among other reasons, to ease the pressure on the Admissions' Office, a generation hence, of applicants who list both parents as being Princeton graduates. So far, pretty much routine. Most colleges shove out such information as a matter of course. But this handbook is special.

Before being distributed, it obtained the imprimatur of the Advisory Council to the Clinic, a fifteen-member body which includes the vice-president for administrative affairs, the associate dean of the college, and the assistant dean of student affairs.

The handbook advises Princeton students on anatomical and sexual nuts and bolts, but there is more to come, as one might have anticipated from the cover design of the handbook which features a clenched-fist revolutionary salute and the slogan "Medicine for the People." "The fact that Zero Population Growth claims to direct its propaganda primarily at white, middle-class Americans," explains the Princeton handbook, "does nothing to eliminate the factor of racism which is an inevitable historical aspect of the U.S. population-control movement, financed and directed by America's white ruling class."

The handbook touches on quite a lot of extra-sexual points, for instance, pollution. "We are the villains because we drive to work in the only transportation system made available by GM, Ford, and Chrysler. We are the villains because America's biggest industry is the war industry, that bleeds taxpayers dry and exists only for death, destruction, and ecological tragedy."

But even as the handbook has solutions for unwanted

pregnancies, it has them for such social tragedies: Maoism. "For solutions, we have to turn to new methods of governing ourselves. The 700 million Chinese accomplished this by overthrowing their foreign exploiters, by taking control of their own natural riches. . . . Nothing short of equally basic social change in America and in the countries it exploits is going to bring solutions to our terrible problems of hunger, pollution, crime in the streets, racism, and war."

Meanwhile, the *Princeton Alumni Weekly* is carrying on a spirited investigation of life on the Princeton campus. Miss Susan Williams, of the Class of 1974, writes in a column "On the Campus" that the best guess is that 30 percent of the Princeton girls live with Princeton boys regularly, and an equal percentage irregularly.

Now this can become troublesome, says Miss Williams. Not because there is anything wrong with such arrangements, but because they can be simply inconvenient. "Those who must fare with an actual roommate of the opposite sex," she explains, "everyday find themselves coping with more pressing exigencies. One girl, trapped in a one-room double, described how 'they hung a curtain down the middle of the room and then played the stereo loudly until 3 A.M. every night to drown out other noises.' And sometimes it can be just plain tiresome and frustrating to have to relate to an unrequested interloper among one's chosen roommates."

"One still hears it said," concludes Miss Williams—"not by students but by outsiders or older people, that students aren't engaging more in sex than they ever did; they just talk more freely about it. Somehow, though, it's hard to believe that a generation ago a woman could say that '30 percent of my friends are living with one person, and another 30 or 40 percent are sleeping with others.'"

Now here is a suggestion I would like to make to the authors of the Princeton handbook. The Maoist Revolution happens to be quite extraordinarily orthodox, not to say prudish, in sexual matters. In the People's Republic of China, men and women are quite thoroughly celibate until they marry, and, like free love, prostitution is proscribed. So why don't Princeton Maoists begin their revolution by cleaning up sexual immorality in Princeton? Isn't that a good idea? *Then* they can move on to hunger, pollution, crime in the streets, racism, and war. I bet they never thought of that. But there will be future editions of their Birth Control Handbook.

XII.

Morals, Manners, Mannerists

Vietnam Blindness: What Is
Morality?

January 8, 1973

THE SWEDES are puzzled that Mr. Nixon has suspended the conventional exchange of ambassadors between the two countries. All the Prime Minister of Sweden did was link the American bombing of North Vietnam with Nazi massacres in World War Two and describe the bombing as a "form of torture" reminiscent of atrocities committed at Katyn, Lidice, and Treblinka.

One would think that the problem is exclusively Swedish, i.e., that in Mr. Olof Palme they have a Prime Minister, presumably very gifted in other matters, who is however incapable of orderly thought when it comes to Vietnam. After all, the obsession has been with him for a very long while. It was five years ago that he marched side by side with North Vietnamese in the demonstration against—well, southern resistance to North Vietnamese demands is the only historically objective way of putting it.

But it isn't a Scandinavian disease. Perhaps Mr. Palme, whose country pemitted Nazi troops to march back and forth between Finland and Norway, is psychologically ill at ease with the historical fact that Americans fought to save Europe while the Swedes practiced nude bathing, or whatever. But that is a narrow observation, because it hardly disposes of Mr. Palme's American counterparts, who have no inferiority complex about the Second World War.

Consider Mr. Wilfred Sheed, a learned and morally acute, if not acutely moral, novelist and critic, a man of exquisite gift for distinction. He wrote last Sunday: "To some of us, this war is the greatest sin we ever expect to find ourselves involved in, and our private spiritual lives are comparatively trivial next to the task of stopping it." I would not have believed such a sentence could have been uttered at the LBJ

389

Unbirthday party in Chicago in 1968 by Paul Krassner. But there it is. I had not known what escalation meant until discovering from Mr. Sheed that there are forces in the world, let alone forces Mr. Nixon has been loosing, which are capable of reducing private spiritual life to triviality.

What do these people see and read and whom do they mix with? Miss Pauline Kael, the movie critic, may have given us the clue to the polarization about which we have heard so much. At a meeting of the Modern Language Association during Christmas Miss Kael offered this introspection: "I live in a rather special world. I know only one person who voted for Nixon. Where they [i.e., the Nixon supporters] are I don't know. They're outside my ken. But sometimes when I'm in the theater I can feel them."

Such a presence as Miss Kael occasionally feels, sitting anonymously in a theater with her, wrote a letter last week to the New York *Times.* It says, really, all there is to say.

"I do not want to argue about the political wisdom of our active participation in the tragic Indochina conflict, about the correctness of the domino theory or the skill of our military operations. But one major issue is simply begging for scrutiny and clarification. It is the moral aspect of this particular war.

"Let us suppose for a moment that East Germany has invaded the Federal Republic, with a formidable array of the most modern Soviet arms, under the guise of helping local Communists and with the avowed aim of overthrowing the existing regime. Villages would be burned, provincial capitals reduced to shambles by devastating artillery fire, servants of the Government summarily executed and relatives of West German soldiers killed.

"Moreover, parts of Switzerland and Denmark would be occupied to better infiltrate the war zone. On top of it all, they would pretend that there are no East German troops in the West.

"Armed support of West Germany in such circumstances could be found too risky and strategically inadvisable, as during the Hungarian and Czechoslovakian tragedies of the last decade. But—except for the Communists—scarcely one voice would be raised to condemn our possible intervention as immoral, all loss of life and prisoners of war notwithstanding.

"Comparisons are never perfect. U.S. stakes in Europe are much higher than in Southeast Asia, and so are the risks. Yet, the fundamental issue is the same: Shall we or shall we not come to the help of friendly nations invaded by totalitarian neighbors? And if we do, can our action be called immoral?

"All wars are brutal and inhuman. But 130,000 people would not have died during a single raid in Dresden if Hitler had not invaded and devastated half a dozen European countries, killing millions in the process. Not a single bomb would have been dropped on Hanoi if Hanoi had not invaded and devastated South Vietnam, Laos and Cambodia."

Reexamining the Pot Sanctions

December 15, 1972

IT IS EASY to denigrate any cause by the technique of putting it alongside other, nobler causes. Thus a decade or so back Mr. John Roche elegantly dismissed the fear of guilt by association as ranking, by his hierarchy of fears, between Fear #25 and Fear #27, the former being Mr. Roche's fear of college presidents, the latter his fear of being bitten to death by piranhas. The trouble with the technique is that it does not make room for ad hoc preoccupations: for individuated concerns. Somewhere, somebody is being eaten by piranhas, or is worrying about that possibility. Somewhere, somebody less secure than Professor Roche actually worries about the disposition of his college president. Surely that is the point, namely that an obliging community should be willing to devote itself to matters that do not rise to the status of eschatology. For instance the crazy pot laws.

I do not see why we cannot proceed on the assumption that although the fear of marijuana, the need for marijuana, and the ignorance of marijuana are neither (a) the central concern of a balanced society; nor (b) the most urgently needed social indulgence; nor (c) the area of legislative obtuseness about which there is the greatest concern—still I say: the critic of the marijuana laws is entitled to his obsession. I for one find the arguments of such a critic as Mr. Richard Cowan, for example—or Professor John Kaplan, or Dr. Joel Fort—not merely plausible, but overwhelming.

It is true, as some observers point out, that the attitude of American society toward pot is in flux. But does that mean that one oughtn't therefore to accelerate such analytical progress as we are making? It was in 1969 that Senator Barry Goldwater came out for the legalization, or more precisely the decriminalization, of the use of pot by consumers. Senator Goldwater! Three years after he did so, a young man was busted at an upstate college in New York, found to be in possession of marijuana. He resides now at Attica. Attica! Let us assume that no important politician—no President, Vice President, aspirant President, aspirant Vice President, beleaguered governor, ambitious committee chairman—will bestir himself by a sensible paragraph written or spoken in behalf of reform in the draconian laws that govern the use of marijuana: even so, common sense would in due course probably assert itself, and the laws will be modified. But that kind of resignation hardly becomes those who feel the afflatus to do what they can to steer public opinion, and are prepared to do so even in anticipation of a hard weather helm. The critics of the pot laws insist quite simply that there are no arguments of force or gravity by which to justify the treatment routinely given to people who use marijuana here and there in the United States. I flatly agree with them.

Even as I agree with such acute monitors of the controversy as James Burnham and Jeffrey Hart who insist that science is not only hubristic but childish to the extent that it finds itself saying that the case for the harmlessness of pot is substantially established. The scientists who say that kind of thing remind me of the scientists from whose computers issue the judgment that a man is under the influence of alcohol and therefore unfit to drive a car when the alcoholic content in his blood is .002—or whatever. This even though everyone knows someone who, if his intake is only .00002 alcohol, is a menace, vehicular and social. Even as we all know one or more people who, even if their alcohol content is .2, can manage to superintend world wars and compose great speeches—even if not quite adequate peace terms—with great competence. Thus we know that pot is a psychic poison to some people, young people in particular; and the hell with those who, consulting their laboratories, gravely find otherwise: they are wrong.

Do we therefore legalize pot? Not, I should myself recommend, in the sense that the legalization of pot is caricatured by the opponents of it: pot at the Automat, for a quarter. But the President's Commission, which reported in last spring, did not advocate legalization when it came out for decriminalization for the user—a distinction that is not conceptually idle. I.e., it isn't silly to say that the user should not be molested, even though the pusher should be put in jail. It was so, mostly, under Prohibition, when the speakeasy operators were prosecuted, not so the patrons. Thus it is, by and large, in the case of prostitution; and even with gambling; and most explicitly with pornography, the Supreme Court having ruled that you can't molest the owner of pornography, even though you can go after the peddler. The gentle animadversions of the law are not useless. They do become, however, a greater menace than any benefaction they propose to perform when they are taken too literally, and I understand this to be what the critics of the pot laws are fighting against, and I am on their side, not 1,000 percent, which would make my point suspect, but a conservative 100 percent.

The Perils of Thinking
Out Loud About Pot

January 1973

JUST AFTER the Associated Press made news out of a commentary I wrote in *National Review* about the need for changing the pot laws ("Buckley Alters/ Position on Pot") I had a letter from a young man who ran for Congress on the Republican ticket last November and very nearly made it. "I am in substantial agreement, but admit I must lose the habit of *thinking* as cautiously as a politician must *speak.*" I haven't heard it said better. The public exercises, in particular over a politician, a genuine tyranny, the conservative justification for which is: It is right that public figures should not express themselves, concerning an issue of grave social moment, iconoclastically. Translated, that means someone who wants to go to Congress (particularly on a Republican label) shouldn't say: "I haven't decided for sure what my position is on the pot laws. There is a lot of medical evidence coming in, and a lot of analysis being done, and I might find myself, in the days to come, advocating certain reforms in the marijuana laws." My friend worried about frozen habits of mind that come from having run for office. "I must, at least when not running for office, resist the habit of arresting my capacity to think," he says.

What's the story on the marijuana laws?

The story is, I think, this: In the past four or five years, millions of middle Americans (I call them that for convenience) suddenly found out that marijuana was something with which their own children were experimenting. Up until that time, roughly, marijuana was neatly packaged in the imagination with the hard stuff, heroin, opium, the more recently discovered LSD, that kind of thing, and on late-night movies you would occasionally see Dick Powell tracking down the swarthy drug peddlers to their native lairs in mysterious and perfidious Egypt and Turkey and Iran. The domestic victims were the social reprobates who hadn't learned any better, and the thing to do was to flog them with the law, and wait for the strictures of Harry Anslinger to reach their untutored ears.

Then, as I say, dozens of millions of Americans began to discover that the people they were in favor of sending to jail included, by theoretical extension, their own sons. Along the way, some conspicuous icons were smashed. Several teenage sons of the most prominent families in America were busted. They weren't sent to jail, but were reprimanded and let out on probation, and Mr. and Mrs. America's teeth were on edge.

A liberal Congressman from New York, Mr. Edward
Koch, at the beginning of this period proposed to a committee of the House of Representatives that a panel of experts
be commissioned to study the latest available evidence on
marijuana, with the view to recommending changes in the
law if such changes were indicated. Mr. Koch might as well
have asked the Congress to look into the question whether
the laws against matricide should be reconsidered: no one,
but no one stepped forward to co-sponsor the measure. The
months went by, and one, then another, then a third, finally
whole carloads of Congressmen changed their minds and in
due course the Presidential Commission on Marijuana was
impaneled, and last spring it came in with its recommendations. The commission said that the laws that call for impris-
oning people caught smoking pot should be repealed, but
that the people who sell pot should continue to be prosecuted and sent to jail. President Nixon (let's face it, this was election year, and by that time he could see that Counterculture
George loomed as his probable adversary) pointedly
snubbed the report, advising the public that under no circumstances would he advocate the decriminalization of marijuana use. The public has a way of compressing the meaning
of positions that touch on major emotional issues. Eight
years ago Senator Goldwater said that atomic defoliation was
one way of exposing the trails down which the North Vietnamese were infiltrating into South Vietnam, but that he
tended to oppose that way of doing it. The headlines had
Senator Goldwater "advocating" the use of atomic "weapons"
in Indochina. Mr. Nixon, two years after he reached the
White House, used the word "bums" to describe those
hopped-up militants who had taken to using bombs in order
to terrorize the campus—young men and women, said the
President, to be sharply distinguished from those who protested by peaceful means. He was forthwith described as having declared that student protesters were, as a class, "bums."
The Presidential Commission has been denounced as being
"pro" marijuana.

Even though Middle America has come to realize it and to
accept it (there is really no alternative to accepting it)—that
in all probability their sons and daughters, at some point in
high school or in college, are going to experiment with mari-

juana—they feel it is important to compensate by reinforcing their public position against marijuana, and the symbol of that position is the permanence of the laws. Their feeling, by the way, is not intuitively lacking in social intelligence. It is lacking in a lot of things, but not necessarily that. In Connecticut there is a statute dating back to the seventeenth century which prescribes the death penalty for sodomy committed with an animal (the question was not even raised whether it is a consenting animal). Frankly, I do not know whether the crime is being committed, and I do not even know whether the Sex Institute at the University of Indiana keeps up to date on the matter, but I do know (a) that no one is being electrocuted in Connecticut for having committed that crime and (b) that no politician is running for office on the need to repeal that particular law. Better—the public is saying in effect—to ignore the law's existence rather than to set right something the mere mention of which is kind of grubby, and the cause for raised eyebrows at the expense of the reformer. Once upon a time it took great courage for a British feminist to speak with passion to the elderly members of the House of Commons pleading for repeal of the laws disabling illegitimate children. "There are no such people as illegitimate children, honorable sirs, there are only illegitimate parents," was the famous line. A few generations later, Greer Garson was portraying the reformer in a popular movie. But not even Paul Newman can raise the question of medieval attitudes toward sodomy without, well, raising public suspicions about the odd allocation of his reformist energies. It is something of the same thing with marijuana reform.

So the same people whose elected representatives really wanted to know what an expert panel thought about the use of marijuana by their children more or less concluded that merely to open up the question of changing the laws might be interpreted as laxity on the subject in general. And, in California, a referendum was placed on the ballot, asking the public to express itself on whether the laws against marijuana should be repealed. The proposition was torn to pieces on election day. The voters unquestionably went home thinking they had struck back at pot. There is a sense in which they did.

Here is how the antipot people feel about it, and I struggle now to avoid saying the obvious things because the obvious things are so well known, and so boring. A little bit less than obvious is this: the public tends to react toward syndromes. It is a perfectly excusable way to act and, by the way, a very economical way to act. If the same man who (let us take an example from the forties and fifties) on issue after issue has sided with the Soviet Union—on the need for the United States to initiate a second front before General Eisenhower thought we were ready, on the undesirability of admitting Chiang Kai-shek to the summit conferences, on the good reasons Stalin had for overrunning Czechoslovakia, on the mercenary and colonialist reasoning behind the Marshall Plan, on the agrarian purity of Mao's movement in Mainland China: if that man, with that record, comes out against America's developing a hydrogen bomb, then the typical newspaper reader is quite reasonably going to discount his advice as prompted primarily by his habit of siding with the Communists on all matters of public controversy. Even if it happened that on that one issue the advocate was motivated by reasons unrelated to the strategic purposes of Soviet foreign policy, the chances of his getting people to listen to his arguments are very small. I am neither surprised that this should be so, nor particularly dismayed. The public doesn't have the time, the resources, or the patience to treat all the arguments raised by every politician or opinion-maker discretely: it tends to situate them in the general context of that person's performance.

Accordingly, people who are neither ignorant nor unresourceful nor lazy tend to believe that those who have come out for the repeal of the tough marijuana laws are really up to something more than compassion for young people who are occasionally caught experimenting with the weed and are sent to jail. The advocates of reform—they reason—are really consistent agents of the counterculture. They are the ones who, by and large, favor repeal of all the obscenity laws. They want abortion on demand. They want amnesty for draft dodgers. They want every known protection for criminal defendants. They reject the ideals of America and the standards of America. They are—the enemy.

I speak not about Archie Bunker, whose amiable stupidity is, I think, the greatest intellectual rip-off in theatrical history. It isn't Archie Bunker, for instance, who wrote to me after I sided with those who have come out for decriminalization, to say: "Polemics aside, that is the reason for the push for decriminalization. The young refuse to learn the value of hypocrisy, vice's tribute to virtue. Most of the pot users in the country are getting away with it, no question about that, so why can't they admit they already have what they want and not pomposify their position by claiming the stamp of legality for their aberrations?" Not quite so sophisticated, but by no means primitive is the lady from California who writes me, "Let's not kid ourselves. The campaign to legalize marijuana is a step toward legalizing hard drugs. Degrees of harmfulness may be debated—about alcohol, ordinary smoking, driving faster than the speed limit, and many other things. The importance of the law against marijuana is that it is a signpost which indicates society believes marijuana to be harmful. Remove this and other signposts (against porno, for example), and the jungle will certainly become more natural."

I think it is fair to say that the overwhelming majority of those who are against any reform in the present marijuana laws are, in fact, not in favor of the vigorous prosecution of the marijuana laws. In other words, they are opposed to their own children going to jail. In taking this ambivalent position toward the law they are of course making a statement, irrespective of the lack of rigor or of consistency. That statement says this: We desire that the supreme law of the land dig in against marijuana. We recognize that to implement that law rigorously is not feasible, and that if it were feasible it would be cruel. We recognize also that every now and then there is going to be the exemplary prosecution, the young man who finds himself face to face with the literal-minded judge in the provinces. It having been established that the young man was indeed smoking marijuana when the arresting magistrate detained him, the judge looks into the statute book under, "Marijuana, illegal possession of, . . ." adjusts his bifocals, notes that he is at liberty to give anywhere from one to five years, and settles on three years as a moderate application of the law. Next case.

Too bad, but that's life. After all, only one out of one hundred people who exceed the speed limit is caught and fined—is that a reason for eliminating the speed limit? Only one out of a thousand tourists bringing in a little extra loot is caught by the customs officials—does that mean you should repeal the customs laws? A few go all the way, for instance the student who writes me from Ohio Northern University: "It is the very leniency of the punishment which increases the number committing the crimes." He, of course, is wedded to the rationalist superstition that there is a correlation between the severity of the sentence and the incidence of the crime. Thus: double the fine (or the prison sentence) and you halve the offense. Curiously it is not the curmudgeons alone who are tempted by the argument. A Princeton student whom I greatly hurt by revising my position wrote, "I guess this area is just another in the series where a minority is allowed to push their will on the majority. I tell you, one of these days I'm going to kick back—but hard. Or, perhaps, that will be the next balloon [I was the first, he had already told me] that went down the drain. Oh, my soul, why canst thou not stop weeping." Because, I fear, the young gentleman's soul is besotted with sentiment, and needs to dry out under the analytical rays of reason.

Reason tells you, I think, several things at the expense of both sides of the controversy. At the expense of the diehards, it tells you simply this, that the public conscience will strain at a system of justice that is utterly capricious. I know people (a) who believe in law and order; (b) who believe in the strong antipot laws; (c) who know that their children have smoked pot, and would protect them against a magistrate dispatched to bring in said children as resolutely as if they were braves doing the work of Sitting Bull. At the expense of the doves, it tells you that the counterculture operates most deviously, its subversive purposes to perform.

What will happen, under the circumstances, is that those who oppose the repeal of the laws will gradually diminish their call for the law's implementation—rather like the jaded bottle laws in the dry states. Inasmuch as there is no real economic imperative for the legalization of marijuana smoking, there is no clear lobby for institutionalizing it, as was the case with alcohol, so intimately related to the tavern, the nightclub, and the country club. Pot smoking has been a privately exercised vice: why not keep it that way, the hardliners are saying in effect. I doubt that in the future anyone running for district attorney, or judge, will be substantially imperiled by the charges of the opposition that he failed to prosecute, and imprison, people who were smoking marijuana. The law's desuetude: the untidy recommendation, in effect, of those who would leave the laws alone, in order to ignore them. The philosophers among them hope to make the subtle cultural point: This Society Disapproves of Marijuana. The Archie Bunkers are not aware of philosophy: but straddling a hypocrisy is a calisthenic one learns early in life: they have got so they can do it before breakfast.

Those, I think, are the terms of the forthcoming treaty between the hawks and the doves. Senator Aiken suggested a few years ago that we should assert simply that we had won the war in Vietnam—and withdraw. We could use our great resources to mystify the ensuing situation, get all mixed up about who was representing whom, and simply cling hard to the illusion. The antimarijuana hawks take a position not dissimilar: hang on to the marijuana laws, ignore them as much as you can, put up with the occasional moral inconvenience of the law applied at the expense of the desultory victim—and relax in the knowledge that the catechism is unchanged.

The others, and I am on their side at this point, reject the uses of individual victims for the sustenance of a legal chimera; and recoil against altogether cynical uses of the law. Not because we are purer than the manipulators, but because we fear the attrition of the law's prestige. There are very good arguments for taking the law seriously. These arguments call for modifying the crazy penalties currently prescribed for the idiots who smoke marijuana.

Capital Punishment

May 8, 1972

THERE IS national suspense over whether capital punishment is about to be abolished, and the assumption is that when it comes it will come from the Supreme Court. Meanwhile, (a) the prestigious State Supreme Court of California has interrupted executions, giving constitutional reasons for doing so; (b) the death wings are overflowing with convicted prisoners; (c) executions are a remote memory; and—for the first time in years—(d) the opinion polls show that there is sentiment for what amounts to the restoration of capital punishment.

The case for abolition is popularly known. The other case less so, and (without wholeheartedly endorsing it) I give it as it was given recently to the Committee of the Judiciary of the House of Representatives by Professor Ernest van den Haag, under whose thinking cap groweth no moss. Mr. van den Haag, a professor of social philosophy at New York University, ambushed the most popular arguments of the abolitionists, taking no prisoners.

(1) The business about the poor and the black suffering excessively from capital punishment is no argument against capital punishment. It is an argument against the *administration* of justice, not against the penalty. Any punishment can be unfairly or unjustly applied. Go ahead and reform the processes by which capital punishment is inflicted, if you wish; but don't confuse maladministration with the merits of capital punishment.

(2) The argument that the death penalty is "unusual" is circular. Capital punishment continues on the books of a majority of states, the people continue to sanction the concept of capital punishment, and indeed capital sentences are routinely handed down. What has made capital punishment "unusual" is that the courts and, primarily, governors have intervened in the process so as to collaborate in the frustration of the execution of the law. To argue that capital pun-

ishment is unusual, when in fact it has been made unusual by extra-legislative authority, is an argument to expedite, not eliminate, executions.

(3) Capital punishment is cruel. That is a historical judgment. But the Constitution suggests that what must be proscribed as cruel is (a) a particularly painful way of inflicting death, or (b) a particularly undeserved death; and the death penalty, as such, offends neither of these criteria and cannot therefore be regarded as objectively "cruel."

Viewed the other way, the question is whether capital punishment can be regarded as useful, and the question of deterrence arises.

(4) Those who believe that the death penalty does not intensify the disinclination to commit certain crimes need to wrestle with statistics that disclose that, in fact, it can't be proved that *any* punishment does that to any particular crime. One would rationally suppose that two years in jail would cut the commission of a crime if not exactly by 100 percent more than a penalty of one year in jail, at least that it would further discourage crime to a certain extent. The proof in unavailing. On the other hand, the statistics, although ambiguous, do not show either (a) that capital punishment net discourages; or (b) that capital punishment fails net to discourage. "The absence of proof for the additional deterrent effect of the death penalty must not be confused with the presence of proof for the absence of this effect."

The argument that most capital crimes are crimes of passion committed by irrational persons is no argument against the death penalty, because it does not reveal how many crimes might, but for the death penalty, have been committed by rational persons who are now deterred.

And the clincher. (5) Since we do not know for certain whether or not the death penalty adds deterrence, we have in effect the choice of two risks.

Risk One: If we execute convicted murderers without thereby deterring prospective murderers beyond the deterrence that could have been achieved by life imprisonment, we may have vainly sacrificed the life of the convicted murderer.

Risk Two: If we fail to execute a convicted murderer

whose execution might have deterred an indefinite number of prospective murderers, our failure sacrifices an indefinite number of victims of future murderers.

"If we had certainty, we would not have risks. We do not have certainty. If we have risks—and we do—better to risk the life of the convicted man than risk the life of an indefinite number of innocent victims who might survive if he were executed."

Lenny

November 25, 1974

THERE IS A movie out on the Life and Hard Times of Lenny Bruce. It is technically a superb production, done in black and white, following the technique of the strung-out posthumous flashback, the style of *Citizen Kane*. The acting is superb. More exactly, the performances are superb, because the principal, Dustin Hoffman, is quite simply unconvincing, and this is to his credit. Alec Guinness doing Adolf Hitler was unconvincing. Perhaps the reason is this, that Hitler was unconvincing.

Unconvincing characters can in fact convince, but this requires the proper historical setting. In the case of Hitler, things like national paranoia, a breakdown of civil government, storm-tossed national emotions on a Wagnerian scale. In the case of Lenny Bruce, it required a nation riding on a frenzy of iconoclasm, where grown-ups, sitting around a bar, felt a sense of liberation on hearing taboo words spoken out loud, smuttily, leeringly, by a "comedian."

There was a lot of that kind of thing in France in the days before the Revolution, when De Sade had his following, and black masses were an aristocratic sport. But reading De Sade now is like reading pathology, and listening to Lenny Bruce is like a visit to one of those clinics where they keep two-headed children until, mercifully, they die off. Lenny Bruce died,

morphine needle at his side, and the wonder of it is that they
sought in the movie to make a hero out of him. I can be made
to feel sorry for Lenny Bruce, but not to admire him. The
worst of it is when grown-up movie producers try to make a
hero out of him.

Why?

I never heard Bruce, and I assume that he must have had
some genuinely funny lines. But in the movie, there were
only one or two. And for a movie a third of which consists in
exact reproduction of Lenny Bruce routines, that simply is
not enough. Well then, was there something of a philosophical nature to be learned from Bruce's experience? I cannot
imagine what. It is true that what would put you in the cooler
a decade ago if you said it in public appears nonchalantly today in mass circulation magazines; so that if you want to say
that Bruce is pathetic because he went to jail back before the
Warren Court issued general instructions to protect the pornographers, then I say: thanks, but my reservoir of sympathy
is otherwise spoken for. I think there is a good case for letting obscene comedians go ahead and be obscene before
their audiences, but my wells of retroactive sympathy do not
run for those who, in their haste to get the law changed,
spent time in jail and lost on lawyers' fees a lot of the money
they earned by pandering to obscenity.

And then the writer of *Lenny* seems to want to make another philosophical point, though he doesn't quite know how to
make it. It is that Lenny was really a wholesome man, coming
out for a direct approach to life, one that is free of hypocrisy.
Count me out. I like it the other way. If Sam and Jane are
having an adulterous affair, I shall proceed as if I did not
know about it, and I much prefer it that they should hypo-
critically defend monogamous institutions than attempt to
flaunt their own libertinism: Hypocrisy, La Rochefoucauld
said, is the tribute that vice pays to virtue.

The fact of the matter is that Lenny was a mess. He
brought unhappiness to all those he touched intimately. He
didn't have as much to say about life in his twenty-year stand-
up monologue as Samuel Johnson will tell you in one page of
any of his works. His search for sensation took him to drugs,
and that humiliating death, naked in the garret, at the age of
forty. I hear it rumored that the movie suppresses some of

Lenny's unattractive traits, such as his turning stoolie on his drug-addicted friends for personal convenience. And his call for candor was often perverse. At one hectic moment he enthralls his youthful audience by motivating the actions of Mrs. Kennedy at Dallas on the day of the assassination in a way that is not only cruel, but unproductively cruel. There is even hypocrisy in his own muddled philosophy, as when, in the nightclub sequence, he uses "nigger" and "wop" and "kike" affecting to defuse the words when, in fact, he is disingenuously exploiting them. Lenny Bruce was probably mad, and mad people can under certain circumstances be entertaining, in time and place. But it is mad to admire them and sick to find them enduringly funny.

The movie begins with the young Lenny Bruce as a $90-a-week stand-up comedian in a strip joint, telling jokes so awful the customers don't even look up from the bar to notice them. "So I went down to the store and said I wanted to buy some crocodile shoes. And the salesman said: What size are your crocodile's feet?" It turns out to have been the funniest line in the movie.

The Ennobling Dirty Movie

January 19, 1973

COMES NOW the news that a new movie starring Marlon Brando will bring explicit sex to, so to speak, the feature film, the whole of it in this case under the ardent patronage of Miss Pauline Kael who says that the debut of *Last Tango in Paris* will rank artistically with the debut of Stravinsky's *The Rite of Spring*. *Time* magazine has done a cover story on the picture, describing in quite sufficient detail the couplings and the writhings of Mr. Brando and his victim and acknowledging—indeed pressing the point—that it isn't love that drew them together, but that he finds love, and so on, and so forth.

The film was banned in Italy, whereupon one of those colloquies was arranged between Alberto Moravia and Jesuit theologian Domenico Grasso (where *do* they find those Jesuits?). Moravia—whose novels one recalls were placed on the Index by Pope Pius XII—said guess what. Right. And Father Grasso said that really the movie, whose sex scenes are "valid," is a life and death struggle between Eros and Thanatos, and is redeemed because the film's director, Hot Pants Bertolucci, gave Eros the edge. Father Grasso concluded that it is "an appreciable work, especially if the people who see it are mature, capable of grasping the idea underneath." Especially if the people who see it are Pauline Kael.

I do wish Adults would read *Trousered Apes*. It is a slender volume by a professor of literature, just now published in America by Arlington House, and it has not made the cover of *Time* magazine. In England it was the nearest thing to a surreptitious volume since the days when pornography was effectively banned. Suddenly London looked up over its reading glasses and noticed that C. P. Snow, of all people, had hailed it as a book of enormous importance, "perhaps the beginning of a major argument of the Seventies." Malcolm Muggeridge said about Duncan Williams' book, *"Trousered Apes* [the title is taken from C. S. Lewis] is a cogently argued, highly intelligent, and devastatingly effective anatomization of what passes for culture today showing that it is nihilistic in purpose, ethically and spiritually vacuous, and Gadarene in destination."

That last, if you had to boil down Mr. Williams' thesis, is it. You can't get away with it forever, he says. You cannot build art around the absurd, the perverse, the animalistic. There are artistic reasons why this will not work, he explains, with wonderfully deft illustrations and citations. And there are philosophical reasons. But the primary reasons are, really, biological. A race cannot hate itself, mock its ideals and institutions, and—survive. He is not, mind you, talking about survival in the Golden-Age-of-Literature sense. He is talking about life and death, period. He quotes Toynbee: "A failure of creative power in the minority, an answering withdrawal of mimesis on the part of the majority, [bring on] consequent loss." That disunity, in an age impatient for apocalypse, would usher in either abject and formal defeat at the hands of a superpower; or, more likely, the kind of disintegration perfectly captured by Walker Percy in his novel, *Love in the Ruins.*

Professor Ernest van den Haag long since made the point about pornography that it should exist, must exist, but that it is important that it should be sold under the counter, the point being that that is where it should be situated by the common consent of civilized society. Dirty movies should look the way that two-stroke outboard engines sound. They say that *Tango* is not even erotic, merely animalistic and depraved; but of course animalism and depravity make art— ask Sartre. Read Sartre on Genet.

In San Francisco a section of the movie page in the morning newspaper is fastidiously reserved for ads from "Adult Theaters." In what way, one wonders, is it adult to desire to see *Bijou*, advertised as "the most ambitious and successful porno film, gay or straight . . . ever." Come to think of it, the ad in question specifies "for mature adults." Immature adults will satisfy themselves with the double feature *Throat* and *Teen-age Fantasies. Adult! Mature!* I propose a new law to Governor Reagan. All movies must be clearly marked: "Warning: Eros does not, in this film, prevail over Thanatos."

The quote from Burke is almost a cliché, but Professor Williams, in his brilliant study, recalls it in perfect context, "Men are qualified for civil liberty in exact proportion to their disposition to put moral chains upon their own appetites. Society cannot exist unless a controlling power upon will and appetite be placed somewhere, and the less of it there is within, the more there is without. It is ordained in the eternal constitution of things that men of intemperate minds cannot be free. Their passions forge their fetters."

On the Use of "Dirty" Words

April 14, 1973

I GUESS I was seven when I first heard the maxim that only people with a small vocabulary use "dirty" words. I am forty-seven and have just received a communication from a reader delivering that maxim as though he had invented it. The trouble with the cliché is (a) it isn't true; (b) it doesn't take into account the need to use the resources of language; and (c) the kind of people who use it are almost always engaged in irredentist ventures calculated to make "dirty" words and expressions that no longer are, and even some that never were.

The first point is easily disposed of by asking ourselves the question, Did Shakespeare have a good vocabulary? Yes; and he also used, however sparingly, profane and obscene words.

The second point raises the question of whether a certain kind of emotion is readily communicable with the use of other than certain kinds of words. Let us assume the only thing it is safe to assume about the matter, namely, that every emotion is experienced by everyone, from the darkest sinner to the most uplifted saint. The sinner, having no care at all for people's feelings, let alone for propriety abstractly considered, lets loose a profanity not only on occasions when his emotions are acutely taxed, but even when they are mildly stirred. The saint—or so I take it from their published writings—manages to exclude the profane word from his vocabulary, and does not resort to it under any circumstances. It was for the saint that the tushery was invented. "Tush! tush!" the saint will say to his tormentors, as he is eased into the caldron of boiling oil.

Nonsaints, it is my thesis, have a difficult time adopting the manners of saints; and even if they succeed most of the time in suppressing obnoxious words, they will probably not succeed all of the time. Moreover, as suggested above, they are up against a community some of whose members are always seeking to repristinate the world of language back to the point where you could not even say, "Gosh, Babe Ruth was a good baseball player," because Gosh is quite clearly a sneaky way of saying God, the use of which the purists would hold to be impermissible under any circumstances—indeed they, plus the Supreme Court, reduce the permissible use of the word to the innermost tabernacles.

The context in which a bad word is used does much to determine the quality of its offensiveness, and the usefulness of the word. Reviewing Norman Mailer's first novel many years ago, Professor John Roche objected that the recurring use of barracks language, while it reproduced faithfully the language of the barracks, in fact distorts the prose for readers outside the barracks set who are emotionally or psychologically interrupted every time they run into a word they are not used to seeing on the printed page. It is as if a poet were handicapped by the miscadencing of his verse by a reader who suddenly paused at unexpected places, as if to walk around a puddle of water.

I had reason to reach, a while back, for a word to comment upon a line of argument I considered insufferably sanctimonious. "Crap," I wrote: And the irredentist hordes descended upon me in all their fury. I have replied to them that the word in question is defined in a current dictionary in several ways. That among these are meaning 2: "nonsense; drivel: *Man, don't hand me that crap.* 3. a lie; an exaggeration: *Bah, you don't believe that crap, do you?*" Notwithstanding that the word has these clearly nonscatalogical uses, there is an Anglo-Saxon earthiness to it which performs for the writer a function altogether different from such a retort as, say, "Flapdoodle."

There are those of us who feel very strongly that the cheapest and most indefensible way to give offense is to direct obscenities wantonly, and within the earshot of those who seek protection from that kind of thing. There will always be a certain healthy tension between Billingsgate and the convent, but in the interest of the language, neither side should win the war completely. Better a stalemate, with a DMZ that changes its bed meanderingly, like the Mississippi River.

The Disintegration of the *Playboy* Philosophy

February 6, 1974

IT WAS widely supposed that the Supreme Court decision of a year ago would put an end to the controversy over abortion. It appears not. There is very considerable agitation to permit the House of Representatives to vote on a constitutional amendment, and here and there legislators are discovering that the resolute opposition to abortion-on-demand is neither an exclusively Catholic hang-up, nor the preoccupation of career causists who, having in recent years gone through the impeachment of Earl Warren and the resistance to fluoridated water, are now arrived at the abortion issue, and are pitching their tents until a fresher cause comes up.

At the crux of the dispute surely is the question whether abortion is a matter of private morality. Granted the argument extends beyond that even if one answers the first question in the affirmative. Whose morality? That gets into the question whether the mother has absolute rights over the fetus. But the very first question is the critical one, and here and there one finds evidence that there are those who, not themselves opposing abortion, begin to understand that the opponents, if they are right, are right on a universal point. I.e., if the taking of the life of a fetus licentiously—indeed, unwincingly—is wrong, then it is wrong irrespective of whether the mother thinks it is right.

That didn't use to be *too* hard a distinction to insist upon, but it has lately got to be very difficult, in part because of the individualization of ethics, of which of course the sexual revolution has been the driving wedge. I am indebted to Mr. M. J. Sobran, Jr., for his exquisite essay on Hugh Hefner's *Playboy*. In four pages he does more damage to the philosophical pretentiousness of that magazine than has ever been done anywhere, by anybody.

Here, for instance, was a *Playboy* editorial, scolding the Supreme Court for its recent decision on obscenity. "The obscene is a subjective concept, existing only in the minds of the beholders. . . . There are ultimately 200,000,000 qualified judges of obscenity in the U.S. and . . . each has a right to his [effective] opinion"—raising the question, as Mr. Sobran points out, "what can 'qualified' possibly mean? Or 'obscenity'? Or 'right'?"

Look at the trouble even *Playboy* gets into. "When in a survey of current porn films, Contributing Editor Bruce Williamson tried to put his foot down, there was nowhere to put it. Straight and even gay films were okay with him, but films of bestiality [Linda Lovelace's leading males, it transpires, aren't always humans] and sex with children were, he said, 'weirdo junk' which 'even dedicated swingers' 'might' find 'hard to stomach.' He didn't go so far as to call for police action, or even to speak of a 'shock to the conscience.' He couldn't: he could only sniff, mustering up the withering contempt of the tastemaker, that kiddie and doggie sex are sort of infra dig, or infra dog, as the case may be."

Of course. If 200,000,000 Americans are absolute arbiters of porn, then indeed it is presumptuous to pronounce something as being obscene: indeed, presumptuous even to use the word. The argument can be made, and is made, by deeply sensitive people that abortion-on-demand is all right by them. This is a responsible position. But it becomes irresponsible to extend that argument to saying: A position that argues against abortion-on-demand is presumptuous insofar as it seeks to exert authority other than over the person making it.

It is the point of argumentation to convince others: that Linda Lovelace's movies are pornographic, for instance; that bestiality is more than merely offensive to *Playboy's* tastemakers; that abortion-on-demand is a violation of human metaphysics. It is the argument that needs to be listened to, rather than foreclosed, by the thoughtlessness of the *Playboy* philosophy.

The Shocking Report of J. Edgar Hoover

February 28, 1975

I HOPE THAT somewhere along the line hard investigation will reveal that the reports of J. Edgar Hoover's lubricious renditions to Lyndon Johnson of the moral habits of some of his important critics will prove to have been exaggerated. I say this because I have a great respect for J. Edgar Hoover which is diminished by these distasteful stories, and I'd prefer it if history proved that they were exaggerated, over against the alternative of permanently lowering my esteem for Mr. Hoover—I know no franker way to put it.

It is pretty sleazy stuff: the head of America's FBI telling, in barroom style to the President of the United States, which of his critics in Congress slept with whom, after putting away how many pints of gin, all which information having been gathered through the use of electronic surveillance or tailing done by FBI agents. I do, however, find paradoxes in the accounts of these episodes which reveal something of the perplexed current position on the public morality.

A spokesman for the FBI insisted that only such Congressmen were investigated as were up for a federal position. For instance, if the President considered naming Congressman Jones to a federal judgeship, the FBI is required, under the law, to run a "security check" on Jones. Now this is first and foremost a check to ascertain whether, by any chance, Mr. Jones is on the payroll of (a) the Soviet Union, or (b) ITT, not of course necessarily in that order of gravity. A category below is an examination into the question of his rectitude in such matters as paying his bills, cheating his investors, that kind of thing.

Then there comes that third category, loosely put together under the heading of "morals."

It is said, for instance, that Mr. Hoover reported to President Johnson that Congressman Jones (any similarity between my Congressman Jones and any Congressman by the same name is, I hope it is understood, purely coincidental) visited a particular brothel on his most recent trip to a great American municipal center. And that Congressman Smith got so smashed at some public affair or other that when it came time to pronounce his oration, he could hardly be understood (a great improvement, I would say, over the orations of most Congressmen, but that is beside the point). Over all of this, it is reported, Lyndon Johnson was given to chuckling with great, lascivious satisfaction at his knowledge of other men's intimate foibles.

Now in discussing these episodes, the commentator for *Time* magazine referred airily to the transcribed "peccadilloes" of the gentlemen in question. Now a peccadillo is a slight offense, a petty fault—like, say, slurping your soup, or picking your nose, or neglecting to use the object pronoun after a preposition.

But of course if this is so, then one wonders why there is so much agitation over the collection, and then the relaying to the President, of these slight offenses and petty faults? If, let us say, a Congressman being considered for a diplomatic position regularly fails to use an underarm deodorant, here would be an example of a petty offense which however would have some bearing on his suitability to be situated between, say, the queen and the Archbishop of Canterbury on some future occasion. But a peccadillo that is less than professionally incapacitating is, one would suppose, not only none of the FBI's business, it shouldn't have any capacity to shock.

Yet it does. I cannot imagine a Congressman running for reelection, and saying to the voters: "I work every day and every night of the week in the public interest, except Saturday nights which I spend in a brothel." The public, one gathers, doesn't share the urbanity of *Time* magazine on what constitutes a peccadillo. And without passing judgment on whether the public, or *Time* magazine, is correct under the aspect of the heavens, if there is such an aspect, it is certainly the case that we have here an awful muddle of sorts: people being shocked by the revelations, by the head of the FBI to the President, of unshocking activities.

The Problem of Unbought Tributes

October 4, 1972

I NOTE THAT Mr. Mark Spitz has embarked on a $5,000,000 career as adviser to the American community on what to eat, wear, drink, smoke, see and hear. The *fons et origo* of his authority to counsel us on such matters is that he can move his body through a given body of water at approximately one second of time less than the runner-up, who will never be heard from again, whoever he is.

It is all quite customary, and accepted with good nature everywhere. There is going on, in the city I inhabit, a blitz these days featuring Mr. Joe DiMaggio. He is running on about the interest rate at a local bank. Mr. DiMaggio knows about as much about interest rates as I know about baseball: never mind. One would think, to judge from the television commercials, that Chet Huntley is an aeronautical engineer, whose career was briefly interrupted by NBC. Never mind.

At the national convention in Miami, a liberal academician given to uninhibited thought leaned over to the moderator of a national news program who had introduced a forthcoming commercial by personally endorsing the product, and whispered, "Why do you *do* it?" "Because," he whispered, "they *insist* on it." *"Try saying no,"* said the professor. I doubt that he will bother to try saying no: the producers would not take no for an answer.

It is all deplorable, and faintly dishonorable, I suppose, though it is quite generally excused, except by the most rigid keepers of the public probity. An exclusive club in New York City is reputed to have denied membership to an industrialist who innocently posed with a bottle of whiskey in his hand in an advertisement in which he was identified as a Man of Distinction, enticed to do so by a procurer who promised in return everlasting patronage for the Red Cross, or the Boy Scouts, or whoever. But the stigma, like the Scarlet Letter, is evanescing, and no doubt before too long the gentleman in question, who has since departed this vale of tears, will be elected to honorary, posthumous membership in the gentlemen's club.

There is another problem, whose tentacles have choked me. It has to do with what is permissible in the way of gratitude. We all express our complaints (though not as often as we should). But how, publicly, to express our enthusiasms? A year or so ago, having arrived in Switzerland, I pulled out the electric portable typewriter I bought ten years ago to keep there, and plugged it into the alien current apprehensively as I do at the beginning of every season, but it jumped instantly to life, performing with the precision of a Saturn rocket. Impulsively I sat down and typed out a letter to the manufacturer: "Dear Sir: I have owned one of your typewriters, model so and so, for ten years. It has given me absolutely faultless service. You have reason to be very proud of your product. You may use this testimonial in any way you see fit. Yours truly, WFB." I never heard again from the typewriter company. No doubt the clerk put the letter in the crank mailbox. On the other hand, perhaps it was pondered and the decision arrived at that no unbought endorsements are worth having. No doubt the company will one day publicize an endorsement of its typewriters by Muhammad Ali.

That last sounds invidious, and is not meant to be. But it would be good to be able to speak one's mind uninhibitedly about the pleasures of certain goods of this world, and as a devoted consumer of them, I would love to hear the unbought opinions of others, on everything from cars that actually stand up (is there such a thing?), to television models that do not require maintenance. The governing ethics as I say are vague on the subject, and it is so widely suggested that one does what one is paid to do, I doubt one can really buck the problem safely. One day I may try it: writing, say, a tribute to fine airline service, or to a ball-point pen (I have discovered the world's best), or to a reference book. But it isn't safe, and one cannot live dangerously in every field.

Truth in Packaging

July 18, 1973

CONCERNING THE Food and Drug Administration, would you believe that the big issue over there is a thing called "slack fill"? Slack fill is loosely defined as that percentage of the cubic space within the package which is not occupied by the advertised product.

The people over at FDA do not sleep at night, one gathers,

for worrying that Post Toasties has too much slack fill. But, say the packagers, what difference does it make if the packagers advertise the net weight within a package of the food they are selling? Suppose you decide, for the fun of it, to put 10 ounces of cornflakes into a package two feet high by two feet wide by two feet thick? The consumer, buying such a package, would do so either because she thought it a boffo way to package a few spoonfuls of cornflakes, or, if she did it in error, she would either demand her money back, which the grocery store manager would probably give her, or the grocery store would politely point out that the ten ounces were plainly listed on the package, and that in fact she had paid for the cornflakes, not for the package, which was simply razzmatazz.

But thus it goes for the shower-adjusters, the felicitous phrase once used to describe the intrusive hand of those who cannot bear to permit you to set the temperature of your own shower. It is, of course, implicit in the exercise by the FDA of its consumerist dogmas that the consumer is certifiably helpless, that if you have a lot of "slack fill" in the package, she isn't going to discover it; or, if she does, that she will not reason over into the cost she is actually paying for the cereal, rather than the space. Accordingly, the gentlemen of the FDA go into retreat for months at a time and emerge with complicated findings, which they seek to use as life and death formulas against the packagers.

For instance, did you know that Kellogg's Corn Flakes has a net weight of 18 ounces, and a percentage of air of 15.5? Whereas Nabisco Quick Cream of Wheat has 28 ounces of net weight and 0.0 percentage of air? If you object by observing that cornflakes in the nature of things use up more air space than quick cream of wheat, or even unquick cream of wheat, you are being elitist.

I like best of all the proposed new mandate for the FDA, as written into a bill submitted last month by Senators Frank Moss of Utah and Warren Magnuson of Washington. This bill says that no package for sale at a grocery store may carry a picture of something that isn't actually contained in a package.

Take, for instance, Quaker Quick Grits. Well, if you go to

buy a package of same you will find on the cover a picture of William Penn, and then the identifying label, and then a frying pan with grits, bacon, and fried eggs. But, the Senators point out, open the package—and what do you find? Nothing but grits—no bacon, and no egg.

Now never mind that I, for one, would not welcome an old fried egg inside a package of grits, and would be incensed with the packager not at *not* finding one in a package marked "grits," but at finding one. But what about William Penn? Open the package and there is not a trace of William Penn. One gathers that the constituents of Senators Moss and Magnuson are the kind who complain that they bought Quaker Quick Grits and did not find William Penn inside.

Speaking of which, one wonders whether these Senators have given thought to the corollary of their statement. All politicians are, of course, packaged for public consumption, and on this point I invite my Maker to cast down a thunderbolt if I exaggerate when I say that more people have been deceived by politicians than by all the packagers since they began retailing frankincense and myrrh.

Should the FDA, or an equivalent of it, inspect all political handouts for discrepancies between that which appears and that which is represented, and that which is actualized, or actualizable? There are the palpable misrepresentations, for instance: the Senators who use a little makeup when they go on television, or when their pictures are taken; those who rub down, a little, the gray in their hair, or perhaps use a little eye shadow.

But of course the most serious misrepresentations are in the printed matter. Whereas cornflakes says 13 ounces when it means 13 ounces, politicians say things like "I will bring peace to our generation," or "I will end discrimination in housing," or "I will bring honesty back into government."

I do hope that someone will attach a rider to the Moss-Magnuson anti-Quick Grits Bill, suggesting that complementary standards be used to guard the consumer against the packaging of political candidates. It will be interesting to know whether, under such a law, we would stand to lose the public presence not only of the fried eggs, but of the Honorable Frank Moss, and the Honorable Warren Magnuson.

Death to Textbook Sexism

November 21, 1972

I HAD AN encounter recently with Ms. Germaine Greer, the antisexist sex bomb who has wrangled with lots of people including Norman Mailer, about whom, incidentally, she wrote the most galvanizing polemic in the recent history of the art (*Esquire*, September 1971).

Miss Greer is a very brilliant woman who, however, in the course of making her case against "sexism" exploits the hell out of sex. The kind of attention devoted to her in *Playboy, Evergreen Review,* et al., is inconceivable except that she obligingly spices her remarks with lascivious sexual detail as reliably as the boilerplate pornographers. I think—I am not absolutely certain but I *suspect*—that she is capable of humor, though her use of it is certainly embryonic; and that she will be rescued by humor. Somebody has got to rescue us from the women's liberation movement, and if Miss Greer gets over her fundamentalist iconoclasm, she might be just the person to do it.

To do what? Well, for instance, to cope with Scott, Foresman and Company. They are the big textbook publishers, and I have here a pamphlet issued by the company called "Guidelines for Improving the Image of Women in Textbooks." How do you define sexism? "Sexism refers to all those attitudes and actions which relegate women to a secondary and inferior status in society. . . ."

The editors warn against stereotypes. "For example, writers should take care that a joke about a woman who is a bad driver, a shrewish mother-in-law, financially inept, etc., does not present these qualities as typical of women as a group."

Mercifully, the editors do not supply examples, though one can use one's imagination. Bob Hope has a line that goes something like this: "I bumped into a car today." Straight Man: "Why?" "There was a woman driver and she stuck out her hand for a left turn." S.M.: "What happened?" "She turned left." In the Scott, Foresman Joke Book presumably the line would be added: "The way men sometimes do."

The editors give examples of sexist language, and, opposite, examples of how to correct the abuse.

For instance, "early man." That should be "early humans." "When man invented the wheel . . ." should become "When people invented the wheel. . . ." Now of course this is something we might be able to get away with when discussing prehistorical inventions. But Scott, Foresman funk the historical problem, unless they are prepared to recommend: "When the Wright people invented the airplane," or "When the Ford human invented the car." Will no one tell the people at Scott, Foresman about the synecdoche?

"Businessmen" is out: "business people" is in. Presumably the singular is a "business person." What do you want to be when you grow up, Johnny? A business person. What do you do with "repairmen"? Not even Scott, Foresman dared come up with "repairperson," so they offer: "someone to repair the . . ." which can be spotted as a syntactical cop-out in sexist *and* nonsexist societies.

The use of the pronoun "he" to do androgynous duty is out. For instance, you can't say, "The motorist should slow down if he is hailed by the police." You have to say: "The motorist should slow down if he or she is hailed by the police" (or policewoman?).

They are so carried away, over at Scott, Foresman, that they appear to have lost all sense of inflection. For instance, the sexist "The ancient Egyptians allowed women considerable control over property" has got to be changed to "Women in ancient Egypt had considerable control over property"—which is, very simply, a totally different statement from the first.

Will they ever make a concession? Yes. "In some cases, it is necessary to refer to a woman's sex, as in the sentence: 'The works of female authors are too often omitted from anthologies.'" I don't know how you could come up with a permissible way of saying: "The works of female authors are too often included in anthologies." I guess you just can't think that. "Galileo was the astronomer who discovered the moons of Jupiter. Marie Curie was the beautiful chemist who discovered radium." WRONG. Try: "Galileo was the handsome astronomer who discovered the moons of Jupiter. Marie Curie was the beautiful chemist who discovered radium." But what if Galileo was ugly? Or, heaven forfend, what if Galileo was really handsome and Marie Curie was really ugly (which I happen to know was the case)?

Miss Greer had better hurry. Her movement is gravely imperiled by the boys at . . . I mean, the boys and girls at, Scott, Foresperson and Company.

Bad Manners in China

March 18, 1972

A REPORT HAS been broadcast about my behavior in China which I hasten to explain, having only just now got wind of it from a correspondent who reproaches me for my "bad manners." And well might she have done so if the facts were as she understood them.

A day or so before leaving Peking (for other parts of China), members of the press were informed that a gift from the government of China awaited each one of us in the White House press office. Thither I repaired in due course to find one-half of the room taken up with what looked like huge individual picnic boxes. I was handed mine, opened it, and examined two pretty, large, Chinese-style vases, made out of metal, and packed in a box approximately the size of Webster's Third Unabridged Dictionary.

It becomes important, for this narrative, to take the time to give out personal information. We were permitted, in China, a single suitcase, plus whatever you could carry on your person. One suitcase is not a lot of space, when you allow, e.g., for all the medicines your wife has provided you after extracting a pledge that you will not under any circumstances submit to acupuncture. Mine was so tightly packed that I had to have help in zipping it shut. On my person I carried a large briefcase with assorted materials, a second briefcase of books and material on China, a camera case with film and binoculars, and a heavy indestructible portable typewriter.

The vases would not have had a chance of making their way into my suitcase, and I would not have been able to wobble out of the hotel if I had one extra large package to handle. So . . . I endeavored to "lose" my gift, and precisely the point I want to make is that I went to extraordinary lengths not to hurt the feelings of my hosts. I therefore checked the package in the hotel baggage room, and left the red plastic check in my shirt, intending there to forget it forever. No such luck. The next day, a Chinese official from the hotel presented me with the red check, salvaged from the laundry. So I put the check in my overcoat pocket and forgot about it. At thirty minutes past midnight, in the press bus headed for the airport, a greatly disturbed Chinese found me in the dark surrounded by my paraphernalia, and advised me excitedly that I had neglected to reclaim a package from the baggage room. How he, or anyone else, knew that the package belonged to me I cannot fathom, having stripped the box of the little card designating it as mine.

In any case, I feigned great horror at my addlepatedness, rushed out to the baggage room, retrieved the package and returned to the bus, to the considerable amusement of my companions, to each of whom I offered the vases should they have room for them, but no one did. So I sneaked furtively to the furthest corner of the bus and slid the package in a corner of it which I felt certain was only examined once a year in broad daylight. You are correct in anticipating the sequel. The plane was about to take off when an official with a box of vases in his hands strode down the aisle, presented me with the package which, he said, must have accidentally slid under the seat while I rode in the bus.

How I finally got rid of the vases is a secret I shall not disclose, except to correspondents headed for China with a limit of one suitcase each.

To clinch the point—that I would precisely not as a matter of principle refuse a perfunctory gift from any host—there was the last night in China. It was just before two in the morning after a very long day—you remember, the day that ended with the loss of Taiwan—and Joe Kraft and I were dozing off, I remember asking him sleepily which was the Hanseatic League—when suddenly there was a stentorian knock on the door and Kraft, groaning, got out of bed, expecting yet one more cable from Washington, asking for a thousand words on the evening's banquet, or whatever. But it was two officials, each one of them bearing an enormous package, like Carmen Miranda's hat box, a gift for each of us from the Revolutionary Council of Shanghai. We were lucky. Some of the boys got theirs delivered at three thirty. The packages were Chinese candy. This was our last air trip, so we could load onto our Pan Am 707 anything we wanted, and that candy is now in New York, gainsaying the report that I would refuse a gift from China.

Candy, I should remark, is a staple in China, and a little saucerful of it, along with hot water, tea leaves and fruit, is in every hotel room. When the Reuters correspondent, not thinking that it would substantially violate the restriction against any news being given out about the impending visit of Mr. Nixon before his actual arrival, cabled London a small item about two U.S. satellite technicians who had contracted pneumonia and were flown to Hong Kong, the Revolutionary Council met to discuss appropriate disciplinary measures against him. For forty-eight hours, no candy was put in his hotel room.

The Poop-Scoop War

May 27, 1972

WHILE PACING up and down waiting for developments on the international war front, I pause to report on the war in New York City between the dog owners and various antidog, or more properly anti-dog-poop, groups.

The issue suddenly burst upon the scene last winter when a middle-aged doctor, coming upon a Doberman pinscher squatting down on the sidewalk opposite his apartment in Greenwich Village, suddenly found himself reaching into his pocket, pulling out a firearm, and shooting the dog quite, utterly dead. This violence was not senseless, in the opinion of those who understood the doctor's frustration. But the dog lovers, greatly aroused, bore down hard and of course the gentleman will be prosecuted, and no one now believes that the final solution to the dog problem was adumbrated by the incident in Greenwich Village.

On the other hand, the dog owners are visibly on the defensive. The issue ties in with the ecological obsession, and indeed the ecologists have now escalated by proclaiming that dog poop has—I forget—either too much acid or not enough acid to help the little trees in New York which dogs love to use as sanitary facilities, so that the argument is now removed from the dog people, who are left, really, without any claim based on the unseen benefits of dog poop casually distributed over the streets and sidewalks of the city.

Comes now something called Children Before Dogs. That organization, one suspects from the fanatical gleam in its prose, is a hardliner, which would really like to do away with dogs altogether.

Anyway, the antidog people are now reviving statutes that have been sleeping soundly for years, which restrict the freedom of dogs, and specifically proscribe certain areas, for instance children's playgrounds in the park, the zoo areas, and what have you. A tactical ambition of the antidog people is to construct a DMZ around the whole of Central Park, a territory the dog people would yield only after bitter resistance. But even if the antidog people win there, their victory can only result in an intensification of the problem somewhere else. I mean, the less poop in Central Park, the more poop elsewhere, which is called Boyle's Law.

In anticipation of this problem, the antidog people are suggesting that dog owners be held instantly responsible for cleaning up everything their dogs do. To this end, American capitalism has developed a little device which facilitates the scooping up of the debris, which is thereafter dumped into a plastic bag. The whole operation would appear to be difficult to consummate with the kind of polish that goes with a stroll down Park Avenue with one's St. Bernard, but the antidog people are not struggling to make it all that easy for the dog owner, the hell with him is their attitude. But now the Dog

Owners' Protective Association charges that the power brokers are really behind the suggestion, that they are trying to create a market for their pooper-scoopers, as they are felicitously called, and are demanding an exposé. American ingenuity has not risen fully to the challenge. For instance, why could they not develop a can of squirt which deodorizes it all, or, better still, turns it into cornflakes, or the nearest alchemical achievement Dupont can come up with?

Mayor Lindsay has actually proposed that dogs be required to perform in their owners' bathrooms, which suggests that the mayor's knowledge of dogs is about on a par with his knowledge of cities: but no one wants to politicize the issue, and for that reason people are careful to move with bipartisan solidarity, whichever side of the issue they find themselves on. For one thing, the pollsters have not discovered exactly where the political advantage lies. It is all very well to say that more people are without dogs than with them. But whereas most people who want the street poop removed are indulging a velleity, those who want their dogs are indulging a passion. So that even if only one-tenth of New Yorkers have dogs, their strength may well be the strength of ten if they find some politician threatening their dogs. Untold prime ministers of Great Britian have fallen for suspected indifference to dogs, let alone for conspiring to constipate dogs. So Mayor Lindsay's foray into the dog war is understandably tentative, and meanwhile the *Village Voice* has helped matters not at all by publishing a recipe for Sweet and Sour Doberman.

XIII.

The Press: Mostly Personal

The Theory of Jack Anderson

April 21, 1972

I SAID to Jack Anderson, "Mr. Anderson, I'd like to know whether you believe that I have the right to go through your files and to disclose their contents in my newspaper column?" And Jack Anderson said, "No. I don't think you have that right because I am not a public official." And I said, with that succinctness for which I am famous: "(a) The Supreme Court, in its rulings on libel, has pretty much dismissed the distinction between a public official and a public figure; (b) there is no question about it that you, Mr. Anderson, are a public figure; indeed (c) you are more influential than most public officials—so if you are entitled to see the files of Presidents and Senators and Cabinet Ministers, why am I not entitled to see your files?" To which Mr. Anderson replies—lamely, I think—that okay, he'll show me his files, if I'll show him mine. To which I reply: No, I won't let you see mine, but my position is consistent, because I don't assert the right to see the private files of the President. But yours is inconsistent because you assert the right to see theirs, while denying them the right to see yours.

So it went—so it goes—and it is very difficult indeed to wrest from Mr. Anderson the theory by which he exercises the right gleefully to disclose and to dwell upon the working papers of government officials. I tried another tack. . . .

Look, I said, I think you are right when you say that there is a conflict of interest implicit in the arrangement whereby the same man who classifies a document as confidential has the sole authority to declassify it, and I grant that that authority is usually exercised in a self-serving way. That is, public officials tend to release documents that make them look good, and suppress documents that make them look bad. Now: wouldn't you agree that by the same token there is a conflict of interest as regards your publication of secret docu-

427

ments? I mean, here you are telling us that you would not in fact give out secret documents that come to you if they imperil the national interest. But as a newspaperman and a sensationalist, aren't you naturally inclined to further your interests rather than your country's interests, even as you accuse the politicians of doing?

Well, said Mr. Anderson, he would like it if a perfectly impartial tribunal (by the way, there is no such thing) were in charge of decisions about what documents should be kept secret and what documents should be declassified.

Okay, I said, but why shouldn't there then be a tribunal that passes on which of the documents that come into your possession should be publicized by you and which should be kept secret? Surely if a tribunal is appropriate to guard against self-serving tendencies of public officials, a tribunal is equally appropriate to guard against self-serving tendencies of newspapermen?

Well, said Mr. Anderson, if the government agrees to set up such a tribunal, I'd agree to go along. So, said I: What is the reason for waiting for the government? Isn't it an approach toward what is desirable to set up a tribunal to pass on your own disclosures?

Dead end.

Mr. Anderson's difficulty, as a theorist, is that he cannot accost the question of public privacy except in terms of evildoing. Now it is absolutely and obviously and unmistakably clear that public officials are very frequently engaged in such evil activity as hypocrisy, cynicism, dissimulation, the whole bit. Everybody who is running for President at this very moment is engaging in the kind of rhetoric that an undereducated mule would not take seriously. But it does not follow from this that a government official is required to send a copy of all his private papers to Jack Anderson, to do with as Anderson sees fit.

When he disclosed the minutes of the special White House group that faced the problem of the India-Pakistan war, Anderson justified himself by saying that there was a great discrepancy between what Henry Kissinger had said was official U.S. policy (namely, neutrality), and what the minutes actually disclosed *was* U.S. policy. The White House denied the discrepancy, whereupon Mr. Anderson gave out the whole of the minutes. Now these included—as an example—the statement by one U.S. official talking at the round table with a dozen assistants of the President: "The Department of Agriculture says the price of vegetable oil is weakening and it would help us domestically . . . to ship oil to India." And, from the Chief of Naval Operations, "The Soviet military ambition in this exercise is to obtain permanent usage of the port of Visakhapatnam." Both of these expressions are, to put it formally, intimate: and their disclosure has nothing whatever to do with the hypocrisy imputed to Henry Kissinger.

What is the theory of our right to hear such spontaneously expressed opinions?—which would simply not have been expressed in the first place if it were known that they would end on Jack Anderson's desk. The gentleman, in fact, has no theory of his right to the information. He has, merely, a squatter's right, and is better off forgetting the theory and confining himself to saying: I'll do it as long as I can get away with it. That is a theory of sorts.

The Proposed Shield Laws

February 17, 1973

DR. FRANK STANTON of CBS has delivered a speech in which he confesses to having slightly altered his opinion about the rights of newsmen. Last October, he says, CBS appeared before Congress to urge enactment of a "shield" statute that would grant specific protections to newsmen. "At that time," said Dr. Stanton, "we did not advocate an absolute, unqualified news privilege. We took the position that there might be extreme conditions under which a court would be justified in compelling the revelation of information or the source of it."

But no grass grows under CBS's feet. "We have since reconsidered that position," said Dr. Stanton. "We now believe it necessary to enact legislation to create an absolute newsman's privilege, which should apply not only to the Federal Government, but to the states, regardless of present shield laws or lack of them."

Concerning the controversy, a few observations:
1. It is hard to believe that CBS really desires an absolute protection for newsmen of the kind so categorically affirmed in the resolute prose of Dr. Stanton. Let us dwell on one or two contingencies:
Johnny Olds has been kidnapped. The kidnapper calls a reporter on the *Daily Eagle*. K tells R that unless he promises not to reveal any information given him except that much which is authorized for use in the public media, he will clam up. R agrees, and relays only in the press K's terms: amnesty for the Harlem Eleven, or whoever. Occasionally, K lets Johnny Olds himself come to the telephone, and Johnny begs R to beg the community to spare his life. Does CBS want a law that prevents the police from requiring the reporter to answer such questions as might lead them to the kidnapper?
Again: A reporter is summoned and told in confidence that if he looks in the trunk of a certain Oldsmobile tomorrow morning, there he will find the mortal remains of Carlo Buono, the notorious capo of the East Side. But—understand—you are not to divulge from whom you got the information, not even that you got it from a leader of the rival family. The hit will be done shortly after midnight, and it will be made to appear that the killer was Buono's own bodyguard. A trial takes place, and Buono's bodyguard summons the reporter to the stand. Do I understand Dr. Stanton to be saying that he should not be interrogated?
2. The absolutization of any protection under the Constitution results in the diminution of another protection, as Sidney Hook pointed out in his book *The Paradoxes of Freedom*. What is needed is not an "absolute" privilege, but the making of some distinctions. It is relevant that there are those who already have warned that distinctions will need to be made if the absolute law is passed, and that those distinctions might then be overweening. For instance, who exactly is

and who isn't a newspaperman, or a reporter, or free-lance television or radio consultant? Nobody much cares nowadays because the distinctions don't mean very much. But they will mean a great deal when particular privileges are invoked. I can hear it now: "Your honor, Mr. I. F. Stone may pose as a reporter. As a matter of fact, all he is is a polemicist for the left: Congress could never have meant to extend to him the immunities intended for objective newspapermen." Such distinctions as these are malevolent. But others are not. The kind of questions that can be asked ought to be defined, to fall short, for instance, of the wide-ranging questions asked of Professor Popkin at Harvard last fall. That is the direction the shield laws should take. And then finally,

3. Surely CBS's emphasis, viewed quite pragmatically, is askew. There is very little suffering going on these days as a result of importunate grand juries going after newspapermen. But there was very nearly a great deal of suffering last fall when CBS was ordered struck by the American Federation of Television and Radio Artists. But what laws has CBS proposed to guard the public from strikes so clearly violative of the spirit of the First Amendment? Dr. Stanton spoke out in order to "protect a basic principle. In this case it is the public's right to a free flow of information." That flow is not seriously interrupted these days by the government, though as always we need to keep our eyes on the government—that enemy of all well-disposed, decent, and industrious men as Mencken put it; but it is time and again choked off, as in New York City three times in seven years, by labor unions exercising powers altogether incompatible with that amendment to the Constitution beloved of Frank Stanton, and me.

What Are the Russians Up To, and How Can We Tell?

November 1, 1974

SUDDENLY WE find out that Liu Shao-ch'i is dead.
When did he die?

We don't know.
How did he die?
We don't know.
Where did he die?
We don't know.

You see, we don't really know anything about what is going on inside Chinese politics. Is that because, as Harriet Van Horne might put it, we went for twenty years trying to pretend that 700,000,000 people didn't exist? No. Because even if you use that silly phrase, we haven't been ignoring the 250,000,000 people in the Soviet Union, not since 1933 when we recognized the regime. And what do we know about the inside of Russian politics? Nothing. I mean, not one blessed thing. What we have is a profession called Kremlinology, which, so far as one can tell from the record, has advanced our knowledge of what is going on inside the Kremlin with about the same statistical accuracy you could have got from consulting the local tea-leaf reader. When Khrushchev was ousted, our Kremlinologists learned about it from the AP. When the last Ping-Pong player has visited China, we will still know nothing more about Chinese politics than we do now.

Which brings one to the solemn warning, issued in New York on October 31, by Senator James L. Buckley. He is on his way to the Soviet Union where, by the way, he intends to discover some non-Jewish victims of Soviet tyranny. He will go to the usual places and meet the usual people and observe—there is a great deal to be said for observing. But being a very intelligent man, he does not expect to return to the United States with a sophisticated idea of exactly what the Soviet military is up to. That kind of information we get only through the use of several devices. The least of these, at this point, is the Central Intelligence agent, because CIA agents who poke about military laboratories in Central Asia are given a bad time. We get the best information we have from our missile technology. From photographs.

Now it was an important part of the SALT agreement that the partners should not engage in efforts to deceive these photographic monitors. In other words, if you were digging a hole for the purpose of putting in it a silo which would contain an intercontinental missile, you must not strew bits of straw around it so as to confuse our monitors and make them think you are storing grain.

Senator Buckley says that some insiders in and out of U.S. Intelligence have recently accumulated a number of grounds to believe that the Soviet Union has been systematically breaking this part of our agreement. This unhappy news combines with something about which there is no dispute, namely, that we greatly underestimated the capacity of Soviet technology to MIRV their missiles when we made the 1972 deal. Under the circumstances, as we move toward the second SALT accord, we face a situation doubly dangerous: (1) an inexact knowledge of what it is exactly that the Soviets have; and (2) a Soviet lead, accomplished by the forward inertia of Soviet technology which the Soviet Union is not going to be anxious to retrench from. It is Senator Buckley's point that in authorizing SALT I, the Senate specifically ordained that SALT II should look to "equivalence," and that unless the White House comes clean now and confirms either (a) that the Soviet Union is forging ahead; or (b) that we have lost our power to establish whether the Soviet Union is forging ahead, Congress is incapable of acting intelligently when it is presented with a proposed agreement involving SALT II.

"To summarize my concerns," said Senator Buckley, "as it appears that the Soviets may be rapidly achieving the capacity to deploy a far greater number of missile warheads than the Congress ever anticipated when the SALT accords were ratified in 1972, and as the Soviets may be initiating measures of concealment that will make it increasingly difficult for us to measure the extent of their aggregate payload capacities and of their capability to intercept United States ballistic missiles, it is imperative that our negotiators take with absolute seriousness the Congressional mandate that the next agreement provide for true parity in strategic forces, and that any such agreement contain more stringent safeguards to assure us of the ability to monitor Soviet compliance." Quite right, though I do wish the Senator would use shorter sentences.

The Ethics of Junketing

December 22, 1973

MY FRIEND Mr. Mike Wallace, a gentleman who is given to protracted concern with scruple, called recently in his diligent way to inquire what are *my* rules concerning "junkets," by which he means trips paid for by someone else. He proposes to do a television program on the subject, and I am grateful to him for his maieutic inquiry about *my* own views, which had not crystallized.

(1) When a columnist is invited on a trip, he should begin by asking whether the host expects that his guest will write about the trip. Obviously if you are invited, say, to look in at the opening of Disney World, your hosts expect that you will write about Disney World. If you are invited (as I along with 1,000 others were) to travel in great luxury to witness the dedication of a new refining plant in a distant Arctic archipelago, your host clearly does not expect that you will write about the plant.

(2) In the second case, then, there is obviously no inhibition in accepting the invitation. In the first, you need to say to yourself: If I find that Disney World is a great bust, will I feel altogether free to say so notwithstanding that the trip down was paid for, as also the hotel bill? That question is only coped with by the injunction: to thine own self be true. But here a qualification is appropriate. Going to Florida and back is not a very big deal, in this peripatetic age. So that the indebtedness of the visiting journalist is not really as heavy as, say, a trip to, well, Mozambique, to examine the policies of the Portuguese government there.

(3) Here the situation becomes more complex, and more interesting. On the one hand there are newspapers that pridefully insist that no journalist should travel to a foreign country at that country's expense because implicit obligations are incurred. That point of view is defensible.

But there is another point of view. It is part of a journalist's duty to move about, and to report to his readers on what he sees. Most often he will use his own money to pay the fare.

But—and here are more subqualifications—sometimes (a) the trip is too expensive to justify the amount of time the journalist reasons he can devote to the subject (how many columns can one write about Mozambique?); and (b) sometimes the journalist is simply not certain whether the trip will produce anything interesting enough to justify the trip.

It is my opinion that in such circumstances the journalist should feel free to accept the round-trip fare, cutting his potential losses to his own time. But—once again—he must know that he will feel free to write as he sees the situation, without any inhibition deriving from the auspices. This is especially difficult because one often tends to lean over backward to establish one's analytical independence, and that is as unjust as to shill. To say the problem is easily solved by simply avoiding the temptation is to take the easy way out.

Some examples, from my personal experience.

I traveled, at the expense of South Africa and the Portuguese government, eleven years ago, to South Africa and Mozambique. I wrote three columns, and a long essay piece. Where I came out on the general subject of South African domestic policies is, I suppose, best situated by saying that a pro-South African committee in the United States made reprints of my essay, while the government of South Africa refused to distribute it.

I traveled over one hectic weekend, at the expense of the government of Northern Ireland, to view the situation there just before Orangeman's Day. It was an excruciatingly uncomfortable trip of seventy-two hours. I wrote three columns, in which I find not a hint of servility to my hosts.

I traveled, at the expense of the United States government, from New Zealand to the Antarctic, and stayed five days, visiting the South Pole, and writing about U.S. operations there. This is one for the naturalists, and though I treasure the experience, I would not undergo it again, even to bring peace with honor to the nations that contend there for scientific advancement.

The general impression is that such jaunts are offered daily to columnists. That has not been my experience. Of course, it is possible that from afar they smell in me that incorruptibility that causes the angels and the saints to chant my name.

On Leveling with the Reader

March 8, 1975

IN RECENT weeks several correspondents, thoughtfully sending me copies, have triumphantly advised editors of newspapers in which this feature appears, that "Mr. Buckley was himself a member of the CIA," and that under the circumstances, that fact should be noted every time a newspaper publishes a comment by Mr. Buckley on the CIA.

Now the Boston *Phoenix*, which is that area's left-complement to the John Birch Society magazine, publishes an editorial on the subject that begins with the ominous sentence, *"William F. Buckley, Jr.'s past is catching up with him. In the 50's he served as E. Howard Hunt's assistant in the Mexico City CIA station. . . ."* Accordingly, the *Phoenix* has protested to the editor of the Boston *Globe,* and reports to its readers, "Ann Wyman, the new editor of the *Globe*'s editorial pages, is now considering whether to append Buckley's past CIA affiliation to his column, which appears regularly in the *Globe*. Wyman intends to consult with other *Globe* editors. . . . The *Globe* may finally be on to him."

If so, it would indeed have taken the *Globe* a very long time, since it began publishing me in 1962, and my CIA involvement (a twenty-five-year-old friendship with Howard Hunt) is, among newspaper readers, as well known nowadays as that Coca-Cola is the pause that refreshes. But one pauses to wonder what is the planted axiom in the position taken by the Boston *Phoenix?*

It is true that I was in the CIA. I joined in July 1951 and left in April 1952. Now the assumption, not always stated, is that obviously anybody who was ever a member of an organization, defends that organization. But one wonders: Why should this be held to be true?—the most prolific critics of the CIA are in fact former members of it.

I attended Yale University for four years. Is it the position of the Boston *Phoenix* that, therefore, everything I write about Yale is presumptively suspect, because as a Yale graduate I am obviously pro-Yale? But it happens that shortly before entering the CIA I wrote a book very critical of Yale. And, as a matter of fact, I have in recent years written critically about Yale on a dozen occasions. So consistently, indeed, that Miss Wyman may feel impelled to identify me, at the end of every column I write about Yale, in some such way as: "Mr. Buckley, a graduate of Yale, is, as one would expect, a critic of that university."

I am a Roman Catholic, and have written, oh, twenty columns in the last ten years critical of developments within the Catholic Church. Should I be identified as a Roman Catholic?

I like, roughly, in the order described, (1) God, (2) my family and friends, (3) my country, (4) J. S. Bach, (5) peanut butter, and (6) good English prose. Should these biases be identified when I write about, say, Satan, divorce, Czechoslovakia, Chopin, marmalade, and New York *Times* editorials?

I wonder if Miss Wyman is being asked, implicitly, to label the religious or ethnic backgrounds of all her columnists? *"Mr. Joseph Kraft, who writes today on Israel, is a Jew."* That would presumably please the editors of the Boston *Phoenix*.

Or, *"Mr. William Raspberry, who writes today about civil rights in the South, is black."*

Or how about: *"Mr. John Roche, who writes today in favor of federal aid to education, receives a salary from Tufts whose income depends substantially on federal grants."*

Pete Hamill, who laughed his head off a few years ago at the hallucinations of Robert Welch, asks in the *Village Voice:* "Is Bill Buckley still a member of the CIA? Have any of Buckley's many foreign travels been paid for by the CIA?" One columnist recently wrote that *National Review*'s defense of the CIA, and my own friendship for Mr. Howard Hunt, might suggest that the CIA had indeed put up money for *National Review* over the years, though he conceded that if that were the case, the CIA was indeed a stingy organization—Mr. Garry Wills knows, at first hand, something of the indigence of that journal. Unfortunately Mr. Wills is the exact complement of Mr. Revilo Oliver, who was booted out of the John Birch Society for excessive kookiness sometime after he discreetly revealed that JFK's funeral had been carefully rehearsed. Both are classics professors by background.

Perhaps one should identify anyone who writes about politics and is also a classics professor as being that? The Boston *Phoenix* and Miss Wyman should ponder that one.

Columnists Are People

December 1, 1974

PEOPLE WHO write newspaper columns are also people, and that is a great, but unexpungeable, distraction. It is sometimes useful to be a people, in addition to being a newspaper columnist—there is no other way, for instance, to have a family, or to drink good wine, or engage avocationally in other practices than writing a column. But let me, just this one time, share my problems with you as a fellow people, giving four examples.

(1) A month ago, a tape was played at the Watergate trial. The voice of President Nixon came in loud and clear, talking to Haldeman, discussing clemency for Howard Hunt. Nixon said: "We'll build, we'll build that son-of-a-bitch up, like nobody's business. We'll have Buckley write a column and say, you know, that he, that he should have clemency. . . ."

Within a very few minutes, my office reached me en route to Boston at an airport. The newspapers had begun to call in, asking the obvious question: "Was Mr. Buckley approached?" "Does he have any comment?" I dictated over the telephone two sentences that were then given by my office to the New York *Post,* the New York *Times,* and the Associated Press: "At no time did any member of the Nixon administration approach me. Besides, I don't need to be reminded to write columns urging clemency even for sons of bitches, as Mr. Nixon has every reason to know from personal experience." The next morning, the charge was carried very conspicuously in the Boston *Globe*—together with my retort. Which I also saw in the New York papers and in *Time* magazine. Notwithstanding, I have received much mail asking why I was silent on the subject raised at the Watergate trial. And two large newspapers have carried letters by readers suggesting that I have been an appendage of the Nixon administration—without any comment from the editor bringing to the writer's attention my brief reply. One more example of the difficulty of catching up with a misleading story.

(2) A month or so ago, I wrote a column on the now famous Goldberg book by Victor Lasky, in which I expressed the view—having now read the book—that although it was of course hostile to Justice Goldberg, it was far from being libelous. I remarked that the only distortion in it was Lasky's statement that Mr. Goldberg was the worst public speaker in the State of New York, since in fact he was the worst in the country. I received a letter from a journalist who covered the campaign advising me that it was going the rounds of the boys in the bus toward the end that "if Goldberg gives one more speech Rockefeller will carry Canada." Mr. Goldberg called me on the telephone and was extremely amiable, and made no criticism of the book, merely of its provenance.

I did not note, in my column, that I am the chairman of the board of the parent company that owns the company (Arlington House) that published the Goldberg book. I did not do this for two reasons. The first was that when the book was first discussed, my position in the corporate hierarchy was widely identified, so that I proceeded on the happy, or if you prefer unhappy, assumption that most people knew about it. The second reason is that never having heard of the book before, I was in no way implicated in the decision whether to publish it. But if I had mentioned my corporate affiliation in the column, I'd have had to go on to make the connecting point, and this struck me, on balance, as unnecessarily self-concerned. Result: a big article in *Editor & Publisher* on whether my omission of my connection was ethically correct. You decide.

(3) Maybe four or five times a year, I am greatly struck by an article or analysis published in *National Review*. Now I am the editor in chief of *National Review*, and its sole owner. So when I mention the article, I give the name of the author—

but leave out the name of the magazine where the article was published, lest it should appear that I am attempting to advertise my impecunious but magnificent journal (150 East Thirty-fifth Street, New York, New York 10016—$15 per year). Then I get mail asking me how could I have been so sloppy as to fail to give the name of the journal where the article I wrote about appeared. . . .

Finally, (4) there is no way to avoid writing, occasionally, about the doings and sayings of James Lane Buckley. How should I identify him? As "my brother the Senator"? That has the obvious disadvantage of calling attention to myself, and the less obvious disadvantage of snuggling up against the cognate cliché, "my son the doctor." So, I resolved to refer to him as "the sainted junior Senator from New York." Hyperbole is a form of self-effacement; but I still get a letter or two, complaining. These I answer by expressing great surprise that the reader is unaware of the beatific character of the junior Senator from New York. But there, now, you share my problems this one time, and I shan't ask you soon again to share them. Many thanks.

XIV.

Religion

1. Chuck Colson and Christianity

June 24, 1974

I HAVE BEEN interested by the leers that greet the news of Charles Colson's conversion to Christianity. They are variously expressed. Those among us who consider themselves most worldly—Mr. Pete Hamill, for instance, or the writers for the *Village Voice*—treat the whole thing as a huge joke, as if W. C. Fields had come out for the Temperance Union. They are waiting for the second act, when the resolution comes, and W. C. Fields is toasting his rediscovery of booze, and Colson is back practicing calisthenics on his grandmother's grave.

It says a great deal about the meaning of Christianity in our culture. Traditionally, it has been those who have sinned the most who are the special objects of Providential grace. The prodigal son is welcomed most by heaven precisely because he has most to atone for.

Ah, but does that mean that we shouldn't be most surprised by the most drastic alteration in known attitudes? If Al Capone had become a Franciscan monk, there is no doubting that that operation would have exhausted huge storage banks of heavenly grace. Or if Anthony Lewis uttered a compassionate word about Richard Nixon, one would certainly take notice, though indeed there are those who would suspect guile: *reculer pour mieux sauter,* as the Frogs say, who know how to step back a little in order to leap forward a lot. But it does not matter who it is, it is possible to suspect guile, as in the case of Charles Colson. If one of the President's conversations had in it: "Let's figure out what our duty is and do it," most people would have suspected that those words were uttered for the sake of the record, maybe after calling in the Secret Service to dust off the hidden microphones. It has all become so twisted that we tend to be particularly skeptical when we detect someone doing something because it is right, even though it is something that is tactically damaging.

443

Concerning Chuck Colson, it seems to me less implausible than it apparently does to others that he should have found Christ. His weakness, as generally identified, has been his heliocentric concern for one person—Richard Nixon. When he told the court that it did not occur to him to challenge Mr. Nixon when told to go out and do something, are we asked to disbelieve that? Not by the critics of Colson, or those of Nixon; indeed that is what they most desire to believe: that everything Colson did that was disreputable, he did at the bidding of someone he treated as Commander in Chief. Whether he'd have served Richard Nixon if Nixon had been not the President of the United States, but chairman of the board of Murder, Inc., we have no way of knowing: no way of knowing whether Colson carried about within himself springs of resistance the devil himself could not overstrain.

But now he says that he has discovered Christ. To say you have discovered Christ, in our secular society, is to say something that causes most people to wince with embarrassment. Christ is something to be discovered only between the hours of ten and noon Sunday morning by Billy Graham, before or after a golf game, or by a bearded young man on the corner of Hollywood and Vine for whom Christ-freaking is a way station between college sociology and Timothy Leary. Or the sort of thing that caused cruel wars in the Dark and Middle Ages because one set of people said Christ had six toes, the other that He had five. For Charles Colson to say that he has found Jesus Christ is like Coca-Cola announcing it has discovered Pepsi-Cola: J. Walter Thompson has to be impeached before that kind of thing is credible.

So much for the *stupor mundi*. And when we need Him most. "I see it as one of the greatest ironies of this ironical time," writes Malcolm Muggeridge, "that the Christian message renouncing the world should be withdrawn from consideration just when it is most desperately needed to save men's reason, if not their souls. It is as though a Salvation Army band, valiantly and patiently waiting through the long years for Judgment Day, should, when it comes at last, and the heavens do veritably begin to unfold like a scroll, throw away their instruments and flee in terror."

2. Abortion

New Thoughts on Abortion

August 2, 1972

PROFESSOR JOHN NOONAN of the University of California at Berkeley teaches both law and philosophy, and is among other things an authority on the history of the abortion controversy. Last week, giving his views on abortion in debate with a vigorous campaigner for abortion-on-demand, he confronted the usual question. The usual question is: "If your wife were raped and made pregnant by an insane Hottentot, wouldn't you desire an abortion for her?" To which Professor Noonan replied calmly that the contingency, so frequently adduced, recalls the aphorism that hard cases make bad law.

He meant by that that legislation ought not as a general rule to attempt to confront extraordinary situations. There are laws against murder, but under certain circumstances murder is renamed, and officially excused. Those who approach human contingency with Thomistic appetites to cover every situation, either exasperate, ultimately; or they end their days in futility: or they make bad law.

The Supreme Court, confronting outrageous behavior by the police in searching the home of Mrs. Mapp, gave us: not a mere reversal of the particular conviction of Mrs. Mapp, a discrete thunderbolt of judicial indignation. No, they gave us a thing called *Mapp* v. *Ohio,* which categorically forbids a trial court to consider any evidence that was discovered in the course of an illegal search. Thus tradition was overturned, and unconvicted crime soared—indeed, a hard case made for a bad law.

Professor Noonan and others who oppose abortion-on-demand ought not to be made to justify their opposition to abortion on what-would-you-do-if grounds. On a famous occasion, defending the cause of pacifism, Lytton Strachey was asked at the Oxford Union debate in the thirties that put Oxford down as resolved not again to fight for King or country: What would he do if he entered his house and found a burly creature attempting to rape his wife? "Why," said Strachey, "I suppose I should try to come between them." Better an ad hoc solution here, than one that seeks to incorporate universal law.

The question about abortion is whether the state should sanction routine abortions. That, at least, is essentially the point being considered in the various states where the abortion laws are currently under review. There are laws against mercy killing. It is, nevertheless, a well-known fact, if not a highly discussed one, that doctors, in hopeless cases, occasionally pull out the tube.

Even so, we stand as a society committed to the notion that old people should be, as a general matter, secure against licentious euthanasia, and to that end there is appropriate legislation. It is Professor Noonan's feeling that the tide is slowly turning. Not toward abortion, but against it: that the moral insights of an alert community are gradually awakening to the fact that a well-developed fetus is a human being, as defenseless, as parasitic, as the nonagenarian, but, like the nonagenarian, a human being nonetheless.

Granted the biological debate will continue on the question of at exactly what point is it reasonable to assume that life has entered the fetus ("ensoulment," they used to call it). About this matter there is disagreement, though continuing research seems to point to earlier "life" rather than later life. Here again we must consider the matter whole. The case against the humanness of old people who have lost their power to think, to control their movements, to experience pain except nervously, could be made if one disdains the central assumption which is that we deal with human life. A fetus is a human life, Professor Noonan contends.

And he reminds us of the very distinguished Americans who not much more than one hundred years ago quite literally believed that the Negro people were not human. That they were therefore a species apart, to be bought and sold, separated or bred, for the convenience of their owners.

The mother is nowadays thought of, by the modernists, as the owner of the fetus in the sense that a slave master was the owner of a slave. Wrong both times. There is no reason, Professor Noonan believes, to be pessimistic about the discovery of the rights of a fetus. We are, after all, only one hundred or so years from discovering the rights of black men.

It is an eloquent insight.

The Court on Abortion

January 27, 1973

SAYS JUSTICE BLACKMUN, speaking for the majority of the Supreme Court: "We need not resolve the difficult question of when life begins. When those trained in the respective disciplines of medicine, philosophy, and theology are unable to arrive at any consensus, the judiciary, at this point in the development of man's knowledge, is not in a position to speculate as to the answer."

But in fact the Court didn't proceed to speculate on the answer, it proceeded to act on an answer it very simply promulgated. Up until three months, said the Court, the human fetus is nothing more than a biological lump of the mother, as expendable as a cyst. From three months to six months, it is something more than just that, but just exactly what, the Court spared us the intellectual embarrassment of stipulating. Then, during the last three months, or more exactly the last ten weeks, the fetus is conceded by the Court as being "viable." That means that even separated from the mother the fetus could develop into a complete human being. Does that mean that beginning at this point the Court confers constitutional protections on the fetus? No. At that point, says the Court, "the state . . . may go so far as to proscribe abortion."

Really, it was an outrageous decision. Concerning it, a few observations:

(1) Because the theological, philosophical, and medical

worlds are divided on just when the fetus can be considered to be "human," why does that mean that the Supreme Court must therefore make the decision? The theological, philosophical, and medical worlds are divided on the question when a human being reaches the age of maturity: and, accordingly, a decision is reached (at age eighteen) not by the theologians, philosophers, and doctors—or by the members of the Supreme Court—but by the politicians, who give their views on the subject, informed by the people.

(2) The notion that we have here a church-state issue in the denominational sense is preposterous. It is everywhere suggested that it is a Catholics-against-the world issue. Yet the most recent national referendums on the matter, in Michigan and North Dakota—both of them states in which Catholics are a minority—ruled against liberalizing the abortion laws. It is quite true that Catholics are particularly mobilized against abortion—why shouldn't they be? Jews are particularly mobilized against genocide—is that wrong? But the notion that opposition to abortion is a Catholic peculiarity not only misses the point; it fails altogether to justify the judiciary's stepping into an argument totally removed from its authority and its competence.

(3) Insofar as the Court attempted to base its line of reasoning on the argument that it is wrong to deny a woman an abortion since statistics show that giving birth to a child is more dangerous than aborting it, the Court was implausible—as one of the dissenters (Justice White) scathingly pointed out. "At the heart of the controversy," he said, "are those recurring pregnancies that post no danger whatsoever to the life or health of the mother but are nevertheless unwanted for any one or more of a variety of reasons—convenience, family planning, economics, dislike of children, the embarrassment of illegitimacy, etc."

In a sentence which will survive in the annals of syntactical inelegance and analytical chaos, the Court said: "Maternity, or additional offspring, may force upon the woman a distressful life and future. Psychological harm may be imminent. Mental and physical health may be taxed by child care." So that is the reason to allow abortion! I should think it at the very least a good excuse to justify infanticide. And the very best of reasons for justifying the elimination of all adolescents as a class. God knows they force upon most mothers a "distressful" life, as the judge put it. The psychological harm of wayward children is not only "imminent," but concrete, as is the "tax" on the "mental and physical health" of their parents.

(4) If it should happen tomorrow that medical science developed a means of protecting the embryo at age six weeks, does the Supreme Court understand its decision as having been invalidated?

The whole of it is dismal, reaching right down to the neglected cuticles of the Court's language. It is, verily, the Dred Scott decision of the twentieth century. One shudders at what a Supreme Court, taking on the responsibility to decide such questions as these, will feel free to rule upon in the years to come. Woe unto these Americans who, because of their great age, threaten distressfulness upon their children.

How to Argue About Abortion

July 14, 1974

THERE IS room for passion in almost every argument, but there is room, too, for dispassion, and those arguments overfreighted with passion tend only to polarize the combatants and tune out those who do not care.

The arguments over abortion have been in this category, and it is a pity. Indeed it may very well be more than a pity, a tragedy: if the moral analysis of the antiabortionists finally prevails upon the national ethos. The arguments over slavery used to be full of passion, and resulted in a civil war. Even so, there were those who were patiently making the rational points on the basis of which the great insight was finally established. Lincoln, debating with Douglas, for instance. And in due course we came to know not only that man was born to be free, but that men brought over in ships from

Africa with black skins were also men: and born to be free. The Civil War settled the political issue. The arguments of Lincoln and others, resting on a distinguished moral and philosophical patrimony, clinched the moral case.

I have seen, I think, the very first attempt to talk about abortion that manages to avoid every one of the bloodcurdling clichés used both by those who believe in abortion and those who oppose it. It is a most remarkable essay by John T. Noonan Jr., and it is entitled, "How to Argue About Abortion."

Professor Noonan shows us here how a subject as sundering as abortion *can* be discussed. What to look for. What the relevant perceptions are. What at all costs to avoid. What are the implications of certain modes or arguments. It is not only a distinguished performance, it is a beautiful performance.

Professor Noonan does some truly marvelous things in a few thousand words. He examines, for instance, the role of perception in the controversy in question. I have myself gagged over the antiabortion material that features pictures of fetuses. I have also gagged at pictures of war that feature mangled corpses. I have always assumed that the reaction of horror and disgust was philosophically irrelevant. Noonan shows, without drawing the same analogy, why in fact it is not. Why in fact perception means so very much in modern intercourse. . . .

> Perception of fetuses is possible with no substantially greater effort than that required to pierce the physical or psychological barriers to recognizing other human beings. The main difficulty is everyone's reluctance to accept the extra burdens of care imposed by an expansion of the numbers in whom humanity is recognized. It is generally more convenient to have to consider only one's kin, one's peers, one's country, one's race. Seeing requires personal attention and personal response. The emotion generated by identification with a human form is necessary to overcome the inertia which is protected by a vision restricted to a convenient group.
>
> If one is willing to undertake the risk that more will be required in one's action, fetuses may be seen in multiple

ways—circumstantially, by the observation of a pregnant woman; photographically, by pictures of life in the womb; scientifically, in accounts written by investigators of prenatal life and child psychologists; visually, by observing a blood transfusion or an abortion while the fetus is alive or by examination of a fetal corpse after death. The proponent of abortion is invited to consider the organism kicking the mother, swimming peacefully in amniotic fluid, responding to the prick of an instrument, being extracted from the womb, sleeping in death. Is the kicker or swimmer similar to him or to her? Is the response to pain like his or hers? Will his or her own face look much different in death?

There is something close to moral and psychological poetry in this passage, and throughout the pamphlet, which friends and foes of abortion will join in acclaiming.

3. The Court

Impasse on the Schools

October 16, 1972

LAST WEEK the Supreme Court, with something very much like a yawn, affirmed the decision of the lower court, which refused Ohio the right to pass along money to the private, church-related schools on the grounds that what Ohio was up to was circumvention. As a matter of fact, that is exactly correct. The Supreme Court has during the past few years honed its fanatical construction of the First Amendment into a fine blade, which cuts through any attempt by any accumulation of parents, priests, ministers, rabbis, school boards or legislatures to stitch together a plan that provides parents with fundamental freedoms to organize their own schools with some reference to religious principle.

Who says A, the philosophers never tire of reminding us, must say B. If it is true that it is a violation of the First Amendment to the Constitution to allow a tax dollar to end up at a parochial school no matter how circuitous the route, then it is true that Ohio has no business permitting parents of private school children to receive the little $90 annual subsidy the legislature of Ohio thought to return to them, in modest compensation for their saving the taxpayers of Ohio the approximately $1,000 per student annual tuition they'd have cost the state by attending the public schools. The decision of last week disposes of most of the public intentions of prominent American politicians for relieving the religious schools of their plight. George McGovern backed, in effect, an extension of the Ohio plan. So did Richard Nixon. So did Nelson Rockefeller. Well, it's gone now. Where do we go from here?

Professor Roger Freeman of the Hoover Institution at Stanford University has been arguing for a very long while a distinction he considers constitutionally crucial. He says: The Supreme Court insists that once a dollar has slipped into the public treasury, you can never get it out for use by a religious-oriented school without constitutional cavil. The only way to do it is to grant the relief before the dollar becomes public property. I.e., before it is taxed. And the way to do that, obviously, is by tax remission.

The courts appear to be hospitable to the argument. In the 1970 *(Walz)* decision arguing against direct subsidies, the court said that "obviously a direct money subsidy would be a relationship pregnant with involvement." On the other hand, "the grant of a tax exemption is not sponsorship since the government does not transfer part of its revenue to churches but simply abstains from demanding that the church support the state."

The good news is that Wilbur Mills caught the signal and though two years ago he was in the Oval Office of the White House pounding his fist in disapproval of the notion of tax remission, this year, mirabile dictu, he emerges as the sponsor of a bill which would provide relief for the private schools by exactly that expedient. The Congress will close momentarily, and it is unlikely that it will vote during this session on the Mills bill, but particularly after the Ohio rejection of last week, it looms as the last hope this side of a constitutional amendment. Essentially, the bill would grant a straightforward tax credit ($200 is the figure they speak about) to any parent who sends his child to a private school. There are any number of variables, i.e., will it be $200 per child no matter how many children; does the tax credit inure even to the benefit of rich parents—and so on. But the principle is comfortably lodged. If it is constitutional for the Congress to say that Mr. Jones' gift of $100 to his church decreases his adjusted gross taxable income, then why can't Congress say that Mr. Jones' expenditure of $500 for his son's education at St. Bartholomew's decreases his tax bill by $200? Who says A must say B. If Congress can constitutionally permit tax deductions for religious gifts, why not tax credits for religious expenses?

We shall see. Meanwhile, about two private schools per day are closing for lack of funds. And taxes increase, as the students go to the public schools. And the frustration mounts.

Dead End with the Court

June 27, 1973

THERE IS a quite general dismay in the afflicted sections of the country following the Supreme Court's perverse decision on the matter of the private schools. What the Court said, in effect, is this: Look, the First Amendment doesn't permit support of religion. Now however deviously you achieve the support of religious schools, that is what you are doing when, as in the state of New York, you permit a taxpayer whose child goes to a private school to itemize a part of that cost as a tax credit.

Now this decision came as a considerable surprise. It upset

a half dozen laws that were either in operation, or poised to go into operation. It upset a Congressional bill that had the approval of the administration, and was working its way quite peacefully through the House Ways and Means Committee, recently liberated from Mr. Emanuel Celler. Paul Blanshard is still alive and has not been heard to condemn the entire thing as a plot to repeal the First Amendment, instigated in Rome.

Moreover, in 1970 the Court had made an enticing distinction in the *Walz* decision, on which toehold the legislators slowly built their structure, and now it too has collapsed.

I truly wonder that all the recent talk is of executive tyranny. At least one measure of the security of any kind of tyranny is the kind of opposition it provokes. When it was widely held that President Lyndon Johnson, and after him Richard Nixon, were waging an unlawful war in Indochina, there was opposition in Congress, in the academy, and in the streets. Today it is everywhere proclaimed that the arrogance of the Executive is bringing on a constitutional crisis, that nothing less than deep surgery will cure the situation and save American democracy.

Who now speaks about judicial tyranny? It appears to be very nearly absolute. It is hard to remember when last the Constitution was amended in order to reverse or to clarify a ruling of the Court. The essential facts in the current situation are these. The Bill of Rights is among other things there to protect this country from the establishment of a state religion. There are fewer Americans who desire a state religion than Americans who want to bring over the Hapsburg Pretender to rule over us.

The overwhelming majority of Americans believe that freedom of religion includes freedom to operate religious-oriented schools. The Supreme Court, in *Pierce* v. *The Society of Sisters,* ruled as long ago as 1925 that it was unconstitutional for any state to establish a monopoly of public schools. Yet a monopoly of public schools is exactly the direction toward which we are headed under the fanatical prodding of a Court that transforms a simple phrase in the Constitution, forbidding the establishment of religion, into a prohibition against elementary toleration of other people's tastes as to where they desire their children to be educated.

The time has now come either for the religious schools to prepare to collapse; or to be open only to the wealthy few; or to pass a constitutional amendment. Rabbi Morris Sherer, who heads a coalition of sectarian and nonsectarian private schools that has pressed for tax credit legislation, has called a meeting in Washington to discuss the alternatives. There are none. One wishes that a few more people in America would accept the authority of the Word of God as compliantly as they do the word of the Supreme Court.

The Need for a Constitutional Amendment

September 7, 1974

PRESIDENT FORD has proposed an amendment to the Constitution to return to the individual states the right to prescribe abortion laws. In other words, to undo the decision of the Supreme Court a year and a half ago preempting authority over abortion.

I hope Mr. Ford's amendment is adopted, but I do so for more reasons merely than because, along with so many others, I thought the decision usurpatory.

The underappreciated point about the Supreme Court is that it has become a kind of moral-secular authority. Adult men and women, staring hard at a clause in the Constitution of the United States that forbids, say, an establishment of religion, and recognizing no reasonable nexus between that prohibition and the recital, at their local public school, of a public prayer jointly formulated by rabbis, ministers, and priests, receive on Monday what might be called a juridical bull from the Supreme Court, and on Tuesday there is compliance.

Their docility is, in the religious sense, exemplary. *If that is what the Supreme Court says,* the most urbane American lawyers, governors, ministers, and journalists will say—*why that is how it shall be.* It is my point that it is something more than compliance that then results. It is something more akin to what, in religion, they call "internal assent." If-that-is-what-the-Supreme-Court-says-that-is-the-way-it-will-be, graduates toward: If that is what the Supreme Court says, that is the way it *ought* to be. The docility becomes religious in character.

The objection that, after all, we have had a number of constitutional amendments in recent years does not affect the insight. Because the amendments, with an insignificant but nonetheless interesting exception, have merely codified popular passions, some of them consolidated (no poll tax), others impulsive and manipulated (no booze). But (save for one largely irrelevant exception—the income tax amendment) there has been no constitutional amendment the purpose of which was to revise the interpretations of a Supreme Court, notwithstanding egregious provocations by the Court, most recently during the fifties and sixties, when it became a commonplace to refer to the "Warren Revolution."

Those who hoped for the status quo ante—in the area of legislative representation, criminal procedure, or freedom of association—spoke big, and filed their proposed constitutional reforms; but, in fact, it was a ritual. They were really waiting for a few popes to die, knowing that only fresh popes could authoritatively change doctrines that were fast being accepted or—received.

The public, under the tutelage of its moral and intellectual leaders—is being trained, as regards the Supreme Court of the United States when it is interpreting the Constitution, to accept its rulings as if rendered ex cathedra, on questions of faith and morals. Thus political candidates for office are routinely quoted as saying that they disapprove (let us say) of busing schoolchildren; but that if the Supreme Court rules otherwise, that of course will be that. It is a far different statement from one, republican in analysis and spirit, which would read: "I am against busing, but if the Supreme Court rules otherwise, I shall abide by its decision—*pending the final*

*verdict on the question by the people through the amendment proc-
ess."*

The durability of the United States Constitution is in part
testimony to the genius of its architects. But it endures also
because it changes. It changes in considerable part at the
shaping of the Supreme Court; concerning those elabora-
tions of the Constitution much poetry has been written,
mostly by those who, at any particular historical period, are
enthusiastic about the direction the Court is taking.

The public needs to experience a release from a subtle
thralldom to judicial morality. The polls are clear on the
matter known as busing, and clear also on abortion when last
there was a state plebiscite on the question. As regards busing, the people are overwhelmingly opposed. The polls are
clear also that the voters are opposed to the total seculariza-
tion of the schools. A constitutional amendment, such as proposed by President Ford, done athwart the will of the Court
for the first time in modern history, would accomplish more
than simply bring relief to the majority who consider themselves victims of judicial usurpation. It would deliver the Republic from a presumptuous ethical-political tribunal which
has come to treat the Constitution with something like an author's possessiveness. Thus is mocked their fellow Americans' powers of thought analysis, and their august commitment to self-rule. Accordingly, the special need for a constitutional amendment, as proposed by the President.

4. Anglican Agony

January 13, 1975

As a Catholic, I have abandoned hope for the liturgy,
which, in the typical American church, is as ugly and as mala-
droit as if it had been composed by Robert Ingersoll and H.
L. Mencken for the purpose of driving people away from the

temples. The modern liturgists, incidentally, are doing a remarkably good job, attendance at Catholic Mass on Sunday having dropped sharply in the ten years since a few well-meaning cretins got hold of the power to vernacularize the Mass, and the money to scour the corners of the earth in search of the most unmusical men and women to preside over the translation.

The next liturgical ceremony conducted primarily for my benefit, since I have no plans to be beatified or remarried, will be my funeral; and it is a source of great consolation to me that, on the occasion, I shall be quite dead, and will not need to listen to the accepted replacement for the noble old Latin liturgy. Meanwhile I am practicing yoga so that, at church on Sundays, I can develop the power to tune out everything I hear while attempting, athwart the general calisthenics, to commune with my Maker, and ask Him first to forgive me my own sins, and implore him, second, not to forgive too lightly the people who ruined the Mass.

Now the poor Anglicans are coming in for it. I am not familiar with their service, but I am with their Book of Common Prayer. To be unfamiliar with it is as though one were unfamiliar with *Hamlet,* or the *Iliad,* or the *Divine Comedy.* It has, of course, theological significance for Episcopalians and their fellow travelers. But it has a cultural significance for the entire English-speaking world. It was brought together, for the most part, about 400 years ago, when for reasons no one has been able to explain the little island of England produced the greatest literature in history. G. K. Chesterton wrote about it, "It is the one positive possession, and attraction . . . the masterpiece of Protestantism; the one magnet and talisman for people even outside the Anglican Church, as are the great Gothic cathedrals for people outside the Catholic Church."

What are they doing to it? Well, there is one of those commissions. It is sort of retranslating it. As it now stands, for instance, there are the lines, "We have erred, and strayed from thy ways like lost sheep. We have followed too much the devices and desires of our own hearts. We have offended against thy holy laws. We have left undone those things which we ought to have done; and we have done those things which we ought not to have done."

That kind of thing—noble, cadenced, pure as the psalmist's water—becomes, "We have not loved you [get that: *you*, not *thee*. Next time around, one supposes it will be "We haven't loved you, man,"] with our whole heart, we have not loved our neighbors as ourselves." "Lead us not into temptation" becomes "Do not bring us to the test."

Well, if the good Lord intends not to bring His Anglican flock into the test, He will not test it on this kind of stuff. As it is, Anglicanism is a little shaky, having experienced about 100 years earlier than Roman Catholicism some of the same kind of difficulties. I revere my Anglican friends, and highly respect their religion, but it is true that it sometimes lends itself to such a pasquinade as Auberon Waugh's, who wrote during the discussions over the Bishop of Woolwich, "In England we have a curious institution called the Church of England. . . . Its strength has always lain in the fact that on any moral or political issue it can produce such a wide divergence of opinion that nobody—from the Pope to Mao Tsetung—can say with any confidence that he is not an Anglican. Its weaknesses are that nobody pays much attention to it and very few people attend its functions."

And it is true that in a pathetic attempt to attract attention, the Anglicans, and indeed many other Protestants, and many Catholics, absorb themselves in secular matters. "The first Anglicans," Chesterton once wrote, "asked for peace and happiness, truth and justice; but nothing can stop the latest Anglicans, and many others, from the horrid habit of asking for improvement in international relations." International relations having taken a noticeable turn for the worse in the generation since Chesterton made this observation, one can only hope the Anglicans will reject any further attempt to vitiate their lines of communication with our Maker.

5. A Personal Statement

December 26, 1974

Mr. Robert Shnayerson
Harper's Magazine

Dear Mr. Shnayerson:
I write [in response to your inquiry] the day after Christmas. I have in front of me a little machine, deposited in my stocking, with which I have been toying. If you pick up a flexible metal strip thinner than your fingernail and ease it into a slot at the upper end of the wallet-sized instrument, an invisible gear clutches it, passing it quickly through, right to left, leaving it limp to the fingers at the opposite end. You grasp it and slide it then into the upper slot where it serves you as dashboard, and what you see, imposed over eight rows of pencil-eraser sized keys, is: GREAT CIRCLE NAVIGATION STD 03A [over the subheading:] LAT LNG calc dist calc hdg. I desire to know what distance I will need to go when, on the last day in May, I weigh anchor at Miami on my sailboat, bound for Gibraltar. I enter the latitude (LAT) of Miami, and the longitude (LNG) (respectively, 25.30, 80.15), and of Gibraltar (5.5, 36.10). I then depress the key (C) that appears directly below "calc dist" (the calculated distance between the two geographical positions whose coordinates have been fed into the computer). The bank of red digital numbers goes into a chaotic frenzy. I don't know how many different numbers actually flash on and off—it would require a slow-slow motion camera to photograph the tracery, and reduce it to figures; and there are split seconds of blackest void, as if the instrument was gagging on the difficulties of the task. But although it seems a very long time, in seven seconds there is sudden calm, and the figure is crystallized, like a tall mountain after a prolonged series of geological explosions: 3831.46 miles, we'll have to sail. In which direction? A great circle bearing is not lightly yielded, and so after depressing the key (D) there is even more commotion, lasting twelve seconds. The course is: 60 degrees 38 minutes.

All of that from the mind of man. It occurs to me, as I ponder the work of Hewlett and Packard, that what strikes me as extraordinary is child's play for Hewlett and Packard, who have answers to scientific problems I shall never know enough to frame. Raising the inevitable question: What is it that strikes Hewlett and Packard as extraordinary? David Hume is famous, among other things, for remarking, in the manner (if not the tone) of Oscar Wilde, that he would sooner believe that human testimony had erred, than that the laws of nature had been suspended. It occurs to me on reflection that the operative word, even allowing for the meiotic tradition of the English, is—"sooner." There *is* a choice. Mine is made, that the order of the universe, the arching of the human spirit, the enduring mysteries of love and the unique serenity of faith, are the result of—Central Planning, which took seven days, not seven seconds, to create a world exciting enough to doubt Him. That is the flirtatious side of God, to reach for a terrestrial metaphor. We should laugh at its presumption, as, after trying it out several times, I can laugh at the black nihilistic teases of Hewlett and Packard. I am programmed to love God and to seek, however vainly, to obey Him, and to trust that the course He laid out for me in the grandest voyage, through time and space, and uncertainty, to infinity and transfiguration, and resolution, is as certainly charted as the toyland course that will lead me from Miami to the Rock of Gibraltar. I shall follow the star of Bethlehem, waywardly; and if I fail to reach it, I shall be guilty of every delinquency save that I ever doubted it was there.

Yours faithfully,
Wm. F. Buckley, Jr.

XV.

Personal

Lillian Elmlark, RIP

(A Eulogy)   June 3, 1973

I DID NOT KNOW her when she was a girl, or even when she was a young woman, married to Harry Elmlark. My impressions of her then are reconstructions, but I do not imagine that they are ill conceived. She was even then, I suppose, both fragile and strong, tentative and resolute, wistful and beautiful. I did not know him either, but one must suppose that the man she married was even then, as now, impossible; and lovely. During the first decade they were adrift, at the mercy of the great currents that were buffeting America, and it was not obvious to any of the academic observers that the Republic would survive. They might with profit have spent an afternoon with Lillian Rosenthal Elmlark. They'd have found there the stuff of this country's enduring strength.

Anyone might have spent an afternoon, with profit, with Lillian Elmlark. There was to begin with the purely feminine charm. Colette wrote that it is given only to a woman convincingly to give her attention not only to what is said to her, but to the person who says it to her. The two attachments were not distinguishable with Lillian: she listened to what you said, and she listened to you. She did so with that combination of diffidence and discrimination which over the years were the alchemy that made her husband Harry endurable, an accomplishment Lillian brought off with that careless skill reserved only to great women. Her responses to life, to what Yeats called the perpetual injustice of life, were at once tender and resigned. When, ten years ago, I first met her, it was instantly clear that unlike the deracinated men so typical of this uprooted century, Lillian was a glad product of a tradition. There was about her a sense of history fulfilled and fulfilling, the maturity of the fully developed human being, the distinctively Jewish blend of pathos and exaltation about which the psalmists sang; the huge capacity for human friendship.

It was just a week ago that Harry told me that although

that which was rational in him begged that Lillian should die soon rather than later, even so he could not imagine a greater desolation than her gone, even if, now, she was only half alive. She never acknowledged the gravity of her illness. The biological compulsions of sickness in due course governed her body. But while she was in control of herself, and this was until nearly the end, her preoccupations were with her husband and her family. Her reticence was with her until the end. She seemed to be saying that she thought it immodest to die. She went to the hospital only at the last moment, and she went there dutifully, concerned mostly to spare her husband and her family extraordinary inconvenience. She died there calmly, peacefully, dutifully.

I thought back, yesterday, of an evening with Lil. It was her birthday, two or three years ago, and there were four of us, Lil and Harry, my wife and I. We were at a splendid restaurant, and Harry was at his best, putting on the act for which he is so famous, affecting an egregious concern for the price of the lettuce, for the indignities of the service, and for the deficiencies of the Republic. Lillian's responses were perfectly tuned. She would sigh, giggle, reproach him stiffly, laugh, demurely change the subject. Harry, emboldened, undertook, on receiving the bill from the headwaiter, one of his economic flights. After reminding us that he had majored in mathematics at the University of Virginia, he reflected that the cost of Lillian's birthday dinner for four people could have purchased 106 TV chicken dinners. Lillian's response was that characteristic blend of feigned embarrassment at Harry's eternal vulgarity, a fugitive amusement over Harry's act, and a protective affection for the man who blew 106 chicken dinners on her birthday, her beloved Harry.

Our beloved Harry. We mourn Harry's loss. The privation is his and his family's, surely not Lillian's. The prophet Isaiah tells us that "the Lord God shall wipe away tears from every face, and the reproach of his people he shall take away from off the whole earth." How do we know that this is so? "The Lord hath spoken it," Isaiah says. "And they shall say in that day: Lo, this is our God, we have waited for him, and he will save us; this is the Lord, we have patiently waited for him, we shall rejoice and be joyful in his salvation."

It is hard to speak, at this moment, of joy in anything, because the fact of it is that, returning from here to Seventy-second Street, Harry will return to an apartment empty of Lillian, and how can one hope to say to him that what matters is less the joy he got from her, than the peace, and happiness, she now has, after the tribulation of the human experience. "Those who have endeavored to teach us to die well," Samuel Johnson wrote, "have taught few to die willingly: yet," he added, "I cannot but hope that a good life might end at last in a contented death."

I pray today not so much for the repose of the soul of Lillian Rosenthal Elmlark, whose loveliness catapults her so confidently into the company of the angels, as for those who are forlorn by her absence, Harry especially, to whom there is left for us to say only that we offer ourselves as poor substitutes for his beloved Lillian, and enjoin upon him the words of the psalmist who, experiencing the distress we are here to record, wrote, "The Lord is close to the brokenhearted; and those who are crushed in spirit, he saves."

Dennis Smith the Fire Fighter

March 20, 1972

ALL OF MY professional life I have listened not disrespectfully—how does one do that to Murray Kempton, or Dan Wakefield?—to the proposition that one cannot truly know a situation without experiencing it for oneself, and never mind the grander applications of that thesis, as they concern, say, sorrow, loneliness, or doubt. I talk about lesser things, and challenge the idea (for instance) that you cannot know about life in Harlem, or about the morphology of Presidential campaigns, or about the life of a fire fighter, without yourself being involved or, failing that, applying yourself as a Boswell, on the scene. I think that Fireman Dennis Smith has written a masterpiece, but hold that for a moment. Can one—short, obviously, of becoming a fireman—know the texture of that existence better than by reading his book? Absolutely not. And, indeed, I'd go further and venture (no doubt to the embarrassment of Fireman Smith) that a reader of his book will end by knowing more of the texture of that profession than do many firemen. This is so because Smith is an artist, defined here as someone who can supply the perspectives with intuitive knowledge of their hierarchy. Smith's success, in this extraordinary book, is a major achievement, comparable to Claude Brown's telling us about Harlem and drugs in *Manchild in the Promised Land,* and Joe McGinniss' telling us (however tendentiously) about Presidential political packaging in *The Selling of the President.*

Smith is a thirty-one-year-old fire fighter who was raised on the East Side in poverty, quit high school at age fifteen, made a living delivering flowers and otherwise, until at twenty-one he realized (quite unambiguously) that he had a vocation. To fight fires. He was, to be sure, drawn to the profession because it is a prestigious fraternity, notwithstanding that (in part, because?) it is, statistically, the most dangerous profession in America—more so than being a policeman, or a miner, or a soldier. There are many more applicants than positions, and one wonders at that, reading this *Report from Engine Co. 82* (Saturday Review Press, $5.95). Granted, the company to which Smith is assigned is the most active in the city, answering over thirty alarms (real and false) in a typical day. (At one point, neophyte Smith decided to try to keep track of how long he would go without a meal's being interrupted by an alarm. He gave up counting after three and one-half months.) Smith was not assigned to Engine Co. 82, in the sense that some marines are assigned to Iwo Jima. After a few years in a relatively tranquil company, he decided that his ardent vocation needed more oxygen, even as there are priests who apply for service as missionaries in South America, or who ask for a transfer to a Trappist order. Smith, with an unusual sense of timing, withholds from the reader until near the end of his book his idealistic dispositions: so that by the time one reaches them, anticipating that now he will disrobe as slowly as any stripper, teasing the last

bit of lust from the reader, and confess that idealism is mostly very hard and dangerous work—he does it all very quickly,
summarily even. Because after a half dozen chapters teem-
ing with smoke and fire and pitch and frozen hose couplings
and a teenage hooker and wild and naked young Puerto Ri-
cans with knives and whips and charred babies and ravished
stepdaughters—you are ready for it; even as, not long after
the age of thirteen, you look back on the movie *Gunga Din*
and recognize that anybody who lets Victor McLaglen talk
him into another term's servitude to the Bengal Lancers deserves nothing better.

Of course, the fashion is to stress the negative, and we
make instant artists out of the Genets, resisting those who,
like Smith, admit to a lingering kinkiness for decency. I sense
that he knows this, and therefore resists any plainspoken endorsement of acts of corporal charity, of the sort high New
York social society has gratefully received from people like
Eleanor Roosevelt and Dorothy Day. But, begging the general pardon, Dennis Smith, high school dropout, can work with
idealism in ways in which those gentle, hard-boiled ladies
never quite could, in part because his narrative and descrip-
tive gifts save him time and again from the colloidal humani-
tarianism of people who are wonderful at legislating or even
administering acts of mercy, but who are public enemies
when they write about them. Dennis Smith, describing a fire
in the bowels of which are stranded a mother and (it will
transpire, dead) child, writes, "We push in, Lieutenant
Welch saying, 'Beautiful, we almost got it, just a little more,'
all the while, and Royce just behind humping the hose, saying 'If you need a blow Dennis, I'm right here.' I can feel the
heat sink into my face, like a thousand summer days at the
beach. We reach the third room, and the fire is extinguished,
defeated, dead. The smoke lifts, and the walls breathe the
last breaths of steam." After that you are ready for human
victims, in the sense in which you somehow aren't when reading (how *do* they get past the third?) the New York *Times'* list
of the 100 Neediest Cases.

And again, why do we need whole academic departments,
when there are fire fighters who can say it in a paragraph?

"I'll never escape from tenements and cockroaches. The

names and the geography may change, but conditions are universal when people are without money. Mrs. Hanratty who lived down the hall from us in my youth is now Mrs. Sanchez; the O'Dwyer for Mayor sticker in the vestibule wall now reads Father Gigante for Congress; and the cry 'Tu eres animal, Rodrigo' now airs through the courtyard in place of 'Jesus, Barney, can't ya ever come home ta me sober?' The smell of dried garbage and urine hasn't changed, but the vomit on the unwashed marble stairs is now mixed with heroin instead of ten-cents-a-shot Third Avenue whiskey. Like chalk to a teacher, roaches are part of my past, and now part of my work. They are under me or on me as I crawl down long, smoke-filled halls. They scurry helter-skelter as I lift a smoldering mattress, just as they scurried between the tin soldiers on the battlefield of my living-room oilcloth. As a child, I would shiver and run from them as I do now, but I was just fearful of them then; now, I resent them. More than anything, they represent poverty to me. More than anything, they are the one facet [unfortunate word] of my youth that I was forced to accept—the ugly, brown, quick-darting companions of the poor. My mother would whisper that she cleaned and sprayed but it didn't help much because they were put in the walls by the builders many years ago, because they had a grudge against the Irish and the Italians. And, anyway, no matter what she sprayed around, the little creatures would learn to enjoy it. I learned that they could be fought, but not defeated. I, as they, adapted." I submit: you have here Daniel Patrick Moynihan, Charles Dickens, Will Herberg, Oscar Lewis and Ring Lardner.

And, though we are singed by hellfire, we experience here and now repose, the homespunness of which, under the discipline of the author, resists the banal—"Tomorrow is Easter. I have the day off, and will be at home with Pat and the boys. My brother and his family will come up, and my mother. My brother will talk about the mentally disturbed children he teaches to read and write, and we will scold our own children for making too much noise. I'll talk about fires and firefighters, and my mother will relate the successes and failures of the guys I grew up with. We'll laugh, and sing songs with the children. The youngest of them will grab at the strings of my guitar and the songs will be interrupted. We will eat heartily, and afterwards the children will ask me to play the bagpipes, and I will tell them I am too tired, and too full. When the table is cleared, the half-devoured ham wrapped securely in plastic, the dishwasher belching its ugly sound, we will sit by the fireplace, joined by the women, and sip brandy and crack nuts, throwing the shells into the fire. It will be a fine day."

And of course the next day will be less fine, like the doctor's, because he too goes from a picnic in the countryside to the operating table at New York Memorial, where he is greeted, as you and I are by orange juice, with a malignant tumor. How does Smith write about the South Bronx? By asking himself, "What would Wordsworth have said of the South Bronx?" And answering the question as brilliantly as he ever performed on duty: "He wouldn't write of hedgerows hardly hedgerows, but of people hardly people." That is Fireman Smith's position.

I don't know anything that has come out of New York City in years that resists better the progressive dehumanization. Or that reminds us more vividly of the formal connection between the spiritual and the material enterprise. "I do not understand," says Smith wistfully, commenting on the refusal of a few fellow fire fighters to join as hosts for a children's neighborhood picnic, "how a man can risk his life in a blazing tenement to save one black child, and refuse to see, to be a part of, two hundred black kids eating ice cream." For Dennis Smith, the phlogistic attractions are inseparable.

Shockley and Shockleyism

A CONTACT WITH Dr. William Shockley serves to remind one how ill poised the academic community is to cope with its own. First they tell you that the colleges are havens for all ideas, that no one has anything to fear in the open society because we shall seek the truth and endure the consequences. Then along comes someone like Dr. Shockley, whose ideas grate on fashionable sensibilities, and the academic community makes a fool of itself by its own standards. Meanwhile, the same community that deplores Dr. Shockley, who is merely an inventive dilettante playing chess with genetics, listens with great respect to Dr. B. F. Skinner who, if his notions about the nature of man were ever believed, would make Dr. Shockley the Mr. Nice-Guy of the academic season.

I do not suggest that Dr. Shockley is harmless. He is in two senses harmful. First, he is a live carrier of scientific hubris. Second, his palaver encourages an Archie Bunkerite racial invidiousness. The same data that can cause Bunker to glow with feelings of racial superiority would be dismissed by such as Professor Ernest van den Haag—as irrelevant.

To begin with, Dr. Shockley doesn't believe in gas chambers for blacks. That will terribly disappoint a significant number of young gentlemen in Yale, NYU, and Stanford, and I apologize for my role as dehobgoblinizer. It is true that sometimes he talks unguardedly about what "should be," and one remembers that desiderata are the seedbeds of totalitarian political movements. But even when Shockley is talking about what should be, it is, as stated, race-free. "Restrictions *should be* placed," he has written, "on the basis of sound genetics without regard to income, class, race, religion or national origin. The breeding of good genetic material, whether the people are rich or poor, is desirable. We want more Lincolns, not fewer." That is Shockleyism.

And that, built on loose data suggesting that in IQ tests measured by Professor Arthur Jensen, Negroes tend to score a few points behind whites, has led to Shockley's doctrine of "dysgenics." Dysgenics, he explains, is "retrogressive evolution through the disproportionate reproduction of the genetically disadvantaged."

Spread out, this says: (a) poor people have more children than nonpoor people; (b) there are fewer bright people among poor people than among nonpoor people; therefore (c) the state should try to persuade poor nonbright people to have fewer children. Persuade? Exactly: Shockley proposes cash incentives for voluntary sterilization. One thousand bucks for each IQ point below 100 if you will submit to sterilization.

What's wrong with that?

It is hard to begin any discussion with rationalists, because there are no reciprocating gears. One might point out that in fact Mr. and Mrs. Lincoln didn't beget any Lincolns, whereas Mr. and Mrs. Carver begat George Washington. Or one might point out that the economic movement of the past decade among Negroes toward economic self-sufficiency is more marked than among whites. Or that, on the whole, bright people have caused the world a lot more trouble than dumb people. Or that the techniques of birth control are rapidly becoming known even among the ignorant, and still surer techniques are on the verge of discovery. And so on.

But meanwhile, how would the country look if everyone had the IQ of, say, a Yale student? Or a Yale president? It is by such as them that the distinctions are regularly blurred: Shockley, who should be condescended to, is shouted down, and his hosts are likened to the mob. Skinner, who should be feared as the dominant contemporary spirit in the movement to dehumanize man, is received fawningly. Poor Shockley. He would probably be treated more sensibly and with more dignity by illiterate blacks in the Alabama countryside, who in their own way have tamed George Wallace.

Harry Truman, RIP

December 6, 1972

FOR A WHILE, Harry Truman was enormously popular among the academic elite. He reached the peak of his popularity after his defeat of Thomas E. Dewey, whose self-assurance in a year that saw his opponents divided into three camps made his defeat all the more satisfying. The academic flirtation with Henry Wallace was brief, and by the time the fall of 1948 came around, Wallace had lost all but hardened fellow travelers and the advanced addlepated. Strom Thurmond, of course, was merely a Democratic embarrassment. They went accordingly to work for Harry Truman, a man they had despised in part because he presumed to sit at the desk of his great predecessor, in part because his vulgarity was always showing through, in part because of the general postwar diplomatic and economic pandemonium.

At one point in the demoralized spring of 1948, when Harry Truman was considered unreelectable, and when Democratic party leaders were urging him not to run again, Senator Claude Pepper publicly proposed that the Democrats nominate General Dwight Eisenhower—and permit him, sight unseen, to write the platform for the Democratic Party.

Then Truman began to fight. And suddenly the tastemakers discovered him. The coarser his rhetoric, the more vituperatively he denounced the Republicans, the more they liked it. One has visions of the ascetic, aristocratic Arturo Toscanini, who used to like nothing more than viewing the old wrestling matches on television about which he would get so excited he would jump up and down on the couch yelling "Keel him! Keel him!" Which is exactly what Truman went on to do to his opponent, as the professors jumped up and down on their lecture platforms with glee.

By the time the end of the next term came, the public had visibly tired of Truman. Senator McCarthy had dramatized the extraordinary postwar diplomatic defeats. We were fighting in South Korea a war which Truman was pleased to call a police action. We had lost China, and it was plain that the Soviet Union had no intention of releasing the countries it held captive in East Europe. The Soviet Union had developed an atom bomb three years before the most pessimistic estimate of when they would do so.

Domestically, Truman's arrogance was wearing the public down. He thought one day on the flimsiest ground to take possession of the steel industry, and was quickly rebuked by the Supreme Court. He was always wrangling with Congress and declining to permit Congressional committees to examine executive records. He had indeed developed a megalomania which was socially embarrassing, at odds with the republican spirit which is especially appropriate to Democratic Presidents.

He chose, wisely, not to run again, and left the White House without anything more than a purely perfunctory exchange with his successor. But as the years went on, so did the rehabilitation of Harry Truman.

At this enterprise his old friend Dean Acheson was tireless, remarking the solid qualities of Truman's character, his decisiveness and courage, the implacable stands he had taken against the Soviet Union in Greece, and against Red China in Korea. He had given the order, against the advice of the great Oppenheimer, to construct a hydrogen bomb. He knit together the network of alliances that still survive, at least formally. He enthusiastically presided over the foreign aid that catalyzed the economic recovery of Western Europe. And like Cincinnatus returned to civilian pursuits, he now devoted himself to his library, to entertaining foreign and domestic visitors, and to occasional acts of charming exuberance like playing the piano with Jimmy Durante. He was hailed as a great President.

For his sake it is good that he was senile during the last few years, so heavy now with displeasure against him and his policies is the critical mood. He, it is said, is more responsible than any man in America for the Cold War, for the internecine alliances, for United States militarism and chauvinism, for a delay in discharging our obligations to racial equality. Thus the pendulum swung, and he wasn't, in ill health, fit, as in the old days, to grab hold of it and hurl it back, knocking over the fainthearted, the revisionists, the ideological egalitarians who are currently in control of the history factories. Harry Truman made many grievous mistakes, but it is not his mistakes that are singled out for criticism, but his triumphs.

Lyndon Johnson, RIP

January 24, 1973

SAN ANTONIO. The lady is middle-aged, shrewd, politically active, impeccably kind, civic-minded, born in Texas and raised here, and she spoke as if she were facing such a problem for the very first time in her life. Well, obviously not the first time: when acknowledged monsters like Hitler and Stalin died, people did not, for the most part, scratch about to find something redeeming to say about them. LBJ was clearly of another category, but the lady now remarked—"What am I supposed to say? I didn't like what I knew about him personally. I didn't admire his domestic programs. And I thought his foreign policy was a mess. So what am I supposed to say?"

I counseled her to say nothing, absolutely nothing at all. Having done so, I regretfully acknowledge that my advice is only one part discretion, nine parts funk. Accordingly, into the breach. . . .

Even if history justifies Lyndon Johnson's determination to stand by South Vietnam, it is very difficult to believe that history will applaud his conduct of the war. We set out, in Vietnam, to make a resonant point. We did not make it resonantly. In international affairs as in domestic affairs, crime is deterred by the predictability of decisive and conclusive retaliation. The Soviet Union knows that it can count on a dozen years between separatist uprisings in its empire because when it moves, it moves conclusively. If the Soviet Union had sent a few battalions into Hungary, and a dozen years later into Czechoslovakia, the Soviet Union would not have made its point.

Johnson, reminiscing in the White House a year before he was evicted, told two reporters that there was no way he might have avoided a showdown in Indochina, that not only John Kennedy (who told him shortly before leaving for Dallas that he intended to make a stand there) but Dwight Eisenhower (who told him in the early sixties that Southeast Asia would be the principal challenge of the Presidency) agreed on the strategic point. But what, one wonders, has been achieved under the circumstances?

To begin with, nobody can predict that, a year or two from now, South Vietnam will still be free. But of greater importance than that, no one in his right mind will predict that the United States, facing a comparable challenge a year or two from now, would respond with military decisiveness. If, in that part of the world, the decision is to gobble up Thailand, what are we going to do about it? Exactly. And if, in another part of the world, they decide to go after Yugoslavia, or even Greece—what would we do about it?

It was the strangest aspect of this strange man that, once having decided on a course of action in Vietnam, he did not pursue it characteristically—i.e., with exclusive concern for its success. By his failure to do so, he undermined the very purpose of the intervention. And if the great Communist superpowers exercise restraint at this point, it will not be because they have learned the lesson of Vietnam in the way that Stalin learned the lesson of Greece and Iran. It will be merely because of the coincidence of their mutual hostility and their desire for American economic aid.

So what of his great domestic accomplishments?

What great domestic accomplishments? He sought a Great Society. He ushered in bitterness and resentment. He sought to educate all the population of America, and he bred a swaggering illiteracy, and a cultural bias in favor of a college education so adamant and so preposterous that if John Milton applied for a job with Chock Full O' Nuts, they would demand first to see his college diploma. The rhetoric of LBJ was in the disastrous tradition of JFK—encouraging the popular superstition that the state could change the quality, no less, of American life. This led necessarily to disappointment, and the more presumptuous the rhetoric, the more bitter the disappointment.

The Great Society did not lead us into eudaemonia. It led us into frustration—and to the lowest recorded confidence vote in the basic institutions of this country since the birth of George Gallup. But: he was a patriot, who cared for his country, who was unsparing of himself, and who acquired at least a certain public dignity which lifted him from buffoonery, into tragedy. And he was the object of probably the greatest sustained vituperation in American political history. He paid a very high price for the office he discharged. And his detractors, as it happened, are America's worst friends, if that was any consolation.

H. L. Hunt, RIP

December 9, 1974

THE DEATH OF Mr. H. L. Hunt, reputedly the richest man in the world, brings to mind some of the tribulations of the defenders of the free market society.

Life would on the whole have been easier for thoughtful advocates of the free market if Mr. Hunt had been a socialist rather than a conservative. For one thing, assuming his character had not changed, he would have been a very stingy socialist, which helps. For another, if he had backed socialist causes, he'd have backed the kookiest of them. Add to which, if he had written and distributed socialist literature instead of conservative literature, he'd have unerringly distributed the most simplistic literature in the field, driving away, rather than toward the desired goal, the intended convert.

I once alluded to Mr. Hunt in a national magazine—a half dozen years ago. "Winston Churchill," I said, "is reported to have said about a tedious socialist of unconventional sexual disposition that he had managed to 'give sodomy a bad name.' Mr. Hunt has done his share among capitalists he has known to give capitalism a bad name, not, goodness knows, by frenzies of extravagance, but by his eccentric understanding of public affairs, his yahoo bigotry and his appallingly bad manners. It is especially ironic that Mr. Hunt has in the course of time employed any number of people professionally devoted to the capitalist ideal, almost all of whom found that their exposure to Mr. Hunt turned out to be the greatest test of their ideological devotion."

Mr. Hunt took great offense, and wrote to many newspapers suggesting that I and my enterprises are surrounded by Communists who *claim* to have deserted the party. The inference was clear (Mr. Hunt was never subtle): in criticizing Hunt, I was doing the work of the Communist Party.

Apart from the damage Mr. Hunt did to the conservative movement, on the whole he led a most useful life. Precisely by becoming rich. It was never so much Mr. Hunt's behavior that rankled the socialist or the dogmatic redistributionist. It was the fact that he was so very rich, so stupendously, redundantly rich. Mr. Norman Thomas, chairman of the Socialist Party, for instance, got utterly carried away by the subject. One time, when I was exchanging views with him at a student forum, he almost lost his voice in indignation at the recently announced calculation that Mr. Hunt was worth $2 billion (give or take $100,000,000, as they say in Texas). Mr. Thomas roared, and fumed, and pawed the ground, and tore at the lapels of his jacket, and belched forth such indignation as the fires of Vesuvius showered upon the people of Pompeii.

We can work ourselves up—can we not?—into a considerable lather against the rich. Not only can we, we do. I confess that I myself get more exasperated by rich people than ever I do by poor people, for the obvious reasons (the rich should know better) and the less obvious reasons (the rich should know better how to enjoy themselves). But even so, what most isn't needed nowadays is a stupendous redundant excoriation of the rich, but rather a defense of the rich—and the sooner the better, before they are made to disappear, which would be very bad news indeed.

The most far-out defense of the rich has been made by that most austere economist, Nobel Prize-winning F. A. Hayek. In the *Constitution of Liberty,* he makes an empirical defense of liberty and therefore of capitalism, and reasons the progressive feature of the income tax out of intellectual existence. He even goes so far as to say that if the rich did not exist, they should quite literally be invented. Society has an enormous stake in its rich—so much so that assuming a society were starting from scratch, everyone equally poor, you would do well to pick 100 citizens and give them each $10,000,000. Because the rich are uniquely situated—Hayek explains what is obvious, yet what is widely unrecognized—they are free to turn their attentions to other matters than getting and spending, even though their capital, used as such, is their most useful economic purpose. Sometimes the rich will spend their money not to buy themselves the redundant wife (like Tommy Manville), or to distribute silly books (like H. L. Hunt), or pay the bills of misanthropic revolutionists (like Friedrich Engels), but to commission another symphony from Mozart (like Lichnowsky), and give money for medical research (like Roy Cullen), or pay the school bills of talented students (like Solomon Guggenheim).

Mr. Hunt built a great fortune. Part of it was luck, to be sure. Part of it was skill, and hard, hard work. The country will miss his entrepreneurial and managerial gifts.

Frank Shakespeare

(Remarks at a Testimonial Dinner)

February 3, 1973

MR. FRANK SHAKESPEARE has now stepped down as director of the United States Information Agency. And several newspapers have dispatched him with considerable rancor. I take leave to dissent. . . .

I met Frank Shakespeare casually, about ten years ago. I knew about him then only that he was a successful young executive in CBS, and that he had a natural affinity for—what he understood to be the purpose of America, viewed from a perspective now almost 200 years old. And a heightened concern for the obligations of America, in a world divided for the most part between those who are hostile to freedom, and those who are indifferent to it. He had gone to Holy Cross College, where he was taught everything there is to learn in the store of human knowledge except the difference between the word "appraise" and the word "apprise," which is the only vulnerability on which the New York *Times* and the Washington *Post* might over the years profitably have fastened. And went directly into business.

A few years later—I divulge a confidence—he approached me to ask my opinion whether I thought Richard Nixon had credentials to serve as President, and to forward a cause we now implicitly acknowledged as having in common. I told him it was my opinion that Mr. Nixon did, and in due course Frank Shakespeare presented himself, in the early months of

1968, to Mr. Nixon and offered to stick with him until he attained the Presidency, or until he lost it.

When Mr. Nixon was elected, he asked Shakespeare to stay with him, and to take charge of the United States Information Agency. I know that he was not disposed to accept the assignment, in part because he felt that it was time now to return to his profession, in part because he felt he had consummated his commitment. He thought not in terms of helping to administer a fresh regime, but of midwifing one. Mr. Nixon, in any case, prevailed; and Shakespeare found himself directing a very large agency, with 10,000 employees, which was never altogether sure what was its function.

The point is hardly settled, what *is* its function. There are various concepts, some of them not easily compressible. I think it accurate to suggest that Frank Shakespeare believes that truth ought to be the tuning fork of our information policy. But in order to make even that statement coherent, it becomes necessary to acknowledge, however soft-spokenly, two things.

One of them is that as a nation we are modestly, but documentably, committed to certain human values, and that necessarily we make judgments with some reference to those values. Another is that the exigencies of diplomacy are not to be confused with the philosophical elaboration of the just society.

My first direct experience with the USIA was in Vienna, to which I went for my first breathtaking experience under the aegis of Frank Shakespeare. The public affairs officers, gathered there from our offices in Eastern Europe for their bi-annual meeting, were passing around, with some amusement, a copy of a column written by Murray Kempton in high glee after reading the freshly published book, *The Selling of a President,* by Joe McGinniss.

McGinniss held Shakespeare up to great ridicule for having said at a staff meeting in the course of the campaign the preceding summer that the Czechoslovakian coup proved yet again that the Soviet Union is not to be trusted to mature into liberalism. I recalled the column in a conversation with Mr. Kempton, a few days ago, and commented that perhaps the trouble with Shakespeare is that he takes Solzhenitsyn seriously. Kempton replied that Shakespeare having served under CBS, no doubt he knew what Ivan Denisovich was talking about.

This is not the occasion to mediate on United States information policy. But it is appropriate to say that against a background of ambiguity as to mission, of concerted and even spiteful opposition by men of another disposition about United States information policy, during a period of great diplomatic upheaval, the symbols of which it is once again not appropriate to recall here, Frank Shakespeare conducted himself in such a way as to earn the quite unabashed admiration of his associates, of whom I was one. I am qualified only to add this, that I have not known a man more thoughtful to his friends, more spontaneous in his enthusiasm, more devoted to his family—or to his religion—or to his country, which is a better country for his service to it.

Sir Arnold Lunn, RIP

June 1974

ARNOLD LUNN died in London on June 2, but at eighty-six was absolutely undaunted, though the flesh had become very weak. He was at work, for the next issue of *Ski Survey,* on an essay on the Olympic Committee's history of the Games. Also on a book—this time on Lakes Thün and Brienz; on several articles, including one for *National Review* and he was expecting, in America, the reissue of his book *Spanish Rehearsal,* about the Civil War. His most recent article had appeared in the *Tablet* only the day before, and his son Peter, and his wife Phyllis, read it aloud to him in the hospital. I can imagine his chuckling over his own words, which greatly amused him, as they did everybody else, save possibly their victims who, come to think of it, probably constituted a majority of readers. He took an unrestrained, unaffected pleasure in his work, which was amiably sarcastic, in the meiotic British tradition, wonderfully well turned, unrelenting but good-natured. He was a most serious man, who saw the humor of every situation.

His career began only months after graduating from Harrow, a few years after Winston Churchill. He wrote *The Harrovians*, an exposé of sorts of public school life, tame stuff by the standards of *The Fourth of June* by David Benedictus, which came along fifty years later about life in Eton; but enough to launch him as a radical young writer. His interest in sports and mountaineering dominated him in those days; and one summer before he was twenty-two he fell while on a solo climbing expedition. For several hours he was without help; then they found him, took him to the hospital, and he blessed himself that (a) the anesthetist was incompetent and (b) he understood Welsh, because he was awake when he should have been unconscious, enough so to hear the doctors making preparations to amputate his leg. This, from his strapped-down position on the operating table, he forthwith forbade, summoning all the authority he could in his youthful voice. The result was a leg deformed, slightly shorter than the companion leg. Athletes and mountaineers of the world wondered what the competition would have been from Lunn if he had had normal legs. Because he scaled everything in Switzerland there was to scale, and raced with the early British ski teams, and was made president of the Ski Club of Great Britain over fifty years ago, and founded the prestigious Kandahar Club in Mürren. It was in those days that he conceived the idea of the slalom, which he introduced into Olympic competition where it has been a fixture ever since. As the years went on, he found skiing more and more difficult, but he persevered, and I skied with him when he was seventy-five years old.

He lived in Mürren during the winter, a ski eyrie that faces, across the Lauterbrunnen valley, the Jungfrau and the dread Eiger. At Mürren he was visited by princes and paupers in his little suite at the Jungfrau Lodge, made available to him by the hotel's owner who recognized that Arnold Lunn had done more for mountaineering and skiing than any Swiss—indeed he was knighted in 1953 by Queen Elizabeth in acknowledgment of those achievements—and that he was broke. To reach him, one rose by funicular, or took the new awesome lift, developed just in time to be exploited in one of the James Bond movies. In Mürren, where there are about 300 residents, he was the most illustrious of them all, and the most beloved and most indulged. When he was eighty-four, Lady Lunn left to visit very briefly her aged mother and gave Arnold his detailed instructions on how he was to behave during her absence. He listened with great attentiveness and apparent docility, and the moment she was off on the funicular, he picked up the telephone and ordered the concierge to produce his skis. The concierge told him forty-five minutes later that he had looked for them in vain, that they must have been lost, after ten years of neglect. But a few minutes after that, very nearly in tears, he confessed that he had hidden them at the express instructions of Lady Lunn who suspected her husband might be just mad enough to try them on.

Sir Arnold used to say that all of mankind is divided inflexibly into two classes. There are the "helpers" and the "helpees." He had discovered early in life that he was a member of the latter class, that no marriage was successful that united two members from the same class. His first wife, Lady Mabel Northcote, was a helper; and when she died, a dozen years ago, he wed Phyllis Holt-Needham who, in addition to all her other qualities, was a born helper: so he knew he was licked. Disconsolately he set out, using the two walking sticks on which he now depended, across the snowy path toward the Jungfrau's dining room when, suddenly remembering his wife's several admonitions, he found his hand slipping down his front to verify that he had remembered to button his fly. But experiencing nothing there at all, he concluded he had his pants on backward. It was all he could do to survive the three days of her absence, and she was never absent again, and was with him when in the early afternoon, failing to rally, he died in the Catholic Hospital of St. John and St. Elizabeth near London.

He must have found it an inconvenient time to die. Two days later he was to have spoken at a golden jubilee dinner of the Kandahar Ski Club, of which he had been the central

PERSONAL   485

figure since its founding. "Phyllis has told me nòt to be controversial in my speech," he had written me. "I must be amusing. I thought after the president had proposed my health as founder of the club to begin my speech saying, 'Phyllis tells me I must not be controversial. So I will begin by expressing cordial agreement with all the very nice things the president has said about me.'" He'd have laughed greatly, telling his friends this. I think he must have spent half his life laughing. During the other half, in addition to the usual things, he wrote fifty-four books, discovered Christianity, and, for his friends, reminded us more than any man I have ever known what is meant when one talks about the irrepressibility of the human spirit.

His road to orthodoxy was, as so often is the case, the road of the militant agnostic. During the 1920s he engaged in spirited debate with Christians, among them Father Ronald Knox. It was thought the exchanges with Knox were so brilliant and of such general interest that they warranted publication as a book. This was done, and Lunn and his votaries were satisfied that they had had the better of the argument. But Knox's arguments, not inconceivably by grand design, overcame Lunn himself, and presently he left the comfortable world of skepticism for a career as a brilliant and persuasive Christian apologist. (His book *Now I See,* published in 1933, was a part of the casual reading of Hugh Kenner when he was a boy, and thirty years later he wrote Lunn to tell him he had succumbed to its arguments.) It was the failure of his contemporaries to concern themselves for the evangelistic function of Christianity that Arnold Lunn could never understand, and against which he railed to the end, criticizing altar boys and Popes. He remarked in a recent letter that "I expect to be the first Catholic excommunicated for orthodoxy."

He was always writing, in his private and published letters, about the Christian mission, and the importance of individual protest. As a high functionary in the skiing world during the thirties, he had succeeded in applying pressure in behalf of Jewish athletes. Why are things now so different, he wondered. "In today's *Times,*" he wrote last December on his chattering old typewriter, whose faded imprints were more difficult to discern than his quaking hand, "I have a letter. Here it is: 'Professor Obolenski's letter on the continuing persecution of Christians in Russia will remind Christians living in security of what we find it too easy to forget. Why is Christian esprit de corps so pitiful compared with Jewish and African esprit de corps? Why are there no demonstrations of Christians, ecclesiastical and lay, in Downing Street to demand the cessation of persecution in Russia, and above all why are there no Sunday prayers in Christian churches for persecuted Christians?' . . . The usual answer is that protests make things worse for the persecuted. But that depends on the protest and its backers. I achieved one positive result, with help from others, on a protest, when I got leave for Schneider to leave Nazi Austria."

The general collapse of standards he was enough the historian not to be surprised by. But the acquiescence in their collapse by Christian ministers could not expect to do less than bring a letter to the *Times,* or to one of his friends. "Yesterday's paper recorded a case of paedophobia [a term Lunn liked to use for 'fear of children']. . . . One of the results of what is fraudulently described as the permissive society. Our age differs only in being more permissive of fornication, etc., and less permissive of any attempt to prevent youth doing what it pleases. 'The legitimate users of the playing field,' we are told by the minister about the recreation area under his charge, 'have better things to do than to arrange the disposal of the youngsters' discarded contraceptives.' Some of these youngsters are 'only 11, or 12.' . . . The moral? In this, as in all else, never blame the sinner, blame the community. The rector wrote his article 'to stimulate the community into providing more social amenities. . . . Our problem is to find better recreational facilities for these children.' Unfortunately, it may be difficult to convince these children that there can be a better recreation than fornication."

He found, as other modern critics, notably Malcolm Muggeridge, have done, a high piquancy in the forms and implications of the great sexual revolution. Last summer he wrote: "The Jellicoe-Lambton scandal puts our avant garde progressives in a dilemma. You see, it is 'progressive' (1) to approve of fornication, adultery, and homosexuality; (2) to disapprove of aristocracy and aristocrats. So what is the current avant garde line when a lord commits adultery with a call girl? I see no nice solution so far as Lord Jellicoe is concerned, but as all convinced progressives are enthusiastic egalitarians, the difficulty of combining one and two might be resolved in the case of Lord Lambton, for he habitually went to bed with two call girls, which few could afford. Egalitarianism, my dear Bill, demands one man, one call girl."

His letters, even on the most solemn matters, almost always ended with a smile. "P.S. Could you tell me whether it is improper to address an American on an envelope as A. B. Smith Esquire, rather than as Mr. Smith? A newly appointed American concierge here at the hotel in Switzerland thought that 'Esquire' was a family name and assumed it must be a very large family, to judge by the number of letters addressed to different persons of the Esquire clan. All such letters were filed under 'E.' It was only when his 'E' partition was overflowing that he asked the manager just when would all these different members of the Esquire clan be arriving."

Though he mixed by preference with ski folk, and students, and indigent poets, he knew the high and the mighty, and was never depressed by finding good qualities in them. "I do wish you could have met the Princess [of Liechtenstein]. In this egalitarian age she has far far more than any reasonable allowance of charm. I know so many charm-deprived people to whom surplus charm might be allotted. I would like to be appointed Minister of Charm Allotment in the next Labor Government." But no one visiting the tiny suite in Mürren ever overwhelmed him. On one occasion Marshal Montgomery hove in, and tried to take over the Kandahar Ski Club, the flagship of Arnold's enterprises. He reminisced about it a few years later. "My own relations with Monty ended rather less friendly than they began. He was my first wife's, Mabel's, first cousin, and normally signed himself 'Bernard.' At the last Kandahar party, Robin Day of BBC was a guest, and he reminded me that in a reply to one officious letter from Monty signed 'Montgomery of Alamein,

Field Marshal' I signed myself, 'Arnold of Kandahar, Snow Marshal.'" Monty gave up on the Snow Marshal, and left Kandahar alone.

I am a member of the Kandahar Ski Club. In order to qualify, it is required that you should descend that terrible mountainside in less than a specified number of minutes— too much for a skier who came to the sport in middle age. "Why are you not a member?" Sir Arnold asked me one day. I explained. Sitting at his desk, he executed a form, asked me for three guineas, gave me a club receipt and the envied badge for my ski parka. "You are now a member." How? I asked. "Under Rule 13, my dear Bill. Nepotism."

When I say I treasure my Kandahar badge, I use the word loosely—I haven't any idea where it is, as a matter of fact. But I treasured the gesture, in context of Arnold's unfailing good humor during the afternoon and evening we would spend together every year at Mürren, and I wrote him so once. "You have occasionally implied that I had rendered you a service," he wrote back. "I have tried very hard—for it makes me more comfortable to believe you—to recall any real service that I have ever rendered to you. Of course I have sometimes made you laugh, and that is a trivial service of sorts. Our friendship dates from a banquet at which I claimed that we in England are more democratic than you in the U.S.A., that whereas you provide careers only for the talented in Congress, the House of Lords provides a career for the untalented. Well, well, if my alleged service to you is as one who has made you laugh, never in all time has a laughmaker been more rewarded. And the greatest reward is all that your friendship has meant to me."

Gratitude was the source of his energy, and of his faith, and of his humor. After commenting, in a letter last Christmas, about the indifference of men toward the plight of each other, he closed with an uncharacteristic solemnity, valedictory in its effect on me. "Every night when I curl up in bed I try not to take for granted that I have a roof over my head and a pillow below my head, and to contrast my immense good fortune in love and friendship with the millions in misery and the millions persecuted, and my letter to the *Times* is not only intended to awake Christian conscience but as a trivial token to quiet my own."

The editors of *National Review* extend their deepest sympathy to Lady Lunn and to his children, on the death of a devoted husband and father, an illustrious Englishman and Christian, our esteemed colleague, and my devoted friend.

Henry Regnery
(Remarks at a
Testimonial Dinner)

April 12, 1972

WHEN I learned that I would be preceded by Russell Kirk and David Collier and Jack Kilpatrick and Vic Milione and Stan Evans and Eliseo Vivas, I wondered why Louis Dehmlow hadn't, while he was at it, arranged to produce Ezra Pound. To present me at the end of this list of speakers is, to say the least, dramatically insecure. It was Abraham Flexner who remarked that For God for Country and for Yale was surely the greatest anticlimax in the English language. But I am here, as we all are, to register our solidarity on a very important attachment—to a man who has been important to all of us in one way or another, indeed to some of us in a combination of ways: as a friend, a publisher, a mentor—in my own case all three. I have not only read books he suggested I read, but even written books he suggested I write: and this requires a very special relationship with someone, such as brought us here tonight.

It is a night for reminiscences, and I think it is accurate that I have known him longer than any of the speakers here tonight, having met him even before Russell Kirk did. I am especially happy about the fecundity of his noble house, inasmuch as I remember, during the very dark days just after

God and Man at Yale appeared, that Henry was wondering whether any writer would ever again consent to write for a publishing house which had midwived such an outrage. It is characteristic of Henry that when he reached this slough of despondency, he didn't do what most of us incline to do—to call out for help, or reassurance, from our friends. I still have the letter from him, advising me that he had devoted the night before—after seeing the first rash of reviews—to re-reading the book. He concluded that he had been correct to publish it and, so far as I know, never gave another thought to the reviews nor to his decision to launch the book, not even when the University of Chicago took the occasion to affirm academic freedom by discontinuing its Great Books contract with the Henry Regnery Company.

It is hard to recall, in the light of later experiences, how much fun it used to be to publish a book. When I came to Chicago to meet Henry and discuss such matters as jacket design, it was automatically assumed that I would stay at his big house in Hinsdale, where over the course of several years I, and subsequently my wife and I, spent so many evenings. I think I should pause, in deference to historical accuracy, to record that there was a certain risk in those days in spending the night with the Regnerys. To begin with, it was during the years of the Regnerys' martial Quakerism—if Professor Vivas will permit the oxymoron. Translated, that meant: no booze. This posed a quite awesome prospect for a young author only a few months graduated from Fraternity Row at Yale University. But Providence has a way of stringing out its little lifesavers in strategically opportune ways—and sure enough it transpired that across the street from Henry, in another big house, lived a most informal and exuberant gentleman, an artist named Kenneth, who had befriended Henry and, by the expansiveness of his temperament, Henry's friends, known and unknown, ex officio. So that at approximately six o'clock in the afternoon, Kenneth would throw open his shutters and, at the top of his lungs, cry out, "If Henry has any guests staying with him, Thee-all can come over for a drink." That disposed of that problem.

The other problem was that Henry's guests sometimes tended to sleep later than Henry's five children. Depending

on my mood, I give different answers to the question I am
sometimes asked: When did you stop publishing with the
Henry Regnery Company? When I feel provocative, I say:
Some time after I stopped sleeping with the wife of the president. In due course I chivalrously divulge that Susan was
then six years old, and she and her two brothers and her little
sister would all four of them come to bed with me at about six
o'clock in the morning and giggle with apprehension when
they heard their mother's footsteps coming to relieve the beleaguered guest. I would do my sleepy best to entertain
them, but they were thoroughly spoiled. Because the bed in
question was often occupied by Roy Campbell, and *he* would
begin instantly, on being boarded by the children, to improvise great tales of giants and giant killers which would hold
them enthralled; and not long after I used to stay there, they
would find themselves under the covers with Russell Kirk,
who would tell his tales of ghosts, in accents baroque and
mysterious. I could not hope to keep them so much excited
by tales of Keynesianism at Yale.

They were as I say very happy days, in which book publishing was something of a personal partnership between publisher and author, each contributing his skills, like one of
those communes we nowadays celebrate. I remember hus-
tling for *McCarthy and His Enemies*—a speech in Milwaukee,
driving up in Henry's car, with Regnery officials Bill Strube
and Kevin Corrigan, Henry at the wheel, the trunk loaded
with books, which we hawked shamelessly after the speech
was concluded. I think we sold seventy-five books that night,
and when, long after midnight, we finally reached Hinsdale,
exhausted, it was with grins on our faces, as if we had drilled
a gusher. . . .

Henry has spoken, in a published piece about his experiences, about the "dismal" sixties, which is how he refers to
the decade that introduced Camelot, the *Playboy* philosophy,
and Mario Savio. Usually when one refers to an unhappy
decade, it is in order to highlight the happy contrast of the
succeeding decade. But concerning the seventies, Henry
Regnery is not at all optimistic, not at all. "The threat of extinction," he surmises, "is now much greater than it was then:
those bent on destroying civilization are better organized,

and the defenses are weaker." He tells us that there won't be—I use his language—any "money or glory" in it—but, he says, "we have inherited a great and noble tradition, and it is worth fighting for."

On that proposition we are all, I assume, agreed—at least, all those of us who paid $25 to attend this dinner. On the other hand, it is also obvious that by no means everyone is agreed that this is so. It was ten years ago that I heard the most succinct statement on this point, by a fashionable young literary iconoclast, who put it this way: once upon a time, it was worth dying—for two reasons. The first was that heroism was rewarded in another world. The second was that heroism was rewarded by the memory of man. However—he said—now that we know from the scientific evidence that there is in fact no other world, no future world, no Christian heaven; and now that we have invented weapons which are capable of destroying all of mankind and therefore all human memory along with it—what is the reason left to run the risk of death and war?

This is a blunt way of saying it, and by no means suited for mass consumption. After all, the average man is not absolutely convinced that H. G. Wells was that much more on top of history than, say, Christopher Dawson; or that George Bernard Shaw had the better of the argument with G. K. Chesterton or C. S. Lewis. And besides, to make the point that we have weapons enough to vaporize mankind is not to dispose of the point that just as after a war there would almost surely remain weapons unused, so would there remain human beings unkilled: so that the potential uses of heroism survive even in the secular context.

Henry is right, when he generalizes that it will be hard to teach people to oppose the effronteries of the modern world. Henry published a book called *In Defense of Freedom,* by Frank Meyer, who would have been here tonight, except that he died two weeks ago. Even in the early sixties, Meyer's metaphysical defense of objective freedom was—somehow—just a little bit embarrassing, and even to the finest of people, the finest of friends, the most ardent of counterrevolutionaries.

"If the Republican Party does not find a way to appeal to the mass of the people," Whittaker Chambers wrote to me after the election of 1958, "it will find itself voted into singularity. It will become, then, something like the little shop you see every now and then in the crowded parts of great cities, in which no business is done, or expected. You enter it and find an old man in the rear, fingering, for his own pleasure, oddments of cloth (weave and design circa 1850), caring not at all if he sells any. As your eyes become accustomed to the gas light, you are only faintly surprised to discover that the old man is Frank Meyer."

In Russia it costs a month's wages to buy a novel of Solzhenitsyn in the black market. And there are old men—and old women, and young men and young women, who in the far reaches of their vast country, transcribe by hand, from Radio Liberty, which they risk prison by listening to, the new novel of Solzhenitsyn, word after word, sentence after sentence, a process that takes months to complete: resulting not in thousands of copies, but dozens or perhaps a few hundred: the oddments of cloth, circa the golden age of civilization, viewed synoptically. It is worth *everything* to preserve those oddments, to make them available to those who are graced with a thirst for them: or—nothing is worth anything at all. Henry Regnery was never confused on this point, so that as long as people are free to remember, there will be those who take thought, and will give thanks to those who came before, and thought, as Henry has done, with loving care to preserve the tokens of hope and truth.

Jozsef Cardinal Mindszenty

April 1, 1975

CARDINAL MINDSZENTY, primate of Hungary, was convicted in February of 1949 of all the usual things you can convict somebody of if you torture him long enough, deploy skilled

forgers, phony defense lawyers, paid and intimated witnesses, and, for the sake of a little plausibility, if you succeed
in sowing abroad just that hint of doubt—not about
Mindszenty's innocence: that was quite widely taken for
granted—but about his guilt. "When I subsequently went
through foreign books, newspapers, and magazines that
dealt with my case and commented on my 'confession,' I realized," the ingenuous prelate tells us, "that the public must
have concluded that the 'confession' had actually been composed by me."

I contribute to the memory bank my own recollection. I
was a student at Yale, one of a few dozen who felt that the
conviction of Mindszenty at the show trial was an offense
against human sensibilities so brazen that a quiet protest was
imperative, to which end we reached out, under the leadership of the head of the Protestant undergraduate council, for
what I can only think to call the purest man in the community, a slightly deaf philosopher of awesome erudition, super-
natural eloquence and overpowering goodness. His lecture
at Battell Chapel, late one afternoon, expressing grief at the
profanation by the puppet government in Hungary, clings
even now to the memory; but lo and behold, Professor Calhoun did, in passing, regret the apparent collusion between
Cardinal Mindszenty and the pretender to the Habsburg dynasty, greatly stressed at the trial, which we discover on reading this book consisted of a single civil encounter between
Archduke Otto and Cardinal Mindszenty, in Chicago, over a
half hour period, for the purpose of trying to raise American
money to help starving Hungarians. From this grew the legend that the cardinal, among other crimes against the state,
was scheming with reactionary elements for the restoration
of a reactionary dynasty.

The memoirs tell the entire story, and cannot, I think, be
disbelieved. They are, for one thing, insufficiently inflamed.
It would be easier, than to fail to accept this as the exact record of the momentous events of a Christian whose fate au-
gured the fate of Eastern Europe, to reconstruct the chemicals in a color film, for the purpose of giving distorted impressions of the hues and tones of a landscape. Cardinal
Mindszenty writes without passion—"I have avoided any

provocative or polemical tone which might prompt base vengeance on me personally or on the church," not because he feels dispassionately, but because he is very old, and very wise, and very experienced, and he knows that he is addressing a world which cannot bring itself to care efficaciously for the suffering of his countrymen because compassion and impotence are, after a point, incompatible; and when, finally, the same man who, as a cardinal of Milan, walked the streets with a cross on his back on the day Mindszenty was condemned, to register his solidarity with his fellow cardinal, as Pope relieved Mindszenty of his primacy, athwart Mindszenty's protests, the cardinal knew that there was no one left, in this world, to plead to: though one likes to feel, on reading this plainspoken book, that the plain words will reach out and move the Prime Mover, in ways they cannot move even His most conscientious servants on earth. An earth in which the Archbishop of Rome is resigned to the necessity of humiliating his adamantine Hungarian cardinal, for the express purpose of avoiding the risk of humiliating his oppressors.

Cardinal Mindszenty, it is appropriate to record, believes that he got away easy in the prisons in which he was kept for the seven years before taking refuge in the American Embassy during the brief Hungarian uprising in 1956. "I must say that physical torture was applied to me much more restrainedly and circumspectly than in the case of many other prisoners"—because it was needed physically to effect his survival, for the purposes of the show trial. His moderate treatment at the Communist prison in Budapest is elsewhere described. "The tormentor raged, roared, and in response to my silence took the implements of torture into his hands. This time he held the truncheon in one hand, a long sharp knife in the other. And then he drove me like a horse in training, forcing me to trot and gallop. The truncheon lashed down on my back repeatedly—for some time without a pause. Then we stood still and he brutally threatened: 'I'll kill you; by morning I'll tear you to pieces and throw the remains of your corpse to the dogs or into the canal. We are the masters here now.' Then he forced me to begin running again. Although I was gasping for breath and the splinters of the wooden floor stabbed painfully into my bare feet, I ran as fast as I could to escape his blows."

When the trial was over, and the long prison term began, the tortures were of a different kind, and students of the subject can spend useful hours on several chapters in this haunting diary. I like especially the totalitarian genius for useless torture. "In May 1950 [my mother] had a picture taken of herself for me, wrote a dedication on it, and sent it to the minister of justice with a request that it be turned over to her imprisoned son. I did not receive the picture until five years later. Aside from a photograph of Pope Pius XII, it was my only picture from the world outside. I put it on my table and kissed it every night."

And I am most struck by one phrase in this flat book with its tombstone prose, its haunting pictures (opposite page 225 there is one of the cardinal as eloquent as any painting of St. Sebastian), its horrifying record of the decomposition of Western purpose. One of the reasons given by a courier from the Vatican why the Cardinal must leave the American Embassy in Budapest was so that he might publish his memoirs—whose publication, by the way, was subsequently discouraged. The monsignor, the Cardinal recalls, added that "I could keep the manuscripts with me and in case of my death have them turned over to a priest who enjoyed both my confidence and that of the Holy See. He even promised that the Vatican *would pay for the necessary typing expenses.*" I cannot imagine that the typing "expenses" taxed the resources of the Vatican; nor, I suppose, can I hone a contagious indignation at the subsequent neglect of the man singled out only two years ago by 130 members of Parliament in England as "the most prominent freedom fighter in Europe," who had gone to jail fighting Nazi and Communist tyranny. Pope Paul, a year before stripping the cardinal of his authority, embraced him in Rome and told those in attendance, "I am giving His Eminence my cardinal's mantle so that it will protect him from the cold in that cool country and will serve as a symbol of the love and respect I have for him." There is no reason to question that love or respect. But the cardinal's end—"total exile" is how he puts it—was predictable. While he was a resident in the embassy, Vice President

Nixon stopped by; but did not call on him. Nor, a few months later, did two sisters of President Kennedy. Cardinal Mindszenty understands, and there is nothing, really, that can be done for him in the few months or years he has left to live, though we can perhaps wrench from our mortification at our neglect of him a little pride at the overlap in our lives.

Death of a Christian

January 22, 1975

A DAY OR TWO before Thanksgiving, Charles Pinckney Luckey of Middlebury, Connecticut, Congregational Church was making his ministerial rounds, as usual on his motorcycle, when suddenly, rounding a corner, he lost his balance and fell. He arrived home to his three vacationing sons—two from college, one from nearby Taft School—a little bedraggled. But this didn't matter much—he was always a conspicuously informal dresser, though never affectedly so; in fact there was no trace of affectation in him, which is one reason why he was so greatly, and quietly, popular with the congregation, even as he had been at Yale, and Taft.

What vexed him was that he should have lost his balance. A perfect physical specimen at fifty, tall and rangy and handsome with a face of a thirty-year-old and the physique of a long-distance runner. So he went to the doctor suspecting he had something wrong with his ears, knowing like the rest of us only Boy Scout medicine, which tells you that when your balance is off, something is wrong in your ear canal. The doctor examined him, couldn't find anything, and everyone hoped whatever it was would go away.

It didn't. Within a week or two he began to lose his vision, at an alarming rate. In three weeks he was blind, and beginning to lose motor control on his left side. A legion of specialists had by that time surveyed his wilting frame, and a name was spoken which squirts ice water even among hardened doctors, because there are only a half dozen recorded cases of it and it is most gruesomely and implacably lethal. They call it Creutzfeld-Jakob disease. Something about a galloping attrition of the nerve endings. Prognosis: one–three months. Cause? Nobody knows, though there was much speculation. Could he have got it eating strange fish in the Yukon on his camping trip this summer with the boys?

They took him to Columbia Presbyterian in New York, to "confirm" the diagnosis. One suspects the altogether understandable reason for the trip was to give the medical students a chance to examine someone suffering from such an exotic disease, rather like the gathering of the astronomers to gaze at a once-in-a-lifetime comet. It was only there that he yielded to depression, as they poked about and asked him questions, to measure, scientifically, the physical and intellectual deteriorations. Before, and after, he was obstinately cheerful and affectionate, dictating to his secretary every day letters of farewell to his friends, letters exalted by a curious dignity that attached to him even as a teenager. He preached his last sermon, propped up by his seventeen-year-old son at the lectern, on the Sunday before Christmas to a congregation wracked with pain and admiration.

The crisis came shortly after. He called his secretary and dictated a paragraph which he sent to a few friends, and which was pronounced by the retired, aged chaplain of Yale University "the most moving credo to the Christian faith written in my lifetime."

"What"—Charlie dictated—"does the Christian do when he stands over the abyss of his own death and the doctors have told him that his disease is ravaging his brain and that his whole personality may be warped, twisted, changed? *Then* does the Christian have any right to self-destruction, especially when the Christian knows that the changed personality may bring out the horrible beast in himself? Well, after 48 hours of self-searching study it comes to me that ultimately and finally the Christian has to always view life as a gift from God, and every precious drop of life was not earned but was a grace, lovingly bestowed upon the individual by his Creator and so it is not his to pick up and smash.

And so I find the position of suicide untenable, not because I lack the courage to blow out my brains but rather because of my deep, abiding faith in the Creator who put the brains there in the first place. And now the result is that I lie here blind on my bed and trust in the succeeding, loving power of that great Creator who knew and loved me before I was fashioned in my mother's womb. But I do not think it is wrong to pray for an early release from this diseased, ravaged carcass.

"Lovingly given," he closed the statement, diffidently, "to my congregation and to my friends if it seems in good taste."

It seems to me in very good taste, and I pass it along, with the good news that at least that final prayer was answered. The coma began two weeks later, and on January 21, he died. There had been no personality change. That, all the dreadful powers of Creutzfeld-Jakob couldn't do to Charles Luckey.

Index

ABC, 256, 324
ABM systems, 336
Acheson, Dean G., 331–32, 475
Adams, Sherman, 111
Aereo Mexicana, 180
Agnew, Spiro T., 38, 43, 80, 84, 120, 152, 165, 330–31, 332, 333, 364, 365, 379
Aiken, George D., 400
Air France, 173–75
Algeria, 204
Algren, Nelson, 112
Ali, Muhammad, 415
Allende, Salvador, 321, 362
Allott, Gordon, 99
Alsop, Stewart, 139
American Economics Association, 74, 281
American Federation of Television and Radio Artists (AFTRA), 255–59, 431
American Motors, 62
American Party, 350
Americans for Democratic Action, 72, 74
America's Cup, 225–26, 228
Amin, Idi, 212
Anderson, Jack, 79, 106, 118–19, 342, 359, 427–29

Andrew (Prince of England), 182
Angola, 212
Anslinger, Harry J., 394
Anson, Robert Sam, 81
Apollo XI, 248
Arab powers, 200, 202, 204. See also individual listings
Ashbrook, John, 22-23
Athens (city-state), 241
Atkinson, Ti-Grace, 334
Atlantic, 35
Attlee, Clement, 27
Autonomous University (Guadalajara), 179–80

Baker, Bobby, 165
Bangladesh, 359. See also India-Pakistan war
Bantustans, 207
Beame, Abraham D., 330
Beard, Dita, 277
Becket, Thomas à, 106, 128
Bellow, Saul, 298
Benedictus, David, Fourth of June, The, 483
Berger, Raoul, 150; Executive Privilege, 148
Berlin, 34, 268
Bernstein, Leonard, 92

501

Berrigan, Daniel, 152
Bertolucci, Bernardo, 406
Beveridge, William H., 262
Bismarck, Otto von, 129
Black, Hugo L., 323
Blanshard, Paul, 454
Boggs, J. Caleb, 99
Bowersox, Jerry, 233
Bozell, Patricia Buckley (sister), 333, 334
Braddock, James, 224
Bradlee, Benjamin, 164–66
Brakhage, Jane, 355
Brakhage, Stan, 355
Brando, Marlon, 405
Brandt, Willy, 56, 201
Breslin, Jimmy, 363
Brewster, Kingman, 364, 365, 366, 367, 375, 376
Brezhnev, Leonid, 46
Brown, Claude, Manchild in the Promised Land, 468
Brown, Edmund G. "Pat," 109
Bruce, Lenny, 403–05
Brundage, Avery, 237
Buchanan, James, 92
Bucher, Lloyd, 378–79
Buchwald, Art, 88, 93, 94–95
Buckley, Christopher (son), 231
Buckley, James L. (brother), 21, 80, 93, 122, 124, 144, 145, 285, 286, 303, 304, 320, 335, 341, 367, 432, 433, 440
Buckley, John W. (brother), 335
Buckley, William F., Jr., 21–22, 23–25, 26, 88–93, 119, 139–41, 161, 211–12, 217–18, 227–35, 244, 246, 255, 282, 290, 292–93, 298, 303–71, 414–15, 420–22, 427–28, 434–35, 436–37, 460–61, 478, 481, 488
Bukharin, Nikolai I., 364
Bunker, Archie, 398, 400
Burchett, Wilfred, 28
Burger, Warren E., 164
Burgess, Anthony, 379–81
Burke, Edmund, 270, 407
Burnham, James, 62, 392

Burton, Richard, 297
Butts v. Satevepost, 323
Byrd, Robert C., 158–59

Calhoun, John C., 68, 72
Calhoun, Robert L., 494
California, 271
California v. Krivda, 88
Cambodia, 128, 391
Campbell, Roy, 491
Canada, 204, 237, 238, 239, 243
Cannon, Jimmy, 218
Cape Shoalwater (boat), 233, 234
Capone, Al, 443
Capote, Truman, 297–98, 339
Cardozo, Benjamin N., 88
Carver, George Washington, 473
Castro, Fidel, 118, 120
Cavett, Dick, 234, 255
CBS, 257, 258, 294, 429–31
Celler, Emanuel, 454
Central Intelligence Agency (CIA), 48–49, 118, 432, 436–37
Chafee, John H., 341
Chalfont, Lord Arthur Gwynne Jones, 213
Chamberlain, Neville, 58
Chambers, Whittaker, 280, 281, 317, 492–93; Odyssey of a Friend, 337
Chapin, Dwight L., 106
Chappaquiddick, 122, 127, 259
Charles I, 116
Chaucer, Geoffrey, 311–14, 331
Chavez, Cesar, 284, 378
Chesterton, G. K., 181, 366, 458, 459, 492
Chiang Ching, 31, 83
Chiang Kai-shek, 397
Chile, 263, 362
China, 474. See also People's Republic of China; Taiwan
Chisholm, Shirley, 71, 382
Chomsky, Noam, 34–35, 273, 306
Chou En-lai, 24, 29–30, 35, 39, 40, 48, 83, 222, 223
Churchill, Winston, 41, 56, 95, 96, 478

CIA. *See* Central Intelligence Agency

City College of New York (CCNY), 379–80

Civil War, U.S., 450

Clark, Ramsey, 88

Clark, Tom C., 88

Coe, Frank, 280, 281

Coffin, William Sloane, Jr., 366, 367

Cold War, 57–58, 66, 199, 475

Colette, 465

Collier, David, 489

Colson, Charles W., 132, 443, 444

Committee for Cultural Freedom, 28

Committee to Re-elect the President (CREEP), 125, 126–27, 130

Communism, 38–39, 42, 55, 57. *See also* individual countries and leaders

Connally, John B., 84–85

Connelly, George G., 328, 329

Conrad, Joseph, 248

Conservative Party, 329–33

Considine, Bob, 26

Conte, Silvio O., 291–93

Corrigan, Kevin, 491

Council on Foreign Relations, 360

Cowan, Richard, 392

Crane, Les, 319

Cronkite, Walter, 25, 258, 290, 291

Csonka, Larry, 219–20

Cuba, 34, 239, 242

Cullen, Roy, 480

Cultural Revolution (Chinese), 26–27, 29, 31, 32, 33, 35, 36, 48, 222, 279

Curtis, Carl T., 156

Cyrano (boat), 228, 229–35

Czechoslovakia, 44, 178, 180, 390, 397, 476, 481

Daley, Arthur, 242

Daley, Lar, 100

Daley, Richard, 91, 92, 165

Dame Pattie (boat), 228, 229

Daniel, Clifton, 54

Davenport, Guy, 318

Davis, Angela, 178, 239

Davis, Garret, 117

Davis, William, 177

Dawson, Christopher, 243, 492

Day, Dorothy, 471

Day, Robin, 73, 487

Dayan, Moshe, 92, 197

Dean, John W., III, 111, 128–29, 130, 131–32, 133, 134, 135, 138, 141

De Gaulle, Charles, 35, 95, 145, 173, 243

Dehmlow, Louis, 489

Democratic National Convention, 67, 69–77, 82, 95, 129, 197

Democratic Party, 61, 70, 72, 73, 74, 75, 79, 82, 84, 85, 90, 91, 105, 106, 107, 108, 109, 110, 125, 198, 264–65, 330, 474

Denmark, 390

De Sade, Donatien, 403

De Sapio, Carmine, 33

Dewey, Thomas E., 473

Dickens, Charles, 470

DiMaggio, Joe, 218–19, 220, 414

Dirksen, Everett M., 267

Doar, John, 158

Dolgun, Alexander, 45–46

Dominick, Peter H., 83

Donahue, Francis, 365, 366

Douglas, Mike, 161

Douglas, Stephen A., 449

Douglas, William O., 88

Douglas-Home, Alec, 116, 210

Dresden, bombing of, 95, 96, 391

Dulles, Allen, 378

Duncan, Isadora, 183

Durante, Jimmy, 475

Eagleton, Thomas F., 77, 78–79, 84, 92, 135

Eastern Europe, 52, 58, 238, 494. *See also* individual listings

Eastern Seaboard Establishment, 48, 142, 261–62, 263

East Germany. *See* German Democratic Republic

Eastland, James O., 71

Eden, Anthony, 116
Edward VIII, 145
Egypt, 200
Ehrenburg, Ilya, 42
Ehrlichman, John D., 125–26, 131, 132
Eisenhower, Dwight D., 52, 68, 111, 134, 147, 148, 153, 172, 260, 262, 267, 397, 474, 476
Eisenhower, Julie Nixon, 160–63
Elizabeth II, 78, 182, 222, 483–84
Elliott, Osborn, 88, 89
Ellsberg, Daniel, 106, 117–18, 119, 138, 262, 309, 383
Elmlark, Harry, 465–67
Elmlark, Lillian Rosenthal, 465–67
Engels, Friedrich, 479
England, 38, 115–16, 145, 181–84, 201, 204, 210, 241, 261, 293, 424
Ervin, Sam J., 123. See also U.S. Senate Select Committee on Presidential Campaign Activities (Ervin Committee)
Esquire, 323, 324, 327–28
Ethiopia, 37
Evans, M. Stanton, 489

Fabian Society, 182
Fairbank, John, 48
Faulkner, William, 182
Federal Bureau of Investigation (FBI), 332, 412, 413
Federalist Papers, 116
Federal Trade Commission (FTC), 295
Felker, Clay, 316–17
Fiedler, Leslie, 298
Fields, W.C., 443
Figaro (boat), 249–51
Finland, 389
Firing Line, 304, 306–7, 310, 319
First World War, 33
Fischer, Bobby, 237, 238, 239, 244
Fitzgerald, F. Scott, 219
Flagstad, Kirsten, 218
Flexner, Abraham, 489
Fonda, Jane, 31, 273, 377–79
Food and Drug Administration (FDA), 415–16, 417

Ford, Betty, 54–55
Ford, Gerald R., 56, 145, 153–55, 163, 268, 269, 287, 455, 457
Ford, Henry, 249
Fort, Joel, 392
France, 145, 147, 204, 223, 243, 403
Franco, Francisco, 43, 44
Freeman, Roger, 452
Friedman, Milton, 138, 171, 273
Fulbright, William, 34, 35, 36–37, 38, 53
Fulbright Reservation, 34
Furtseva, Yekaterina Alekseevna, 178–79

Galbraith, John Kenneth, 48, 71–72, 74, 75, 88, 89–91, 92, 98, 101–2, 106, 150, 197, 198, 244, 245, 279–80, 281, 282, 283, 286–88, 309, 322–27, 340; Affluent Society, The, 91
Gallup, George H., 92, 307, 383, 477
Gallup polls, 23, 121, 124
Garson, Greer, 396
Geneen, Harold, 277
Genet, Jean, 407, 469
George III, 115
German Democratic Republic (East Germany), 390
German Federal Republic (West Germany), 390
Germany, Nazi, 53, 81. See also Hitler, Adolf; Nazis
Ghana, 38
Gleason, Jackie, 297
Goldberg, Arthur J., 439
Goldwater, Barry, 65, 74–75, 81, 91, 98, 101, 108, 120, 139–40, 141, 142, 172, 223, 267, 273, 341, 392, 395
Goldwater, Barry, Jr., 321
Graham, Billy, 151, 317, 442
Graham, Fred, 87
Graham, Katharine, 54
Gramm, Philip, 284
Grasso, Domenico, 406

Grateful Dead, 86
Great Britain. *See* England
Great Society, 477
Greece, 38, 43, 44, 223, 475, 477
Green, Donald, 233, 235
Greene, Felix, 28
Greer, Germaine, 418, 420
Gregory, Dick, 382
Gromyko, Andrei A., 50–51
Guggenheim, Solomon, 480
Guinness, Alec, 403
Gunning, Rosemary, 330

Haldeman, H. R., 125–26, 131, 132, 438
Hamilton, Alexander, 115, 116, 117, 164
Hammill, Pete, 437, 441
Harris, Louis, 92, 307
Hart, Jeffrey, 392
Hartz, Jim, 287
Harvey, Mike, 234
Hayek, Friedrich A., *Constitution of Liberty, The*, 479
Hazlitt, Henry, *Economics in One Lesson*, 265
Heath, Edward, 362
Hemingway, Ernest, 219
Henry II, 106, 128
Herberg, Will, 470
Herrington, Gregg, 81
Hewlett-Packard, 461
Hiss, Alger, 30, 331–32, 333
Hitler, Adolf, 34, 41, 43, 53, 56, 58, 81, 157, 183, 201, 327, 391, 403, 476
Hoch Paul, *Rip Off the Big Game*, 221
Ho Chi Minh, 38
Hoffman, Dustin, 403
Holt-Needham, Phyllis, 484–85
Hook, Sidney, 298; *Paradoxes of Freedom, The*, 430
Hoover, J. Edgar, 81, 129, 411–13
Hope, Bob, 418
Hruska, Roman L., 156
Hume, David, 461
Humphrey, Hubert H., 61–63, 64–65, 68, 70, 71, 72–73, 85, 90,
166, 198, 264, 265, 286, 382
Hungary, 239, 242, 390, 476, 495
Hunt, E. Howard, 117, 118, 119, 120, 436, 437
Hunt, H. L., 67, 478–80
Huntley, Chet, 414
Hutchins, Robert M., 33

Iacocca, Lee, 85
India, 118–19
Indianapolis 500, 226
India-Pakistan war, 118, 428
Indochina, 34, 53, 56, 66, 197, 390, 395, 454, 476. *See also* individual listings
Indonesia, 204
Ingersoll, Robert G., 317, 457
Internal Revenue Service (IRS), 260
International Covenant on Civil and Political Rights, 49–51
International Covenant on Economic, Social and Cultural Rights, 49–51
Invisible Hand Society, 359
Iran, 204, 477
Iron Curtain, 43
Israel, 57, 92, 93, 197–200, 202
Italy, 37, 184–86, 202, 204, 239, 242, 405
ITT Corporation, 277, 297–99
Ivan the Terrible, 223

Jackson, Andrew, 72, 102, 156
Jackson, Henry M., 51, 52, 56, 81, 89, 261
Jackson Resolution, 51
Jane Chord, 355–56
Japan, 204
Javits, Jacob K., 147, 265
Jay, John, 164
Jefferson, Thomas, 121, 149, 369
Jellicoe, Lord George Patrick John Rushworth, 487
Jenkins, Walter, 111
Jensen, Arthur, 472
Jewish Defense League, 51
Jews, 51–52, 53, 55, 57, 81, 271, 335

Jimmy the Greek, 76
John XXIII, *Mater et Magistra,* 319
John Birch Society, 436, 437
Johnson, Andrew, 116, 117, 154, 156
Johnson, Lyndon B., 72, 81, 101, 111, 116, 123, 133, 147, 160, 165, 198, 223, 262, 285, 305, 339, 365, 378, 389, 411–12, 454, 475–77
Johnson, Samuel, 404
Jones, T. Harding, 381–83
Jordan, 200

Kael, Pauline, 390–91, 405, 406
Kahn, Roger, 218, 221
Kant, Immanuel, 218
Kaplan, John, 392
Katyn massacre, 389
Keating, Kenneth, 342
Kempton, Murray, 467, 481–82
Kennedy, Edward M., 77, 109, 122, 127, 130, 259, 260, 264, 294, 335–36
Kennedy, Jacqueline, 323, 405
Kennedy, John F., 77, 85, 123, 133, 139, 143, 164–67, 268, 273, 323, 339, 369, 378, 437, 476, 477
Kennedy, Robert F., 62, 80, 166–67, 200
Kenner, Hugh, 140, 193, 251, 356, 357, 358, 485
Kenya, 211–13
Kenyatta, Jomo, 211, 212–13
Keynes, John Maynard, 74, 89, 262
Khrushchev, Nikita S., 176, 243, 432
Kilpatrick, Jack, 489
King, Billie Jean, 224
King, Martin Luther, Jr., 34, 45, 68
Kirk, Russell, 489, 491
Kissinger, Henry A., 21–22, 46, 52, 53, 56, 57, 208, 209, 222, 242, 243, 343, 356, 428, 429
Klein, Herbert, 24
Knapp, Robert, 383
Knox, Ronald, 485
Koch, Edward, 395
Korea, 34
Kotz, Hick, 80

Kraft, Joseph, 40, 421–22, 437
Krassner, Paul, 390
Ku Klux Klan, 161
Kunstler, William, 239, 262
Kuo Mo-Jo, 37
Kuykendall, Dan, 144

Laird, Melvin, 71
Lambton, Lord Anthony Claud Frederick, 470
Land, Edwin, 272
Lane, Mark, 378
Laos, 391
Lardner, Ring, 470
La Rochefoucauld, François de, 404
Lasky, Melvin, 343, 347
Lasky, Victor, 439
Last Tango in Paris, 405–6
Lattimore, Owen, 47–49; *Solution in Asia,* 47–48
Laugh-In, 303, 304
Lausche, Frank, 140
Leary, Timothy, 442
Lebanon, 34
Leinster, Duke of, 181–82, 184
Lekachman, Robert, 293
Lenin, Vladimir I., 46, 241, 288, 338
Leningrad, siege of, 241
Lenny, 403–5
Levin, Bernard, 183
Lewis, Anthony, 53, 150, 441
Lewis, C. S., 335, 492
Lewis, John L., 22
Lewis, Oscar, 470
Lewis v. AFTRA, 258
Lichnowsky, Prince Karl, 479
Lidice massacre, 389
Liddy, G. Gordon, 129, 130, 136, 159
Lincoln, Abraham, 121, 124, 193, 267, 449, 450, 473
Lindsay, John V., 76–77, 189, 260, 330, 366, 424
Linkletter, Art, 83
Liu Shao-ch'i, 431–32
Lockheed Corporation, 62, 288
Lombardi, Vince, 225

Long March (Chinese), 30, 243
Loomis, Edward, 356
Louis, Joe, 224
Lovelace, Linda, 411
Luce, Henry R., 367
Luckey, Charles Pinckney, 497–99
Lunn, Arnold, 482–89; *Harrovians, The,* 483; *Now I See,* 485; *Spanish Rehearsal,* 482
Lydon, Chris, 81

Macaulay, Rose, 31–32
Macmillan, Harold, 100, 116
Madison, James, 149, 164
Magnuson, Warren G., 416, 417
Magruder, Jeb Stuart, 129, 138
Mailer, Norman, 95, 318, 319; *Naked and the Dead, The,* 408–9
Mangope, 207–8
Mano, D. Keith, 351
Manolete, 226
Manville, Tommy, 479
Mao Tse-tung, 29, 30, 31, 32, 36, 40, 41, 43, 44, 48, 51, 55, 147, 198, 222, 223, 242, 280, 281, 349, 397
Maoism, 385
Mapp v. *Ohio,* 88, 445
Marchi, John, 330
Marcuse, Herbert, 239
Markmann, Charles Lam, 307–8; *Buckleys, A Family Examined, The,* 307
Marshall, George C., 263
Marshall Plan, 397
Marx, Karl, 338
Massachusetts, 98–99
Mather, Cotton, 93, 146
Mau Mau, 209
McCarthy, Eugene, 70, 77, 91
McCarthy, Joseph R., 47, 49, 148, 280, 474
McCarthyism, 48–49, 280
McCord, James W., 111
McCormack, John W., 166
McGinniss, Joe, *Selling of the President. The.* 470, 481
McGovern, George S., 38, 61–62, 63, 64, 65–66, 67, 68, 69, 70, 71,

72–73, 74, 75, 76, 79, 80–82, 84–86, 88, 90, 91–92, 93, 95, 96, 97, 98, 99, 100–1, 102, 105, 106, 107, 110, 119, 137, 138, 171, 178, 198, 199, 223, 267, 270, 271, 272, 278, 377, 382, 395, 452
Meany, George, 134, 273
Mencken, H. L., 431, 457
Merritt, Danny, 229, 231, 234
Mexico, 179–81
Meyer, Frank, 492–93; *In Defense of Freedom,* 492
Middle East, 35, 93, 197–294, 292, 294. *See also* individual listings
Milione, Victor, 489
Mill, John Stuart, 44, 115
Miller, Jack, 99
Miller, Lawrence K., 328–29
Millett, Kate, 298
Mills, Wilbur, 97–98, 452–53
Mindszenty, Jozsef, 493–97
Minuteman missiles, 42
Miranda decision, 88
MIRVs, 433
Mitchell, John N., 111, 129, 136–37
Mitford, Jessica, 307
Mobil Oil, 290
Moi, Daniel Arap, 213
Molotov, Vyacheslav M., 244
Monroe, Marilyn, 220
Montgomery, Bernard Law, 487–88
Moravia, Alberto, 406
Morgenthau, Hans, 53
Moscow Trials, 28
Moss, Frank E., 416, 417
Moynihan, Daniel Patrick, 470
Mozambique, 212, 435
Mozart, Wolfgang Amadeus, 479
Muggeridge, Malcolm, 67, 78, 182, 406, 444, 486
Mundt, Karl E., 81
Mungai, Njeroge, 211–12
Murphy, Patrick, 87
Muskie, Edmund S., 65, 99, 105
Mussolini, Benito, 37
Muzorewa, Abel, 210
My Lai, 277. *See also* Vietnam War
Myrdal, Gunnar, 297, 298

Nabokov, Vladimir, 90
Nader, Ralph, 117, 172
Namath, Joe, 363
National Gallery of Art, 53
National Labor Relations Act, 259
National Labor Relations Board v.
  General Motors Corp., 258
National Right to Work Committee,
  256
National Students Association
  (U.S.), 34
NATO, 93
Nazis, 241, 247, 389
New Deal, 70, 248
New Journalism, 368
Newman, Paul, 396
Newsweek, 166
New York City, 189, 190, 366,
  422–24, 431
New York City Police Department,
  87, 190–91
New York City Public Library, 90,
  92
New York *Times,* 93, 137–39, 140,
  294
New Zealand, 435
Nicholas II, 111
Nigeria, 204
Nisbet, Robert, 138
Niven, David, 322, 323
Nixon, Pat, 83, 163, 222
Nixon, Richard M., 21–23, 24, 26,
  27, 29–31, 33, 34, 38, 39–40, 41,
  42, 43, 44, 48, 52, 55, 66, 69, 73,
  81–82, 88, 93, 94, 95, 97, 98, 99,
  100, 101, 105, 106, 109, 110, 111,
  112–14, 116, 120, 121–22, 123–
  24, 125–26, 127–28, 131, 132,
  133–35, 137, 138, 139, 140,
  141–43, 144–45, 146–48, 149,
  150, 151–53, 154, 155, 157–61,
  162–63, 164, 165, 166, 173, 176,
  212, 222, 223, 225, 236, 240, 242,
  243, 256, 259, 260, 262, 264, 265,
  266, 270, 272, 282, 285, 287, 288,
  292, 330–31, 337, 339, 349–50,
  365, 378, 379, 382, 389, 390, 395,
  422, 438–39, 441, 442, 452, 454,
  480–81, 496–97

Nkrumah, Kwame, 38
Nobel Peace Prize, 57
Nock, Albert Jay, 40–41
Noonan, John T., Jr., 445, 446,
  447, 450
Normandy invasion, 273. *See also*
  Second World War
Northcote, Mabel, 484
Northern Ireland, 435
North Vietnam, 34, 56, 57, 63, 66,
  268, 378, 389, 391, 395. *See also*
  Vietnam War
Norway, 389

O'Brien, Lawrence F., 107, 108,
  117
Occidental Petroleum, 293–94
Oliver, Revilo, 437
Olom, Louis T., 341
Olympic Games, 183, 226, 240,
  241, 242–43, 482
Oppenheimer, J. Robert, 475
Orwell, George, 56; *1984,* 31–32
Ostpolitik, 56, 201
Oswald, Lee Harvey, 378
Otepka, Otto, 139
Oxford Union, 445–46

Pakistan, 118–19
Palm Coast, 297–98, 299
Palme, Olof, 389
Pan American Airways, 186
Panic, The (boat), 228
Papadopoulos, George, 43, 44
Pasternak, Boris, 33
Pastore, John O., 152
Paton, Alan, 207
Patton, Thomas, 166–67
Paul VI, 496
Pauling, Linus C., 323
Pearce Commission (English), 210
Pearson, Drew, 359
Pegler, Westbrook, 146, 248
Peking University, 32–33, 36
People's Liberation Army (Chi-
  nese), 35–36
People's Republic of China, 21, 23,
  24, 25–33, 34, 35, 37, 38, 39–41,
  42–44, 47–49, 51–52, 53–55, 56,

198, 209, 221–22, 223, 242, 243, 247, 262, 279–82, 342–43, 397, 420–22, 432
Pepper, Claude, 474
Percy, Walker, *Love in the Ruins,* 189, 263, 407
Persian Gulf states, 203
Philby, Kim, 280
Pierce v. *The Society of Sisters,* 454
Pius IX, 133–34
Pius XII, 406, 495, 496
Playboy, 409–11, 491
Poland, 239, 242
Polo, Marco, 39
Pompidou, Georges, 147, 173
Pool, Ithiel de Sola, 138
Popkin, Samuel L., 431
Porter, Katherine Anne, 318
Portugal, 212
Pound, Ezra, 219
Powell, Dick, 394
Presidential Commission on Marijuana, 395
Presley, Elvis, 86
Princeton University, 381–83, 384, 385–86
Profumo, John, 116
Prohibition, 393
P'u Chih-lung, 37
Pueblo, 378
Puerto Rico, 239, 242

Quemoy, 34
Quinn, Peter A., 258

Raines, John, 295, 296, 297
Rand Foundation, 189
Raspberry, William, 437
Reagan, Ronald, 21, 93, 142, 407
Rebozo, Bebe, 260
Red Cross, 370
Red Detachment of Women, 31, 36, 55, 342
Red Guards, 32
Reedy, George, 116
Regnery, Henry, 489–93
Rehnquist, William H., 88
Renaissance, 227

Republican National Convention, 82–84, 129
Republican Party, 67, 70, 71, 94, 95, 96, 97, 98, 99, 101, 106, 107, 108, 109, 154, 155, 262, 264, 266–67, 330, 474, 492–93
Reston, James, 27, 48, 54, 65
Reynolds, Alan, 293, 294
Rhodes, John, 266, 267
Rhodesia, 209–11, 212
Ribbentrop-Molotov Pact, 41
Rickenbacker, William, 348
Riggs, Bobby, 224
Roche, John, 197, 391, 409, 437
Rockefeller, "Happy," 83
Rockefeller, Nelson A., 64, 65, 83, 145, 166, 439, 452
Rockne, Knute, 267
Rogers, William P., 35
Rolling Stones, 86
Romania, 38
Romney, Goerge W., 66
Roosevelt, Eleanor, 62, 93, 471
Roosevelt, Franklin Delano, 68, 82, 95, 98, 121, 133, 146, 248
Roosevelt, Theodore, 267
Rose, Jonathan, 367
Rose, Pete, 220
Ross, Edmund G., 156
Rostow, Eugene, 375–76
Ryumin, M. D., 45–46

Sakharov, Andrei, 53
Salinger, Pierre, 64
Salisbury, Harrison, 48
SALT talks, 147, 242, 243, 255, 256
Sartre, Jean-Paul, 407
Saudi Arabia, 202, 203, 204
Saulnier, Raymond, 138
Savio, Mario, 491
Scandinavia, 202. *See also* individual listings
Schlesinger, Arthur, Jr., 38, 48, 100–1, 102, 109, 110, 298, 304–6
Schmeling, Max, 224
Schultz, George P., 282
Scott, Dred, 449
Scott, Foresman and Company, 418, 419, 420

Scott, Walter, 367
Scranton, William, 69, 142
Seale, Bobby, 239
Second World War, 33, 201, 241, 273, 389, 397
Segal, Erich, 351
Segretti, Donald H., 166
Sevareid, Eric, 257, 258, 259
Sex Education, Counseling and Health Clinic (Princeton University), 384
Shakespeare, Frank, 480–82
Shakespeare, William, 315–16, 408
Shaw, George Bernard, 183, 492
Sheed, Wilfred, 389–90
Shnayerson, Robert, 460
Shockley, William, 225, 355, 471–73
Sinatra, Frank, 226
Sinclair, Upton, 279
Sirica, John J., 111, 117
Six-Day War, 197
Skinner, B. F., 472, 473
Slocum, Joshua, 248
Smith, Dennis, Report from Engine Co. 82, 467–71
Smith, Gerald L. K., 248
Smith, Ian, 209, 210
Smith, Margaret Chase, 99
Snaith, Cleody, 251
Snaith, William, 248, 249, 250–51
Snow, C. P., 406
Snow, Edgar, 30–31
Sobran, M. J., Jr., 410
Solzhenitsyn, Aleksandr, 44–45, 46–47, 49, 179, 233, 241, 493, Day in the Life of Ivan Denisovich, A, 52, 481–82; Gulag Archipelago, The, 45
South Africa, Republic of, 207–9, 212, 270, 435
Southeast Asia, 197, 391, 476. See also individual listings
South Korea, 474, 475
South Pole, 435
South Vietnam, 34, 56, 57, 58, 62–63, 151, 197, 198, 199, 263, 268, 391, 395, 476. See also Vietnam War

Soviet Union. See Union of Soviet Socialist Republics
Spain, 38, 43, 44, 223
Sparkman & Stephens, 249
Sparta, 241
Spassky, Boris, 237, 238, 239, 244
Spitz, Mark, 220, 239, 413–14
Spock, Benjamin, 382
SST program, 66
Stalin, Joseph V., 28, 35, 41, 46, 338, 397, 476, 477
Stanton, Frank, 261, 344–45, 348, 429–30, 431
Starr, Peter, 231, 234
Stassen, Harold E., 65, 142
Steibel, Warren, 304
Stein, Andrew, 284–86
Steinem, Gloria, 350
Stevenson, Adlai, 376, 377
Stigler, George, 138
Stone, I. F., 431
Strachey, Lytton, 445–46
Stravinsky, Igor, Rite of Spring, The, 405
Strube, Bill, 491
Students for a Democratic Society, 365
Stuyvesant, Peter, 297
Sukarno, Achmed, 130
Sullivan, Silky, 220
Sullivan v. New York Times, 323
Susskind, David, 319
Sutton, Willie, 135–36
Sweden, 389
Swift, Jonathan, 285, 358
Switzerland, 390
Syria, 202
Szasz, Thomas, 138

Taft, Robert A., 262, 267
Taiwan, 42, 43, 421
Talese, Gay, 220, 368
Taylor, Austin C., 370–71
Taylor, Elizabeth, 86, 297
Taylor, Kathleen Elliott, 370–71
Terence, 354–55
Terrill, Ross, 27, 35–37, 38, 309–10
Tet Offensive, 89. See also Vietnam War

Thailand, 92, 477
Thieu, Nguyen Van, 38, 66, 81, 89, 198
Tho, Le Duc, 57
Thomas, Norman, 98, 479
Thompson, J. Walter, 444
Thurmond, Strom, 140, 473–74
Tibet, 38
Time, 293, 294
Tito (Broz, Josip), 38
Tobin, James, 282
Tonkin, Gulf of, 321
Topping, Seymour, 48
Toscanini, Arturo, 217, 218–19, 474
Tower, John G., 140
Townsend, Robert, *In the Name of Profit*, 277, 278; *Up the Organization*, 277
Toynbee, Arnold, 406
Treblinka, 389
Trotsky, Leon, 90, 91
Truman, Harry S., 110–11, 148, 473–75
Truman Doctrine, 93
Tuchman, Barbara, 37, 48
Tuck, Dick, 108–9
Tufte, Edward R., 383
Tumin, Melvin, 297
Turkey, 263
TWA, 186–87, 188

Uganda, 212, 270
Ungar, Sanford J., 317–18
Union of Soviet Socialist Republics (USSR), 28, 33, 34–35, 45–47, 49–51, 52–53, 56–57, 67, 175–79, 199, 201, 202, 209, 221, 223, 237, 238, 239, 240, 241, 242, 243, 244, 247, 262, 278, 280, 338, 397, 429, 432, 435, 474, 475, 476, 481, 493
United Jewish Appeal, 71
United Nations, 49, 50, 63, 147, 161, 197, 210
United States, 22, 33–35, 41–42, 46, 52, 53–55, 56–58, 61–102, 107, 114–15, 116, 118–19, 121, 128, 147, 158, 197–204, 223, 237, 238, 239, 240, 241, 242, 243, 244, 262,

263, 270, 271, 272–74, 277, 278, 283–84, 289, 379, 389, 391, 392, 397, 428–29, 432, 435, 457, 474–75, 476–77, 480
U.S. Coast Guard, 233, 235, 236, 237
U.S. Congress, 96, 97, 99, 107, 116, 120, 123, 126, 148, 150, 154, 155, 159, 190, 193, 203, 226, 243, 255, 263, 265, 266, 268, 271, 272, 273, 285–86, 292, 294, 395, 410, 412, 433, 453, 454, 474
U.S. Constitution, 116–17, 121, 123, 145, 160, 164, 255, 256, 321, 431, 452, 453, 454, 455, 456, 457
U.S. House Committee on Un-American Activities (HUAC), 31
U.S. House Judiciary Committee, 154, 155, 156, 158, 159, 164, 332, 401
U.S. House Ways and Means Committee, 454
U.S. Information Agency, 175–78, 343, 481, 482
U.S. Justice Department, 114, 148, 332. *See also* Watergate
U.S. National Security Council, 118–19, 263, 359
U.S. Post Office, 188–90
U.S. Senate Foreign Relations Committee, 52
U.S. Senate Select Committee on Presidential Campaign Activities (Ervin Committee), 123, 125, 126, 133, 146
U.S. Sixth Fleet, 92
U.S. State Department, 54, 55
U.S. Supreme Court, 87, 88, 120, 121, 154, 160, 200, 271, 323, 327, 393, 401, 404, 408, 409, 427, 445, 447–49, 451, 452, 453–57
Universal Declaration of Human Rights, 49–51
University of Chicago, 490
Updike, John, 219–20

Van den Haag, Ernest, 401, 407, 472
Van Doren, Charles, 331

Van Horne, Harriet, 432
Venezuela, 204, 295
Victoria (Queen of England), 223
Vidal, Gore, 322–28, 329, 335
Vietnam War, 66, 72, 79, 81, 87, 89,
    95–96, 139, 178, 225, 265, 272,
    277, 278, 285, 365, 378, 389, 477.
    See also North Vietnam; South
    Vietnam
Vivas, Eliseo, 489
Voegelin, Eric, 310, 311
Voice of America, 341–43
Vonnegut, Kurt, Jr., 95; Slaughter-
    house Five, 95
Vorster, John, 207, 208

Wakefield, Dan, 218, 467
Wallace, George C., 67–69, 71, 82,
    171, 210, 473
Wallace, Henry A., 66, 473
Wallace, Mike, 434
Walters, Barbara, 28
Walz decision, 452, 454
Warner, H. B., 33
Warren, Earl, 70, 87, 88, 163–64,
    348, 410, 456. See also U.S. Su-
    preme Court
Warren, Frank, 229, 231
Washington, George, 40, 242
Washington Post, 294
Watergate, 48, 55, 105–9, 110, 111,
    112, 114, 117–20, 121–23,
    124–26, 127–37, 138, 140, 141,
    143, 146, 149, 154–60, 165, 212,
    222, 259, 260, 261, 266–67,
    438–39
Watson, James, 297
Waugh, Auberon, 459
Wayne, John, 83, 273
Webb, Beatrice, 75
Webb, Sidney, 75
Weicker, Lowell P., Jr., 127,
    135–37, 138

Welch, Robert, 437
Wells, H. G., 492
Western Europe, 201, 202, 475.
    See also individual listings
West Germany. See German Feder-
    al Republic
Westmoreland, William, 375–76
Whig Party, 266
White, Byron R., 448
White, Theodore H., 23–25, 33
Wicker, Tom, 166
Wilde, Oscar, 124, 461
Wilkins, Roy, 208
Will, George, 318
Williams, C. Dickerman, 123
Williams, Duncan, Trousered Apes,
    406, 407
Williams, Susan, 385
Williamson, Bruce, 410–11
Wills, Garry, 270, 355, 368, 437
Wilson, Woodrow, 28, 33
Wilsonianism, 33, 37–38
Wolfe, Tom, 368
Wolkinson, Herman, 148
Wordsworth, William, 471
World War I. See First World War
World War II. See Second World
    War
Wyman, Ann, 436, 437, 438

Yale Daily News, 365, 367, 368–69
Yale Political Union, 375–77
Yale University, 42, 364–65,
    367–68, 369, 375–77, 437
Yankelovich, Daniel, 92, 307
Yeats, William Butler, 357–58
Yugoslavia, 38, 477

Zambia, 335
Zero Population Growth, 384
Ziegler, Ron, 24, 125

OSR

REFERENCE